# Silver in the Sun

A.D. (Tony) Parsons has worked as a professional sheep and wool classer, an agricultural journalist, a news editor and rural commentator on radio, a consultant to major agricultural companies, and an award-winning stud breeder of animals and poultry. He owned his first kelpie dog in 1944, and in 1950 he established 'Karrawarra', one of the top kelpie studs in Australia. In 1992 he was awarded the Order of Australia Medal for his contribution to the propagation of the Australian kelpie sheepdog.

Since 1947 he has written hundreds of articles, many in international publications. His technical publications include *Understanding Ostertagia Infections in Cattle*, *The Australian Kelpie*, *The Working Kelpie* and *Training the Working Kelpie*, now regarded as classic works on the breed. His previous novels are the bestselling *The Call of the High Country*, *Return to the High Country* and *Valley of the White Gold*.

Tony lives with his wife not far from Toowoomba in Queensland and successfully showed merino sheep and wool until 2005. He still maintains a stud of kelpies.

Also by Tony Parsons

*The Call of the High Country*
*Return to the High Country*
*Valley of the White Gold*

# TONY PARSONS

# Silver in the Sun

VIKING
*an imprint of*
PENGUIN BOOKS

VIKING

Published by the Penguin Group
Penguin Group (Australia)
250 Camberwell Road, Camberwell, Victoria 3124, Australia
(a division of Pearson Australia Group Pty Ltd)
Penguin Group (USA) Inc.
375 Hudson Street, New York, New York 10014, USA
Penguin Group (Canada)
90 Eglinton Avenue East, Suite 700, Toronto, Canada ON M4P 2Y3
(a division of Pearson Penguin Canada Inc.)
Penguin Books Ltd
80 Strand, London WC2R 0RL England
Penguin Ireland
25 St Stephen's Green, Dublin 2, Ireland
(a division of Penguin Books Ltd)
Penguin Books India Pvt Ltd
11 Community Centre, Panchsheel Park, New Delhi – 110 017, India
Penguin Group (NZ)
67 Apollo Drive, Mairangi Bay, Auckland 1310, New Zealand
(a division of Pearson New Zealand Ltd)
Penguin Books (South Africa) (Pty) Ltd
24 Sturdee Avenue, Rosebank, Johannesburg 2196, South Africa

Penguin Books Ltd, Registered Offices: 80 Strand, London, WC2R 0RL, England

First published by Penguin Group (Australia), 2007

1 3 5 7 9 10 8 6 4 2

Text and cover design by Karen Trump © Penguin Group (Australia)
Cover photographs by Bill Bachman
Inside back cover art, 'Kanimbla', by Holly Parsons
Typeset in 13/18 pt Adobe Garamond by Post Pre-press Group, Brisbane, Queensland
Printed in and bound in Australia by McPherson's Printing Group, Maryborough, Victoria

National Library of Australia
Cataloguing-in-Publication data:

Parsons, A. D. (Anthony David), 1931– .
Silver in the sun.

ISBN 978 0 670 07031 2.

I. Title.

A823.3

www.penguin.com.au

Oven-hot the sun beats down,
Through silver leaves of silver trees.

Tony Parsons


Do the shearers still go riding up the Warrego to work,
Where the Thurulgoona woolshed flashes silver in the sun?
Is there racing at Enngonia? Is Belalie still a run?
Do the Diamantina cattle still come down by Barringun?

W. H. Ogilvie


For there's haste and there is hurry when the Queensland sheds begin;
On the Bogan they are bridling, they are saddling on the Bland.
There is plunging and there's sidling – for the colts don't understand
That the Western creeks are calling, and the idle days are done,
With the snowy fleeces falling, and the Queensland sheds begun!

W. H. Ogilvie

# Author's Note

Two themes were foremost in my mind as I wrote this novel. The first concerns the promotion and marketing of Australian merino wool to the rest of the world. The Australian wool industry's inability, up to now, to manage a professional marketing campaign has led to a massive downturn in sheep numbers, especially in Queensland (where this story is set), where they fell from a peak of twenty-two million to a current low of five million.

The second theme explores the problem of declining rural populations and, I hope, acknowledges the efforts of many people to promote their towns and villages through projects such as the Spirit of the Bush and Tidy Towns, to name just two.

*Silver in the Sun* also touches on the importance of medical research. Australia has had, and still has, some of the world's most brilliant medical researchers, yet public money allocated to this field is, to say the least, scant. Successive federal governments have thrown money into far less deserving areas, while medical research projects operate on shoestring budgets. The fact that researchers have achieved so much with so little says volumes for their ability and dedication.

While on the subject of medical research, my first acknowledgement must go to the Commonwealth Serum Laboratory's toxicologist, the late Dr Struan Sutherland, whose epic work to produce an antivenom for the funnel-web spider brought him world recognition. This remarkable man also invented the pressure immobilisation technique of first aid for snakebite, and developed a venom detection kit to enable doctors to ascertain which antivenom should be administered to a snakebite victim. I am indebted to Dr Sutherland and Dr James Tibballs for their paper 'Management of Snake Bites in Australia and New Guinea', which was written for the Royal Flying Doctor Service in 2002.

It would be impossible to calculate the cost of snakebite to Australia's agricultural industry. I have lost valuable working dogs, some irreplaceable because of their breeding, and I'm sure thousands of other livestock owners could say the same. Horses are particularly vulnerable to snakebite. I lost my last mare in this fashion. Of course, there's also the human cost of encounters with these reptiles. I've had three narrow escapes myself. According to the noted snake handler Ram Chandra, only one person had ever survived a taipan bite before an antivenom was developed.

Three people deserve particular thanks for their contribution to my imperfect knowledge of Australian parrots. The first is Mr Roger Turnbull, Senior Wildlife Ranger with Queensland Parks and Wildlife, who gave me the whys and wherefores for the keeping of parrots. Mr Des English, President of the Downs Bird Breeders Association, filled me in on the care and feeding of various parrot species; and noted bird expert Mr Bob Branston of Hannam Vale, New South Wales, gave me a considerable amount of information about the peculiarities of some parrots and why certain species can't be housed together. Bob also gave me some valuable advice about the rarest and most endangered species.

Bill and Rosemary Benjamin of Clifton, and Peter and Ruth Harvey of Highfields, reminisced with me about their sojourns on the Queensland merino stud properties Burenda and Terrick Terrick respectively. In our declining years, Peter and yours truly showed sheep and wool at the same shows and Peter often transported my sheep. He is one of nature's gentlemen.

I was very fortunate to meet Jenny Milson of Longreach, the author of a book on Queensland vegetation. Jenny made it her business to find and photograph for me the 'silveriest' trees she could find on her trips around Queensland's 'big' pastoral country. Very many thanks, Jenny.

My daughter, Holly, found time to produce a map of the layout of Kanimbla homestead and its outbuildings, which to some extent mirrors properties known to me. She's a busy person, so I'm very appreciative of her input.

I must also thank Toowoomba motelier Mr Bill Klaassen for his advice regarding motel construction. Over the years he has been the proprietor of several motels, sometimes building them from scratch. Bill is a very knowledgeable man in this field and a good friend too.

Once again the Penguin team have been great, including publishers Ali Watts and Kirsten Abbott, and editors Nicci Dodanwela (who almost had her first baby at her desk) and Miriam Cannell. Producing the cover is always a challenging task, and designer Karen Trump went to great lengths to ensure that the book had visual appeal. They're a special team and they all have special gifts. They make a difference.

A. D. (Tony) Parsons, OAM
East Greenmount, Queensland

# Prologue

The mirage floated endlessly – a lake across the dull grey of the western road. Ian noticed that it had been with them from early morning, and while the country had changed, the lake remained – always suggesting the possibility of water, yet always receding before their gaze. Timber changed with the soil, from gidgee and false sandalwood to whitewood and boree on the Mitchell grass country and then to mulga on the red soil further west. Magpies warbled and crows cawed, pecking imperiously at the carnage of dead roos beside the road.

And then as suddenly as it had appeared, the lake vanished. To the right of the coach a long line of red gums masked for a time a lovely stretch of river. The road crossed a bridge, swung away slightly to the north-west and the township of Murrawee was before them.

To Ian, the little town looked much like many others he had passed, except for the trees in the paddock on its outskirts – two silver-leafed trees growing in the red soil, the sun shining down on them at just the right angle to make the leaves shimmer.

# Chapter One

The big brown and gold coach stopped in front of the shop, on a wide bitumen road with verges of yellow-red sandy soil. In the days when there was a rail service, most visitors to Murrawee came by train, and there was always a noisy throng awaiting its arrival. But this was the first decade of the twenty-first century, and many Queensland rail links were no longer used; just about everyone owned a vehicle and road transports carted the essential freight.

A corrugated iron verandah shaded the footpath outside the shop and kept the gentle August sun off the window. In this shade, an old black kelpie with one flop ear lay asleep on a corn sack. The dog lifted its grey muzzle and briefly inspected the single passenger alighting from the coach, before returning to sleep. 'Moss' had once been a very good sheepdog, but after ten years of hard work in murderously hot paddocks, his owners had retired him to end his days in town.

The passenger watched as the coach driver pulled a large leather suitcase and army-style kitbag from the luggage compartment beneath the coach and dropped them at his feet. 'Be seeing ya, young fella,' the driver said as he slammed the compartment door shut and climbed back into the coach.

Several bored-looking passengers gazed at the tall, fair young man for the last time before the coach pulled away. A well-groomed elderly woman, who had been sitting across the aisle from the young man, sighed. Watching him heave his kitbag over his shoulder she was reminded of the good-looking young man she had married. Occasionally – very occasionally these days – you struck a man with real class. This young fellow had heaps of it, and she wondered what he was doing in this backwater. He must be the son of a grazier, she thought, or perhaps he had a girlfriend who was a grazier's daughter. She sighed again and wished it were possible to roll back the years.

The young man watched the coach disappear into the distance before turning and looking into the shop window. A fly-specked square of yellow cardboard proclaimed in faded red letters that the shop was the depot for McCafferty's Coach Services. According to a large overhead sign, the place was also a café.

Perennially hungry, he turned from his inspection of the window and was about to ascend the two steps into the café when a stout, dark-haired woman appeared in the doorway. The woman's keen brown eyes appraised the new arrival. She observed that he was very tidily dressed in well-cut dark grey corduroy trousers, a light-coloured shirt with dark blue tie and a navy jumper.

'G'day,' she said by way of greeting. 'Have a good trip?'

'It was all right, thank you,' the boy answered.

Nice accent, Helen Donovan thought, obviously English and educated, but not posh. Aloud she said, 'Old Leo's laid up with a crook foot and he's asked one of the neighbours to pick you up and take you out to Kanimbla. They'll be an hour or so yet 'cause they're at a sheep sale. Leo said for you to wait here and have a feed with us.'

The boy looked at her and nodded. 'Thanks. I don't mind waiting. Is Mr Blake hurt badly?'

'I think he might have broken a bone or two in his ankle – it's in plaster. It's his right foot so he can't drive,' the shopkeeper explained.

'I see. I'd appreciate some lunch if that's all right,' the boy said.

'Right as rain. You can have steak or chops or a mixed grill or snags with vegies or salad, or plain cold meat and salad.' And in the next breath, 'What am I going to call you?' She knew he was more than a jackaroo or station hand and that he was related to Jack Richardson, who'd owned the biggest property in the district – Kanimbla.

'Ian,' he said. 'Just call me Ian.'

'If that's all right,' she said.

'It's all right. Why shouldn't it be?'

'We-ell . . . Jack Richardson was always Mr Richardson and you're a relation, aren't you?' she asked.

'I'm a relation but I don't want or expect to be called Mister,' he said. 'I'll have some steak and salad, please.'

'Would you like a drink of something while you're waiting?' she asked. 'Maybe an orange juice or a squash?'

'An orange juice would be great,' Ian said. 'Are you here on your own?'

'Most of the time. I've got a daughter that comes and helps with the cooking at busy times. My husband has the mail run. Done it for twenty years. Ray'll be back later on,' she explained.

Ian nodded. 'Does he take the mail to Kanimbla?'

'Yeah, twice a week, Tuesdays and Fridays. The mail and just about anything else that anybody wants delivered.'

The woman retreated into the recesses of the shop to reappear with a tall glass of orange juice. She put it down on a yellow plastic-topped table and the boy smiled his thanks and sat down. 'I'll be back before long with your lunch – er – Ian.'

'Thank you.'

But Helen Donovan lingered to look down at the young man as he took his first sip of juice. 'Did you know Jack and Linda Richardson?' she asked.

'I knew them, but I can't say I knew them very well. I met them three or four times. The first time was after my parents were killed, when I was eight. They met me when I arrived in Sydney. That was before I went out to Warren. Uncle Jack got me that position.'

If he had been asked for his opinion of his uncle, he would have had some difficulty framing a diplomatic answer. Jack was unfailingly friendly and generously concerned for his nephew's welfare in Australia, but Ian was never really comfortable in his uncle's company. It seemed to him that his Uncle Jack had an attitude problem. He projected an image of class superiority that did not go down well. He had great looks, a voice that had retained its educated cultivation, and the trappings of a very wealthy man, but there was an urgency about the way he lived that disturbed Ian. It seemed that despite the favourable circumstances of his life, his Uncle Jack was one of the most discontented people Ian had ever met. He had a higher opinion of his aunt than his uncle, with the reservation that she seemed perfectly happy to follow wherever her husband wished to go. But Linda Richardson was childless, and her husband had become her life.

Helen Donovan thought that she had never met such a well-mannered young man. Most of the young blokes who came into the café were polite enough but likely to be half-drunk. She was dying to find out all she could about Ian because the district was still agog at the recent death of the Richardsons in a light plane crash. They had no children and the great property's future was the major item of interest in the district. Would it be put on the market? Even Leo Blake, who had been Jack Richardson's right-hand man, couldn't tell them who owned the property now. The rumour was that it had been left to the Anglican Church.

After grilling Ian's steak and putting together a salad, Helen Donovan, ostensibly dusting the shop shelves, watched as he ate his lunch. He ate quite slowly and carefully, which was not at all how most of the young men ate when they rushed in for lunches or evening meals. They usually devoured their food, talking as they ate. They didn't play up too much because Helen was known far and wide as a woman who could give as good as she got. Then there was the fact that Ray Donovan was a very tough man who had fought in the ring. Singly, or as a pair, Ray and Helen Donovan spelt trouble for any young fellow who stepped out of line. But they didn't mind a bit of good-humoured chiacking. And the young blokes helped to keep the café afloat. Helen felt sorry for them, really. No wonder they spent their evenings drinking – Murrawee didn't have much to offer young people any more.

'Would you like anything else?' Mrs Donovan asked when she saw that Ian had put his knife and fork together on his plate. The young man intrigued her. He was hardly more than a boy, yet he wasn't a boy. There was a quiet dignity about him that suggested a maturity beyond his years. And, like just about every resident of any Australian country township, Helen Donovan had a lively curiosity. The café was the major source of gossip and information in Murrawee and people would expect her to know more than anyone else about Kanimbla and its future. This was her chance to glean some vital info.

The young man looked up at her and smiled gently. 'It was delicious, thank you. And no, I don't need anything else. I'm not used to having dessert in the middle of the day.'

'Would you like to read a paper while you wait?'

The young man smiled again. 'Actually, I'd prefer

to talk about Kanimbla. That is, if you have the time, Mrs . . . er . . . '

'Donovan. I'm Helen Donovan and me husband's Ray,' she reminded him.

'Have you lived here long?' Ian asked.

'All me bloomin' life. Me dad and mum had the café and shop before they retired. Ray and I took it over. I went to school here.'

'So you must know the district very well?'

'I reckon I do. I know just about everyone and what they're up to. I know the ones I can trust with credit and the ones I can't. I know the alcos and I know who's been fooling around. Everyone comes to me for the latest,' Helen said.

'Perhaps you'd be kind enough to tell me what you know about Kanimbla and Mr Blake,' Ian suggested.

Helen pulled a chair away from Ian's table and sat down rather heavily. Ian looked at her and decided that she was not unattractive. Her hair was still dark and wavy and it was kept in place by a large gold clip. Her skin was verging towards olive and her eyes were a deep brown. Her khaki skirt and lemon blouse were half-hidden by a yellow apron with a red border.

'Kanimbla's the biggest property in the district. It's not as big as it used to be in the old days because some of it was sold before Jack Richardson came on the scene. Because it was a major merino stud it wasn't resumed for soldier settlement after the war, which was a good thing as most of the blocks they handed out were far too small to make a living off.'

Helen was delighted to have an attentive audience, and such a good-looking one at that.

'I reckon Jack and Linda Richardson were the closest to royalty of anyone who ever lived in this district. Jack was the son of a Pommy aristocrat and Linda was from a family just as classy as him. They never had kids – Linda had some kind of health problem. Jack lived it up pretty well – though you probably know all this. When Jack took over the place he had Leo Blake there from day one. Leo's a really good man. He's been the manager there for years and been running the place on his own since the crash. There's not a person in the district that would say a bad word about Leo and Judy. Judy's a bit younger than him. Leo won't stand for any nonsense but he'll give a fella a go if he thinks he's got some good in him.

'Do they have any children?' Ian asked.

'Two girls. There's Joanna. She's married to a fella who's got a cattle place over towards the coast. He's a nice bloke and they've got a boy and a girl. Now there's another baby – unplanned, mind you – and that's why Judy isn't with Leo. His crook foot happened the day after Judy went to help Jo,' Helen Donovan explained.

'What about his other daughter?' Ian asked.

'Rhona lives in the city. She isn't married. She's a doctor of something, not medicine,' Helen said.

'A PhD, perhaps?' Ian suggested.

'Something like that. She's at Sydney University. Jack Richardson had a few clashes with Rhona. She didn't have

8

much time for Jack, said he wasn't much of a man, just lucky to be born with a silver spoon in his mouth. She rarely came back to Kanimbla while Jack was here, usually only when she knew he'd be away. She might not have come at all if it wasn't for Leigh Metcalfe,' she said.

'Who's Leigh Metcalfe?' Ian asked.

'If you take notice of Rhona, Leigh is one of Australia's best writers and he's a poet of sorts too. Some people say they had an affair, though nobody really knows. Leigh probably didn't want to cross Leo, though it wasn't for lack of trying on Rhona's part. She's a touchy woman, and brainy,' Helen said.

'So where does Leigh fit into Kanimbla?' Ian asked, intrigued that there was a celebrated writer in the region.

'He lives on Kanimbla. He's got a house up the river and keeps an eye on things at that end of the property. He's not a full-time employee but he gets some kind of wage, as well as what he earns from his writing.'

'Interesting,' Ian said. 'So what else can you tell me about Kanimbla, Mrs Donovan?'

'Well now, it has the best merino sheep and the best Shorthorn cattle in the district. It was one of the original properties when this part of the country was first settled. There's leg irons in one of the cellars. They were used when convicts worked there. I don't know how many there were, but some died there.'

He'd hoped to learn more about local opinion of his late uncle but Mrs Donovan hadn't given him much of a picture. And any further conversation was halted by the arrival of two customers. One was a tall man with broad shoulders, obviously a grazier from his attire and wide-brimmed hat. His companion was a girl who Ian judged to be about his own age. Beneath her grey Akubra, her long dark hair fell in soft curls and had been tied loosely with a simple band. She was dressed in blue jeans and a blue checked shirt. Ian guessed that she was the man's daughter.

'G'day day, Helen. Got our order ready?' the tall man asked with his eyes on Ian. The girl's grey eyes were also on him. Visitors were a rarity.

'It's all ready, Mr McDonald. How are you, Fiona?' the shopkeeper asked.

Before Fiona could respond the tall man lifted his eyebrows in an unspoken question and nodded towards the young man at the table.

'This is Ian, Mr McDonald. He's going out to Kanimbla with Alec and Trish Claydon. Ian, this is Mr Lachie McDonald and his daughter, Fiona. They're almost your neighbours.'

The young man rose to his feet in one smooth movement to shake their hands. The older man's hand was rough from years of hard work but the girl's was very soft. As he shook her hand, and met her gaze, her eyes sparkled in her tanned face and it dawned on Ian that she was quite stunning.

'Going out there to work, Ian?' Lachie McDonald asked. Kanimbla usually employed at least two jackaroos and sometimes three.

'Something like that,' Ian answered with a smile.

'First job?' Lachie pressed.

'Not quite. I jackarooed on Wongarben at Warren for a year or so,' Ian said.

'I reckon you'll get on well with Leo. He's a tough task-master but he's also very fair. We might see you around, Ian.'

Lachie turned and walked to the shop's counter. Fiona smiled in Ian's direction, nodded and followed her father. Ian resumed his seat just as a large car drew up outside.

'Your taxi has arrived, young man. You should have an interesting drive,' Lachie chuckled. He and Fiona left the shop with boxes of groceries in their arms. They were trailed by Helen Donovan, who also carried a box of groceries under each arm, the weight of which seemed not to concern her in the slightest. Outside, Lachie spoke briefly with the new-comers and jerked his head to indicate Ian's whereabouts.

A sandy-haired man of medium height but thick build came barrelling through the shop doorway. He had the appearance of someone in a great hurry, or perhaps some-one with great energy. He was followed more sedately by his taller wife, whose youthful figure could still turn heads. Dressed to emphasise her best features, her fawn skirt pro-vided a fair glimpse of her long, smooth thighs. Her eyes registered mild shock when they rested on the handsome young man at the table.

Ian got to his feet again and extended his hand. 'Hello,' he smiled. 'You must be Mrs Claydon.'

'And you must be Ian,' she returned a brilliant smile. 'Sorry we're late. The sheep sale dragged on a bit and Alec would stay. And stay. Oh, this is my husband, Alec.'

Alec's handclasp was very firm and it was accompanied by a slight pat on the young man's upper arm. 'Welcome to Murrawee, Ian. Not that there's a lot here to provide you with a welcome.'

'There's not much wrong with it so far,' Ian said quickly. 'I've had a nice lunch and Mrs Donovan has been entertaining me very well.'

Helen's brown eyes glistened. It had been a while since anyone had come right out and paid her a compliment. Ian's words were not lost on Trish Claydon either. She reckoned she knew men, and here, she decided, was a very different kind of young man to any she'd met in a long while.

Ian turned and shook hands with the shopkeeper. 'Thank you very much for the lunch and for looking after me so well, Mrs Donovan.' He handed her a twenty dollar note and thanked her when she gave him his change.

'It was a pleasure, Ian. I hope I see you again before long. Give my regards to Leo and tell him I hope he's on deck again pretty soon. And don't forget what I told you. Leo's been known to eat jackaroos – but only smart-mouthed ones,' Helen said, smiling.

'I shouldn't be in any danger then,' Ian said as he collected his suitcase and kitbag and followed Trish out the door, leaving Helen to puzzle over his remarks.

# Chapter Two

'So you're a relation of Jack Richardon,' Trish said to Ian as soon as the Fairlane was cruising down the wide, dusty road.

'That's right.'

'Will you be staying long?' she asked.

'I don't know yet, Mrs Claydon.'

'I suppose it will depend how well you get on with Leo. He can be quite – er – forceful,' she said, and smiled.

'It won't, actually,' Ian answered politely but firmly. 'How well or otherwise I get on with Mr Blake won't make any difference to how long I stay.'

Trish wasn't sure how to respond to this. The boy sounded older than he looked. Before she could say anything, he changed the subject.

'So how far is it to Kanimbla?'

'Fifty-two ks,' Alec got a word in.

'Fifty-two *kilometres*,' Trish corrected.

'Christ,' Alec said under his breath. 'Why does she have to correct every damned thing I say?'

Ian felt the atmosphere in the car grow tense. Unabashed

by her husband's obvious irritation, Trish pressed on. 'Is this your first job, Ian?'

'It's not exactly a job, Mrs Claydon,' he said, but offered no further information. Trish thought that perhaps he had come for an extended holiday. His accent sounded English, and she knew lots of young Brits came to Australia on working holidays and stayed for months or even years.

'Are you English?' she asked.

'I was born in Australia – my mother was Australian – but I lived with my grandfather in England. I went to school at Harrow.'

'Is that like Eton?'

'Similar,' Ian said with a slight smile.

'Well, you must come and see us at Bahreenah while you're here,' Trish said warmly. 'We're your closest neighbours and Alec is a very keen merino breeder. We're using Kanimbla rams.'

She could have added that these days her husband was keener on his sheep than he was on her. Alec had become so predictable. Who wanted to talk about sheep all day? If only Alec were more like Leigh Metcalfe.

Ian attempted to diffuse the atmosphere in the front of the car. 'There seem to be lots of kangaroos here. Are there any emus?'

'Heaps,' Alec answered. 'They're murder on fences. Pretty good dog tucker, though. Roo meat's okay if you don't mind the worms. Don't know how you could eat it, but some do. Give me a good fat wether any day.'

'We have some nice horses at Bahreenah. Both our girls ride. They're away at Abbotsleigh. That's in Sydney,' Trish said.

'I know about Abbotsleigh,' Ian said.

'You do?' she said, surprised.

'Oh, yes. There were girls at Warren who went to Abbotsleigh,' he said.

'Of course.' Trish turned in her seat to face Ian, 'So do you have a girlfriend?'

Ian had got used to the forthrightness of the bush community during his time at Wongarben, but was still unprepared for this question. 'Ah . . . no. I don't have time for girls right now.'

'That's the shot, Ian,' said Alec firmly. 'Get your life sorted out before you start worrying about girls. They'll still be there a few years down the track.' Alec was very impressed with this young bloke. He seemed to have his head screwed on pretty well.

'Huh!' Trish snorted and turned to face the front. 'Oh, 'I thought all boys were keen on girls.' God, but he was nice-looking, with his fair hair and serious hazel eyes. No doubt he had a girlfriend hidden away – maybe back in England. 'Not long to go now,' she said.

Ian nodded. The wide plain had given way to low hills and to his right he saw the line of the river. Flocks of white cockatoos were perched on many of the gums edging the river. They were like a white frosting on the dark green of the trees.

15

Alec turned off the main bitumen road and drove up a narrower tarred road that presently branched into two. 'All that country on the right for as far as you can see is Kanimbla. That's Bahreenah on the left. The Kanimbla homestead and woolshed are at the end of this track. You'll see them in a tick.'

Ian tried to take in the array of buildings as the Fairlane moved slowly down the track. There were so many they resembled a small village: the imposing homestead with its wide verandahs, sweeping lawns and huge shade trees, a smaller bungalow that he presumed was the manager's residence, and more cottages further down the track. Away to one side was the huge woolshed. There was another big building that Ian subsequently discovered was the ram shed. There were other buildings too: a big hayshed, a massive machinery shed and a separate fuel shed. Behind the main homestead there were stables and horse yards.

'That homestead's a bloody bottler, eh? Take a few bob to build it today. Eight bedrooms and three bathrooms. You can dance in the lounge room. There used to be three servants in the old days. There was a maid with Mrs Heatley when the Richardsons lived here. Now there's only Mrs Heatley. She's the housekeeper. Then there's an old fellow who looks after the gardens and lawns, feeds Jack's horses and dog, and kills for the homestead. He's been here a good few years. Leo will fill you in,' Alec said.

The Fairlane pulled up outside the bungalow. There was a mesh fence at the front of the house and a taller fence along

16

the sides and behind. Roses dominated the front garden, which was obviously the object of much attention as there wasn't a weed to be seen. A grey-haired man sitting in an easy chair on the wide front verandah stood up and with the help of a crutch came down the three front steps to meet them.

'Alec, Trish,' the man greeted them.

'G'day, Leo. We've brought your visitor,' Alec said. 'Ian, this is Mr Blake.'

'G'day, Ian. Have a good trip?' Leo Blake asked.

'It was all right thanks, Mr Blake,' Ian said.

'Sorry I couldn't be there to meet you. Mrs Donovan look after you?'

'Very well. She's a nice person,' Ian said.

'That she is. You can drop your gear off here and we'll take it up to the homestead later,' Leo said. He noted the look of surprise on the Claydons' faces; they had probably expected Ian to be lodged at the old jackaroos quarters.

'I suppose you're ready for a drink o' tea and a bit of something to eat?' Leo queried.

'I had a good lunch in town, Mr Blake. But a cup of tea would be nice, if you're having one,' Ian said.

'You like to stay a while?' Leo asked the Claydons.

'Thanks, but we'll be going, Leo. I've got a few things to do before dark,' Alec answered.

'Thanks again,' Leo said.

'Yes, thanks for the lift,' Ian echoed.

Trish moved close to Ian and placed a hand on his shoulder. 'Be sure to come and see us. The girls will be home on holidays soon. I'll give you a call when you've settled in a bit.'

Ian nodded, feeling a sudden urge to move out of her reach.

Alec lifted his right arm in a gesture of farewell as he turned the car in a circle and headed back down the narrow road. Ian watched the car until it was out of sight and then looked at Leo Blake and grinned tightly.

'An interesting drive up?' Leo asked, smiling too.

'You could say that.'

'Look I'm sorry I couldn't be in Murrawee to meet you. Our older daughter is having a baby. Judy, my wife, is over there with her,' Leo explained.

'It was fine, really. I hope your ankle is much better,' Ian said. He liked the look of Leo Blake. Close to six feet tall and solidly built, he had a very strong face with nicely shaped nose and steely blue eyes. His face was tanned and the skin below his eyes crisscrossed with fine wrinkles. His grey hair was cut short but there was still plenty of it. He was wearing grey gaberdine trousers and a creamy-brown checked shirt. His slipper flapped as he moved with the crutch.

'It's more a hindrance than anything else. Let's go inside and I'll put the kettle on.'

Ian opened the mesh door for Leo. 'I can get the tea if you'd like to keep off that foot. I got fairly handy while I was at Wongarben,' Ian said.

'I'm not that useless, but thanks anyway. Judy left a big cake – it's in that red tin in the cupboard,' Leo pointed towards a large walnut dresser. 'I don't mind a beer at night, but there's nothing like a drink o' tea during the day. I suppose you learnt to drink at Wongarben?'

'Not really. Mr Murray was fairly strict. The other jackaroos, Harry and Tim, used to drink a bit. They liked B & S balls and always came back looking very seedy,' Ian said.

'And what did you do while Harry and Tim were away chasing girls?' Leo asked as he filled the kettle. 'If Warren is anything like Murrawee, there isn't much to keep young people busy in their free time.'

'I used to go riding with Mrs Murray. She loved horses, and Mr Murray wasn't so keen on them. He preferred his dogs – he had some good kelpies. I started to do a bit of study too, as well as a lot of reading, and a bit of writing,' Ian said.

'Is that a fact? I like a good yarn myself, especially the Upfield novels. But you mentioned writing. What kind of writing?' asked Leo.

'Stories about the bush – the landscape, the animals,' Ian said quietly. 'English was one of my best subjects at school.' He could have added that he was Harrow's finest student, but that was not his way. His grandfather had advised him never to blow his own trumpet, and especially not in Australia. Ian could also have said that he had spent what little spare time he had in his final year studying Australia's wool industry.

'Surely you would have been distracted by girls?'

'I didn't meet anyone who caught my eye,' said Ian.

'While we're on the subject, I'll give you your first piece of advice. Watch yourself with Trish Claydon. She can be unstoppable, and you wouldn't want to get on the wrong side of Alec Claydon. He hits pretty hard.'

'I don't want to get on the wrong side of anyone, Mr Blake. Mrs Claydon is a married woman, and Alec seems like a good man.'

'Alec's all right. He's good with stock and a good neighbour too. It's bad luck he's lumbered with Trish.' Leo slid the cup of tea towards Ian. 'But that's enough about them. It's time you gave me the drum on where you fit into the picture. I realise you're Jack's nephew and that's about all I know. When the solicitors talked to me they said you'd give me the rest of the story. So over to you.'

# Chapter Three

Ian put down his cup and extracted an envelope from his shirt pocket. 'This should explain everything, Mr Blake.'

Leo slit open the envelope with his pocketknife and began reading its contents. When he had read both pages through once, he re-read them to ensure that he had everything clear in his mind. He then leant back in his chair and looked steadily at the young man who sat across the table from him.

'Do you prefer Boss or Mr Richardson?' Leo asked with a gleam in his eye.

'Mr Blake, if you call me either, we'll have our first argument. Ian will do just fine. And as the letter states, you are still more or less the boss here, until I'm twenty-one. You have financial and managerial control unless I object, and then I have to take it up with the accountants. While I own Kanimbla on paper, I need to learn the ropes from you – providing you're willing to give me the benefit of your experience.'

'I suppose you realise how lucky you are to have Kanimbla dropped in your lap,' Leo said bluntly.

'Yes and no,' Ian said. 'The accountants went over it with me. Kanimbla is a big property and if it was sold, stock and all, it would realise a lot of money. That money, invested wisely, would produce a better dividend than the property is returning right now.'

Leo nodded. The young bloke was obviously no fool. 'I can't dispute that. Things are tough. Wool is way down and it's our main money-earner. Stud cattle are okay, but they're secondary to our sheep. Your uncle was toying with the idea of planting cotton but I was against it.'

Ian frowned. 'I wouldn't touch cotton. It requires high levels of chemicals and extensive irrigation, an environmental no-no, not to mention the ill will you create amongst your neighbours. Cattle properties need to be quarantined because of chemical-spray drift, and the run-off can pollute rivers and kill fish. It just seems daft to grow cotton on the world's driest continent.'

Blake looked at Kanimbla's new owner with growing respect. 'Your uncle thought that he could use cotton earnings to keep the merino stud going until the wool business picked up. But it will be a relief to your neighbours to know that they don't have to contend with cotton growing on the Big Plain. Right now there's a few worried blokes I can tell you.'

'If we were to farm anything, it would be soy beans or chick peas or some other food crop. Australia is still importing half of its food requirements and legumes are kinder to the soil than most crops.'

'Too hot and dry for those,' Leo said.

'We'd grow them under irrigation. Anyway, that's all in the future. So what are the latest livestock numbers?' Ian asked.

Leo took a small red notebook from his shirt pocket and glanced down at a page. 'According to my figures, Kanimbla is running 38 200 sheep, which includes 2100 stud ewes. And we're running just over 1000 Shorthorn cows, which is roughly equivalent to another 5000 sheep.'

'The accountant's figures were less than this,' Ian said.

'You always supply figures that are under the number of stock you actually run because if you lose stock you still have to pay on the figures you've supplied, whether it's to the accountants for tax purposes or for the rural boards,' Leo explained.

'But the property is only returning two per cent on its estimated value.' Ian's statement was more a question.

'A lot of places aren't returning even that,' Leo said.

'That's true, but many of these are far too small for Australian conditions. It seems to me that many owners here regard farming more as a way of life than as a business with the potential to show profitable returns. They simply like the life and don't see themselves doing anything else. But back when wool and beef prices dropped, some of the big pastoral companies – and I mean companies running huge numbers of sheep and cattle – sold all their properties. Some of these companies had a long association with the land, but they simply walked away from it because they couldn't entertain a return of two per cent on capital. And shareholders placed their money elsewhere,' Ian said.

'You've been doing your homework,' Blake said.

'I think it's important to understand the wider context,' Ian answered. 'Let me put my cards on the table, Mr Blake. The truth of the matter is that although you believe I'm very fortunate to have been left this property by my uncle, I don't have any great desire to be here. I think that to be good at something you need to have a passion for it and I haven't yet developed a passion for the land. I had a pathway drafted out for me that was not of my choosing and it included a spell of jackarooing. I did it because it was what my father wanted. I promised my grandfather that I'd abide by my father's wishes.

'You're probably thinking that I'm an ungrateful sod because there would be any number of young men who would give anything to be in my position. But they would be the kind of men with land and stock on the brain. I wasn't ignorant about stock before I went to Warren, and I learnt a lot more while I was there. Obviously, Australia's seasons and its way of running stock differ greatly from Britain's, and I still have a huge amount to learn. But I've come to terms with the basics.'

Leo shifted in his chair. 'Well, this is a nice how-do-you-do. Here was me thinking that you'd be Kanimbla's saviour, and now you tell me you aren't even sure if you want the place! So if you don't see yourself as a grazier and merino stud master, what do you see yourself doing?' Leo asked.

'Going to Cambridge,' Ian answered.

'University?'

'That's right. My father and mother were both zoologists, though they had medical degrees as well,' Ian said.

Leo whistled. 'What were they doing when they were killed?'

'They were studying African hunting dogs – part of an overall study of the Canidae family. That's the world's indigenous dogs. They were planning to come here to study the dingo,' Ian said.

'And do you want to become a doctor too?' Leo asked.

'Doing a science degree as well as medicine gives me more options,' Ian replied evenly.

'You'd need to be a brain to do that, wouldn't you?' Leo said.

Ian hesitated before answering modestly. 'I did pretty well at Harrow, Mr Blake.'

'Well. If you don't stay here, I know your uncle would have been very disappointed. Jack was a tearaway in many respects but he was strong on family ownership of properties. He used to talk to me about places in England that had been owned by the same families for hundreds of years. He and Linda were pretty devastated about not having a son to take over here, though they tried not to show it,' said Leo.

'The point I'm trying to make is that I'm not sure that I can do what I really want to do and play around with sheep and cattle,' Ian said.

'You wouldn't need to do much playing around, as you

put it. Your uncle certainly didn't. He was always somewhere else (mind you, it cost a packet!). We bring in teams
to do the lamb and calf marking and the mulesing, so you
don't have to be involved in that area of management. You'd
want to get yourself involved with the ram selling, though,'
Leo said.

'But isn't ram selling a kind of treadmill?'

Leo didn't try to hide his annoyance. 'I wouldn't exactly
describe showing and selling rams as a treadmill! There are
a lot less interesting occupations than trying to improve the
merino's genetics. Computers have added a whole new dimension to sheep breeding – cattle breeding too, for that matter.'

Ian felt suddenly tired. 'I'm sure they have and no doubt
you're right about it being an interesting occupation. Look,
I'm not going to make any sudden decisions. I'm committed to being here until I'm twenty-one and then I'll review
the situation. What I'd like now is to have a shower. Where
could I do that please?'

'Mrs Heatley will show you. She's back in residence now
and is expecting you. She'll give you your meals and look
after you. I'll give you a tour of the place over the next few
days so you get an idea of the layout. There's horses in the
stables and if you're a rider you could use them to have a
look around the closer paddocks. Always let someone know
if you're going bush on your own, though. There's a utility
in the big garage behind the homestead, and a Mercedes.
They're yours now.'

Ian nodded.

'I don't want to come across as a bloke who keeps hand-ing out advice,' Leo continued, 'but I suggest that sometime over the next few weeks we organise a function so that you can meet the neighbours. Some of them use our rams. Your uncle and aunt were very keen on the social side of things. Kanimbla is the kingpin property in this area and always has been. People look to it for some kind of leadership,' Leo said.

'Was my uncle respected?' Ian asked.

'That's not an easy question to answer. The toffy graziers respected him because of his aristocratic background. But to be honest, if I hadn't been here . . . '

'Maybe they'd have bought their rams elsewhere?' Ian suggested.

'That's about it, and I'm not saying that to big-note my role here. Truth be told, your uncle and aunt were often away for months at a time and they left the running of Kanimbla to me.'

'You can rest assured I won't be gadding about, Mr Blake.'

Leo continued, 'What I will say for Jack is that he was usually willing to take advice where Kanimbla's management was concerned. He saw the need to computerise our sheep-breeding programs and that's made a huge difference.'

Leo got up from his chair and slipped the crutch under his armpit.

'I'll take you down to the homestead now and you can meet Mrs Heatley. I should warn you that she might seem a bit grim to begin with. She didn't have much time for your uncle and might decide to tar you with the same brush.'

'She does sound a bit daunting. If she didn't like my uncle and aunt how did you persuade her to come back here?' Ian asked.

'Mrs Heatley's had a hard life. Her husband managed a property not far from here, but he was killed in a car crash. He was a boozer – ran right off the highway. Then she lost her son Miles in a motorbike accident, when he was about your age. That's how she came to be the housekeeper here. She has a house in Murrawee, but she likes Kanimbla,' Leo explained. 'She gets on very well with my wife. They go for walks together and can talk the legs off chairs.'

'How very sad she lost her husband and son. But I'm pleased she's back at Kanimbla – good show!'

'You sound just like your uncle. Jack used that expression even after all his time here. Still very English, he was.'

'I suppose I should say "Bewdy!" or "She'll be right, mate." What do you think? I mean, what would I be expected to say from my lofty position as owner of Kanimbla?' Ian asked.

'It depends on how ocker you want to be. It could be "You beaut!" or maybe just "Good-oh".'

'Good-oh,' Ian smiled.

Leo Blake was relieved by Ian's smile. At the outset he'd thought the young fellow might be a little too serious for his age.

'My ute's in the garage. If you get it and throw your gear in, we'll go down to the homestead. I suppose you *can* drive?'

28

'Of course. I drove everything I could at Warren, even a bulldozer.'

Leo raised his eyebrows.

'We were putting in extra dams and I had a go at it. But I much prefer horses to vehicles,' Ian said.

'So did I in my younger days. They're miles the best way to break in sheepdogs, too. From a horse, I mean. In those days labour costs weren't what they are today. Vehicles and four-wheelers are quicker but putting a dog on a motorbike doesn't teach him anywhere near as well. Are you interested in dogs?' Leo asked.

'Oh yes. Grandfather's manager had a couple of good border collies and he showed me how to train them. And there were plenty at Wongarben.'

'That's good. You can take over Gus, Jack's old kelpie.'

Kanimbla had been built when labour costs were low, so the original builders could afford to erect a very considerable homestead, by Australian standards. It had been added to over the years, but this had been done so well that it was difficult to pick the new part from the old. It was single-storeyed, of timber construction with a galvanised iron roof, and surrounded on three sides by the gauzed verandahs that were a feature of most houses in the district, and necessary unless you wanted to be perpetually brushing away flies. Kanimbla was nothing like Ian's grandfather's house in Cambridgeshire, which was of brick and stone with a slate roof, and two-storeyed with all the bedrooms upstairs.

As he drove along the red gravel drive to the front of the house, Ian noted the vast lawn, gardens and shrubs, gazebo and swimming pool. Majestic red gums lined the bank of the river beyond.

'This is nice,' Ian said.

'Yes,' Leo agreed, 'it's not a bad place to be at the end of the day.'

They pushed open a gauzed door and stood on the verandah. Leo pressed the buzzer and somewhere inside the house a bell rang. This brought almost immediate results.

'Mrs Heatley, I'd like you to meet Jack's nephew, Mr Ian Richardson,' Leo said as the housekeeper opened the front door. Ian took a deep breath, unsure what to expect. Glenda Heatley was a tall, rather elegant woman in her early fifties. Her fair hair was turning grey and she had grey eyes to match. Her longish face and fine chin suggested a serious demeanour.

'Mr Richardson. Welcome to Kanimbla,' she said in a rather businesslike way. 'It's nice for one of the family to be in residence for a while.'

It seemed that she imagined Ian to be staying only temporarily, but Leo soon put her to rights about that.

'Ian is Kanimbla's new owner,' he continued. If Mrs Heatley was staggered by this announcement, she didn't show it.

Glenda Heatley had been a teacher of what used to be called home economics, which included cooking and sewing, and she was a virtuoso of both. When her husband died, she accepted the position of housekeeper at Kanimbla rather than moving back to Brisbane. The homestead had been a very lively place when Jack and Linda were around, and despite her difficulties with Jack, Kanimbla came to be her life. Following their tragic accident, Leo had told her that he couldn't keep her on full-time until the will was sorted out. So she'd driven out to Kanimbla one day a week to dust and clean the many rooms on rotation, and in her free time, to supplement her income, she'd sewed everything from exquisite baby clothes to ravishing ball dresses and wedding gowns.

'I see,' she said stiffy. 'I've got you in the main guest bedroom tonight but I'll shift you into the master bedroom tomorrow,' she said.

'Anywhere will do for now,' Ian assured her. Mrs Heatley wasn't as icy as he expected, but she hadn't given him the warmest of welcomes either. Perhaps she had some kind of residual gripe about how his uncle and aunt had treated her. He decided he'd try and find out, as he didn't want to live in the same house with a sour housekeeper.

'I'll have dinner with Ian tonight, Mrs Heatley. Let's make it for seven. Ian could do with a decent night's sleep after that coach trip, so lay on breakfast for seven if you could. We'll spend tomorrow morning close by, have an early lunch and then head out to see Leigh,' Leo said.

'Very well, Mr Blake,' the housekeeper said.

When Ian returned from delivering Leo back to the bungalow, he found Mrs Heatley waiting for him at the front door.

She led him through what he learned was the reception room for guests into a ballroom with full-length windows that overlooked the front lawn. Further back, various hallways led to bedrooms, bathrooms and the huge kitchen.

'This has an en suite,' Mrs Heatley said, showing him into a tastefully furnished bedroom. 'Pop your luggage in here, have your bath and then I'll show you the rest of the house. All the bedrooms have doors that open onto the verandahs so you can leave them open when the nights are warm. There's a buzzer by your bed. I'll come and get you when I hear it.'

The en-suite bathroom, like everything else about the homestead, was quite large and there was a spa bath with shiny taps that looked like quite a recent addition.

Ian ran a bath and tried to relax, but there was so much to think about. Apart from his concern about whether he would ever be up to the job of managing the property, even if he wanted to, he was also anxious not to present himself to his employees as a complete novice. He'd learnt the hard way that many Australian men were very critical of 'Pommies' – despite the fact that Australia's first white settlers had come from England – and that their criticism could be quite scathing. He knew that whatever he did, he'd have to do it pretty damned well to avoid being called some fairly descriptive Australian names!

After a long soak, Ian buzzed for Mrs Heatley and she appeared so quickly he thought she must have been waiting for him. He took only a perfunctory interest in the many rooms he was shown through. He had been brought up in a grand mansion in England so he was quite used to a large residence. He sparked up when he found that his late uncle's study contained a decent collection of books and one of the latest computers.

'This was your uncle and aunt's bedroom,' Mrs Heatley informed him. It opened onto a wide verandah beyond which was a sweeping lawn, a rose garden and many shrubs. The most striking item in the bedroom was a massive four-poster bed.

'It's very impressive,' Ian said.

'Air-conditioned too,' she said. 'Now I'll show you where the dining rooms are.'

The main dining room was adjacent to the ballroom and the dinner table provided seating for thirty people. The kitchen was down another hallway and next door to it was a smaller, more intimate dining room with seating for eight. 'Your uncle and aunt ate here unless there was a big function,' Mrs Heatley explained.

Ian nodded. 'And the kitchen?'

'It's through that door,' Mrs Heatley said, pointing.

Ian walked through the door into the kitchen and nodded appreciatively. Every item was in its place and the whole room was as clean as a new pin. There were long benches for food preparation and three different types of stove – electric, gas and combustion. At the far end of the kitchen stood a solid wood table covered by a brightly patterned cloth. There were two chairs and he guessed that Mrs Heatley probably ate her meals here.

'Did my uncle and aunt have any of their meals here?' he asked.

Mrs Heatley shook her head. 'Never. They mostly ate next door and sometimes on the verandahs.'

'I'd like to have my breakfasts here . . . if that's all right with you, Mrs Heatley,' Ian said.

'If that's what you'd prefer, Mr Ian,' she answered. She had decided that she would call him Mr Ian, which seemed to suit him better than Mr Richardson.

'Does Mr Blake eat anything special?' he asked.

'Only good plain food. Mr Blake is a steak and chops man. He likes fish too, when we can get it,' the housekeeper said.

'I'll leave it to you, Mrs Heatley. I'll eat just about anything except curry,' Ian said.

Mrs Heatley was a woman who did everything with great enthusiasm and thoroughness. If she liked someone, she liked them a great deal; and if she disliked someone, they were left in no doubt about her feelings. With Ian Richardson, however, she felt she needed more than one afternoon to make up her mind about what kind of man he was. He might well prove to be an inconsiderate gadabout like his uncle, but something told her that this was unlikely and that there was a great deal more to him than met the eye. In any event, she certainly wasn't the only one keen to find out more about Kanimbla's new owner.

# Chapter Four

As a boy of eight, Ian's world had crashed about him when the plane carrying his parents had nose-dived into the African plain. He had been left with bearers at the base camp until the police came to inform him that both his parents were dead. His father and mother had been rather eccentric, though loving parents who had taken him with them all over the world, and it took him some time to comprehend that he would never see them again.

At first, neither he nor anyone else knew what his future might hold. Stickers on crates belonging to his parents suggested that they had an association with Cambridge University in England, and communication with the university finally unearthed the wills of Laurence and Helene Richardson, held by a prestigious legal firm in London. The wills contained detailed provisions for Ian's education, but of more immediate concern was the direction that he was to be looked after by his elderly paternal grandfather. General Sir Nicholas Richardson had had a distinguished military career and was a director of several companies. A widower, he lived alone at Lyndhurst, a very beautiful and productive property beside the River Ouse in Cambridgeshire.

Sir Nicholas, who had raised four sons and lost three of them – two in war and now Laurence in Africa – was chuffed that his youngest and brightest son had chosen him to look after his grandson. But the will provoked a contretemps between Sir Nicholas and his eldest and only surviving son, Jack. Childless, Jack and his wife Linda wanted Ian quite desperately. Their desire to adopt the boy was strengthened further after they flew to Britain to see him. Linda thought him an enchanting child and devastatingly bright. At Linda's urging and because he loved her dearly, Jack took legal advice in an attempt to wrest Ian from Sir Nicholas's guardianship, but it was a fruitless undertaking. Under the terms of Laurence's will, Ian's fate was sealed. Ian was to be brought up by Sir Nicholas and schooled at Harrow. After leaving school, he was to do a stint of jackarooing in Australia. At twenty-one, he would be free to choose the career he wished to follow. It seemed that while Laurence and Helene Richardson wanted Ian to have a taste of Australian rural life before committing to any career, they did not consider Jack's lifestyle conducive to good parenting. Jack's expulsion from Harrow and a series of drunken escapades featuring women and fast cars didn't help his cause.

So, from Nairobi, Ian was escorted to London by a junior member of the British diplomatic fraternity, from where he was taken to Lyndhurst. For three years he was tutored at his grandfather's home before going to Harrow. Sir Nicholas was a wise old bird and knew that Ian would find it rough at boarding school. He knew his grandson had exceptional qualities, but that he needed to learn how to fit in. Sir Nicholas believed that Harrow would be the making of Ian because it would prevent him from retreating so much into himself as to become a kind of hermit.

Harrow was a great school with a rich tradition, but for Ian, boarding there was akin to being exiled to another planet. He was an individual in a place where you were required to conform to a great many rules. Ian hated it, at least in his early years. He had few friends his own age and had begun to imagine that there might be something seriously amiss with him. Unlike his classmates, he was not interested in girls or sports such as rugby, and unlike his grandfather, he was not drawn to a career in the military.

It was only the libraries at Harrow and Lyndhurst that helped make his life endurable. Sir Nicholas had inherited a massive library to which he had added some hundreds of books, and Ian habitually lost himself in this Aladdin's cave of literary riches. He was exceptionally well read when he enrolled at Harrow, and as the school library was well stocked, he was able to keep up his reading there.

Ian also lived for the holidays, when he could walk through the meadows and along the river at Lyndhurst, and help his grandfather oversee the property. Sir Nicholas kept a fine stable of horses, and Ian came to love these majestic animals. As an ex-cavalryman, Sir Nicholas saw to it that his grandson could ride a horse with the best in the country. They often rode together and keen judges were heard to pronounce that there was nothing between them as to either seat or style. Ian could even ride and jump bareback, with his hands behind his back, thanks to Sir Nicholas's cavalry training.

Initially in awe of his grandfather, Ian grew increasingly fond of him over the years. The old man didn't hand out many bouquets, but when he did Ian knew that he had earned them. Occasionally, Sir Nicholas would lay his hand on the boy's shoulder – a signal that he was especially pleased with him. Used to assessing and commanding thousands of men, Sir Nicholas saw the steely resolve beneath his grandson's reserved demeanour – the boy never skited, not even when he topped his first year at Harrow.

'Jolly good show,' Sir Nicholas had said.

'What is, Grandfather?' Ian had asked.

'Your results, Ian.'

'Oh, that. I'm glad you're pleased,' the boy had said.

And that was that.

Sir Nicholas realised that his grandson was far brighter than he had been at the same age, and probably even smarter than Laurence, and took every opportunity to offer the wisdom of his own experience. He was particularly concerned that Ian might fall prey to alcohol. 'Stay off it if you can. Not easy, I know. It was damned difficult for me, in the mess especially. You've got to be very strong. People will think you're anti-social, but you can show them it's possible to have a good time without liquor.'

The old man held very definite views about a wide range

of topics, and was not shy of sharing them with his grand-son. 'Australians are an irreverent lot. Got to admit they're damned fine soldiers, though. Lack a lot in discipline but don't seem to need it. They've done a first-rate job settling the country, considering what they started with. Australians judge a fellow on the job he does. Understand?'

'Yes, Grandfather.'

'It's important, since you'll be going there.'

'I understand, Grandfather,' Ian said.

'Good show, Ian,' Sir Nicholas said and rested a hand on the boy's shoulder.

Sir Nicholas and Ian were sitting on a bench watching the ducks on the river. Behind them, new lambs gambolled on the rich pastures of what had originally been fen country.

'You know that the family has been in wool process-ing a long time, Ian,' Sir Nicholas began. 'Well, soon after Australia was settled – largely by scoundrels from here, remember – we began to hear that it had a flourishing wool industry. Our mill received some samples of this wool. It was very fine and soft, and produced lovely cloth. We heard that there was unlimited land waiting to be taken up so my great-grandfather decided to send his youngest son, Gavin, to have a look at what opportunities there were for acquiring land. It's a long story, Ian old chap, so I hope I'm not boring you,' Sir Nicholas said.

'You could never bore me, Grandfather,' Ian said.

'Because most of the immigrants were settling in New

South Wales, the Queensland Government began its own immigration program in the early 1860s, offering land to immigrants who paid for their own passage. This meant that people with money or influence back in Britain often managed to secure large areas of land. That's how Gavin Richardson acquired Kanimbla, and it's been held by the Richardsons from that day to now. It came to me from my father and I passed it on to your Uncle Jack. I hoped it would be the making of him.'

Ian was pleased that his grandfather had confided in him. If he had been a less respectful boy he would have taken issue with one aspect of his grandfather's story. He knew from his extensive reading that many of the 'scoundrels' his grandfather had referred to had been transported to Australia for pitifully small offences brought about by Britain's woeful social system. He had enjoyed reading about Australia's history and was amazed that the country had travelled so far in little more than two centuries.

Sir Nicholas had devoted his whole life to family and country. Yet he was not a dour man or devoid of humour. He had a rich laugh and enjoyed a good story as much as anyone. The Lyndhurst property was only a fraction of the size of Kanimbla, but it was exceedingly productive. Its peat-black reclaimed fen country produced heavy crops of wheat, corn and potatoes and the pastures turned off high-quality prime lambs and vealers. It was profitable enough to employ a manager and a farmhand plus a housekeeper.

Ian would never forget the day that Hooper, Sir Nicholas's

former batman and then driver and handyman, came to collect him in the Rolls Royce. Sir Nicholas was very ill, and had been taken to a private room in a nearby hospital. He managed to dredge up a smile when Ian entered the room and came to stand by his bed. Hooper stood to attention just outside the door. A sister stood beside Ian and watched Sir Nicholas carefully.

'Grandfather!' Ian breathed and took the hand lying on the blue counterpane.

'Ian, lad, it's good to see you,' Sir Nicholas said faintly. 'Sit down, there's a good fellow. See you better that way.'

'I never thought you'd get sick, Grandfather,' Ian said.

'No good gilding the lily. It's my Last Post, lad. Want to say a couple of things before I go.'

'Shouldn't you be saving your strength?'

'Doesn't matter now, Ian. Want you to know what a joy you've been to me. Damned pleased your father sent you to me. Lyndhurst is yours, Ian,' Sir Nicholas said in a voice that was not much more than a whisper.

'Thank you, Grandfather.' Ian paused, 'Does that mean I don't have to go to Australia after I finish school?'

'Afraid not. We have to follow your father's orders. You can do what you like once you're twenty-one. Understand?'

'I understand. Oh, Grandfather! Thank you for everything . . . for looking after me . . . well, for everything. I'll never forget you. And whatever I do, I'll try to do it well. I wish you were going to be here to see it,' Ian said, his voice breaking.

'I've had a good innings, Ian. I could have been killed many times. Saw others killed all around me. Been lucky, lad. Keep a straight bat and play down the line,' Sir Nicholas said.

'I'll do my best, Grandfather.'

Sir Nicholas closed his eyes, exhausted from the effort of speaking.

Ian stayed with Sir Nicholas until the end. Hooper brought the lad a cup of tea and sandwiches and then resumed his vigil outside the door. Several hours later, the sister woke Ian to tell him that his grandfather had finally passed away. Ian got up and went outside to tell Hooper. The ex-soldier came in and saluted before the sister covered the old general's face.

Jack and Linda Richardson flew to Cambridgeshire for the funeral on what was to be their last trip to Britain. If Jack was disappointed about not inheriting Lyndhurst he didn't say so. He knew that he had fallen far short of his father's expectations, and that Sir Nicholas had been more than fair in his treatment of him. He would never forget the climactic meeting where Sir Nicholas had read him the riot act and sent him out to Australia to take over at Kanimbla. 'You're a bounder and a fool, Jack,' his father had told him. 'For all that, I think you've got a bit of good stuff in you. Be damned disappointed if you haven't. I'm giving you Kanimbla, which is more than you deserve. But it's your last chance. If you make a mess of it, you're on your own.'

Jack knew he had to make a go of this opportunity, and

arrived at Kanimbla full of enthusiasm and energy, even if some of that seemed, at times, misplaced. Still, over the years, Kanimbla had made Jack a fair living and he'd become a well-known figure in the Australian pastoral industry. Linda was a strong woman who always called a spade a spade. The fact that she loved Jack had not blinded her to his faults, and she never shied away from expressing her opinion. If she had been otherwise, Jack would probably have gone to the devil. In many instances, she had been responsible for toning down his wild behaviour.

When Jack and Linda met a teenage Ian at Sir Nicholas's funeral, they were even more impressed than they had been with the newly orphaned eight-year-old. Linda thought Ian was the nicest young man she had ever met. 'I'd be very proud to call Ian my son, Jack,' she said to her husband.

'Well, he was obviously a hit with the old man,' Jack replied. He remembered, with shame, the terrible dressing-down he had received from his father after being expelled from Harrow. He knew that his behaviour had been a black mark against not only himself but his whole family. Now it seemed that his nephew had more than redeemed the Richardson name by covering himself with glory at Jack's old school.

Jack shrugged. 'I don't begrudge Ian the old place. Laurie would have got it anyway, so what's the difference?'

'What we have to think about now is who will inherit Kanimbla should anything happen to us,' said Linda, practical as always. 'You haven't made a change to your will since we were married.'

Jack felt that the question was academic, since he never considered his own death, but he was keen to reassure Linda.

'If I go first, the place is yours while ever you want it. If you don't want it, put it on the market,' he said. 'And if we both disappear off the face of the earth, that's easy – Kanimbla will go to Ian.'

How cruelly ironic that this is exactly what would happen.

# Chapter Five

'Should I wear a tie for dinner, Mrs Heatley?' Ian asked.
Despite her coolness, Ian felt himself drawn to Mrs Heatley,
who reminded him of Mrs Peake, the housekeeper at Lyndhurst, and he was determined to win her respect.

'I don't think a tie will be necessary. Mr Blake doesn't
concern himself too much with dressing up. An open-
neck shirt and a pullover will be fine. You'll be having an
informal discussion so it's not like a dinner party. I'm sure
you wouldn't want Mr Blake to think you're a toff first-up,
would you?'

'Not at all, Mrs Heatley,' Ian smiled. 'I want to start off
on the right foot.'

Mrs Heatley nodded her approval. She sensed that her
new employer was relying on her to ease him into his new
role as boss, and she liked being needed. 'I'll make up the fire
in the study and you can sit in there after dinner. Most of the
stock records are kept there.'

As Mrs Heatley had predicted, Leo arrived tie-less. They
went straight into the small dining room. The manager took

the beer Mrs Heatley handed him and saw that his new employer had been given an orange juice.

'Settled in?' Leo asked.

'With Mrs Heatley's help. She obviously knows everything, even down to what you prefer in the way of food.'

'No mystery there. Nothing flash. My daughters tell me I have boring tastes. Of course Rhona says worse than that. She reckons I'm a dinosaur,' Leo chuckled.

'Oh, why?' Ian asked.

'I'm one of the last of a dying breed, Ian. I'm like the old drovers – we've just about had our day. I'm too much of a bushie for Rhona. She mixes with so-called New-Age men. They can all argue like bush lawyers but if you asked them to put up a length of fence they'd die of fright. I had a mate of Rhona's here, setting up the stud merino records. He was a genius on the computer but didn't have a clue about the day-to-day running of the property. It cost us a heap of money, though I admit it's been worth it in the end. Jack couldn't follow the computerised records but the overseer here didn't have any trouble. When Rhona comes up she checks on the system and makes any necessary changes,' Leo said.

'I should be able to handle that side of things,' Ian said, and then added hastily, 'once Rhona shows me the systems you've set up, of course.' He didn't want Leo to think he was a know-all.

'Well, I'm relieved. I'm not saying the computer isn't the way to go, it's just that it's not my game. That aside, being able to call up all the sheep records so easily is a huge improvement. I'm not such an old fogey that I fail to recognise that. You can measure fleece weights and tell which ram is leaving the best progeny. Big factor when you're selling rams,' Leo explained.

Over dinner, which began with a light vegetable soup followed by steak and then fruit salad, the conversation veered away from rural subjects for a while as Leo sought to discover more about Ian's background.

'So you went to Harrow. Good school?'

'Some people say it's one of the best in Britain. Harrow and Eton both have their champions. Winston Churchill went to Harrow. He might have been as unhappy – at least in his early years – as I was. I always felt quite out of place,' Ian said.

'How did you finish up?' Leo asked.

'Oh, I topped my year,' Ian said quietly.

'Phew!' Leo whistled, 'I knew you did well . . . Actually, I wasn't thinking so much of your results as whether you came to terms with being there.'

'I never felt at home. And this isn't meant as a criticism of Harrow because I wouldn't have been at home at any school. I just couldn't imagine myself in the armed services. That's where lots of my classmates were headed. Harrow has a special course to prepare you for an army career. My grandfather was a general and he was knighted for his military contribution but he understood that I wasn't like him. I'm too much like my father, Mr Blake,' Ian said.

'So why did your father insist that you spend time in

Australia? Why couldn't you have gone straight to university?' Leo asked.

'He wanted me to experience the Australian side of our family history, I guess. To see what life on the land might be like. I don't know, maybe to give me more options. He wasn't to know that Uncle Jack would leave me Kanimbla.'

'It seems to me that you're in the fortunate position of having a choice of careers. If you don't like the land you can go back to England and do something at Cambridge, and you've got a home there into the bargain. Looks like you'll never be short of a quid,' Leo said.

'I realise that having money is important and that it makes a difference to one's lifestyle, but it isn't my top priority. I'm much more interested in doing something that makes a contribution; that's what will really give me satisfaction,' Ian said.

'That's a very mature point of view,' Leo said.

'My grandfather always encouraged me to do something I feel passionate about. I'll admit there are all sorts of other things I could do – like completing the research my parents began. But Kanimbla has been left to me so I'm honour-bound to give it a try.'

'I think I understand,' Leo said. 'Judy and I went through this with Rhona. She was far too brainy to do just any job. We let her have her way and now she has a PhD and I don't know what else. I wouldn't say she's any happier than Joanna with her three kids and her cattle-mad husband, but she's doing what she wanted to do and we didn't stand in her way.'

Ian realised how difficult this decision must have been for Leo, and admired him. He also found himself hoping that the opportunity to meet Rhona might arise before long. She sounded interesting.

After dinner, Ian and Leo moved into the study where Mrs Heatley put a pot of tea on the hearth and left them. The study was a biggish room and apart from the book-shelves lining two walls, the furniture included a comfortable brown leather settee and two matching lounge chairs. There were large framed photographs of merino rams and ewes and splendid horses. In one corner stood a long desk on which there was a computer, scanner, copier and fax machine. A telephone and reading lamp sat on a separate, heavy writing desk. The fireplace was a massive affair, capable of handling large logs. Ian liked this room and looked forward to spending time in it. He had begun studying a science degree externally soon after arriving at Warren, and this would be a pleasant room in which to continue his studies.

Leo took a sheet of paper from his shirt pocket. 'Here's a mud map of the property – you'll need to know the full layout of the place to find your way about.' Leo paused for a moment before resuming. 'Let's start with people. Ben Fielder looks after things around the homestead, feeds and shoes the horses, and feeds the dogs. He's an old bachelor and very reliable. He lives in a small cottage near the stables.

'Next there's Jim Landers, who is the overseer and stud master here. Jim's a bottler, looks after all the stud sheep – everything from preparing the sale sheep to artificial insemination. Jim's got a great wife in Karen, and they have one child. Billy's nearly three – I think you'll like him.

'There are three jackaroos – Peter Cross, Ted Beecham and Gerald Bradshaw. Peter is the senior jackaroo and he works mainly with Jim Landers but they all do anything that's going. They're not bad blokes but, like most young men, they play up a bit from time to time, usually when they get a belly full of beer. They live in the jackaroos' quarters and there's an old shearers' cook who gives them their meals. That's Jack Greer. If you want to learn anything about inland fishing, Jack's the fellow to ask.'

Leo paused and gave his young boss a keen look. 'Got all that?'

Ian nodded. 'So far, so good.'

Leo continued. 'Then there's Norm Higgins, our station hand or boundary rider or whatever you like to call him. Norm's a cousin of Helen Donovan at the Murrawee store. He used to be a butcher but got sick of it and asked your uncle for a job. Norm's been here about ten years. His wife Kathleen is all right too. Norm is almost as keen on fishing as Jack Greer. They're always talking about the 'big ones' they've caught. Norm and Ben kill and cut up all the meat we use,' Leo said.

'That's handy. Norm being a butcher, I mean,' Ian said.

'Very. He makes sausages for us, too – they're the best! Now we come to Leigh Metcalfe,' Leo went on.

'Ah, yes, Mrs Donovan talked about him earlier,' Ian said eagerly.

'Leigh lives right up in what we call the gorge country. It's nothing like the New England or Monaro country, but it's fairly spectacular. He's on a rise right above where the river breaks out of the gorge on to our plain. It's a beaut spot. When you see what Leigh has done there, you'll understand what I mean. I should explain that Top River was once cut off from Kanimbla. The chap that bought the land built the house Leigh lives in, but he did no good – went broke, actually. Your people (that was before your uncle came here) bought it back. It's not far from an old shack that was built many years ago. That shack is on a dirt track that connects Top River with Bahreenah and the main western road,' Leo explained.

'So what does he do up there?' Ian asked.

'He looks after the top end of Kanimbla. But he does more than that. He's also our resident dingo expert and helps to keep them in check – otherwise we might not be able to keep running sheep. If that happened, and it's happened elsewhere, we'd have to go over fully to cattle,' Blake explained. 'Leigh's got a dog that's almost human. Unreal, Shelley is. He's a German shepherd – we used to call them Alsatians in the old days – and he can smell dingoes a mile off.'

'I see,' Ian mused. 'Mrs Donovan told me that your daughter has a very high opinion of Leigh's literary abilities.'

'Who am I to argue with a PhD?' Leo grinned.

'Is Leigh a full-time employee?' Ian asked.

'Not exactly. I pay him on the basis of two days a week.

He lives rent-free and gets his fuel and meat for nix. If we need him for more than two days in a week, I pay him casual rates. In his free time, he writes and does a bit of bird-watching. He's just about a walking encyclopaedia on Australian birds. Especially parrots,' Leo explained.

'Does he live alone?'

'Oh, yes. Leigh doesn't like being around people. He went up there mainly to get away from them. He tried to get your uncle to let him buy fifty acres around the house and river,' Leo said.

'What did Uncle Jack say?' Ian asked.

'He said he'd think about it. I told Jack that while we owned the house Leigh was beholden to us, but if we allowed him to buy it, he could thumb his nose at us. I'm not saying that he'd do that but he could,' Leo said.

'What's he like?' Ian asked.

'I suppose a lot of people would describe him as a bit strange. He either talks a lot or doesn't talk at all. It depends on the company. My wife gets on well with him and reckons he's handsome in a rugged kind of way. Rhona says he has a magnetic personality when he makes the effort. I've never had any trouble talking to Leigh but I stick to basics.'

'Does he have a girlfriend?'

'Why do you ask?' Leo said with a frown.

'It was just something Mrs Donovan said,' Ian answered casually.

Leo gave Ian a hard look before answering. 'If you heard that Leigh and Rhona were having an affair, then I can tell you that they weren't. I told Leigh that if he so much as laid a finger on Rhona, he was out on his ear. He assured me that he hadn't touched her and that he wouldn't. Rhona and I had a big row about it. She can be a real pain,' Leo said tightly.

Ian was beginning to feel more comfortable with Leo and wanted to find out as much as he could. It was clear that there was a lot more to this district than merino sheep. 'Couldn't she have told you to mind your own business? I mean, your daughter is a grown woman and is quite probably involved with men in Sydney.'

Leo didn't seem put out by the directness of Ian's question. 'I don't doubt that she is, but I don't have to work with them. I didn't want my daughter being seen as another scalp on Leigh's belt, especially right after Trish Claydon had been sleeping with him. Women are only a game for Leigh. I wanted better than that for Rhona.'

'Have you read any of Leigh's work, Mr Blake?' Ian asked, changing the subject.

'Some,' Leo answered. 'I read one of his novels and some of his poems. There's some I like and some I don't. Important-looking people have been out here to talk to Leigh, so he must rate fairly high. You'll probably get on very well.

'Well, that's the team, Ian. Now I'll tell you a bit about the country. We grow some oats and lucerne for the stud sheep. We use the river for irrigation. We've got an allocation of water and we use most of it. So far we haven't had a problem with salinity but some places have. Of course they're a fair way from here and every place is different.

'Basically, we're trying to produce a nice-handling, medium wool on a big-framed sheep. By that I mean a well-crimped, soft wool that micron tests finer than it looks. I'll get Jim Landers to talk to you about the stud side of things but I suppose that after your stint at Warren you'll probably have a fair idea of the basics of merino breeding. Warren used to be one of the great stud merino areas,' Leo said.

'I got a crash course,' Ian smiled. 'Mr Murray was very helpful and I picked up quite a lot. But I've got a great deal to learn.'

'I wouldn't worry too much about that. Some people catch on very quickly. It depends how keen you are. Now this is what I've arranged for tomorrow. We're going to have morning smoko down at the shearers' quarters. Everyone will be there at ten to meet you. That's everyone but Leigh. He won't come in, but we'll be seeing him after lunch tomorrow. Lunch will be here. You can poke about the house in the morning, maybe have a look at the horses, and pick me up just before ten,' Leo said.

'Sounds good,' Ian agreed.

'There's one other thing. I mentioned your uncle's dog, Gus. You'll need a dog and I suggest you take him,' Leo said.

'What is he, kelpie or border collie?' Ian asked.

'Gus is a kelpie and a damned good one. A MacLeod kelpie. Your uncle and I went down to Merriwa in New South Wales to look at a top ram and we saw this young dog that David MacLeod had going fairly well. We bought the ram – for a lot of money, I might add – and Jack asked David whether he could buy Gus too. So David sold him the dog. When Jack was killed I took him over. You couldn't have a better dog. He'll work anything from a chicken to a bullock, but Jack used him mostly to hold small mobs of rams when clients came to inspect them. It made him feel like a dinky-di stockman when sheep clients praised his dog.'

'How old is Gus?' Ian asked.

'He'd be about seven now. He's a great casting dog. David has bred for cast in his dogs – unlike here where it's quite flat, they need good casting dogs in their high country. They still use horses there. Motorbikes have ruined casting ability in sheepdogs, though you can't deny that bikes have their place,' Leo said.

'So who's this David MacLeod? Are his sheep as good as his dogs?'

'As good as you can get.'

'Are we still buying rams from him?'

'We bought two and used them in artificial insemination programs. They brought our wool up a lot and fined down the micron too. Big-girthed rams they were,' Leo answered.

'But this isn't fine-wool country,' Ian noted.

'No, it's not. But we've been trying to produce a super-medium wool rather than wool just on the strong side of medium. We've just about achieved that and maintained the size of our sheep,' Leo said. He looked at Ian closely, sensing that the young fellow knew more about sheep and wool than he was letting on. 'So you know a bit about wool?'

'My grandfather was a director of a woollen mill in Bradford,' Ian said. 'I'd go through the mill with him sometimes, during school holidays, and I guess I picked up a bit there. I can't say I know a lot about wool in Australia, but Mr Murray was a great help at Wongarben. He was very critical of the way Australia has promoted its wool. I don't know the subject well enough yet to say whether I agree with him, but I'm inclined to think he was right,' Ian said.

Leo poured himself another cup of tea. 'We don't have much to do with that side of things, though Kanimbla has contributed a lot of money in wool levies. I'm not interested in agri-politics. There's those that are and good luck to them – someone has to look after the growers, or the politicians would walk all over them. Now, about tomorrow. I'll get Ben Fielder to meet you at nine and show you around the stables and other buildings.'

Ian nodded. 'When are you expecting Mrs Blake?'

'That's a good question. Another few days, I'd reckon,' Leo said. 'No doubt she'll take the chance to visit the art gallery in Toowoomba on her way home. Judy's a bit of an artist herself.'

'You must both have dinner with me,' Ian said. 'I've seen some of the great paintings in the London art galleries.'

'Judy would like that, and if you can talk art, so much the better,' Leo grinned.

'What about your daughters? How often do you see them?' Ian asked.

'Joanna and her family visit us two or three times a year.

Rhona might come once, although since she's been helping on the computer she's been coming every six months or so,' Leo said.

'I'm wondering whether they'd like to come when we put on this function you suggest I give. They probably know a lot of the neighbours and might like to meet up with them again,' Ian suggested.

'That's a nice idea. Joanna and Rick would probably come. Their two older kids are away at boarding school,' Leo said. 'But how it would fit in with Rhona's movements I wouldn't have any idea. She's a lecturer at Sydney University. She gets sabbatical leave sometime in the near future and knowing her she could be headed for Peru or Africa or anywhere. Kanimbla wouldn't be high on her list of priorities, Ian.'

'Let's work on that proposition anyway. You could get Mrs Blake to talk to Rhona. If she comes, she can go over the computer programs with me,' Ian said.

'Good idea. I'll get Judy to work on her.' Leo stood up to leave and then turned back to Ian. 'There's one more thing I'd like to nail down. Your uncle was always referred to as Mr Richardson, never Jack. You're probably a bit young to be called Mr Richardson, but I don't want anyone taking liberties with you because of your age. Have you got an opinion on the matter?' Leo asked.

'I'd prefer they call me Ian. Just Ian,' he replied. 'I'm sure the men you've got working here wouldn't be here if they didn't meet with your approval. You had my uncle's trust and you have mine, Mr Blake.'

'Thank you, and for what it's worth, I think you're going to be all right. We'll settle for Ian and see how it goes. Oh, and one last thing. If you're keen to keep up your studies, you should have plenty of time. The staff do all the hands-on work. Your main job will be to familiarise yourself with the merino stud and to get to know our main ram buyers,' said Leo.

'That's a relief. As to how I'll shape up here, only time will tell. Time is the best judge of most things.'

After driving Leo home and before retiring for the night, Ian went out on to the long front verandah. The exterior lights were on, and bathed the grounds in a warm light. The lawn was extensive and stretched to the bank above the river. The gum trees growing along the bank provided a contrast to the lower Australian natives and other shrubs that grew in profusion around the lawn. A large gazebo contained a barbecue and a sink, and wide benches on which to lay out food. On the far side of the lawn the swimming pool was surrounded by buff-coloured paving, and at the river end of the pool, a low table and chairs sat in a small, covered area.

Ian walked across the lawn, stood beneath a gum and looked down at the murmuring river, its surface glowing silver in the half-moonlight. Then he turned and looked back at the gardens. This was, he concluded, a beautiful spot – a kind of Eden set in the midst of a much less idyllic landscape. He imagined what it would be like here when guests covered the vast lawn and some of them swam in the pool.

The gazebo would be full of food and drink and, as dusk closed in, this would be a magical place. He walked slowly back to the verandah to find Mrs Heatley watching him.

'Do you like what you see, Mr Ian?' she asked.

'Yes,' Ian said. 'I was trying to imagine what it would be like with a lot of visitors.'

'We never had any complaints. Your uncle used to fly in all sorts of delicious food – fresh seafood, whole hams. Nobody who was invited liked to miss coming here.'

'Well, it seems I'll be expected to have some kind of a party to announce my arrival,' Ian said.

'You sound reluctant.' Mrs Heatley didn't miss much.

'I don't like crowds – I didn't at boarding school. But, as my late grandfather used to say, "one's personal likes and dislikes often have to be put to one side".'

What he didn't add was that his grandfather had also said that you can't really judge the worth of a person until you see them placed under pressure. And Ian knew that there was going to be plenty of pressure in his new position at Kanimbla.

# Chapter Six

Ian woke to the carolling of magpies. One bold bird was perched on the rail of the verandah outside his window. It was one of Mrs Heatley's pets and was used to being fed scraps of meat and cheese. This was not what people were supposed to do with wild birds, according to the wildlife people, but Mrs Heatley didn't know anything about that. She liked to feed the birds and would go on feeding them for as long as she stayed at Kanimbla.

There were stewed peaches and cereal, and orange juice in a jug waiting for Ian when he walked into the kitchen. This was followed by bacon, eggs and tomatoes on toast. It was a tasty breakfast and Ian ate with a good appetite, knowing his first full day on Kanimbla would probably be long and tiring.

Ben Fielder was the first of his staff that Ian met that morning. The tall, quietly spoken man had been sitting on a bench at the back of the homestead and was halfway to his feet when Ian waved him back to his seat. It was difficult to estimate Ben's age. He had a salt-and-pepper beard and moustache, but his blue eyes sparkled beneath his wide-brimmed hat and seemed to belong to a much younger man. He was tidily dressed in corduroy trousers and a dark green shirt, and his laughing-side boots were tolerably clean. A pipe and tobacco pouch bulged from his shirt pocket.

'How long have you been here, Ben?' Ian asked, taking a seat beside him.

'Just on twelve years now – er – Ian,' Ben replied.

'And how do you find it?' Ian asked.

'It's a good place to be. There's some that would say it's too quiet for them, but I've had my fair share of excitement in life and I don't need it any more. Anyway,' he added as an afterthought, 'I've still got some nice horses to look after.'

'What is there in the way of horses?' Ian asked.

'There's a few thoroughbreds, and some that are a mix of thoroughbred and stock horse. The boss and his missus used to ride a lot. They played polo and polocrosse. I was told to keep their horses looked after and I have. They're not all shod but a few are. Do you ride?'

Ian nodded. 'Yes. My grandfather taught me. I'd love to do some riding here.'

'Praise the Lord. It's a damned waste. Those horses have been jumping out of their skins for work. I can't exercise them all myself. You can have a dekko at them now, if you like,' Ben said.

They wandered down to the stables, about a hundred metres from the homestead. The buildings were scrupulously clean and bales of lucerne hay were stacked at one end.

A black-and-white cat of enormous proportions sat licking itself on a bale and regarded the visitors with interest.

Ian thought the horses were a grand lot. Bays and browns with bright eyes and shiny coats. 'You've done a great job with them,' he said to Ben.

'Lovely things, horses. Expensive, but lovely. I hate to see a horse neglected. Mr Blake told me I was to keep them in shape just as if Mr Richardson was still here. There's saddles and gear in the room beside the stables. Some of these might be a bit lively for a while.'

'Do you think I could come back for a ride this evening, Ben?'

'I'll have Major saddled up and waiting for you,' Ben said, his face collapsing into a wrinkly smile.

'Thanks. You'll be at the smoko?' Ian asked.

'I'll be there.'

'Then I'll see you soon. Oh, by the way, would you mind looking after Gus for me?' Ian asked.

'Sure. I had Gus here before Mr Blake took him up to his house. Gus is a great dog. I'll get him and bring him down for you,' Ben said.

'Thanks a lot, Ben. If you have any problems come and see me any time,' Ian said.

He left Ben and drove Leo's ute up to the manager's bungalow.

'How's the ankle this morning?' he asked Leo.

'Much the same as yesterday,' Leo said with rueful grin. 'It's a pain in the bum, to put it bluntly.'

'Yes, I can imagine. Are we going up to the quarters now?'

'Presently. I've got a few more things to discuss with you before we go. I've drawn up a program of things we do each month. Some things might have to be changed from time to time but there are fixed events such as shows and shearing. You work everything else around those,' Leo explained.

Ian perused the list, then folded it and put it in his shirt pocket. 'Not much slack time,' he remarked.

'Not much,' Leo agreed. 'How did you get on with Ben?'

'Quite well. He seems a decent old chap. The horses are a credit to him. They look wonderful,' Ian said.

'Ah well, if Ben knows about anything, it would be horses. In fact, I think his problem has been knowing *too* much about them,' Leo said.

'You mean he was crooked?' Ian asked.

'He used to work as a trainer and I suspect he wasn't absolutely honest where horses were concerned. He boozed a fair bit, too, before he came here. But he's been right as rain at Kanimbla. He's got a rent-free cottage and a few horses to look after, so he's happy. I told him if he drank he was out,' Leo said. 'Right, let's go and meet the gang and have a feed of Jack Greer's tucker.'

'I had a pretty good breakfast,' Ian said, then looked at his watch and grinned. 'But that was a while ago.'

There was a hum coming from the shearers' quarters as Ian walked and Leo hobbled towards it. The long building

63

was made of timber with a galvanised roof. With a kitchen at one end, the set-up was similar to the shearers' quarters at Warren, but larger. The jackaroos' cottage was a little distance away.

The dining area was very large and a long table ran nearly the full length of the room. Backless benches lined both sides of the table that was, perhaps in Ian's honour, covered by white paper. There were numerous plates of scones, biscuits and damper and, at a separate, smaller table, a large stainless-steel urn of boiling water.

Jim Landers, the overseer and stud master, was in his early thirties, of average size with fair hair and blue eyes. He had learned the stud sheep business at Terrick, one of Queensland's leading merino studs, and was highly regarded in the merino business.

Norm Higgins, the ex-butcher, was a tall, lean man with dark hair and grey eyes. It was said of Higgins that he could catch fish where nobody else could.

The three jackaroos, Peter Cross, Ted Beecham and Gerald Bradshaw, were all sons of graziers and wore faded white moleskins and checked shirts. Ian would immediately christen them the Belted Trio because they each wore a plaited belt from which hung a knife pouch – apparently a mandatory item of bush apparel.

The last of the men was the station cook, Jack Greer. Greer was rather wild in appearance with longish grey hair, fierce blue eyes and the build of a weight-lifter. His physical presence was softened only marginally by his snowy white apron. Ian remembered what Leo had told him about Greer's prowess as a fisherman and that there was keen rivalry, fish-wise, between him and Higgins. He learned that it was generally conceded that, as a fisherman, Higgins was Greer's superior. It was also said that if Higgins could catch 'em, Greer could cook 'em, and his fish meals were to die for. Greer's past was something of a mystery, though he had apparently been a ship's cook for some years. This group, together with Mrs Heatley and Leigh Metcalfe, were Ian's employees. They were, in Leo's words, 'not a bad lot'.

The low mumbling of the men ceased when Ian and Leo walked through the door. Leo nodded. 'Thanks, fellas. This is Mr Ian Richardson, the new owner of Kanimbla and our new boss. You'll be calling him Ian at his insistence, but what he says goes.' Leo, despite his crutches, had an air of strength and authority. He did not have to lay it on with a shovel; the men obviously understood him well. Ian looked at his men's work-worn faces and knew he'd have a job to prove himself. Not one of them had had much time for his late uncle, and here he was, the scoundrel's nephew and a young bloke into the bargain. He could imagine them thinking he was just lucky to be born with a silver spoon in his mouth and that there was no way he'd know the drill out here. He'd soon fall in a heap and run back to England with his tail between his legs.

Yet, over the generous smoko and mugs of hot tea, Ian talked with his people and learned a little about each of them. They, in turn, learned a little about him, although Ian didn't make a speech or say too much about himself. Before leaving the group, Ian complimented Greer on his cooking and said that he had enjoyed a real Australian smoko. This pleased the old cook no end and later, he agreed with the others that 'young Richo seems a pretty good bloke'.

'That went off all right,' Leo said as they drove back to the homestead.

'Like you said, they're not a bad lot,' Ian said.

'There's quite a mix. Four blokes out of private school and three from the school of hard knocks. You never know how long they'll stay, but Jack, Ben and Norm have been here a fair while. They break out every now and again, but you expect that from blokes that live in the bush for long periods. They're pretty loyal really. I mean, they don't mind working extra hours when the need arises. Of course you need to do the right thing by them too. There's got to be a bit of give and take,' Leo said.

'It would be nice to meet Jim Landers's and Jack Higgins's wives. You might check with them and find out when it's suitable for me to visit the cottages,' Ian said.

'I'll do that.' Leo tried not to look surprised. Jack Richardson had never been inside any of the cottages.

After lunch they drove north-west of the homestead, staying roughly parallel to the river. The road was gravel and in reasonable condition. The vegetation, both grasses and trees, was varied. Leo pointed out the different timbers as they drove along. 'There're hundreds of types of trees and shrubs out here. It will take you years to recognise them all. Broadly speaking, there's black-soil country and mulga country. The mulga country is a lot lighter. There's Mitchell and buffel grass on the black country. Oh, and saltbush. There's several varieties of mulga including one called bitter mulga. If you clear mulga country it will grow what the old fellows call Prince of Wales feather but some call mulga oats. It has a feathery top and you'll know if sheep have eaten it because their piss is red. You need to be able to distinguish the useful stuff like mulga and wilga and myrtle from the poisonous stuff.

'The timber is mainly boree gidgee interspersed with dogwood, leopardwood, whitewood and broom. There's some bloodwood too – it's the favoured tree for the Major Mitchell cockies to nest in.'

Leo pointed towards a clump of trees on his side of the road. 'That's acacia – there are quite a few species. The easiest way to remember the various trees is from their bark and the colour and shape of the leaves.' Ian made a mental note that the acacias had narrow, grey-green leaves and smooth grey bark. Such a lot to learn, he thought, and all so different from the verdant pastures of England . . .

Absorbed in Leo's description of the vegetation, Ian had hardly been aware that they had left the flatness of the great black plain and were now on higher, rocky ground above the river, which had disappeared into a gorge.

'How long ago was the phone line put in?' Ian asked. He'd noticed it when they'd left Kanimbla but had lost sight of it along the way.

'A fair while before there were any mobile phones. Unlike the road, it follows the most direct route,' Leo explained. 'Now, turn in there,' he instructed and stabbed a finger towards a track that diverged from the main road. Ian turned off to the right and almost immediately saw a bungalow on a rise beside the river. The bank below the bungalow had been dug out and carefully stepped with wide planks, with the last step disappearing into the river's brown water. A small boat equipped with an outboard motor was anchored to a steel ring on one step. It hardly moved on the tranquil river.

'What a beautiful place! Who did all that work?' Ian exclaimed, pointing to the riverbank.

'Leigh did it. He got a couple of loads of second-grade timber and worked at the bank for maybe six months. Not bad, eh?' Leo said.

'It's terrific,' Ian agreed.

The timber bungalow was long and narrow, with an iron roof. A verandah facing the river ran the entire length of the building. There was a hammock and a wide table and a few chairs on the verandah. A man and his dog came down the steps and looked up to where Ian had stopped the ute.

'You can drive down a bit further and you'll find a place where you can turn and park,' Leo said.

Having brought the ute to a halt, Ian handed Leo his crutches and turned his attention to the man on the steps. His long hair, once very fair, was now liberally streaked with grey, and his beard was also pied. He was dressed in green gaberdine trousers and a red checked flannelette shirt. He

68

was shoeless and, like his trousers and shirt, his black socks cried out for a darning needle.

'G'day, Leigh,' Leo called as they approached.

'G'day, Leo. How's the foot?' the man responded.

'Not the best, but coming along. This is Ian Richardson.'

'All the way from dear old England,' Leigh said as he shook hands with Ian.

'Not directly. Via Warren. I've been in Australia for a year or more,' Ian said. He noted that Leigh's calm, brown eyes seemed at odds with his rather wild appearance.

'And that's Shelley,' Leo said, pointing to the German shepherd. 'He's not up to Gus as a sheepdog, though Leigh can get him to work sheep. But he's the smartest dog I've ever known, and I've seen a lot of dogs in my time.'

Ian studied the big ash-grey dog. 'I knew a lady in England who had a German shepherd. She called him Byron because she liked his poetry.'

'Shelley wrote the loveliest verse in the English language,' Leigh said with a gleam in his expressive eyes, 'the most gorgeous and the most lyrical. His imagery is unequalled.'

Ian felt his heart leap. It was as if he was hearing again his English master at Harrow as Leigh recited:

*'Higher still and higher*
*From the earth thou springest*
*Like a cloud of fire;*
*The blue deep thou wingest.*
*And singing still dost soar, and soaring ever singest.'*

Ian continued, reciting the next stanza:

*'In the golden lightning*
*Of the sunken sun.*
*O'er which clouds are bright'ning,*
*Thou dost float and run;*
*Like an unbodied joy whose race is just begun.'*

Leigh nodded as he considered the tall young man standing beside Leo.

'Pygmies. That's what modern poets are when compared with Shelley. We'll never again see anyone who can write poetry like Shelley or Keats. But we can only write what's in us,' Leigh said.

Leo, who had been leaning on his crutches during this exchange, nodded and smiled. 'I've talked to Ian about your role here, Leigh. He understands where you fit in. And I've explained about the dingoes.'

'How many dingoes would you catch in a year, Leigh?' Ian asked.

'It varies a fair bit. I killed thirty-odd the first year. Only a few young ones this year. Why do you ask?'

'Before they died, my father and mother were studying various species of Canidae – native dogs. They were planning to come to Australia to study the dingo.'

'Imagine that!' Leigh paused. 'Pity they're such a bloody menace here. Sheep are easier to catch and kill than roos,' Leigh said.

'How do you kill them?' Ian asked.

'Any way I can. Getter-gun and traps. They're harder to find in the steeper country, but once they come out onto the plain, I get them sooner or later. Mostly sooner. If there's one about, Shelley lets me know,' Leigh said. '"Yellow dog, pale and fleeting, beneath the stars I hear your yodelled greeting." I can't remember who wrote that, but it's damned good.'

They sat down at the table on the verandah and Leigh brought them freshly squeezed orange juice. 'Got a tree out the back,' he explained.

'What made you come up here?' Ian asked, intrigued.

'I suppose I can write better here. Of course, you can write anywhere, but you can write better in some places than in others. No matter where you go, you can't entirely escape from the fools of this world and what they're doing to the country. I tried to get as far away as I could from the cities and the cars and the crime and the greed. I wanted to be entirely divorced from politicians and public servants and bureaucracy. I suppose I could have gone farther out but I'd have a job to find a place to beat this one.'

'Seeing this place, I can't imagine you studying in the city. How did you cope?' asked Ian.

'Buried myself in my work, I guess. Never had much time for people en masse, but I was stuck with them at uni. I got away from that when I did my masters.'

'I know what you mean,' Ian concurred. 'I never thought I'd get used to Harrow, but I learned to cope, eventually.'

Leigh was unlike anyone else Ian had met since coming to Australia. There was a kind of magnetism about him. Leigh's place, Ian sensed, was somewhere he would be able to come to – escape to – if he needed. It was like finding a rare gem in an unexpected locality. It was only later that night that Ian realised why Leigh might be so attractive to some women. It wasn't that he was wonderfully good-looking, but that he possessed a kind of smouldering intensity or suppressed energy. It was what he *promised* that was attractive.

Following tea and damper cooked on the fire (the only electricity at the bungalow, which was a long way from the power grid, was produced by a generator), the conversation ranged across a great variety of topics. Ian found himself explaining that the school library had been his retreat at Harrow. 'I mean, I really did fall in love with books. Through all the wars and the obscene waste of life, there were writers and poets whose works will probably be read while ever there is life on this planet. Look at the regard Australians have for Lawson and Paterson. I was fortunate that there were a couple of masters at Harrow who understood that I was, like you, an individual. They couldn't do a lot about it but at least they understood. And Harrow did give me a great foundation of learning, which is what my father and mother wanted for me,' Ian said.

'You're absolutely right about the language, Ian,' Leigh said with a gleam dancing in his brown eyes. 'Cromwell took an army to Ireland and slaughtered close to sixty thousand of its people. He left a legacy of hatred for the English that has lasted over four hundred years. In much the same period, certainly during part of the seventeenth century, William Shakespeare produced the greatest plays in the English language. As Ben Jonson wrote, Shakespeare was "not of an age, but for all time". Two Englishmen and yet so different. One slaughtered people by the thousand and the other produced immortal verse. And who is remembered most today? Who is held in the highest regard? Certainly not Cromwell!'

Leo glanced down at his watch and frowned. 'We should be going soon, Ian.'

Leigh, who sensed that Ian wasn't at all anxious to leave, suggested they might like to stay for tea.

'Mrs Heatley is expecting us for dinner tonight, Leigh. We'll come again soon,' Leo said.

'Ian can come out any time he likes and I'll enlarge his knowledge of dingoes,' Leigh said.

Ian and Leo walked along the steps beside the river to the ute, with Leigh and Shelley following close behind.

'That's a great dog you've got there, Leigh,' Ian said.

'When you get a German shepherd, you get a quantum leap in canine intelligence. They think and they remember. Did you know that there used to be a ban on their importation to Australia?'

'You're kidding,' said Ian.

'No fear. It was put on in 1929. They were called Alsatians in those days, and they had to be sterilised in Western Australia. Plain stupid. Probably the brainiest dog in the world and it was banned,' Leigh said with disgust.

'Why?' asked Ian, interested.

'People claimed that they had wolf blood in them, and that if any went feral and crossed with the dingo, it would be calamitous for the sheep industry. A bloke called Kaleski wrote a chapter about them in a book, predicting all kinds of dire consequences if we allowed Alsatians to proliferate in Australia. Bloody funny when you consider that all dog breeds go back to the wolf, and that some cockies cross cattle dogs with dingoes anyway,' Leigh said.

'Who was responsible for the ban?' Ian asked.

'Some of the reigning powers of the pastoral industry got to the politicians and persuaded them to take action. In those days the wool industry ruled the roost. In some places, kids couldn't even keep white rabbits as pets.'

Ian was astonished. 'Really?'

'Yep. They were seen as a threat during a big campaign to reduce wild rabbit populations. Bloody stupid when you consider that anything white wouldn't last five minutes in the bush.'

'So what happened about the German shepherd?' Ian asked. He was beginning to understand that if you got Leigh talking, he was likely to range over a dozen subjects, all of which he seemed to be able to discuss in great depth.

'Well, they were banned for a fair while – up until the war – yet all this time they were doing great police work, like finding lost kids. No great disaster could be sheeted home to Alsatians, either, except that every time a dogger killed an odd-coloured wild dog, the Alsatian got the blame. The ban did, however, affect their breeding, because fewer numbers had led to poor temperament and some were becoming fear biters.'

'So what happened when the ban was lifted?' Ian wanted to know.

'A lot of German shepherds were imported by show breeders, who were looking for angulation. And what they got was a lot of dogs with crook hips. But that's show breeders for you. They've stuffed up just about every useful dog breed to put it into the show ring. The founding breeds of German shepherd were a bit like oversized kelpies – straighter in the back than the breeders wanted, and not fancy enough for the show cranks.

'Now we've got these dangerous, pea-brained fighting breeds that are taken out into the bush to hunt pigs and roos. Some of them get lost, and don't tell me *they* won't be a menace if they cross with dingoes. Shows you things can change. They banned the cleverest breed in the world, and then allowed these fighting mongrels into the country,' Leigh said with obvious disgust.

Ian looked at Leigh Metcalfe and thought he was an amazing bloke. Would he learn something new every time he came to Top River?

'I'd love to hear more, Leigh, but I think we'd better be going,' Ian said reluctantly.

'Be seeing you, then,' Leigh said and raised his hand in a theatrical gesture of farewell.

'Wow. Was all of that true Mr Blake?' Ian asked when he and Leo had come down off the ridge onto the plains country.

'I reckon so. He's a walking encyclopaedia on some subjects. If anything takes his interest, he studies it in detail.

Don't get him started on parrots or you'll need to stay a night,' Leo smiled.

As soon as he'd dropped Leo at his bungalow, Ian made for the stables. The shadows were lengthening now and it was much cooler. He found Ben grooming a horse. Major, a bay with a small white spot in the middle of his forehead and two white socks on his hind legs, was already saddled and waiting for him.

'I reckoned you'd be here soon as you got back from Top River. I could tell you were bustin' to get on a horse again.' Ben grinned, holding out the reins.

'Was it that obvious? Ian grinned back. He took the reins and, with little apparent effort, vaulted into the saddle. He walked Major around an adjoining yard until he had the feel of him and then put him to a trot. The old horse trainer watched the young man critically, but it was clear that Ian was no mug on a horse.

'I brought Gus down – thought you could take him for a run, too,' Ben said.

'Will he follow me?' Ian asked.

'I reckon so,' Ben said.

He walked up to the end of the stables where a handsome black-and-tan kelpie was watching horse and rider with great interest.

'You can take the road to Top River and about two miles along you'll find a track down to the river. There's a rough picnic spot there. Two miles up and back would be enough if you haven't been on a horse for a while. It pays to ease back into riding,' Ben advised.

Ian smiled to himself. Not so very long ago he'd ridden a long way further than four miles.

'I did a fair bit of riding while I was at Warren, Ben,' he said.

On a good horse – and as soon as he felt Major move under him he knew that he was top quality – four miles was only a hop, step and jump. As soon as he was clear of Kanimbla's buildings Ian put Major to a slow, swinging canter. He looked down and saw Gus keeping pace just behind.

It seemed no time at all before the track Ben had mentioned appeared on his right. A circular table made from rough-sawn timber stood alongside two log benches, and there were two more benches closer to the river. Ian dismounted, hooked Major's reins on a scrubby tree and walked down to the riverbank. Gus was a couple of feet out into the stream, lapping delicately at the water.

Ian sat down on one of the benches and took in the scene. It was, he thought, real outback country, though its harshness was softened by the tranquillity of the brown water. There was gentle birdsong up and down the river and, occasionally, the harsher calls of white cockatoos. Ian looked down as Gus emerged from the river and sat beside him.

'We're both a long way from home, aren't we, Gus?' The dog cocked his head at mention of his name. 'We'll be spending a fair bit of time together, so I hope we'll be good mates.'

Gus moved close enough for Ian to stroke his head, and they sat silently for several minutes.

'Well, I suppose we'd better be getting back,' Ian sighed eventually. 'This isn't a bad place for a picnic.'

On the way back along the track, Ian spotted a fallen tree out to one side. 'Let's see what you're like as a jumper, Major.' He put the big horse at the log and Major flew over it like a bird.

Ben watched as his new boss cantered Major back down the road towards him. He had a wonderful seat and a great pair of hands.

'Go okay?' Ben asked as Major came abreast of him.

'Major's a good horse, Ben. He can jump, too,' Ian said.

'Had a go, did you?'

'I couldn't help myself, I'm afraid.' Ian dismounted and handed over the reins. 'Are all the horses up to Major in class?' he asked.

'They're all pretty good. Your uncle wouldn't have anything that wasn't. Gus follow you all right?'

'No problem. We're going to get on just fine,' Ian said, stroking the dog.

Ben watched as Ian walked beside the horse yards and down to the homestead. He reckoned he knew horses and it was clear that whoever had taught Ian Richardson to ride had known his business, too.

After a quiet dinner in the kitchen, Ian asked Mrs Heatley to sit down with him for a few minutes.

'Mrs Heatley, I wanted to ask you about the reception for the neighbours which Mr Blake is expecting me to give. He suggested waiting a couple of extra weeks and putting it on during the school holidays so that some of the children could come too. Mrs Blake is going to draw up a list of people I should invite. He thought an evening barbecue would be best. Do you look after the food for a function like this? And what help do you need and all that sort of thing? Could you have a think about it and let me know?'

'Very well, Mr Ian.' Glenda was impressed by Ian's respectful approach. It was so different from the way his uncle had handed out instructions.

'Mr Blake told me that his daughter might be persuaded to come back for it,' Ian added as an afterthought.

'Might she indeed? Very unlikely I should think. He probably meant Joanna and her husband, but I doubt that she'd come either with a new baby. Rhona would be too outspoken for your party, and anyway, it wouldn't be the kind of function she'd drive all this way to attend – not unless there was a man she had her eye on. I think you can forget about expecting Rhona to come.'

'She sounds like a handful,' Ian laughed.

'That's an understatement,' said Mrs Heatley dryly. 'Rhona left here in high dudgeon last time she came, after a big row with your uncle. He suggested that she was more welcome elsewhere. In this case, I didn't blame him.'

'What happened?'

'I don't know, exactly, but Rhona can be outspoken to the

point of rudeness. She wasn't allowed to get away with much while she was growing up because her father wouldn't stand for any nonsense. He never had to touch Joanna, but Rhona got some whacks. The bush didn't suit her – but she's in her element at the university, I believe. She can have her affairs there and her parents don't have to know. It isn't my place to say this, so please excuse me, but if Rhona Blake comes here, you be careful, Mr Ian. Don't be taken in by her.'

'Now look here, Mrs Heatley, I don't want you apologising for giving me advice. I don't have a mother or a sister and I haven't had much experience in some areas of life. I'm very grateful for any advice you can give me so please keep on giving it. Now, if you don't mind, I'll head for bed – it's been a long day.'

Mrs Heatley smiled. God love him, she thought. Imagine Jack Richardson having a nephew as nice as that young fellow. I'll wring Rhona's neck if she goes anywhere near him.

# Chapter Seven

There were four cottages in a row beyond Leo's residence. They were separated by a road that led across the plain to Leigh's bungalow. The first cottage was the largest of the four and by tradition was reserved for Kanimbla's overseer. When Ian arrived on Saturday morning, Jim Landers was working in his vegetable garden, which consisted of neat beds planted with a variety of vegetables, all watered by a sprinkler system designed to reduce water usage and time spent watering. The garden was behind the cottage and was, as Ian was to discover, an example of the stud overseer's know-how and thoroughness.

Jim, sweat running down his face, pushed his old Akubra up on his forehead and greeted Ian with a grin. 'One of my weekend chores,' he explained.

'It's a credit to you, Jim. I've never seen healthier-looking vegetables. Of course, I can't say that I'm an expert in vegetable gardens, but this one looks a treat,' Ian said.

'Sheep manure – you can't beat it! Grow anything. Plenty of it under the sheds. Come and meet Karen and Billy,' Jim said. Ian was pleased to be out in the fresh air again. He'd spent the morning at his computer, writing a paper for his science course.

They walked around to the front of the cottage and up the steps, where they were met by an obviously nervous Karen. She was blonde, slim and very pretty, and seemed overawed to be entertaining the new owner of Kanimbla. Just behind her was a small boy with a head of golden curls and warm brown eyes.

'Ian, this is my wife, Karen,' Jim said. 'And this is Billy. Don't let his looks fool you. He might look angelic but he's full of mischief.'

'Karen, how very nice to meet you. And you too, Billy – a pleasure!' Ian said, shaking Billy's small, chubby hand. Then he went on, 'Mrs Heatley sent some biscuits and muffins for smoko. I'm sure you don't need them but you'd know what Mrs Heatley is like,' Ian said.

'That was nice of her,' Karen said as she took the two tins from Ian. 'We'll have smoko on the verandah, if that's all right. The flies won't bother us there.'

When Ian saw the spread Karen had laid out on the gauzed verandah, it was obvious that they would have no need of Mrs Heatley's contributions. There was a sponge cake, scones, Anzac biscuits and shortbread.

'Wow! You shouldn't have gone to all this trouble, Karen,' Ian protested.

'It wasn't any trouble. Jim likes his food and I only made a couple of extra things,' Karen insisted.

'So how long have you been in this area, Karen? Did you grow up here?'

'No, I'm a city girl, originally. I grew up on Sydney's North Shore. I met Jim through one of his cousins in Dubbo – I was staying at her place to go to a picnic race meeting. We went to school together,' Karen explained.

'And how do you like living at Kanimbla?'

Karen didn't respond, but looked shyly across at her husband.

'Karen finds it a bit quiet, Ian,' Jim answered for her. 'She also understands that it takes a few years for a fellow to obtain a top job. I mean, like a manager's job. I've got an uncle with a property near Gilgandra in New South Wales. He never married and his health is not too good so I suppose there's a chance that he might leave it to me.'

Karen's eyes lit up. 'We'd be near Dubbo, which is a good-sized city with lots to do.'

'Well let's hope that it doesn't happen before I've got to know you,' Ian joked. 'So what do you do with yourselves at weekends?'

'We occasionally have a weekend in Toowoomba but mostly it's Roma for our shopping. We've made some good friends in the district and we exchange visits. We go fishing and have picnics and there's always the TV. That's made a huge difference,' Jim said.

'It's still a bit dull,' Karen said and grimaced.

'Yes, but we know it's not for ever,' Jim said. 'Something will come up eventually. It's just that managers' positions on places like Uardry and Egalabra and Boonoke don't become vacant very often. The managers of those studs – Rowand Jameson who was at Uardry, Alec Ramsay who was at Haddon Rig and Peter Harvey at Terrick – they're legends now.'

'Is that what you want to do, manage a big stud?' Ian asked.

'Next to owning my own place, that's the best option,' Jim said. 'Those large parent merino studs helped shape Australia. The big properties depended on those studs to supply consistent lines of quality rams that suited their country.'

'What do you mean "suited their country"?' Ian asked.

'It's fairly simple. The secret to producing good wool is finding the strain of sheep that suits your country. Some sheep do well in certain areas but not so well in others. The old saying "horses for courses" very much sums up sheep breeding,' Jim explained.

Ian turned back to Karen. 'So what happens in Murrawee, Karen?'

'Not very much,' she answered. 'There's a good hall there but it's hardly used now. There's an oval or park where they hold horse days occasionally – the gymkhana is probably the biggest event of the year. There's a primary school. There's no doctor. The closest doctor and hospital are at Roma. I'm always worried about whether we could get Billy to Roma in time if he was hurt badly,' Karen said.

'So what do young people get up to? I mean, what is there to do?'

Karen laughed, 'You mean apart from drinking? I don't

know. Having Billy means we don't go out much. You could talk to Fiona McDonald, though. She's just left school.'

Ian looked out to the front lawn, where a blue swing hung from a rusting iron frame. It was beneath a tree with rough bark – he thought it might be an ironbark. He noted the shape of its leaves, determined to learn to identify these trees.

'Does Billy like his swing?' he asked Karen.

'Oh, yes, he loves it,' she replied.

'I want you both to know that if you've got a problem, you're not to hesitate to come and discuss it with me,' Ian told them. 'If you've got any suggestions, bring them to me too.'

He turned to Jim. 'I'd like you to come and see me when you can, Jim. I'm keen to know the ins and outs of the stud business. When I get settled in, I'd like you and Karen to come and have dinner with me. Thanks for the great smoko, Karen,' Ian said as he stood up. 'Perhaps Billy and I could have a swing before I go?'

Karen looked down at her small son. 'Would you like that, Billy?' she asked.

'Mmm,' he answered, nodding his head until his golden curls shook.

Ian and the little boy went outside and across to the swing. Billy launched himself at the seat with undisguised eagerness and was trying to get some momentum up before Ian even got to him.

'Here we go, Billy,' Ian said with boyish enthusiasm.

As the swing came back he remembered fondly the words

of the 'Road-Song of the Bandar-Log' from Kipling's *Jungle Book* and repeated them for Billy:

*Here we go in a flung festoon,*
*Half-way up to the jealous moon!*
*Don't you envy our pranceful bands?*
*Don't you wish you had extra hands?*

Billy squealed with laughter at the strange words and asked to be pushed higher. Ian was sad when his time was up. He had to coax the little boy, who took his hand, back to the bungalow.

On his return trip to the homestead, Ian called in at the manager's residence. Leo had his leg up and was reading a newspaper.

'I've had an idea. I want to install a swimming pool,' Ian said without preamble.

'You've already got a decent swimming pool,' Leo said.

'At the homestead, yes, but I want to install one for the staff. This is a very hot place and, unlike the coast, we don't have beaches and the river's not suitable for swimming. I want the pool for Jim and Karen and for Billy and for anyone else who wants to use it. I think it would do a lot for morale. We can appoint someone to be responsible for its maintenance. We can afford it, can't we?' he asked.

'I have no doubt we can afford it. What kind of pool do you have in mind?'

'The Murrays had a relatively inexpensive pool with concrete surrounds. I'd like a shade shed down one side. Will you get some quotes for me?' Ian asked.

'Sure. It would give me something to do while I'm out of action,' Leo said.

'Good show,' Ian said, pleased.

When Leo rang through to the homestead to say that Judy was back, Ian immediately invited them down for an afternoon cuppa.

'You might have told me he was so good-looking,' Judy complained to her husband later.

'What's that got to do with anything? The most important thing about a man is how he behaves, not how he looks,' Leo said.

'Leo, you've been with sheep and cattle far too long. Don't you realise what effect Ian is going to have on the women of this district?' Judy said.

'From what I've gauged of him so far, Ian isn't the slightest bit interested in women. He's got his mind on other things.'

'Oh, how little you know about women!' Judy exclaimed. 'Do you honestly believe that Ian Richardson – young, good-looking, unattached and the owner of Kanimbla, not to mention some great mansion in England – will be allowed to get away with being single? Not on your life!'

The next day, Judy gave Ian morning smoko on the bungalow's back verandah. Leo had departed with Jim so she'd asked if Ian would like to see some of her paintings. Judy was an attractive woman with dark, curly hair that was showing some grey, and warm, brown eyes that could light up a room. Ian enjoyed her cheerful nature and her sense of humour.

'I like your paintings, Mrs Blake. I really do. The later impasto ones are the best I've seen since I came to Australia,' he told her.

'Do you think so? I've been experimenting quite a lot,' Judy said.

'It shows,' Ian said.

'Who is your favourite artist?' she asked.

'Oh, Turner, by a mile,' he said.

'I suppose I should ask you why,' Judy said.

'Because he aimed for the stars. He sought to paint what nobody else had painted, to take painting to a new dimension.'

Judy nodded. She didn't often have a conversation like this at home.

'Turner did for painting what Shelley did for the English language, if you know what I mean,' Ian added.

'I know what you mean,' replied Judy, who had once been a teacher of secondary school English.

'Leo told me that you were eventually hoping to go to Cambridge University,' she said.

'That was my intention . . . '

'So Kanimbla doesn't appeal to you?'

'It's too early to tell.'

'But not to the same extent as Cambridge?' Judy probed.

'I'm committed to Kanimbla until I'm twenty-one. It's what my father wanted, and I promised my grandfather.

I'm doing a science degree, or at least part of one, by correspondence. That way I've got a leg in both camps, so to speak.'

'Well, I hope you can manage. It sounds like a bit of a juggling act.'

'I'll do my best.'

Judy had no doubt that Ian's best would be very good indeed. She was also more inclined now to her husband's view that Ian would have little time for romance. There were going to be some very disappointed young women in the district.

# Chapter Eight

It was several weeks since Ian's arrival and he had spent many hours crisscrossing Kanimbla with Major and Gus – the kelpie had already become a constant companion. Lyndhurst would have fitted many times over into Kanimbla's horse paddock and it was taking Ian some time to come to terms with the size of the property. He felt responsible, as owner of the property, for understanding how it was run, and his mind was full of all the new details he was trying to retain each day. To a boy brought up in the lush Cambridgeshire countryside, Kanimbla was, in many respects, forbidding country. There was the heat, the droughts, the snakes and the dingoes . . . and that was just for starters. He'd also driven into town and had a long look around, chatting to Larry Phillips at the hotel and getting a feel for life in Murrawee.

To say that Fiona McDonald was surprised to hear Ian Richardson's voice on the phone one evening was the understatement of the year. When she'd recovered from the shock, she realised he was inviting her over to Kanimbla to discuss something. Her mind raced. What on Earth could it be?

'Why not bring a horse and we can take a ride along the river road. Maybe have smoko,' Ian added.

'That would be lovely,' Fiona answered.

Fiona McDonald had thought quite a lot about the young man she'd met at Helen Donovan's store. Despite her looks and her background, Fiona had never had what she would describe as a boyfriend. None of the boys who'd taken her to films and parties had ever lingered in her memory. The hazel-eyed young man she'd met in Murrawee, however, had made a deep impression. The news that he was actually the new owner of Kanimbla accentuated his appeal. She was thrilled when he rang, and wondered if his call signalled an interest in her.

And so, the next morning, she found herself riding down the river road beside Ian. At the picnic spot, they sat on one of the log benches overlooking the river and Ian produced a flask of hot tea and some of Mrs Heatley's homemade biscuits. Gus sat close to Ian, and he shared his biscuit with the dog.

Fiona turned to Ian, and took a deep breath, 'So what is this mysterious thing you wanted to discuss?'

Ian met her gaze and cleared his throat. Fiona McDonald was the first girl his own age he had met since coming to Kanimbla. He wanted to start making friends, and she seemed the obvious first choice. More to the point, Fiona had been away at boarding school in Sydney and would have a useful opinion on the decay of the township. Ian knew he would need some allies if he was going to achieve anything, and Fiona seemed the perfect candidate. However, he found himself shaken up by Fiona in a way that he had not expected. She was more beautiful than he remembered – tall and slim in her jeans and shirt. He forced himself to concentrate on the purpose of their meeting.

'Well, I've had a good look around Murrawee, and it seems to me that certain improvements could be made to ensure the district's prospects.'

'What do you mean?' Fiona was puzzled. He looked so young, yet he spoke in such a formal, almost old-fashioned way.

'Well, I know I haven't been here long, but I can't help noticing that Murrawee seems to be losing businesses to bigger towns. It's a real shame.'

'I know what you mean,' Fiona agreed. This was a subject dear to her heart, and she forgot her nervousness for a moment as she spoke her mind. 'We've still got a policeman but no doctor and little chance of getting one. If it wasn't for the doctors with overseas qualifications who are willing to work in rural areas, even some of the bigger towns wouldn't have a doctor.'

'I've been thinking about this a bit, Fiona. Maybe it's because I've lived in a country where village life is still pretty much alive and well, but the shock of seeing this town slowly dying made me wonder if it's not too late to do something. I wondered what changes might get people interested in their community again, and thought I'd ask you, seeing you're the kind of young person that needs to be encouraged to stay.'

Fiona looked away, momentarily embarrassed by his gaze. She sensed he was attracted to her. She also felt pleased and flattered that he'd asked for her opinion, and tried hard to think of an appropriate answer. 'It would be great if there was more to do, more to attract visitors maybe. I don't know. Maybe a lovely park where people can stop for a picnic, or a playground for kids. Or even somewhere nice to stay. The gymkhana is very popular, and brings lots of people to town; perhaps we could have a sheepdog trial as well.'

'What a great idea, Fiona. Kanimbla could certainly help with that; we've got the sheep and the manpower.'

Fiona felt pleased that she had been able to suggest an idea that Ian liked. Later, when she stood by her vehicle and horse float ready to leave, she thanked him for a very nice morning. Did she imagine that his hand stayed closed around hers for longer than might be expected for a cordial farewell? It was something for her to think about.

That evening, Lachie McDonald sat with his daughter on the verandah of his property, Nelanji, as they enjoyed a drink. Lachie had had a busy couple of days and the two, who'd become much closer since Maisie had died, hadn't had a chance to catch up for a couple of days.

'I had a lovely morning with Ian, Dad,' she said. 'We went down to the picnic place beside the river and had smoko while we talked. Ian wanted my views on Murrawee.'

'What do you mean "views"?' Lachie asked.

'He's interested in what it's like for us, living here,' she explained. 'He seems so quiet, but his mind is racing all the time. Mrs Blake told me that he won all sorts of prizes at school. His father and mother were both scientists. Maybe he sees something that he thinks is not right and he wants to do something about it.'

Lachie leaned back in his chair and looked at his daughter. She looked especially happy today, happier than he'd seen her in a long while. 'But what do you think of him?' he asked.

Fiona blushed, 'Well, I think he's very sweet. He's trying hard but he doesn't seem to fit in at Kanimbla.'

'But do you like him?' Lachie persisted.

Fiona wondered what her father was driving at. 'Yes, I like him. How could you not like him? He's very well educated, has lovely manners and a cute sense of humour. Besides which he's very nice-looking . . .'

'And he owns Kanimbla,' Lachie added.

Fiona ignored her father's comment. 'Anyway, I hardly know him, and he won't be interested in a country girl.'

'Why wouldn't he be interested in a girl like you?' her father asked. 'I'll bet there are plenty of young blokes who think you're pretty special. Anyway, Ian's made the first move, hasn't he?'

And, remembering the way he had looked at her, she had to admit to herself that this was true.

# Chapter Nine

'If you take two more steps to your right, there'll be bits of your legs strewn all over the paddock,' Leigh Metcalfe said sharply.

Ian came to an abrupt halt beside the fence that led upwards from the river. They were on a faint pad leading away into the timbered infinity of the Kanimbla river paddock. He glanced across at Leigh and was met by a look that was at once a cross between a grin and a frown. Leigh pointed towards the ground and Ian could just make out an almost invisible length of line stretched tautly across the pad.

'If you hit that cord, it pulls the trigger of the getter-gun. That's it there, just to your right at the end of the log. It fires a shotgun cartridge and it's set at about chest height for a dog. There's another couple of them in this paddock. That's why I left Shelley at home. A bloke needs to know where he's planted them or he could be in big trouble,' Leigh explained.

'How do sheep and cattle manage? Don't they run into them?' Ian asked.

'There are no sheep in this paddock. It's a kind of buffer zone. When I'm using the getter-guns, Leo musters the cattle into the next paddock. That way I can leave the guns and not have to worry about them. The roos and emus set them off, and so do the pigs. If I hear them go off, I come over and investigate.'

'So how exactly do they work?' Ian was fascinated.

Leigh explained that the guns were quite simple and involved a length of galvanised steel pipe, a nail for the firing pin and a shotgun cartridge. 'You don't get as many dogs with these as you do with ordinary traps. Ten-Eighty poison is still the most effective agent of all, but it's a real bugger. I don't like using it because it kills more than just the dogs. But graziers hate dingoes so much that, in their eyes, the end justifies the means. It's easy to get that way when you have to destroy sheep that have had their guts torn out. It's hard enough to make a living in the bush without dogs ripping up your sheep.'

'Steel traps seem awfully cruel,' Ian remarked to Leigh. 'Surely science can devise a trap that doesn't cause as much pain and suffering.'

'Steel traps have been allowed up to now because of the damage that dingoes cause and because the grazier mob have exerted so much influence. But things are changing and some people are beginning to object. I can see the day when steel traps will be banned, so we'll have to come up with an alternative soon.'

'What about shooting?' Ian asked.

'That's one option, but you have to see a dog to shoot it,

and a lot of the time dingoes are only about at night. They're not as easy to spotlight as roos. If they're in tall grass, it's almost impossible to see them,' Leigh explained.

'Can't the numbers of dogs ever be reduced?'

'That depends on a lot of things. It depends on the type of country, for starters. Then there's the fact that in the old days, dingoes used to have only one litter a year. But now they're starting to interbreed with domestic dogs and the cross-bitches can have two litters a year, so that's adding to the numbers. Also, the cattle producers don't tend to be as diligent about getting rid of the dogs as the old sheepmen. Some of them seem to think that dingoes aren't a problem. That's until they check out their calving percentages. If there's a shortage of game, dingoes aren't averse to tackling calves. We've lost several calves here,' Leigh said. And before Ian could formulate another question, he sped on, 'I reckon some graziers are their own worst enemies. A big percentage of them never tie up their dogs. They're simply bad dog keepers. Some people should never be allowed to own one dog, let alone a heap of them. Then there's the shooters who lose their pea-brained biting dogs in the bush. I doubt we'll ever rid the country of wild dogs. There's too much rough country and too many national parks where dogs can breed up. The best we can do is to keep the numbers down – even that takes a lot of effort. Dogs and sheep simply can't exist together.'

'So how did you learn so much about dingoes?' Ian asked.

'By living with an old dogger. I went bush so I could write about the country – something Lawson did – and I ran into this old dogger and ended up camping with him for more than a year. Camped pretty damned rough, I can tell you, but I loved it.'

Ian gazed into the paddock of yellow grass and rough-barked timber. From a distance he heard the bellowing of a cow. Closer, there were crows cawing. He wondered whether there were any dingoes around now.

'You wouldn't see one of the yellow mongrels even if it was only a hundred yards away,' Leigh said as if reading Ian's thoughts. 'But if we had Shelley with us, you'd know if there was one about. He's never wrong. I never saw a dog that hates dingoes as much as Shelley. The hair on his back bristles when he smells a dog, and when he gets close, his lip curls.' Leigh paused. 'Well, you seen enough? If you have, we'll head back to the house and have a feed.'

'Mr Blake tells me that you're quite an authority on native birds,' Ian said as they wandered back.

'Yeah, well, I know a bit about them. Made it my business to learn what I could. Australia's got more parrots than any other country – between fifty and sixty species. Africa has only about a quarter of that. I became interested in cockies when I first read that some varieties were either endangered or had actually become extinct. The poor buggers have taken a hammering since they stuck the Union Jack up at Port Jackson – every mad bugger with a rifle used cockies for target practice in the old days. Not that you'd think so when you look at the numbers of white cockies along this river now. Other species, especially those that aren't widespread, haven't been so lucky. Then there's the numbers that are smuggled out of the country because they're worth a bundle overseas. A lot of them die in the process – awful,' Leigh said.

Ian marvelled at the contrasts in the man walking beside him: a celebrated writer and poet who killed dingoes one day and studied birds the next. Yet he felt comfortable with Leigh, and found himself confiding that he found western Queensland a very different place to England. 'I'm not sure I'll ever come to terms with this part of the world,' he said.

'Of course you'd find it different. But how do you think the first settlers from Britain found it when they arrived? The indigenous population were hunters and gatherers. The landscape and the vegetation were like nothing the white men had ever seen in their lives. And the weather could change from devastating drought to raging floods virtually overnight!' Leigh said. 'Don't sell this country short,' he continued. 'Sure, you can't run the stock per acre that you can in Britain, but we've produced our share of wealth. And a lot of it is very sweet stock country. It's an amazing place. You'd think there was very little life along these western rivers, but when the big rains come, all that changes. A river can be almost dry – maybe only a string of muddy waterholes – but after the rains, life reappears as if by magic. First the water fleas, yabbies and frogs, and then the water birds in their thousands. I tell you, it's just amazing.'

By this time they had reached the house and Leigh asked how steak, onions and a piece of damper would go down.

'It would go down very well,' Ian said. He'd spent a

couple of hours walking the paddocks that morning and was hungry as a horse.

'Right. It won't take long to burn a bit o' steak. What do you fancy to drink? Tea do?'

'Tea will do fine,' Ian said.

'It'll be tea with condensed milk because I don't see much bottled milk here. It's a bit early for the other stuff. What's your usual there?' Leigh asked.

'I usually stick to orange juice, but I don't mind a beer at the end of a long, hot day,' Ian said.

'You won't get into too much trouble if you stick to that regime. Of course, it depends if you can stick to one,' Leigh said with a grin.

They sat at the big table on the verandah and watched the river while they ate their simple but very tasty lunch. Shelley sat at the top of the steps and surveyed everything. Leigh noticed that Ian was watching the dog.

'He's keeping nit,' Leigh said, nodding towards Shelley.

Ian looked puzzled.

'"Keeping nit" actually means watching for the police when something is going on that shouldn't be. Like two-up – that's a gambling game you play with coins and it's illegal except on Anzac Day. So, to play it on any other day, one fellow has to keep nit,' Leigh explained. 'It's an old-fashioned saying now, but you'll still hear it now and again.'

'I see. I'm not up to speed with all the Aussie sayings,' Ian apologised, 'but I've heard a lot in the past year.'

'Not to worry. You'll get there. A lot of it isn't fair dinkum

Australian anyway. Not any more. The American influence is very strong – "guys" instead of "blokes" and that sort of thing. What say we take the boat and go for a cruise upriver? We might get a fish or two,' Leigh said.

'Sounds great. How far would we go?' Ian asked, torn between wanting to spend more time with Leigh and needing to get back to his studies.

'Oh, just a few miles. We might see something interesting – there's a lot of wildlife out there. I put the electric motor on the tinny this morning. It's quieter than the six-horse fuel job,' Leigh explained.

'Does Shelley go with you?' Ian asked.

'Bloody oath, he goes. He sits in the front and if he sees anything he doesn't like, he growls,' Leigh said.

'What doesn't he like, apart from dingoes?' Ian asked.

'Just about everything on four legs or two, except sheep. He doesn't mind sheep. He doesn't like roos and he doesn't like emus and he hates pigs almost as much as he hates dingoes,' Leigh explained.

Ian decided he could do with seeing a bit of the river, and they wandered down to the tinny, Leigh carrying handlines, some raw meat to catch bait, a bottle of water and two small cushions. 'The seats get a bit hard on your backside after a while,' he said.

'And here's me thinking you were a tough-as-nails bushie!' Ian laughed.

'I like a bit of comfort when I can get it. No need to suffer unnecessarily.'

The tinny's engine purred to life and they moved effortlessly into midstream. The river here was almost as wide as the long stretch near Murrawee, though it could hardly be called a large river. After a few minutes Leigh ran the tinny in beside a bank and tied it to a dead log. 'Time to get some bait,' he said. He tied some pieces of the raw meat to a couple of lengths of green cord, handed one to Ian and dropped the other into the water. 'If you feel something at the meat, pull the line up slowly and we'll see what you've got,' he said.

Inside ten minutes Leigh had three yabbies in a billy, but try as he might, Ian couldn't get one into the boat. 'Not to worry,' Leigh said. 'We'll have a go with what we've got. Here, I'll bait a line for you.' Then, 'Hang on, while we're here I'll see what's under the bark of that old red gum.'

Leigh jumped out onto the bank and proceeded to examine what lay beneath some loose strips of bark on the massive trunk of the ancient tree. He returned to the boat with two grubs in his clenched fist. 'Funny fish, these freshwater blokes. Sometimes they'll bite on just about anything and sometimes they won't bite at all. But grubs will often do the trick.'

They pushed off again and cruised along the gum-lined river. 'No wonder the Aborigines stuck to these rivers. Shade from the heat and plenty of ducks and fish. Look, there's a mob of woodies,' said Leigh, pointing ahead to where a small flock of subtly coloured, pale brown ducks floated on the river. Suddenly, the flock took off noisily like a squadron of planes.

'Nothing like a bit of water, is there,' offered Leigh. 'Water conservation is just about the number-one priority for Queensland – except that the dopey politicians lack the vision to realise it. There's more votes in building sports stadiums in the capital cities. But there'll be a day of reckoning, you can depend on it. With the dry years we're getting now, and more and more people moving here, water is going to become our most precious commodity.'

'I guess the English don't realise how lucky they are,' said Ian. 'A lot of Cambridgeshire used to be covered by water.'

'Yeah, fen country. It's been drained for agriculture now, hasn't it?' Leigh asked.

'That's right,' said a surprised Ian. Most of the people he'd met in Australia hadn't known a lot about Cambridgeshire.

'I've been there. Been to Cambridge Uni. And seen a lot of those lovely little villages,' Leigh said.

'You didn't tell me that,' Ian said.

'Yeah, well. You don't spill all your beans first-up. I'll bet Murrawee was a shock to your system after those Cambridgeshire villages. I reckon it would have gone down like a lead balloon, eh?'

'It's not a very lively place, that's for sure. But do you think it has to be as dead as it is? I mean, surely there are things that could be done to make it more attractive. Tourism is a big thing in Australia these days, but travellers must bypass Murrawee because there's nothing to see. How can you hope to keep young people in the bush when there's no entertainment for hundreds of miles? No wonder the small country townships are slowly dying,' Ian said.

'There's a store, a pub and a garage and a big campdraft once a year. That's enough for most people,' Leigh said.

'I've asked a few locals how they find it living here. It must be pretty dull for the Landers, with a young son. Fiona McDonald said that there's nothing going on except parties and the occasional B & S ball at the bigger towns – and they don't appeal to everyone,' Ian said.

'Ah, talked to Fiona, did you? Now there's a catch. Have much experience in the crumpet department?' Leigh asked in one of his frequent and unexpected changes of subject.

'The what?'

'Women,' Leigh said.

Ian paused, 'Not much.'

Leigh raised his eyebrows.

'I suppose I've never met the right girl. Actually, to be honest I've never really met any girls,' Ian said quickly.

'A bloke in your position could have girls galore. All young and willing, too,' Leigh said with a smirk.

'And all wanting to be the mistress of Kanimbla, I guess,' Ian said. 'No, I'll wait until I'm ready. And when I do decide to get married, I'll be looking for a very special woman.'

Leigh clearly wasn't going to give up. 'I can put you in touch with a couple of women who just like the sex – you don't have to marry them. They'd be falling over each other to get to you. It'd be like all your Christmases had come at once,' Leigh smiled.

'Thanks, but no thanks, Leigh. I don't have time for a relationship.'

'But how do you manage *not* to think about women?'

'Oh it's not too hard, I just think about something else. My grandfather told me he used to do things like memorising the names of all the men in his company or all the officers in the battalion,' Ian said.

'A real pukka sahib, was he?' Leigh asked.

'I suppose so. He had a set of standards he lived by all his life. Loyalty to one's country and one's friends was at the top of the list. And not doing anything he would be ashamed of was a large part of that.'

Watching the river drift by, Ian became lost in his thoughts. He was feeling a little guilty. He hadn't been entirely honest with Leigh about girls. Or, more specifically, about one girl . . . It was certainly true that he hadn't had anything to do with girls, and that he hadn't thought much about them either. But Fiona McDonald had changed all that. She was not only the first young woman he had talked to at some length, but also the most attractive. She had a very warm personality that endeared her to just about everyone she met. Leo told him that there'd never been any question that she would be school captain, as she was regarded as the most outstanding student of her final year. And Ian simply enjoyed her company. She wasn't worldly wise – apart from her school excursions, she'd seldom been away from Nelanji – but she was a naturally inquisitive and intelligent young woman, and could give an opinion if asked for it. Ian felt very relieved at having Fiona so close to Kanimbla and hoped they would become great friends.

Ian's thoughts were interrupted by Leigh, who apparently had a fish on his line.

'Woo-hoo!' Leigh exclaimed as he hauled in a seven kilogram Murray cod. 'This one's a beauty. Can you blame a bloke for wanting to live here? I've got the river at my door, I can fish when I like and there's birdlife galore. There are no traffic lights or traffic jams to concern me. I've got space to write and if a woman wants a bit of fun I can accommodate her without having to worry about a nosy neighbour.'

'How well you paint the picture,' Ian said with a laugh. 'I must say, it's been an interesting day and we haven't once mentioned Shelley or Lawson! But I'm afraid you'd better point this craft back towards your Shangri-la. I've got some planning to do – I'm to give a party at the homestead. Not my idea of fun, but it's expected, apparently.'

'I assume you mean for the grazier types, not the hoi polloi?' Leigh grinned.

'I suppose so,' Ian returned the smile.

'You'd better not invite Rhona Blake – she can upset a party in two sentences. For starters, she thinks most of Queensland's politicians are second-rate and that the National Party crew are at the bottom of the pile. As all your guests would vote National Party, you can imagine how well her views would be received!'

'We'll cross that bridge if we come to it,' Ian said. 'It's been a great day, Leigh. Thanks.'

'Don't forget what I told you. If you feel you need a bit of fun . . .' Leigh trailed off, with a twinkle in his eye.

'Are you going to clean that fish?' Ian changed the subject.

'Course I am. I'll split it down the middle. Mrs H knows how to cook the buggers,' Leigh said.

After a delicious fish dinner and before retiring that night, Ian added to the diary he'd been keeping since arriving in Australia. He wrote some of the lines of poetry Leigh had shared during their long conversation:

*Oven-hot the sun beats down,*
*Through silver leaves of silver trees.*
*The red earth gasps in muted shade,*
*Bereft of the faintest breeze.*
*Oh, will the daylight never fade*
*So we can dream of crystal streams*
*Before new day invades our dreams?*

One day, Ian hoped to turn the diary into a book. He would call it 'Sojourn in Australia', or perhaps he'd substitute 'Oz' for Australia. Leigh would certainly appear conspicuously in it. He was, without a doubt, the most unusual character Ian had ever met and he felt fortunate to be the employer of such a man. He wondered what the reaction would be if he invited Leigh to his party. It was the kind of thing you wouldn't hesitate to do if giving a party for the literati, but in western Queensland, it was a different matter. A pity. If Leigh were there, the conversation would certainly extend way beyond sheep and cattle and the weather. And if both Leigh and the formidable Rhona Blake were in attendance, that really *would* be a situation. Ian wondered what word Rhona would use to describe the masculine equivalent of crumpet. Even though he hadn't met her yet, he felt sure that she'd have one . . .

# Chapter Ten

Little Billy Landers bubbled over with excitement as the big yellow bulldozer rolled off the low loader and began gouging into the red-brown earth. Soon he would be able to swim in a pool close by his home. His excitement, however, reached fever pitch when the dozer's laconic, gum-chewing driver lifted him up to the controls.

That was only the beginning. Thereafter came a flurry of activity with the delivery of the pool shell, the laying of the concrete surrounds and the erection of a safety fence and shelter. Of course, Billy's biggest moment came when he was given the honour of the first swim. He stood with Ian, Jim and Karen on the pool's edge in his fluoro floaties and then threw himself into the water and began to thrash around, squealing with delight. Ian looked down at his soaked trousers and grinned ruefully. 'Now you'll have to learn to swim properly, Billy,' he said.

'This is going to make a big difference, Ian,' Karen said gratefully.

'I hope so,' Ian smiled.

Lachie McDonald was a man with his feet partly planted in the old days and the old ways but whose mind was flexible enough to accept new ideas and adapt to changing circumstances. He'd had some difficulty coming to terms with things like the feminist movement and the explicit sex scenes that were shown on television and he probably would have avoided them altogether except that he had a very intelligent daughter with a questioning mind.

When Maisie died, Lachie worried about his own mortality and how Fiona would cope if she were left on her own. Fiona was the apple of her father's eye. It had taken years for Maisie to fall pregnant and Fiona was their only child. Father and daughter were very close. When his newly motherless daughter had told him she would be putting off going to university in the coming year, Lachie decided it was time they had a down-to-earth discussion. This took place on the Nelanji verandah one warm evening. Lachie was drinking beer and Fiona had started with a gin squash.

'Fiona, if something were to happen to me, what would you do?'

'Why should anything happen to you, Dad?' Fiona asked, startled. After her mother's death, this was almost too much to think about.

'We can't presume that it won't. You've put off going to university for the time being, but would you go if anything happened to me? And would you sell Nelanji? You'd have to employ a manager if you intended to keep it and go to university.'

'Dad, such questions!' Fiona exclaimed. 'I haven't thought about any of those things. Sell Nelanji? It's been in your family for three generations. Anyway, you might marry again, and it would go to your wife. You're not ancient,' Fiona said.

Lachie shook his head. 'I'd never find someone to replace your mother. It's you that concerns me. This isn't the most desirable place in the world for a young woman to spend her best years and certainly not a place to spend them alone. Your mother wanted you to have an education. I don't want you to regret that you didn't.'

'I've decided to stay, Dad, for the time being. Please put it out of your mind. I can handle it,' Fiona said, patting her father's arm.

Her father was a dear, Fiona thought to herself. After her mother died, he'd told her that if she was going to stay home and work on the property there were less pleasant aspects of farm life that she needed to know. She remembered how embarrassed he'd been when he'd asked her to handle the rams' testicles and explained that the larger a bull's scrotum, the more fertile he was likely to be. 'You can't be a dumb-cluck on a property, Fiona,' he had said in a blustery way to cover his awkwardness. 'You need to know about such things.'

He really was a dear because of course she already knew about these things. Maisie had made sure her daughter was educated about the facts of life. Fiona had been relieved that she'd had her first period in the Christmas holidays before she left for boarding school in Sydney, because her mother had been there to offer help and advice.

In her final year, when she was school captain and much admired by most of her peers and younger girls – 'Fiona McDonald is just lovely,' they said of her – she was often approached for advice by girls whose parents seemed too busy to listen to their problems. Fiona was well aware that some of the older girls had been on the pill. It wasn't considered anything unusual now. Some of the girls had even slept with more than one boy. Fiona hadn't slept with a boy yet, but she knew that she would if she met the right one. She'd only just met Ian Richardson, but something told her he might be the one.

It had always been her mother's wish that she enrol in university – she hadn't wanted to see her daughter stuck in western Queensland, and certainly not before she'd had the opportunity to sample a different lifestyle. But after her mother's death, Fiona had been reluctant to leave her father and so postponed her enrolment. In a vague kind of way Fiona had imagined that she would one day marry a grazier and spend the rest of her days on a property. She loved horses and enjoyed working with dogs and stock.

Fiona was suddenly jolted out of her reverie. So *that* was where her father's questions were leading. He was thinking that if she married Ian, it would be the perfect solution. She would have a very nice young husband, live in a big homestead on a famous property, and be able to take trips to Britain while living not far from her father whom she would be able to visit quite regularly. Fiona began daydreaming again. It was a lovely idea – imagine the wedding! And they could go anywhere in the world for their honeymoon . . . The only problem was, she just couldn't seem to picture Ian Richardson ever sharing her dream.

## Chapter Eleven

'So, what's he like?' Rhona Blake asked her mother. She had arrived at Kanimbla only an hour or so earlier, showered, drunk two gin and bitters to get the taste of dust out of her mouth, and was now stretched out on a sofa in the Blakes' air-conditioned lounge room.

'Ian is very nice,' Judy Blake said.

'Nice? What do you mean by *nice*?'

'He's done some good things since he arrived,' Judy said.

'Like what?'

'Well there's the swimming pool.'

'That's a positive development but hardly a luxury, Mum – I should think that a pool would be a necessity if you want to get people to work for you in this country. What else has he done?' Rhona asked.

'I don't monitor all of Ian's movements. You can ask your father what he's done around the property. I've heard whispers that he's interested in pulling Murrawee out of the doldrums. There's talk of a sheepdog trial. I know he spends a fair bit of time with Leigh Metcalfe,' Judy said.

'Well now, no doubt Leigh will extend young Mr Ian's knowledge in certain areas,' Rhona laughed.

'You can get that out of your head. Ian told your father that he's not the slightest bit interested in girls. Though I suppose he did invite Fiona McDonald over here . . . ' Judy trailed off.

'Ha, if it's not girls, it'll be boys,' Rhona said unkindly.

'You've become far too cynical, Rhona. There are some very genuine people in the world and I believe Ian Richardson is one of them,' Judy said.

'I suppose it's easy to be nice when your future holds no money worries,' Rhona said.

'Well, you can make up your own mind about Ian. We're invited down to the homestead for drinks this evening. Ian thought you'd prefer to have a quiet dinner with us on your first night home,' Judy said.

Judy glanced at her daughter and stifled a sigh. Rhona, nearing thirty, was wearing white shorts and a blue tank top – both very brief. Her dark hair matched her mother's but her eyes were grey like her father's. Rhona was so different from her mother. Sometimes Judy wondered what went on in her daughter's mind. She really had no idea.

'I'm sure you'd be interested to know that Trish Claydon told Helen Donovan at the store that she reckoned Ian was the cutest fellow she'd ever seen out here.' Judy resorted to a bit of gossip, which she knew Rhona would like. 'And I think Fiona McDonald might have her eye on him. Well, she'd be silly not to.'

Rhona's laughter pealed across the room. 'Now there's a contrast in style – Miss Goody Two Shoes and the Wicked Witch of the West! Well, Trish should know – she's broken in more than one young bloke in this district.'

'Don't talk like that, Rhona. Anyway, I think Ian has far too much common sense to allow Trish Claydon anywhere near him,' Judy said.

'Is Trish still having it off with Leigh?'

'I've no idea, but if Alec catches them there'll be big trouble.'

'I'll never understand how that marriage survives,' Rhona remarked.

'The only reason Alec doesn't divorce Trish is that he knows he'd lose half his property and half his stock. Leo says Alec would prefer to lose an arm or a leg to losing all that. Alec loves his property and he's nuts about his sheep. But the word is that Alec has just about reached the end of his tether with Trish, so there could be a big row before long,' Judy said.

'Trish has had a good run,' Rhona said, 'but she started early.'

'You only know what people have told you. A lot of it would be exaggerated,' Judy said.

'I doubt that anything anyone said about Trish Claydon would either be an exaggeration *or* do her justice,' Rhona said.

'So, you haven't found a nice man to settle down with and start a family?' Judy teased.

'Most men I meet are so dull, Mum. They're only any good in small doses. And as far as having kids goes, why would you want to bring more kids into a world like this one? The chances of me finding a partner suitable enough to make me want to settle down in this fly-blown part of the world would be a thousand to one against. And what would children do here? They'd just have to be packed off to boarding school . . . No wonder Trish has affairs. A woman could go off her head here if she didn't have a bit of excitement. I don't know how you've stuck it all these years.'

'Rhona!' Judy cautioned.

'Well, it must have been bloody awful.' Rhona made a face.

'If you love someone and want to share their life, you go where they go and make the best of things. Your father is a good man; one of the best. You know how well thought of he is in the pastoral industry. It takes years to earn that kind of respect. So don't look down your nose at him because you've got degrees and he hasn't. Leo paid for your education and put you through university. He did his duty as your father even though you made his life quite difficult at times. Please don't argue with him and make your stay unpleasant,' Judy pleaded.

'You know I'd never do that,' Rhona said mildly. 'So is Dragon Lady back at the homestead? And what does she think of Ian?'

'I think you should ask her yourself. But I wouldn't wear

those shorts to the homestead, Rhona.' Judy sounded a little anxious.

'Oh, I wasn't planning to, Mum.'

When Leo returned, Rhona was dressed in a red skirt and a tailored white shirt.

'Hi, Dad,' she said breezily and gave her father a quick kiss on the cheek.

'Hello, stranger. You look a million dollars.'

'Thanks. How's the ankle now?'

'It's okay. Almost forgotten. Have a good trip?'

'Tiring. Thank God for air-conditioning. How are you coping with the new chief?' Rhona asked.

'He's young and inexperienced, but he's a bright bloke.' Leo turned to Judy, 'I'll have a shower now. It's six-thirty, isn't it?'

'Casual. No tie,' Judy said.

'Good. Are we taking anything? Leo asked.

'Only ourselves, dear. Glenda would be insulted. It's a "welcome back" drink for Rhona,' Judy said.

'Dad sounds cheery,' Rhona observed after Leo had left the lounge room.

'He's been a different man since Ian arrived. It's almost like he's acquired a son and he's showing him how to take over the place. I just hope he won't be too disappointed if Ian leaves,' Judy said.

'You think he'll go back to England?' Rhona asked.

'Perhaps. His parents went to Cambridge and Ian has

spoken of it rather feelingly on more than one occasion,' Judy said.

'Interesting . . .' Rhona mused.

Ian was on the front verandah waiting to greet the Blakes when they arrived. In his grey trousers and blue shirt he appeared impossibly young to be the owner of Kanimbla.

'Rhona, how nice to meet you. I've heard so much about you,' Ian said as they shook hands.

'I hate to think what!' Rhona was momentarily taken aback by his good looks. 'I know I'm a big disappointment to my long-suffering parents.'

'Hardly a disappointment from what I've heard. A BA with honours *and* a PhD,' Ian said and laughed. Rhona laughed too, but rather dryly.

'My academic achievements don't rate very highly in comparison with my sister's three children,' she murmured as she stood aside so Ian could greet her parents.

They stayed on the verandah, where they took their drinks from a traymobile and sat down in comfortable chairs not far from the pool. 'We should be having a pool party. It's hot enough for it,' she said in her uninhibited way.

'If it stays hot, we can have a party before you go back,' Ian said, unfazed. 'But feel free to use the pool any time you like while you're here.'

'Thank you. It was a good move deciding to put in a pool for the staff,' she said.

'Yes. I reckon they'll need it,' Ian said, before turning his attention to Leo. 'How do things look in the back paddocks, Mr Blake?'

'The feed is drying off, but there's plenty of it. I think we should get some of those steers away while prices are good. I doubt they'll get any better,' Leo said.

'If you think so,' Ian said.

Rhona looked at Ian and wondered what on Earth she was supposed to call him. He had called her Rhona but her father Mr Blake.

'Can I call you Ian?' she asked.

'I'll be unhappy if you don't,' he said.

Rhona smiled, 'So how are you finding things here?'

'Without the twelve months jackarooing at Warren I would have found Kanimbla a shock. It's the size of the place that's hard to take in. But we're getting there, aren't we, Mr Blake?'

'We're getting there,' Leo agreed.

'Now that I'm relatively settled, there are a couple of projects I'd like to examine more closely. I don't want to give the impression that I'm a new broom – and a green one at that – who's going to make a lot of changes. But coming here from Britain there are some things I find very strange. There doesn't seem to be much happening in Murrawee township and I'd like to do something to change that,' Ian said.

'Ooh, you'll cop some flak. Anyone who tries to rock the boat here gets plenty of criticism,' Rhona said. 'You need to live in Queensland half a lifetime before you're regarded as a local, if you ever are. I mean, there's native-born

Queenslanders and then there's the "Mexican" imports. Anyone who lives south of the border is regarded as a Mexican, though I doubt that Poms rate any lower than Victorians. Mind you, there are some cracks in the wall of bigotry seeing that Brisbane has a great Australian Rules team with a big supporters base.'

'We'll see about the flak. I want to at least give it a try. What was it that old Labor man said in *Fame is the Spur?* "The shame is not in failing but in never trying," or words to that effect?' Ian said. He was sure Rhona would have read Spring's book and was just about to ask her opinion when she beat him to it.

'What did you think of the book?'

Ian took a moment to form his answer. 'I liked the way it tries to show how people can be changed by circumstances – for instance, by good fortune or money – while other people remain true to their original beliefs. I don't know much about Australian politics, but it seems to me there are examples of both in Australian political history,' Ian continued. 'Being prime minister never changed Ben Chifley. He always remained a quintessential Labor man, an Australian counterpart to Spring's Arnold Ryerson.'

Rhona nodded her agreement. 'That's a very interesting answer from a new Aussie – and a Pommy into the bargain,' she added.

'I'm not a Pommy, Rhona. If I'm anything, I'm an Australian who was educated in England,' Ian said.

It was a mild rebuke, but it slid past Rhona like water off

a duck's back. She tried a new approach. 'I believe you've been seeing a fair bit of our Writer in Residence,' she said. Ian had noticed that she preferred to make up nicknames rather than use people's real names. He thought her sardonic humour seemed out of keeping with her looks.

'I doubt Leigh would give a moment's thought to how others described him. He writes for his own enjoyment, not for praise or acclaim,' Ian said. It was the second rebuke he had handed out to Rhona in his disarming way, and again she hardly seemed to notice.

'Leigh is a poet as well as a writer. Have you read any of his poetry?' she asked.

Ian looked at her and smiled. He knew Rhona was testing him. 'I haven't read enough of Leigh's poetry to venture an opinion. He gave me a few of his early poems, which were mostly written in a conventional, rhyming style. I haven't read much of his later free-verse stuff. But I do love the way he describes this country. "Oven-hot the sun beats down, / Through silver leaves of silver trees..." He's been very helpful to me. We've been playing some mind games and I think my writing is improving a little,' Ian said. He was, as usual, modestly implying that he couldn't write very well at all. It wouldn't have occurred to him to tell her about his achievements at Harrow.

'What kind of mind games?' Rhona asked with genuine interest.

'Well, he might ask me to look at something – say a tree or a dingo caught in a trap – and then he'll get me to write two or three sentences. I must record what I see as if I will never see it again. It's sharpened my senses and brought greater vitality to my writing. Like tearing down a great curtain and finding a new world behind it.'

Rhona looked at this young man with sudden compassion. What a waste, she thought. As much as she had disliked Jack Richardson and the snobby squattocracy in general, she felt drawn to Ian, although she could not yet put her finger on exactly why. She couldn't judge whether he was just an earnest young man bursting to find his creative self or whether it was something more than that.

'How did you feel about coming to Australia to jackaroo?' Rhona asked.

'I wasn't happy about it at first. I'd had my heart set on going to Cambridge.'

'Surely you won't stay here?' Rhona said, oblivious to her father's frown and the shuffling of her mother's feet.

'It's early days yet and I'm still feeling my way, Rhona.'

'So what have you got in mind?' Rhona persisted.

'It's premature to discuss that right now,' Ian said.

'Isn't that a cop-out?'

'Not at all.' Ian wasn't going to allow Rhona to push him into a corner. Instead, he redirected the conversation towards her parents. And when he did finally bring the discussion back to her, it was to ask if she would have the time to go over the current computer programs with him and perhaps, in association with Jim Landers and himself, install a new program for the merino stud.

'Of course, we'll pay you for your time and expertise,' he said.

'That won't be necessary. I'll be pleased to do it,' Rhona said. 'Besides, I wouldn't want anyone else mucking around with my programming.' She looked forward to working on a project with Ian – especially a project where she was in charge. 'Would Thursday morning suit you? I'm busy tomorrow.'

'That would be great, thanks,' Ian replied. 'Now, if you'd like to stay, Mrs Heatley has offered to prepare a cold dinner.'

Judy wasn't happy about making extra work for Mrs Heatley, but Rhona wanted to stay – so they did. In twenty minutes they all had plates of salad with cold beef and ham and two bottles of chilled white wine.

'Yummy,' Rhona exclaimed, with her eye on the bottles, 'a Stanthorpe white. I'd love to try some.' Rhona seemed to have a good knowledge of grape varieties and who made the best wines. Conversely, Leo had no interest in wine and seldom touched it, preferring whisky or beer. Ian poured glasses for Judy and Rhona.

'Mmm, it's not a bad drop,' Rhona pronounced, first sniffing and then sampling the wine before sinking comfortably into her chair.

Three glasses of chardonnay and a great deal of chatter later, Rhona got up from her chair. 'Crikey, it's so hot. All we need for a perfect evening is a dip in the pool!'

'But you didn't bring any bathers, Rhona,' Judy cautioned.

'Don't need any, Mum,' Rhona giggled.

'Don't be silly,' Leo growled. He hadn't said much since dinner because Rhona had commandeered the conversation.

'If Rhona wants to have a dip, that's all right. I'll help Mrs Heatley with the washing up,' Ian smiled. And before anything further could be said, he'd disappeared into the kitchen.

While Ian and a disgruntled Mrs Heatley washed up ('That Rhona – she never comes here but there's trouble'), and Leo and Judy sat on the verandah in embarrassment, Rhona had her swim in her knickers and bra. After Mrs Heatley had taken her a towel and served them all tea and coffee, Leo told Rhona it was time to leave.

As they said goodbye, Rhona gave Ian a lusty kiss on the lips. 'Lovely evening, *Mr Ian*,' she said and laughed.

'I'm pleased you think so,' Ian said, momentarily taken aback, though he recovered quickly. He winked across at Leo, who nodded and walked to the car.

'Thank you, Ian,' Judy said and kissed him on the cheek. Ian could sense her mixture of gratitude and embarrassment.

'It was nothing, Mrs Blake. I enjoyed your company. Actually, would you consider being my hostess for the reception?'

Judy was both flattered and flustered. 'Me? Why me?'

'Because you would be the perfect choice.'

Despite the awkwardness of the evening, Judy went back to their bungalow feeling on top of the world. Being asked to host such a big function was a huge compliment. She wasn't aware that Ian had already discussed the matter with her husband, who had said that Judy would probably be over the moon about being asked. In fact, Leo was just as pleased as his wife. Of course it would mean a swish new dress for Judy, but that was a small price to pay for something that would give her so much pleasure.

'So, what did you think of Ian?' Judy asked, looking in on Rhona as she sat on the side of her bed, brushing her hair.

'Mmm. He's so pure. I could eat him,' Rhona looked away dreamily. All the men she had slept with were either incompetent or arrogantly experienced, and it was a revelation to find that such a virginal male could exist. She yearned for a man she could manipulate where it mattered – usually in bed. For Rhona, men were like an itch that had to be scratched, and occasionally she despised herself for allowing lust to override her intelligence.

'Rhona, he's far too young for you,' Judy frowned.

'I know. But it doesn't hurt to dream a little.'

'Perhaps you should opt for a husband, Rhona,' Judy said, feelingly oddly protective towards Ian, 'or at least a full-time partner. That would be much safer than your casual affairs.'

'You know marriage is not a priority, Mum.'

Judy sighed, 'But love should be. Good night, Rhona.'

Ian went to the study and spread out his papers and books. He had virtually put Rhona out of his head as soon as she'd left the homestead. He'd been impressed by her mind, but not by her pushiness or her flirtatiousness.

Since beginning his science degree by correspondence, he'd tried to devote at least four hours to it every day – sometimes longer, if he felt fresh enough at night. These hours had become his favourite time of day because the acquisition of knowledge exhilarated him. His brain absorbed information like a sponge and, fortunately for him, his memory allowed him to recall virtually everything he read. Time seemed to fly and he had been working for nearly two hours when he looked up to find Mrs Heatley standing beside him with a glass of milk and a neatly prepared sandwich.

'Mrs Heatley, you don't have to wait up and make me supper. I'm quite capable of going to the fridge for a glass of milk.'

'But you wouldn't, Mr Ian. You'd keep going to midnight or later and then go to bed without any supper,' she scolded.

'Perhaps we can work out a compromise,' Ian smiled. 'You could make the supper early and just leave it in the fridge.'

'We could try that, but if I found it there in the morning, I'd be very cross,' Mrs Heatley said with mock severity. She continued to stand beside him and he sensed there was something more she wished to say.

'What is it, Mrs Heatley?'

'Were you happy with the evening? The dinner was put together in such a hurry and perhaps the wine wasn't such a good idea . . .' she began.

'Everything was fine, thank you,' Ian reassured her, 'it really was. The wine was a lovely idea. And I'm glad Rhona the Rebel lived up to her reputation – I would have been disappointed otherwise!'

'Rhona the Rebel!' Mrs Heatley stifled a giggle. 'That's a good one, Mr Ian. She's very fond of calling people names – I know she calls me "Dragon Lady" behind my back. Now, that's one in the eye for her!'

'Well don't let her affect your sleep. She won't affect mine.'

The housekeeper smiled with obvious relief.

'And for goodness sake go to bed and leave me to my protozoa,' Ian said, turning back to his books – and his supper. 'You're spoiling me rotten.'

# Chapter Twelve

It was quite a different Rhona Blake who presented herself at Kanimbla soon after nine o'clock two mornings later. Her jeans, blue checked shirt and hint of lipstick made her seem several years younger.

Ian met her at the front verandah and escorted her into the study. Jim had given him an outline of the extra information that he wanted recorded on the computer, and said he would come at ten o'clock with some new material he'd been working on. In the meantime, Rhona could look over what was already on disk and work out how to add the new material. She figured this out in a matter of minutes and was soon browsing the ram sales and buyers' details, which were also recorded. Ian noticed her scrutinising the screen with a puzzled expression.

'What is it?' he asked.

'Did you know that your ram sales have been dropping steadily for the past four years?'

'What? They can't have!'

'According to this, they have. Not by many the first year,

then down a hundred the second, more than two hundred the third, and over four hundred last year. That's pretty significant, isn't it? Hasn't Dad mentioned it?' Rhona asked.

'No. We're still breeding from the same number of stud ewes as five years ago,' Ian said.

'Then you're either getting lousy lambings or you're dicing more rams.' She scrolled further down. 'Ah, here's the answer. You sold two lots of young rams to Charleville meatworks.'

'Did we?' said a startled Ian.

'I suppose a place this size can wear a $160 000 loss. But if sales keep declining at this rate, I guess you'd need to look at a different strategy for the stud – and for Kanimbla for that matter,' Rhona said.

'Hmm,' Ian frowned. He realised that the wool market was 'sick' but not that Kanimbla had been so much affected by the downturn in prices. And he couldn't understand why neither Mr Blake nor Jim Landers had mentioned the declining ram sales. He asked Jim as soon as he arrived.

'I wanted to discuss it with you, but Mr Blake said that I wasn't to worry you,' Jim explained. 'He said you had enough to concern you at the outset and he'd talk to you about the ram sales later.'

'Surely you must be worried by this downturn?'

'I sure am. But it's not as if we're the only stud affected. Some of the other studs – and I mean some of the biggest studs in Queensland – are closing down their studs and getting out of sheep altogether. They're going to run cattle exclusively,' Jim said.

'Where does that leave Kanimbla?' Ian asked.

'We've still got clients who are going to stick to sheep. I think the answer for us is to reduce the number of stud ewes and concentrate on quality. Maybe have an annual sale of rams and surplus ewes here at Kanimbla. Maybe show sheep farther afield. The thing is that although ram sales have been declining, the quality of the sheep here has improved considerably,' Landers said.

'I think it's time to call in Mr Blake. He said he'd be doing the books if I needed him,' Ian said.

'Do you want me to leave?' Rhona asked.

'No, I want you to stay,' Ian said tightly. He was clearly shaken by what he'd learned.

'Got a problem?' Leo asked when he arrived.

'You could say that. Last year's ram sales are down by four hundred. That's a very significant decline. And now Jim tells me that some of the big studs nearby – including Ter-rick – are going right out of sheep because there's no market for their rams. When were you going to discuss this with me, Mr Blake?' Ian asked.

'After your reception, when you'd had time to settle in a bit. It's not that I tried to conceal it. The big question is whether we retain the stud, albeit in a reduced capacity, or dice it completely. We could run more cattle – while they're bringing the prices they are now, we'd be okay. Or we could go right out of sheep and replace them with cattle —'

'Or grow some cotton,' Ian cut in.

'I thought you were against cotton!' Leo said.

131

'I'm only joking, Mr Blake. Don't worry. We won't be growing cotton on Kanimbla.'

'That's a relief,' Landers said under his breath.

'The bigger picture is that fifteen years ago there were seventeen million sheep in Queensland. Today there are less than five million. This reduced flock leaves a much smaller piece of the pie for everyone. Indeed, the push for finer sheep was probably the last straw for the medium–strong studs. These studs had no market for their rams and no longer regard wool alone as an option. So they're going to cattle. You can't blame them. It's a bad show. And what makes it worse is the effect on the merino sheep and wool infrastructure. For generations the big studs have been the training schools for overseers, managers, sheep classers and judges. They've been responsible for producing hundreds, perhaps thousands, of our best sheepmen. All of that is falling to pieces,' Leo said sternly.

'But how could this happen?' Ian asked.

'Too many morons running the show,' Rhona cut in.

'Rhona!' Leo protested.

'Well, who else is responsible? You might blame the dingoes for some reduction but they've always been here. Or perhaps you could blame the second-rate politicians – but even they're not entirely responsible for a downturn of twelve million in sheep. The truth is that wool is one of the best natural fibres in the world but it hasn't been well promoted and marketed. Even I can see that and I'm not in the wool business,' Rhona said, looking her father in the eye.

'I'm afraid Rhona's right and it's a damnable situation. It's not the stud breeder or what I might term the professional woolgrower who's letting the industry down. There's wool available that has a one hundred per cent comfort factor – it's beautifully crimped with great elasticity. But who knows about it? Even with the downturn, many growers are still paying big money for rams to maintain or improve their wool. There are plenty of growers who still have faith in wool, but they're not being supported by top-class promotion,' Leo said.

'The question is: where does all of that leave us?' Ian asked.

'Well, we've refashioned the stud along the lines of Uardry in Rowand Jameson's day. We've got special, double and single stud ewes. As things are shaping we could probably reduce our stud ewes, but before we actually do that I'd be inclined to use some of the finer ewes to set up a fine–medium family. If we could produce fine–medium wool on good-sized sheep, maybe we'd pull in some new clients.'

'You've just about echoed my thinking, Mr Blake. I'd say it's either a total commitment to producing very high-class sheep or getting out of the business altogether. I doubt there's a middle road. It's tough for me to contemplate dicing stud sheep and I hope we don't take that road,' Ian said solemnly.

'It wouldn't be the finish of Kanimbla because you could run a heap of cattle here, but it would be the end of the place as we know it. We've made a lot of progress with the sheep and I'd hate to see all that tossed away. But I guess the decision is between you and Ian, Mr Blake,' Jim said.

'Thanks, Jim,' said Leo. 'You've put the position very clearly. I agree it's either–or. And I also reckon that in the final analysis it's Ian who has to decide which way we go. It's a lot to put on your shoulders, Ian. There's hard-headed rural men who are pulling out of sheep and there are other hard-heads who are staying with them. But breeding stud sheep is different to breeding flock sheep. You can only survive as a stud operation if you can sell your rams. The big question is whether we can still sell our rams. We can take certain steps to improve our selling situation but we've got to hope that merino sheep numbers don't shrink any further. And that, to a great extent, will depend on how well we promote wool in the future,' Leo said.

Poor bloody Ian, thought Rhona. He'll be criticised if he closes down the stud and he'll be criticised if he spends money to improve it and still can't sell Kanimbla rams. Talk about having no way out.

Ian himself felt a little shaky after these revelations, but knew that he was expected to take the lead.

'I suggest that we work out what we need on the basis that we're going to carry on with the stud,' he said. 'That way, Rhona can continue with the new program while she's here. You could go back to your books if you like, Mr Blake, while we nut out what we want to put into the computer.'

So, until lunchtime, when Jim had to leave, the three of them sat around the computer and looked at numbers. It was exhausting, but they were all intelligent people with different areas of expertise, and after the initial shock of the situation, Ian began to enjoy the process. He ended up feeling quite grateful to Rhona, and invited her to stay for lunch, in the hope that Mrs Heatley wouldn't mind too much.

Ian looked at Rhona as she sat sipping an orange juice on the verandah. She had the habit of licking the corner of her mouth with the tip of her tongue. He had never seen anyone do it in quite the same way. She was an eye-catching woman – very attractive in a slightly harder sort of way than her mother. Perhaps it was her steely grey eyes – just like Leo's – that suggested an inner toughness. Rhona came across as a woman who knew where she wanted to go.

'So, you're getting on well with Leigh Metcalfe?' Rhona asked to get the conversation going.

'He's an interesting person,' Ian said.

'He's certainly opinionated,' Rhona agreed. 'Has he shared his views on the fairer sex?'

'Well . . . ' Ian began.

Rhona smiled mischievously, hoping Ian might be encouraged to continue.

'I didn't prolong that part of our conversation and it isn't something I want to discuss now, if you don't mind,' Ian said, looking away.

'Hmm.' Rhona was disappointed, but decided that she liked him too much to push him further. 'So what are your plans while you're here?'

Ian refused to meet her eye. Despite his intelligence, he wasn't sure what she was getting at.

'I mean, as far as Kanimbla goes,' she said quickly.

'I'm worried about the wool situation. We're producing a beautiful product, and there's hundreds of millions of people in the Northern Hemisphere who have to endure awfully cold winters, yet the wool prices are lousy. I keep racking my brains, asking myself why. There must be a remedy,' Ian said.

'Look, this isn't my area of expertise, but I suspect that a lot of mistakes have been made in the promotion and marketing of wool. I was always against the reserve price – it encouraged more producers to grow more but not necessarily better wool. That stockpile was like a sword of Damocles hanging over the wool producers. In the finish, financing the purchases was too much for the government. I think a product has to stand on its merits and not rely on a subsidy, which the reserve price really was. We criticise the Americans and the Europeans for their subsidies yet the federal government sanctioned the reserve price.

'There are two things essential to selling any product. First, there's the product and its uniqueness or attractiveness. Second, you need to promote these features so people will want to buy it. Never mind the old "Throw another shrimp on the barbie" line. The advertisements *should* be saying, "Now that it's getting colder, throw on a super-soft, warm Aussie jumper." As the daughter of a station manager, surrounded by wool talk from the day I could walk, I've taken some interest in the subject. For years you couldn't buy woollen articles because the top end of the market was all that mattered – woollen blends were discouraged. Every generation needs to be told about wool and why they should wear it. I mean, why do companies selling other products spend so much on promotion? Because they're worried about losing market share! Years ago, in a hearing before the old Prices Justification Tribunal, a major manufacturer of breakfast foods was asked why they needed to spend so much on promotion. If less was spent in this area, surely the price of the product could be reduced? The company's answer was that if they spent less on promotion, a lot of people would go back to eating bacon and eggs!' Rhona finished with a smile.

'So what do you think we should be doing?' Ian asked.

'Wool needs to be promoted better – here and overseas. Growers have contributed a lot of wool-tax money and they're asking what they've got for it. There's enough talent in Australia to produce really worthwhile promotional campaigns, but it hasn't been utilised. The pig industry turned the image of pork around with its new cuts and a striking sales pitch – that's what we need for wool. And woolgrowers aren't the best people to do it; we need top marketers and advertising people,' Rhona said.

'But aren't the lower prices a part of the problem?' argued Ian. 'We could accept lower wool prices if our costs were lower, but they're not.'

'Granted. But don't forget that the fibre business is characterised by substitutability. The wool price is measured against the price of cotton and synthetics. Overseas fibre manufacturers don't concern themselves with Australia's production costs, only with what our wool costs against the price of the other fibres. And we're losing market share,' Rhona said.

Ian looked at her with a new respect. He hadn't expected her to be so switched on about issues in agribusiness.

'Is there an answer?' he asked.

'For you? Sell Kanimbla and go back to Cambridge,' she said with a laugh. 'There are plenty of people with dirt on the brain who'll battle on with sheep and wool for the rest of their lives.'

'The Richardson name would be mud if I sold Kanimbla.' Ian frowned.

'Properties get sold all the time, even the top properties. Someone else would buy Kanimbla and life would go on and you could be doing whatever you fancy,' Rhona said.

Ian stood up and walked over to the window. 'Look, I don't like the idea of selling Kanimbla. It's been in the Richardson family for a long time. What about China? They're buying more wool now. Surely there are good prospects for wool there.'

'China is a great potential market. It has far cheaper manufacturing costs and a huge population that's generally enjoying a higher standard of living. But how well we promote wool in the future will play a big part in determining how much China takes,' Rhona said.

'Mmm. I take your point.' Although Rhona was not in the wool game, what she'd told Ian seemed to make a lot of sense.

'I'm at your disposal while I'm here,' Rhona said and again the tip of her tongue licked the right side of her mouth.

'Hang on a moment,' Ian said and disappeared into the homestead. When he reappeared he handed Rhona a bottle of wine. 'This is from my uncle's collection; it's a small gift to show my appreciation for all your help. You might like to share it with someone special when you go back to Sydney,' he said.

Rhona looked at the bottle and her eyes widened in surprise. 'Grange Hermitage! Gee, I don't know anyone I would describe as special enough to rate a drop of this. Are you sure you want to part with this? Thank you so much, Ian.' She got up from the chair and kissed him on the cheek. 'I think you're pretty special. Don't waste yourself here.'

It seemed to Ian that Rhona's eyes were less steely now and her face softer. She turned, opened the gauze door and went down the steps and across the lawn without looking back. He watched her until she reached the road and then passed out of sight behind the homestead.

'What's that you've got there, Rhona?' Judy asked when Rhona walked into the bungalow carrying the bottle.

'It's a present from Ian,' Rhona said absently, her mind already on other things. 'I just need to throw a few things together. I'll be leaving in a minute, Mum.'

'But I thought you were staying until Sunday . . .'

'I swear if I stay any longer I'll disgrace myself over that bloke down the road!'

'What happened?' her mother asked gently.

'Nothing happened. It didn't have to. Ian isn't like that. He's just the nicest fella I've ever met. I need to vamoose.'

'Your father will ask why you had to leave in such a hurry,' Judy said.

'Tell him I've been called back to uni,' Rhona said, almost running to her bedroom.


The next morning, unaware of Rhona's departure, Ian drove to Nelanji to see Lachie Macdonald. The two men took a seat on the verandah.

'You're a woolgrower, Mr McDonald, and you also have cattle. How do you see the wool situation?' Ian asked.

'Well, it isn't encouraging. Prices are down a lot and that wouldn't matter if costs weren't so high. I've tried to cut costs, but there's a limit to that too. I don't have any full-time employees now and Fiona and I do a lot of the routine work. We bring in contract teams for mulesing and lamb marking but I'm doing the cattle work, thanks to a better yard system. We have pretty good wool, but we don't get the top prices they get in the tablelands. There's only so much you can do in this country. It isn't prime lamb territory and you're really back to wool and cattle. If wool prices get any worse, we could dice the sheep and just run cattle, but I don't like putting all my eggs in one basket,' Lachie said.

'What's happened to the wool industry? Australia produces the best wool in the world but the Australian flock is down by nearly half. Is it because demand is down so prices are lower or is it because our costs are too high?' Ian asked.

'Probably a bit of both. There have been some mistakes made in the promotion and marketing of wool, no doubt about that,' Lachie said.

Ian sat back and absently took a scone from the carefully prepared plate. He wondered where Fiona was. She must have baked these earlier that morning. 'What disturbs me is that since 1950, when the price of wool went through the roof, the Australian wool industry has had a long period to get itself into a stable situation. But for all the money that's been contributed via the wool taxes, we've lost market share and the sheep population is way down. Before I make any decisions regarding Kanimbla's future, I want to be sure I've got a good picture of where we're at,' Ian said firmly.

'I'm a grazier pure and simple. I'm not a marketer except of my own stock, and I don't have the answers you're seeking. There's hardly ever a time that everything goes right for us on the land. And we're all banking on the cattle market staying as good as it is now. What if it doesn't? What if the wool market kicks and you've got rid of all your sheep? These are the kind of management problems we're all faced with. But we're still here and we're managing despite the lower wool prices and the dingoes and the dry times. We've planted some areas of saltbush and that's helped our wool and our carrying capacity,' Lachie said.

'Mmm. Thanks, Mr McDonald. I value your opinion,' Ian said thoughtfully. As he rose to leave he caught sight of Fiona. She looked quite lovely, and despite himself he felt his pulse quicken. She walked towards him. 'Are you staying for lunch?'

'I'd love to, but I'm afraid I can't,' he answered. 'There's an important rep from the Department of Primary Industry coming for lunch. Mr Blake wants me to meet him. You'd think that, situated where we are, there'd be very few callers, but there's hardly a day passes that someone isn't there. Mr Blake says it's my place to meet them,' Ian said apologetically.

'There'll be another day,' Lachie said, seeing the disappointment on his daughter's face.

'Absolutely,' Ian agreed. 'There are a few other things I want to discuss with you and Fiona. Thanks again, Mr McDonald. I appreciate your time.'

Lachie and Fiona watched from the verandah as Ian departed. 'That is one bright young man,' said Lachie.

'A bright young man in an awful hurry,' Fiona said.

'What do you mean?'

'Oh, perhaps I'm only imagining things, but it seems that he's trying to do too much, as if he's racing the clock.'

'You think he'll leave Kanimbla?' her father asked.

Fiona sighed. 'Oh, I hope not. Anyway, there's one thing I am sure of – he didn't come here this morning to see me.'

'I don't believe that for a moment. It might just take him a little while to work out what his priorities are, but I'm sure you're up there in his thinking.'

'I hope you're right, Dad,' Fiona said wistfully.

# Chapter Thirteen

Fiona had heard that Ian was planning a party of some sort and, despite her disappointment in his apparent lack of interest in her, was delighted to receive an invitation. She knew Ian would be busy planning the event, and expected that this would be the next time she would see him, so his phone call came as a surprise.

'Are you doing anything on Saturday morning?' he asked.

'Nothing really important. Why?' she managed to ask calmly, even though she felt her heart thumping hard.

'Can you be over here at about eight?'

'Sure. Yes. Are we riding somewhere?' Fiona asked.

'Not this time. We're going in to Murrawee,' he said.

Fiona wondered why Ian would ask her to accompany him into town – and why he wasn't more forthcoming. But she was very pleased and already couldn't wait till Saturday.

'Are we meeting anyone? I mean, do I need to get dressed up?' she asked.

'Nothing like that. You look very nice in jeans. I'll expect you at eight,' Ian said and hung up.

Fiona put the phone down and smiled.

'What was that all about?' Lachie asked as he finished a plate of lamb's fry and bacon.

'Ian wants me to go into Murrawee with him on Saturday morning,' she said. *He told me I look nice in jeans!*

'Did he say why?' Lachie asked.

'No.'

'Funny. I wonder what he's up to,' Lachie mused.

On Saturday, when Fiona arrived at Kanimbla, Ian was waiting for her beside the Mercedes.

'Hi,' she said as she climbed down from the four-wheel drive.

'Hi, yourself,' Ian said with a smile. She thought he looked gorgeous in his white moleskins, blue checked shirt and wide-brimmed grey Akubra.

'Can you stay for lunch when we get back?' he asked.

'Yes – I'll just need to let Dad know,' she said.

'Great. You get in the Merc. I'll duck in and see Mrs H and ask her to phone your father.'

Once on the road, they drove for a few minutes without speaking. Finally, Fiona broke the silence, 'So how are things coming along for the reception?'

'Fine. I've left it all to Mrs H and Mrs Blake. Parties aren't really my scene. Do you like them?' he said.

'I haven't given one yet. Mum was too sick when I came home from school and then she was in hospital and Dad was away with her a lot. He's been saying that we should start entertaining again, but it's not the same without her.'

'I know what you mean. I lost my parents when I was eight,' Ian said.

'Oh, that's so sad,' Fiona said. 'I'm so lucky to have Dad.'

They travelled in silence again for a while, before Fiona could contain her curiosity no longer.

'Tell me, do you enjoy being mysterious?' she asked with a half-smile.

'Mysterious?'

'This trip to Murrawee – you haven't said a word about why you've asked me,' she said.

'Sorry, but you'll just have to be patient,' Ian said.

'Now you're scolding me,' she said, smiling again.

'Oh. I don't mean to sound scolding. I'm just a little distracted,' Ian said as they arrived in the township, where a one-tonner parked outside the café and two other vehicles outside the pub represented Murrawee's entire traffic fleet.

'Sin city of the west it isn't. Can you imagine a deader place?' Fiona remarked dryly. Every school holidays, when she had come home from boarding school, Murrawee had seemed a little more dilapidated. There was always one less business in operation, or one more vacant house, until all that remained were the bare bones of the original township. It made her sad, but nobody had tried to do anything to stem the exodus. If you couldn't get something you needed in Murrawee, it was easier to drive somewhere else.

Ian bypassed the neglected railway station, drove over the railway crossing at the edge of the village and down a gravel road that led to the river. Here, he stopped the vehicle. They got out and looked up and down the length of its wonderful gum-lined waters. To one side of them was a paddock in which ghost gums and a species of acacia grew.

'A lovely spot, isn't it?' Ian asked.

'It is. So is this what you've brought me to see?' Fiona asked.

'Not exactly. In the middle of that paddock there's a capped bore. You can't see it for the grass. It was one of the first bores ever sunk in this area, but nobody knows why. Maybe it was a test bore for Murrawee in its early days. You wouldn't think they'd have needed bore water with the river so close, but maybe there was a drought at some stage. The point is that it's a hot bore. I'm having it tested for mineral content,' Ian said.

'Why?' Fiona asked.

'What do you think of this paddock?' Ian asked without answering her.

'Um, it's nice and flat, with some good trees on it. What would it be . . . twenty acres?' she suggested.

'Thirty-five, apparently. I'm going to buy it. There's been no rates paid on it for years and council is happy to sell it,' Ian said.

'But why would you want to buy thirty-five acres here when you own Kanimbla?' she asked.

Again, Ian dodged her question. 'Would you describe yourself as an imaginative person?'

'Well . . . ' she began.

'Never mind. Just try this. Imagine a caravan park close to the river, with people fishing, and next to it hot and cold swimming baths. Then further back up the road near that biggest ghost gum,' Ian pointed, 'imagine an aviary with native Australian birds. How's that for starters?' he asked, grinning broadly.

Fiona looked at him, puzzled. Her first thought was that he was having her on. And then she realised that Ian was not a person given to that sort of joke. As fantastic as his proposal seemed to her, Ian was apparently deadly serious.

'What do you think?' Ian asked.

Fiona was lost for words. 'It sounds great . . .'

Ian was on a roll. He was excited to be sharing his ideas with his new friend, and happy that she seemed to be on the same wavelength. 'Later, I think the district should look at building a small motel, even if it's just a few units. Tourists could break their journeys here, maybe stay a day or two.'

Ian's enthusiasm was infectious and Fiona joined in. 'Yes! And if we held a sheepdog trial in Murrawee, it would help the pub and the café, and the garage would probably get some business too.'

'You're right,' said Ian, 'and it's something we could do right away.'

Fiona smiled. This shared project meant she would see a lot of Ian – a prospect that gave her immense pleasure. 'You know I love sheepdogs,' she said. 'Could I help with the organisation of the trial?'

'I was hoping you would. Murrawee could be a very different place to live with just a few small changes,' Ian said enthusiastically.

Fiona's face suddenly dropped. 'Oh dear. Here we are planning huge changes to the town without even knowing what anyone feels about them. How would you put your ideas to people?'

'From what I can gather, people are more concerned about whether Kanimbla intends to grow cotton on the Big Plain. I think my uncle suggested this once when Kanimbla was short of cash, but I never want to see cotton growing here. I understand why people grow cotton, but I couldn't consider it with every one of my neighbours running livestock. I'd like to have a public meeting to put the cotton issue to rest, and I could use the occasion to broach these ideas for improving the township,' Ian said.

He's worked it all out, thought Fiona. Aloud, she asked, 'What does Mr Blake think?' Like most people in the district, Fiona regarded Leo Blake as the lord high priest when it came to just about anything.

'At first he thought I was off my head. Then I think he talked with Mrs Blake, and he agreed that this sort of complex might be able to attract people to Murrawee. I won't be using Kanimbla money to buy this paddock – it will come out of my own pocket. If the district goes along with me, I'll transfer the title into the name of the "Murrawee and District Development Association" or something similar,' Ian said.

'So *that's* why you asked me about improving Murrawee for young people last week!' Fiona exclaimed.

'Your idea for a park was great,' Ian said. 'I took that one step further to include an aviary. Now, would you like a drink of something? We could drop in on Mrs Donovan.'

'That'd be nice,' Fiona agreed. She felt so close to Ian just then, and fought the urge to take his arm. It just wouldn't do to be so bold and possibly embarrass Ian in public.

Helen Donovan greeted them warmly. 'You might have told me who you were, that day when you arrived,' she said, feigning irritation.

Ian smiled. 'I owed it to Mr Blake to tell him first. Besides, you couldn't have looked after me any better than you did.'

Fiona noticed with pleasure the effect he had on Helen Donovan; she was putty in his hands.

'It's very nice of you to say so. I hope you'll be very happy at Kanimbla. Good to see you too, Fiona. I've known Fiona since she was a baby, you know, Ian. She used to hold my skirts and ask for sweets.'

'And you always gave them to me, even though it made my mother quite cross. She didn't approve of lollies,' Fiona smiled.

'Well, I must say they haven't done you any harm, Fiona. What brings you into town?' the shopkeeper asked.

Ian looked at Fiona and rolled his eyes and Fiona knew this meant he wasn't ready to talk about his ideas with the rest of the township. 'I wanted to have a look at the river,' he said to Mrs Donovan. 'Mr Blake told me it was the best stretch of water for a long way.'

'So what did you think?' she asked.

'I agree with him. By the way, do you stock birdseed? Is it something that's easy to come by?' Ian asked.

'You can buy birdseed in small packets or in big bags. We stock both. It's mostly made up of millet, sorghum, corn and grey-stripe sunflower seeds. Queensland grows most of Australia's millet. Are you planning on getting a cockie or a budgie?' Helen asked.

'No. I was just wondering if Kanimbla could grow some seed, but if those grains are in good supply there'd be no need to,' Ian said.

Helen wondered what Ian had in mind. Perhaps he was looking at diversifying into cropping. Glenda Heatley had told her that he was very bright. He certainly hadn't taken long to work out that Fiona McDonald was the pick of the girls in the district.

Mrs Heatley brought their lunch out to the verandah – cold corned beef, green salad, potato salad and a refreshing jug of lemon squash.

'This is a great spot, Ian. Whoever picked out this site for the homestead knew what they were doing, with the river just over there and those lovely trees. And there are so many birds here,' Fiona said.

'It's very pleasant, isn't it? To me it seems so *Australian*. The gums and the blue sky and the song birds . . . even this verandah,' Ian said.

'You haven't told me a thing about England, about Cambridgeshire,' she said.

*Where would I start?* Ian wondered. 'Well, it's dotted about with villages — some of them hundreds of years old and quite beautiful. It never gets as hot as this. If we were having lunch at Lyndhurst instead of here, we'd probably be sitting on the side verandah that Grandfather added to the old place. We'd be looking down at the willow-lined River Ouse. If it was summer, there'd be young cattle on lush pastures. Or maybe ewes with lambs. At the back of the house there's quite a large orchard — I used to love to sit there . . . '

'And I suppose Cambridge University is its crowning glory,' Fiona said.

'Oh, yes. It has picturesque colleges and lovely old bridges that span the River Cam. It was a Roman town and has a fascinating history. There are many historic homes with beautiful gardens,' Ian said.

'And you own one of them,' she said.

'Yes, thanks to my grandfather,' he said.

'I hope you don't think me rude for saying so, but knowing you have Lyndhurst makes it hard for me to understand why you're here, and why you'd want to spend your time trying to resurrect a dying Australian town,' Fiona said.

'That's easy, Fiona. From what I can gather, my Uncle Jack didn't do much for Murrawee. I wouldn't like to be left all this and put nothing back into the community,' Ian said.

'Does that mean that you don't see yourself staying here for the long-term?' asked Fiona.

'Short- or long-term, I'd like to think I was able to help,' Ian said evasively.

'But surely Kanimbla already contributes a lot to the district. It employs several people and supports the only local businesses,' Fiona pointed out.

'But in the larger sense we're not doing enough. The town is going downhill and I'd like to turn that around. Quite apart from what we discussed this morning, I'd like to see someone with medical knowledge take up residence here – perhaps a retired nurse or ambulance officer. We could offer them free rent. And if we could liven up the township, it would be easier to attract that sort of person,' Ian said.

'Oh yes,' Fiona agreed. 'When Mum was at home between her stays in hospital, I felt very nervous. I often wished there was a nurse I could call on for help. It would have been so reassuring . . . '

After lunch they sat quietly for a while looking out across the shade-dappled lawn. 'I'd like to have a look at the river,' Fiona said eventually. 'Will you walk over with me?'

He held the screen door open for her and she waited for him at the foot of the steps. In a gesture that surprised him, she took his hand and they walked across the lawn to where massive red gums lined the river. They stood side by side with their backs against the trunk of one giant gum that had probably been a fair-sized tree even long before white settlement. Fiona leant gently against Ian and her hair brushed his neck.

'It's been a lovely morning, Ian,' she said, kissing his cheek and leaving her face resting against his. Her heart beat fast as she felt his skin against hers. She desperately wanted him to respond, but he simply stood there for a few moments, as

152

if engaged in some internal struggle. Eventually he turned to face her, leaning gently in to kiss her. Fiona closed her eyes and felt herself melting at his touch, wanting the kiss to go on forever, but then suddenly he pulled away and looked towards the river. She felt stunned and embarrassed, and then angry – she could have shaken him. At boarding school she'd been led to believe that boys were never backward where girls were concerned – that they generally came on too strongly, if anything. But here he was sending her mixed messages. Ian turned back to her, touched her arm and pointed up the river.

'See there? It's a brown duck and her ducklings. I wonder where she sat to bring them out.'

At that moment, the last thing Fiona was interested in looking at was a clutch of ducklings! She told herself to calm down. Perhaps he was just nervous. She folded her arms, 'Well, I'd better be getting back to Nelanji.'

Soon after, Fiona drove away from Kanimbla confused. What did that kiss mean? Ian had paid her lovely compliments and sought her opinions on an important project, but did he regard her as nothing more than a friend? Or was he hiding his true feelings? She was no closer to understanding this enigmatic young man.

# Chapter Fourteen

On the eastern side of the great Kanimbla homestead there was a landing field for light aircraft. Jack Richardson had been a pilot and had had two strips laid with bitumen (one east–west and the other north–south), so that the field could be used in virtually all weathers.

From the air, something important was clearly taking place at Kanimbla this October day. There were eight light planes spaced along one side of the landing field, as well as scores of vehicles parked at the homestead and more converging on the front gate along the main road. A casual observer might have guessed that it was either a field day or a clearing sale, but it was neither. In fact it was the first official engagement held by the property's new owner. The event was particularly significant for some of the guests because not only was Ian Richardson a very young man, but he was also unmarried. This made him, arguably, one of the most eligible bachelors in the Queensland pastoral industry.

Invitations had been sent some time before, and had been received with excitement. Jack Richardson had a reputation for holding the best parties in the district and everyone was keen to know whether Ian would uphold this tradition.

There had been an awkward situation concerning the property's employees and who should attend. Judy Blake was the hostess, of course, and Jim and Karen Landers would be there, since Jim was overseer and stud manager. The Belted Trio, Peter, Ted and Gerald, had been instructed to meet the planes and ferry the guests from the landing field to the homestead. Most of the rest of the staff were enjoying a case of beer, courtesy of Ian, at the shearers' quarters tonight, and looking forward to their own celebration (Ian had promised a special barbecue by the new staff pool). Rhona Blake had declined her invitation. She'd met a new man, Graeme, and in the throes of early romance, was unwilling to leave him for the weekend.

According to the elegant but simple invitation, dress was casual – though Judy had warned Ian that this wouldn't stop some of the girls and women from dressing up, as they didn't often get the chance. 'They'll be out to impress you,' she'd said. The invitation also announced that drinks and hors d'oeuvres would be served from five-thirty, with dinner at seven. Those who wished to swim in the pool could do so. Staff would also be available from three o'clock for anyone interested in an inspection of shedded rams.

By five-thirty there were probably a hundred and fifty people on Kanimbla's verandah and front lawn, and perhaps a score of young people in the pool, making the most of the warm afternoon. The girls' attire ranged from modest one-piece costumes to skimpy bikinis. Ted and Gerald, in between meeting planes, could only look on and wish they were in the pool too.

When Fiona arrived with her father, Ian was struck by her composure. He'd never seen her in anything but jeans, but this evening she wore a stunning black dress. In heels, she was almost as tall as Lachie, and as she stood with her shoulders back, Ian couldn't help noticing her long, elegant neck. She'd dressed so well that she wasn't outshone by any of the other women at the party – some of them very experienced party-goers.

Fiona felt proud to be accompanying her father to Ian's reception, and she knew that her father was proud of her too. He'd been delighted when she'd been elected school captain at the start of her final year. He knew that she was well mannered, like her mother had been, and that she attracted admiring glances. She was handy on the property and ran the homestead well. Lachie had appreciated her practical skills and her care for him even more since his wife's death.

'Welcome!' Ian said. 'It's lovely to see you both,' he shook hands with her father, then leant over and gave her a kiss on the cheek. 'You look exceptionally nice tonight,' Ian whispered in her ear. 'Elegant, in fact.'

Fiona felt a fluttering in the pit of her stomach. 'Thank you,' she said with a radiant smile. 'It's going to be a great party.'

'I think you could guarantee that,' Lachie agreed.

'I'll talk to you again soon,' Ian promised. Fiona hoped it would be very soon.

The early evening hummed along nicely with a lot of animated conversation fuelled by a steady intake of liquid refreshments. About six-thirty, there was a stir as the Claydons arrived. Trish never appeared at a function until it was well underway. She liked to make a big impression and knew that other wives would be on tenterhooks, wondering whether she'd be there. Trish knew that many of them despised her flirtatiousness and her outrageously provocative clothing, but she didn't mind. She got enormous satisfaction from the fact that she'd known some of their husbands intimately and they didn't have a clue. Men wouldn't wander if they'd been looked after satisfactorily at home, she thought. But in reality, she was more selective in her lovers than rumour suggested. She liked sex but she sought partners who could elevate the experience beyond the commonplace.

This evening, Trish was flanked by her two daughters, Cyd and Maureen. Alec brought up the rear because he stopped so often to greet people. He was a friendly fellow, if a bit rough around the edges, and there were a lot of people who felt genuinely sorry for him, stuck with Trish.

At eighteen, Cyd, a blue-eyed blonde, was a younger version of her mother. She was wearing a sparkling, slinky dress that revealed her long, tanned legs. She looked rather out of place among the more conservatively dressed guests, but didn't seem to notice. Maureen, Cyd's younger sister by a year, was dressed in a tasteful pair of pale blue pants and a white blouse.

'Now that you've settled in, you must come and see us,

Ian,' Trish said. 'Sometimes the girls and I go away for the holidays – Bali or somewhere – but this time we're all staying home.' Ian tried to avoid looking at the plunging valley that was Trish's cleavage.

'Yes, you must,' Cyd echoed. 'We have a pool too.'

'Are you still at school, Cyd?' Ian asked.

'This is my final term,' Cyd answered. She thought Ian was too good to be true. Imagine having a boy like him next door!

'And you, Maureen?' he asked.

'I have another year to go,' Maureen said.

'Do you have any idea what you'll do after school?' he asked Maureen. She seemed to him to be a very nice girl whereas Cyd was obviously a flirt.

'I think I might do vet science,' Maureen said.

'That's a very worthwhile profession. It opens up a lot of avenues,' Ian said.

By the time Alec reached him, the three Claydon women had merged into the throng. 'Nice to see you again, Mr Claydon,' Ian smiled.

'You're a dark horse, young fellow,' Alec said, referring to Ian's failure to disclose his identity on his first day in Murrawee. He crushed Ian's hand in his iron grip.

'Well I wouldn't want to give away all my secrets at once now would I?' Ian laughed.

Ian made a short speech just before dinner was served. The speech was remarkable not for what he said but for what he didn't. He praised Blake's management both before and after his uncle's death and said how fortunate he was to have such a fine overseer as Jim Landers. He said he had a great staff, which made for good management. About himself, he said virtually nothing. In closing, he said that since coming to Australia, he'd recognised how important it was to have good neighbours, and that neighbours needed to work together in good times and bad. He hoped that Kanimbla would always be regarded as a good neighbour.

The guests weren't quite sure what to make of Ian's words, but most of them had already formed their own opinion of Kanimbla's new owner anyway. Some of the tough older western graziers reckoned that Ian would be too soft for Queensland conditions, while most of the women, young and not so young, thought he was 'just lovely'.

It was at this party that Ian first met Joe Barker, one of the most affluent graziers in western Queensland, and a National Party supporter and benefactor. Joe was a wide-shouldered, stocky man with a broad face, blue eyes and iron-grey hair. Somehow he never seemed well dressed, despite the quality of his clothing, and this may have had something to do with his build.

'I called in to see you a couple of days ago, but you were out,' Joe said when Lachie introduced him to Ian. 'I'm often in the neighbourhood.'

'Joe is quite partial to Fiona's baking,' Lachie said with a smile. 'He liked Maisie's too.'

'I hope you enjoy the food this evening,' said Ian.

'I'm sure I will,' said Joe.

The hired chef had prepared a delicious buffet including coral trout, barramundi and marinated prawns. There was also a magnificent ham, thick steaks of grain-fed beef, and salads galore. Later, guests chose strawberry cheesecake, Pavlova or fruit salad and ice-cream for dessert. And the drinks continued to flow.

There were tables and chairs scattered casually about the gardens and around the pool. The only exception was a table near the verandah where Ian sat with the Blakes, Jim and Karen Landers (with Billy on her knee), and Lachie and Fiona McDonald. Judy had whispered to Lachie that Ian would like him and Fiona to sit at his table. Fiona had been delighted. The truth was that, of all the non-Kanimbla people Ian had met, he felt most at home with the McDonalds.

Fiona didn't get much of a chance to talk to Ian over dinner, as he was preoccupied with making sure all his guests were being looked after, but it was enough for her to be sitting at the table and to be able to catch his eye now and again.

As the evening closed in, Kanimbla's gardens seemed to soften and the air was filled with the fragrance of roses, hakeas and grevilleas. At dusk, the area around the pool and front verandah was suddenly transformed by myriad tiny white lights, and the word 'WELCOME' hung in coloured lights between two sugar gums. There was a brief burst of clapping in appreciation of the garden's metamorphosis. Ian watched as Billy Landers's eyes nearly popped out of his head.

'How fantastic, Ian,' Fiona said and flashed him a quick smile. He smiled back. Fiona, emboldened by a glass of champagne, had then slipped her arm through Ian's as they watched Billy dancing around happily.

'Stay away from the edge, darling,' Karen cautioned, and took her little son by the hand. 'Come on, sweetie. It's long past your bedtime.'

Just after Karen left, there was a kerfuffle at the pool. Cyd, who'd consumed far too much wine, had become giddy, over-balanced and fallen into the deep end. Gerald Bradshaw had immediately dived in and brought her to the surface. Coughing and sick, her sparkling gown sodden and her make-up smudged, she looked very sorry for herself.

'Take her in to Mrs Heatley,' Ian said quietly to Alec, who picked up his sodden daughter and carried her into the homestead. Trish's only comment was that Cyd would have to 'learn how to handle her drinks'.

Later, Ian had a quick word with Fiona just as she was preparing to leave. 'You were the belle of the night, Fiona,' he said with a smile. 'I hope you enjoyed yourself.'

'Oh, yes. The food was great. Apart from Cyd's dive into the pool, I'm sure everyone had a lovely time,' she said.

Just after one o'clock, Ian stood with Leo and Judy and watched the lights of the last vehicle recede down the road. Those who were not leaving until the morning, which included the airborne division, had been found beds throughout the homestead.

'Do you think it was a good night?' Ian asked.

'I'd say it was a great success, Ian; a terrific night,' Leo said. 'I'd better go and talk to Peter and the boys before they push off. They did a great job. Gerald's rescue was beyond the call of duty.'

'I'd echo that,' Ian said. He stood with Judy Blake and watched his manager walk away. 'I haven't had the chance to tell you how nice you look,' he said to Judy, who did look splendid in a long wine-red dress that perfectly complemented her dark hair and lovely brown eyes.

'Thank you. I shall never forget this night,' Judy said.

Ian smiled gently, 'No, thank you for being my hostess and for your understanding. You're a very sweet lady, Mrs B.'

He was really still only a boy, she thought.

When his guests had all departed the next morning and the last of the planes was a speck in the sky, Ian walked his last guest, who was also a client, Finlay Urquhart, to the ram shed. Jim Landers was waiting for them and looked none the worse for his late night.

'How did you pull up, Fin?' Landers asked Urquhart. The two men got on very well.

'No problem,' Urquhart said with a grin. He was fifty or so, but looked much older because his hair was very grey. Urquhart had worked himself into the ground to own the properties he now controlled and was Kanimbla's most important ram client. Lean and shrewd, Urquhart was a very wealthy man, but money hadn't made any difference to the way he treated people. He was straight-from-the-shoulder and his handshake was as good as a signed contract. Some would say that he was one of the last of his kind. Urquhart was a sheep man first and foremost. When the long dip in wool prices had caused many other sheep producers to switch to cattle, Urquhart stuck to sheep. He culled his flocks heavily and sought to improve the cut and quality of his wool. He'd stayed with the type of wool that he knew from experience he could grow profitably. This was from a long stapled, reasonably dense medium-wool sheep – sixty-fours as it used to be called or twenty-one to twenty-two microns in the newer language – of good size and constitution. What Urquhart wanted now was rams with richly crimped white wool and he didn't like too much skin on his sheep. He liked a ram to have a fair front, two or three folds maybe, but he didn't like them overdone.

It was Jim Landers's job to know what Kanimbla's ram clients were looking for, and on this occasion he had drafted off two big pens of the best of the sale rams (after Kanimbla had set aside its own selection). Jim's judgement was spot on. Urquhart couldn't find a ram he didn't like and soon handed his cheque to Leo.

'So you're going to stay with merinos?' Ian asked.

'Yeah, I'm staying with them unless the market collapses completely. I'm trying to breed the best sheep and the best wool I can and keeping a close eye on costs. And I'll say this to you. If you keep breeding rams of the quality you've got here, you should be able to sell them. You might not sell as many, but I'd hate to see you go out of ram breeding altogether. It's taken a fair while to get where you are now. You might need to show them interstate to give yourselves a bigger name, but with sheep of this standard you wouldn't be disgraced anywhere.'

'Thank you,' Ian felt a mental lift hearing such a positive assessment of Kanimbla's rams.

That night, after Ian finally fell into bed, a memory came back to him. It was something he had witnessed in Africa only a couple of nights before his father and mother were killed. He and his parents were sleeping in the same tent. The moonlight illuminated the tent, and through the mosquito net tucked tightly around his bed he could see his parents moving quietly on their bed. They were naked, and he could see the outline of his mother's breasts before his father covered them with his body. Presently, through his sleepiness, he heard strange sounds coming from the bed, but they were not unpleasant. Then there was a *shhh* and a giggle from his mother and silence. Through the gap in the opening of the tent he could see one of the camp fires still burning and away in the distance he heard lions roaring.

Although the memory did not disturb him, he'd imagined that he might not think of his parents much now that he was no longer a boy. It wasn't that he wanted to forget his mother and father; on the contrary, he had used all his powers to try to keep them alive in his thoughts. Small incidents and characteristics were especially dear to him and kept both of them alive in his mind – like his mother's pride that he could spell

'Viverridae', which was the family to which civet cats and meerkats belonged. Sometimes he couldn't understand what his parents were discussing because their words were too scientific, but he understood more than most young boys. He loved to listen to their conversations – often beside camp fires or around bush tables – and they always encouraged him to join in. He knew that the dhole was the hunting dog of India and that there were many wild dogs in Asia. Along with the American coyote – and bears and wolves – they all belonged to the order Carnivora. While at Harrow he'd written an essay on the Carnivora and it had been highly praised. He'd been amazed how easy it had been to write that essay, as if his long-deceased parents were dictating what he should say. Instead of using scientific and technical language, he'd written it as a story.

Ian knew that there was a world that lay just beneath his everyday consciousness. He thought of it as a world-in-waiting. Memories of his parents and of their work contributed to the dissatisfaction that haunted him – nothing seemed *enough*. He wished he knew what his father would have done if Kanimbla had been left to him.

The following morning, after the final guests had left and everyone had pitched in to clean up the pool and garden, Leo, Jim and Ian inspected the landing field. It seemed to have stood up to the spate of arrivals and departures pretty well, considering it had hardly been used for some time.

'Actually, I've been meaning to talk to you about your

uncle's plane, Ian,' Leo said, as they wandered along one of the landing strips. 'It was a write-off after the accident but it was well insured and we need to decide – well, *you* need to decide – whether to take the money or a replacement aircraft. I realise this is probably a painful subject for you but we do need to make a decision. There are certain advantages in owning a plane and having someone on the property who can fly it. It cuts down travelling time a lot, especially if you're going to the Riverina to look for top rams. There's also the emergency aspect – you can't always get the Flying Doctor when you want it, so if there's an accident here we can get to Roma or Toowoomba, or even Brisbane for that matter, fairly quickly. What do you think?' Leo asked.

The thought of flying a small plane terrified Ian. Apart from the fact that both his parents and then his uncle and aunt had died in plane crashes, he didn't trust himself to fly one.

'Flying is the last thing I want to do,' he said firmly.

'I can understand how you feel,' Leo said sympathetically. 'Would you have any objection to buying a plane and letting someone else fly it?'

It was on the tip of Ian's tongue to veto the plane but he valued Leo's judgement and had appreciated the advantages he had mentioned.

'I suppose we should. Does it cost much to maintain one?' he asked.

'There are costs in servicing and maintenance, but you've got to balance those against the expense of someone having to drive long distances and stay at motels those extra nights,' Leo said.

'I get the picture,' Ian said.

'If you agree that we should get a replacement, how would you feel about Jim learning to fly?' Leo asked, glancing at Jim.

Ian looked at Jim who had remained silent while he and Leo were talking. Clearly Leo and Jim had spoken about the subject before. Now, Ian recognised the eagerness in Jim's eyes.

'When do you want to begin your flying lessons?'

Jim smiled. 'Any old time.'

'Have you discussed this with Karen?' Ian asked.

Jim nodded.

'And?'

'She isn't totally onside, but she understands the advantages, and it would ease her anxiety about the lack of medical assistance available around here,' Jim explained. 'And I told her that more people die in car accidents than in planes.'

'All right. Go for it. I understand you need so many hours' flying to get a basic licence. When you've clocked up some hours, let me know and we'll see about getting our plane here,' Ian said. So long as he didn't have to fly the damned thing, or even get in it, he could see the benefits. In the meantime, he decided, he'd see about having a low-cost hangar built to house the plane. He didn't want it sitting out in the open all the time, and parked in a hangar, he wouldn't have to look at it.

167

'Now that's settled, there's something I want to discuss with you,' Ian said to Leo, as they watched Gus enjoying himself in the open space of the field. 'I've been wondering whether we could hold an annual sheepdog trial in Murrawee.'

'What kind of a trial?' Leo asked.

'Not a three-sheep trial, I mean one for farmers – with a long cast and that includes yard work. Anyone could enter. I mean, you wouldn't have to be a member of an association. There are plenty of farmers who reckon they've got good dogs and are always boasting about them. Let's put on a trial for them,' Ian suggested.

'Would you bar the professional sheepdog men?' Blake asked.

'No, I don't think so. But we'd provide prize money for both. We could call it the Western Districts Championship Utility Trial,' Ian said.

Leo looked sceptical.

'How do you propose getting this off the ground?' he asked. 'It would take a fair bit of organising wouldn't it? Especially when you've got a lot on your plate as it is.'

'Fiona has agreed to help. She's very enthusiastic. And there's a way we can get more people interested. You know that public meeting you've been pushing me to have, to lay the cotton issue to rest? Well, I'd like to schedule it, and to add a few other items to the agenda. I've been having a good look at the township and have come up with a few ideas, but I need to know what support I'd have to implement them. If

I get knocked back, well and good. If I get support, I'll propose that we form the Murrawee and District Development Association and that one of its initiatives will be an annual sheepdog trial,' Ian said.

Leo looked surprised. 'Well, this doesn't sound the sort of thing you'd expect from a bloke with his sights set on Cambridge University.'

'The state of the township really bothers me, Mr Blake. Why should I sit by and watch it fall into decay when I can do something?' Ian said. 'So, what do you think?'

'I think you should go ahead and have your meeting and see what comes out of it,' Leo said.

'Good show,' Ian grinned. 'I'll get onto it.'

## Chapter Fifteen

Ian's first summer at Kanimbla was long and hot, and if he hadn't already experienced an Australian summer at Warren it would have been a rude shock. Dry heat, often in the mid-forties Celsius, wasn't something he'd experienced in Britain and his relatively brief sojourn in Africa had been during that continent's winter. While the Kanimbla homestead was air-conditioned and he spent a lot of his time inside working at his science papers, the heat hit him when he ventured outside. He couldn't spend all his time in the study because many visitors called at Kanimbla to either buy or inspect rams and he was expected to meet and in some cases entertain them.

For the first time ever, a Christmas party was held in the shearer's dining room at Kanimbla. Ian had given each of his married employees a ham, the others beer, and young Billy a present. On the evening of Christmas Day, after the heat of the day had abated, Ian joined everyone else for a cold turkey dinner and there were drinks laid on. He didn't drink much and didn't see out the party but the fact that he'd given it and then turned up rather than holding a party at the homestead moved him up a notch in the men's estimation. Jack Richardson had never done anything like that.

During the summer, he had Murrawee builder Frank Morton erect a one-room building he could use as a laboratory. It was adjacent to the stables and was fitted out with a sink, fluorescent lighting, wide desks and an array of beakers, test tubes, trays and of course his microscope. Here he could do staining and testing so that he became familiar with a variety of organisms.

Ian was studying microbiology and human physiology and anything in this field attracted his attention – he was not content to confine his explorations to the task requirements of his course. Infectious diseases were especially interesting because most of them were caused by bacteria and viruses, and working with livestock gave him ample opportunities for acquiring further knowledge. It was typical of him that he rarely mentioned his study to anyone. Fiona, for one, had to dig it out of him.

'What's this about you getting Frank Morton to build you an outside study?' she asked one Sunday after lunch. The McDonalds had been invited for a meal at Kanimbla, after which Lachie had excused himself with 'I'll just leave you young ones to it' and wandered down to see Leo and Judy.

Ian wondered how Fiona had heard about the study. 'Who told you about it?' he asked.

'Haven't you encountered the outback grapevine yet, Ian? There's not much you can keep quiet in the bush.'

'Well, it's not actually a study, Fiona,' he said.

'If it's not a study, what is it?' she persisted.

'It's a very basic laboratory,' Ian said.

'What do you need a laboratory for?' she asked.

'To become familiar with lab equipment, do simple tests, staining . . . just elementary stuff. There are no test animals or anything like that,' Ian assured her.

'Can I have a look at it?' she asked.

'There's not much to see. But sure, you can have a look,' Ian said.

'Now?' Fiona asked and watched Ian's face for a reaction. She wondered if she was being too nosy for Ian's liking. Neither of them had mentioned the kiss by the river again, and Fiona began to think she might have imagined it.

'Well, okay,' he said patiently.

It wasn't until she stood with Ian in his 'elementary laboratory' that she saw a different side to him. The more questions she asked, the more animated he became. 'What's that about?' she asked and pointed to an open book in front of a chair.

'It helps identify bacteria by a gram staining index.'

'Have you found anything interesting?' she asked.

'Nothing startling. There's *E. coli* bacterium just about everywhere, but very few strains are harmful to humans.'

'I thought they were all a worry,' said Fiona.

'Not unless they mutate. One particular strain produces a toxin that damages intestinal lining and is usually transmitted by ground meat contaminated during slaughter or processing. There's no treatment apart from fluid replacement and supportive care.'

Fiona shivered, 'Luckily I'm not a big fan of steak tartare.'

Ian smiled at Fiona's joke. 'For other bacteria, it's important to identify the organism so that you can treat it properly. I've discovered that there's a species of Chlamydia that infects poultry, pigeons and parrots and is communicable to humans. It's called *C. psittaci* and causes severe bronchitis and other pneumonia-like symptoms. Some people call it parrot fever. It requires a blood test for accurate detection, but a lot of doctors don't carry out blood tests and simply hand out any old antibiotic when a specific one is needed,' Ian said.

'I had no idea a cocky could be so dangerous!' said Fiona.

'Only when it's a sick one,' said Ian. 'One day when I'm staining specimens you might care to come and have a look.'

'You mean through the microscope?' she asked.

'Yes. It's not the best microscope you can buy, but it's all right for the time being,' Ian said.

'Is this what you've been studying?' she asked.

'This and other stuff,' he said with a shy smile. 'It's never-ending. Scientists think they've controlled a disease and then it mutates or else it becomes resistant to the available drugs. That's happening with malaria right now. One day we'll be able to vaccinate against malaria just as we do against polio and diphtheria. And maybe we'll be able to do it against AIDS, which is killing millions of people worldwide.'

'That would be amazing.' Ian could see that Fiona was genuinely interested. She had never known Ian to open up like this before. She was impressed with his vision – there was no doubt that science was a subject very close to his heart. But as a magpie warbled from outside the window, she was reminded that this was Kanimbla and a very unlikely place for anyone to study microbiology. Where, for heaven's sake, would this subject take him? That was the big question.

'So this is why we don't see much of you,' she said.

'I guess so,' he admitted with a smile.

## Chapter Sixteen

The iron-roofed weatherboard hall was oldish by Australian standards and was used for just about every meeting of note held in the town. There hadn't been a dance in Murrawee for a long time, but in the days before television, the hall had hosted two or three dances a year. Like the railway station, it would have looked much better with a coat of paint, but no one seemed to have the inclination.

It was a hot night and the lights of the hall attracted a wide variety of flying insects including the odd mosquito. Some sixty people sat in the body of the hall – about half from properties around Murrawee and half from the township itself. Ian had asked the Hall Committee, presided over by Helen Donovan, to have tea, coffee, cold drinks, biscuits and cake on hand for both before and after the meeting. The Committee, first formed in the 1930s, had had an important role in the town for several decades. However, as Murrawee's population declined, and events were fewer, the Committee became less active. The annual gymkhana seemed to be its main reason for survival.

Everyone had been intrigued by the flyer that Ian had had posted around the town and dropped in mailboxes all over the district:

Are you satisfied with Murrawee?

Do you realise what could be done here?

If you are interested in how our township could be improved,

please attend the following meeting:

*Where:* Murrawee Hall

*When:* Thursday 24 February at 7:30 pm

*Convenor:* Ian Richardson, Kanimbla

Also to be discussed: 'To Grow or Not to Grow Cotton'

*\* This is an important meeting and your attendance is especially requested.*

It was just after eight o'clock when Leo Blake asked for everyone to be seated. He and Ian sat at a table up the front. The lights had been dimmed in an attempt to diminish the insect problem.

'I'd like to call the meeting to order,' Leo began. He had a rather formal manner on occasions such as this, but the respect with which he was regarded throughout the district made him the best chairman. 'Before I turn the meeting over to Ian, I'd like to explain that this is more of a discussion evening than a meeting, as such. But please give Ian your attention and he'll explain further,' Leo said and sat down as Ian stood up.

From the hall, Fiona McDonald's eyes focused unwaveringly on Ian. She'd never seen him in a tie before and, although it clearly wasn't his accessory of choice, she thought he looked very handsome in it.

Before Ian could say a word, 'Blue' Delaney was on his feet. He owned a cattle property adjoining Kanimbla's Big Plain. Never a man to mince words, he reckoned he'd get the cotton business settled one way or the other before they got tangled up in other matters.

Blue's strong voice echoed round the hall. 'What some of us would like to know before the discussion gets underway is whether Kanimbla proposes to grow cotton on the Plain.'

The question produced a loud murmur of support from the body of the hall.

Ian nodded. 'A fair question,' he said, speaking very clearly. 'So let me assure you that Kanimbla has no intention of growing cotton on the Plain or on any other part of the property.'

'Have we got your personal assurance on that?' Blue asked.

'As long as I own Kanimbla, there will be no cotton grown on the property.'

The assembled throng murmured their approval. 'I reckon that will ease the minds of a few people here tonight. It's not that we don't understand why people are growing cotton, it's just that some of us have got very heavy investments in cattle and we'll sleep a bit better knowing we don't have to worry about cotton chemicals drifting on to our places,' Blue said, clearly relieved.

'Hear, hear,' came from several places in the hall.

'Good,' said Ian. 'Now that we've got that out of the way, I'd like to come to the real purpose of tonight's meeting. I'll begin by asking you some questions. The first is: How many of you here tonight are satisfied with Murrawee as a township? If you're satisfied with it please raise your hand.'

Ian paused but not a single hand was raised. He wasn't sure whether this was the true response of the gathering, or whether they were unsure of his intentions and wary of expressing an opinion.

He went on, 'If you're not satisfied, how many of you would like to see some improvements in Murrawee?'

The mood was tentative at first, but after a minute or so, about half of those present had raised their hands. This was such a good result, Ian wondered why nothing had been initiated before now.

'Then I'll ask you a third question: How many of you here tonight would be willing to *do* something to improve Murrawee?'

This time almost as many hands were raised. Ian nodded his satisfaction, glanced at a small card in his hand and launched into his proposals for the township.

'Some of you probably think that I've got a colossal hide to come here and ask you to listen to my proposals. I'd have been reluctant to do so except that Mr Blake has assured me that Kanimbla has often taken a leading role where matters affecting its neighbours and the citizens of Murrawee —'

'I've got to take issue with you on that.' Blue Delaney was on his feet again. 'At one time, Kanimbla did do a lot for Murrawee, but that was in the old days. Your uncle Jack wasn't much of a help. He spent as much time away as at Kanimbla. He never really got to know us at all,' Blue said in his usual blunt fashion.

'Yes, I understand that,' said Ian, 'and I'm sorry it has been that way. But my attitude is quite different from Jack Richardson's. I'd like to make up for recent years, and I hope Kanimbla can become a community leader again.'

Looking on, Fiona was amazed that a young man not much older than she was could command an audience so calmly and effectively. She'd enjoyed watching the debating during her school years, although she'd never been confident enough to try it herself, and she had no doubt that Ian would be a brilliant debater. No matter what argument anyone threw at him, he seemed to have a logical response.

'What concerns me, and I'm sure it concerns all of you,' Ian continued, 'is whether Murrawee will survive, or whether it will, eventually, cease to exist as a viable township. Mrs Donovan tells me that there used to be both a butcher and a baker here, as well as a barber and some other small businesses. Now you all have to drive a fair distance for these services. And if we don't do anything soon, there's a good chance that a few years down the track the few surviving businesses will close too. I, for one, don't want that to happen. I realise that Murrawee hasn't been the same since the rail service was discontinued, but I refuse to believe that we can't do something to get things happening here again. I reckon that if we can put in place some schemes that will help us to capture some of the tourist trade that currently passes us by, we'll be well on the way to ensuring Murrawee's future.' Ian paused as murmuring broke out around the hall.

'But what have we got to offer tourists?' someone called from the back.

'Nothing!' said another voice. 'Not a damned thing.'

'Do we even want tourists here?' Blue threw in. 'Murrawee wouldn't be the same with rubbernecks all over the place. That's always supposing there's anything worthwhile for them to gawp at, which there isn't.'

'The question we should be asking is whether we want Murrawee to survive,' said Ian. 'Without tourists, I believe it will become a ghost town in just a few years. We've already had this audience's collective opinion; half of you clearly want to do something to develop the township.'

'You'd have to be a magician to improve Murrawee,' Blue muttered and someone else laughed.

Ian shook his head. 'Not at all. You've got one of the finest stretches of river country in all Queensland on your doorstep. I'm assured that some people come back here every year to camp and fish – and that's with no conveniences available to them. Using this stretch of river as our launching pad, I believe we can create a set of attractions that will entice plenty of visitors to Murrawee.'

Fiona looked at the workworn faces around her and felt suddenly worried that apathy might get the better of her community. Determined to show her support for Ian, she stood up, glancing at Blue before addressing the hall. 'Actually, the river is not all we have to offer. Did you know that in the thirty-five-acre paddock across the railway line, adjoining the river, there's a hot-water bore that's been sealed? Ian's had the water analysed and it's got good enough things in it – minerals and the like – for us to promote its health-giving qualities. We could build two swimming pools there, one hot and one cold.'

Ian smiled at Fiona, who sat down quickly, a little embarrassed at her outburst. He scanned the faces in the hall. It seemed that everyone had become very quiet. Clearly, they were waiting for further details.

'As far as funding goes,' Ian continued, 'there's government money available and other sources too. This project would certainly require some contributions from us, mainly in the way of skills and manpower, but I believe it's quite feasible. If we decide to go ahead, I'll propose that we erect an honour board listing the names of every person and company involved in the construction of the pools in whatever capacity,' Ian said.

'Supposing that we could install these pools, they aren't going to be enough to bring tourists out of their way,' said a male voice from the back.

'No, the bigger towns have swimming pools, and there's the Stockman's Hall of Fame at Longreach, which we could never match,' said another voice.

'You're right,' Ian agreed. 'We'd need more than the pools. If we had a motel reasonably close to the pools, people might be tempted to stick around for a day or two and, hopefully, spend some money in Murrawee. The motel wouldn't need to be anything extravagant – maybe eight or ten units to begin with, and a kitchen. I'm not aiming to take business away from the pub, but the fact is that many people now prefer to stay in motels. And if we can attract tourists, the pub will get *more* business, not less.'

Ian heard the first whispers of agreement.

'I reckon that what we need initially is a caravan park. As you all know, a lot of caravaners use the road through the township, but they don't stop on two accounts: there's nowhere with facilities where they can stay, and there's nothing for them to see. The paddock beside the river is a lovely spot, ideal for caravans. So, in the first instance, I propose that we fence off an area for a caravan park and maybe start the ball rolling by building an amenities block and buying a couple of on-site vans. We'd just need to put up signs on the road so that people would know the place is here.'

'I've often thought of taking a caravan down there myself, doing a spot of fishing . . . ' commented Sean Driscoll, who owned a place beyond Nelanji and was something of the town wag.

'Good on you, Sean!' someone called.

'But we still don't have a major attraction,' said Larry Phillips from the pub. He hadn't raised any objection to Ian's suggestion for a motel because he doubted that it would ever be built. And even if it was, he reckoned it wouldn't affect his business because very few people ever stayed at the pub unless – and this was rare – there was something on, like the gymkhana. And in this case, he never had enough rooms.

Ian took a deep breath. Although his next idea was the one that excited him the most, he was a little nervous about suggesting it. But he also realised that this was the ideal opportunity to broach the subject, so he focused on the audience in the hall and ploughed on.

'I think we should look into the possibility of establishing an aviary for native birds. This country boasts a wonderful array of parrots and other birds and if people had the chance to see them in natural-looking surroundings – trees, rocks, pools with running water, that sort of thing – I think they'd be very tempted to stop here. Besides which, we have a native bird expert – an amateur ornithologist – in our midst, and we could make use of his expertise in this area,' Ian said.

'Who is he?' was the call, though Ian knew that at least some of those present knew of Leigh's interest in birds.

'Leigh Metcalfe. He looks after our Top River country,' Ian replied.

'You mean the writer bloke? I'd heard he was interested in birds all right!' someone called from the back. There was a quick burst of laughter.

Ian ignored the comment, 'Leigh Metcalfe can identify any bird in Queensland, but he's especially knowledgeable about Australian parrots. Of course, the things I'm pro-posing couldn't all be done at once, but if we drew up a schedule and got ourselves organised, we could achieve a lot in the next eighteen months or so – especially if some of us are willing to commit some time and other resources,' Ian said. He sensed the atmosphere in the hall beginning to warm, and he felt a little more confident as he broached his final proposal for the evening.

'Lastly, if you'll bear with me, I'd like to suggest that we stage an annual sheepdog trial. Ian smiled at Fiona. 'This was really Fiona McDonald's idea, and it's a brilliant one.'

Fiona smiled back, pleased that Ian was publicly recognising her input.

'We've got an oval and there's adjoining country that could be used. The trial would carry good prizes – Kanimbla will contribute a worthwhile amount. A lot of local people have the skills necessary to organise an event like this.' Once again, Ian sought out Fiona in the centre of the hall and gave her an encouraging smile. She felt herself blushing in the dim light and hoped no one noticed. 'It would be a fairly big undertaking, but it would put Murrawee in the spotlight, and I think it would give us something to look forward to each year, as a community.'

The hall broke into murmurs again, and the noise gradually rose as people got into discussion with their neighbours.

'I'd like to break now so that you can discuss these proposals amongst yourselves,' said Ian, over the noise. 'And I'm dying for a cuppa! Perhaps we could reconvene briefly after supper. A big thankyou to Mrs Donovan and her hall committee for supplying us with drinks and supper tonight,' Ian concluded.

Blue, however, wasn't finished. 'I reckon we've heard some pretty surprising suggestions from you tonight, Ian,' he said. 'I'm not going to say I'm against them, but what I'd like to know is how much Kanimbla is really prepared to support them.'

Ian nodded. 'The thirty-five acres beside the river where the hot bore is situated – do you agree that it's a good site?' Ian asked Blue.

'Yeah. It's not bad,' Blue admitted.

'I've bought it.' Ian paused to let the exclamations die down. 'And if you agree to form a township development association and set it up legally, I'll donate those thirty-five acres to Murrawee in perpetuity. I'll also pay for a fence for a caravan park and install a couple of on-site vans to kick off the program. How does that sound?' Ian asked.

'It sounds pretty bloody good to me,' Sean Driscoll said, provoking much laughter, which soon subsided into clapping. Ian stepped down from the platform with relief before moving into the hall.

Despite the heat and the insects, supper went on for some time, and got noisier and noisier. Ian found himself bailed up by Frank Morton, the local builder, and Joe Barker, one of the shrewdest graziers in the area.

'Building a motel seems a very ambitious undertaking,' Joe said. 'Would it pay?'

Joe was supposed to have the first dollar he ever made and it was rumoured that he could come up with a million dollars overnight.

'It's been done before, Mr Barker. Farmers have put up the money to build motels. And they've done all right, too. I'm not so much concerned with making a small motel pay as using it to draw people to Murrawee so that the local services get some extra business. I'd be happy for it to break even,' Ian said to Joe. 'We'd pitch the price a bit lower than at the bigger towns – that ought to entice a few. They'd pay to use the pools and to look at the birds.'

'It all sounds fine, but do you think we could pull it off?' Joe asked dubiously. 'It sounds like a big project for a township on its last legs.'

'I don't see why not,' replied Ian. 'New developments are occurring everywhere else. Why not in Murrawee?'

'An eight- or ten-unit motel with a kitchen wouldn't cost a lot, it's true, especially if we used some voluntary labour . . .' Frank began.

'I wonder, Mr Morton, would you be able to work out some costs for us?' asked Ian, keen to get the builder on-side. 'I've had one estimate and I'd be interested to see how yours compares,' Ian said. He was sure Frank wouldn't be able to pass up the chance of some business.

'All right. My quotes are pretty competitive – I reckon you'll be surprised. If you're going for a caravan park, you'd need a toilet block and it might be possible to link up that septic system with what you'd need at the motel, to save on costs,' Frank said, already on the case.

'You're right,' Ian agreed. 'Cost savings like this would make all the difference.'

'Do you think it's a goer, Frank?' Joe asked, surprised by Morton's sudden enthusiasm.

'There's heaps of tourists, local and international, travelling these days and they're all looking for the real Australia, whatever that is,' said Frank. 'A real Australian township with genuine attractions at realistic as opposed to luxury prices . . . well, it could be a goer, Joe. It depends a fair bit on how well it's presented and that will depend on how well people get behind the project.'

'Hmm. Well, Ian's right about the site. That's a great stretch of water. The trouble was that we all got too used to it. It took an outsider to see its possibilities,' Joe said. He looked thoughtful as he walked back to his seat.

As well as being a careful man where money was concerned, Joe Barker was also a passionate Queenslander. Initially, he'd thought that Ian's suggestions were pie-in-the-sky stuff generated by a young English lad who hadn't been in the country long enough to know its real nature. Now, he wasn't so sure. He imagined what it might be like to see a few more businesses in the township again, like in the old days. He realised that the only way they could achieve that was by attracting more visitors.

After about three-quarters of an hour of solid and noisy discussion, Ian and Leo went back to their table and the audience took their seats. Helen Donovan moved to the front of the hall and tapped a glass to get everyone's attention. She wasn't usually one for making speeches, but neither was she backward in speaking her mind, and she felt she couldn't leave without saying something tonight.

'Ah, I'd like to say a few words. I can see that Mr . . . um . . . Ian has put a lot of time and thought into what he's suggesting for our town. And personally, I think his ideas are very exciting. These are things that we could realistically do, if we pulled together. Murrawee is our town and Ray and me don't want it to die. We'll do anything we can to make it a better place. The shame is, we should have done something before now. Anyway, I reckon Ian should be given a vote of thanks for what he's proposed . . . and for not growing cotton,' she said.

There was a moment of silence, before a burst of applause.

Ian had seen Lachie and Fiona McDonald with their heads together, so he wasn't altogether surprised when the tall man stood up. 'I'd like to endorse Helen's remarks, Mr Chairman. Those of us who live here surely have a vested interest in trying to maintain Murrawee as a viable township. Fiona and I would be happy to serve on the kind of development association Ian has suggested. His ideas make a lot of sense. Fiona and I especially like the idea of the aviary. It could generate a lot of interest.'

'Mr Chairman,' Lachie continued, 'you said this wasn't a formal meeting, but I'd like to suggest that we take Ian's proposals a step further by asking all those prepared to serve on a development association to write their names down. If we get enough names, we can get the ball rolling.'

'Sounds fine to me,' said Leo.

'Thank you Mr McDonald,' replied Ian. 'Before you put pen to paper, I just want to make it clear that I'm not trying to railroad any of you with these proposals. This only goes ahead with your support. If you're not with me we may as well call the whole business off. If you are, let's work together to make a town you can be proud of. Thank you.'

Ian sat down to hearty applause.

Leo looked at Ian and grinned. 'Looks like you might have started something,' he said.

'Finishing it is what really matters,' Ian replied.

Nelanji homestead was large and comfortable – nowhere near as grand as Kanimbla, but up there with the best of the homesteads in western Queensland. Fiona's mother had created a beautiful garden, a living testament to her dedication and creativity. The homestead didn't have Kanimbla's natural advantages of a tranquil river setting with towering red gums, and had had to be developed from flat scrubby plain. It took a good deal of trial and error to find trees and shrubs that could stand up to the harsh conditions. Most of the homestead block was encircled by a shelter break of tough cadagi (sometimes called the widow-maker because of its propensity to drop branches), silky oaks, golden rain trees, tipuana (often referred to as racehorse trees because they grow so fast, and considered weeds by the authorities), and white cedars. There was an inner line of grevilleas, hakeas and murrayas and adjoining the lawn there were beds of pelargonium, lavender, roses and blue-flowered plumbago. The garden's crowning glory was a towering purple bougainvillea, interlaced with mauve wisteria that covered a long-dead tree. The back portion of the block was devoted to a couple of tidy beds of spinach and other vegetables. There was no great stretch of lawn because, as Fiona would later explain to Ian, it took too much dam water to keep a lawn green (bore water was too hard) and it made more sense to keep the dam water for the rest of the garden.

Since offering to help organise Murrawee's first sheepdog trial, she had been making some calls, and was keen to discuss some of the details with Ian, so had invited him for a meal.

Fiona was shifting a spray when Ian arrived and gave him a dazzling smile when he complimented her on the garden.

'It was all Mum's doing really. We've just kept it going. Dad says that he still feels close to Mum when he's out here. And he does his share. He brings the sheep manure and if we pass a nursery he's happy to bring home anything I need. We really appreciate Mum's foresight and hard work when the westerly winds blow like mad. Of course it hasn't got Kanimbla's grand setting,' Fiona said.

'It's a beautiful garden, Fiona,' Ian said warmly. And he thought how happy she looked in it. As she walked towards him, tucking a stray curl behind her ear, he noticed a little smear of dirt on her cheek and wanted to reach out and wipe it away. The longer he knew her, the more beautiful she seemed to become. He looked away, anxious not to betray his feelings. He wasn't sure if he would stay on at Kanimbla, and he was so busy – there didn't seem to be time for anything but work or study. He didn't want to hurt Fiona. It would be better for everyone if they were simply good friends.

'It's beautiful at sunset when the murrayas release a lovely orange scent,' Fiona said. 'Well, we'd better go inside.'

After leaving school and deciding to stay on at Nelanji instead of going away to university, Fiona had become more closely involved in the day-to-day management of the property, which was no small operation. There were fifteen thousand sheep and seven hundred Shorthorn cows, requiring a great deal of stock work, though big jobs like mulesing and lamb marking were carried out by a contract team. A lot of the jobs could be done on horseback and this suited Fiona very well.

She'd found that she needed dogs to move the sheep and cattle and, until she arrived home from boarding school, the only dogs on the place were her father's. Recently, Lachie had bought her a young kelpie, Glen, who she'd been working hard to train. She'd bought a couple of books on training sheepdogs and, as her knowledge increased, so did her interest. She had even wondered, occasionally, whether she might eventually work some dogs in trials. There were a few women trialling and they'd had their share of success.

After drinks on the verandah, Fiona took Ian to show him her horses and the shearing shed. There wasn't a lot to show, but Fiona did want a chance to get Ian on his own again.

Her mother had told her that if a fellow was really interested in a girl, then his gaze would hardly stray from her. If she looked at him, his eyes would meet hers and both would know that something wonderful had happened. On this occasion, Ian was impeccably well mannered. He spent plenty of time looking at and discussing her horses, and once even took her hand to help her over a fence. But nothing more.

'Tell me about the bay,' he asked.

'That's Star. He's a lovely natured horse – a thoroughbred and stock-horse cross. He's got a great canter.'

'And the brown one?' Ian stroked the beast's neck.

'That's Tex. I do most of the stock work on him. He's an Australian stock horse. And the grey pony was one of my early horses. She's retired, of course, but I could never sell her. I love horses.'

'I can see that,' Ian smiled.

He was so unlike other boys, especially compared to the boys she'd heard about from her friends at school. Fiona noticed that his eyes strayed all over the place, taking in the property and its facilities, and only looked in her direction occasionally. In blue jeans and a light shirt that didn't hide her figure, she wasn't dressed to kill, but she was definitely dressed to interest – and Ian seemed very uninterested. She returned to serve dinner deeply disappointed, and found it hard to concentrate on being a good hostess.

She'd gone to a great deal of trouble with the meal: they began with a salmon entrée that she'd tried out on her father the previous week, followed by a ham salad with chive-flavoured potatoes and then dessert. She'd tossed up between fruit salad and a meringue pie with ice-cream, and had finally settled on the pie because she knew that Mrs Heatley often served fruit salad. Also, meringue pie had been one of the last dishes her mother had taught her to make, and it was a favourite of her father's.

'How are the plans for the sheepdog trial coming along?' Lachie asked Ian.

'Well, I've been thinking we should aim to hold it in September. May would be better, but we won't have time to organise things for May this year. Fiona has started making some calls and I'm hoping she will play a big part in its organisation.'

Fiona hesitated, 'I love the idea, Ian, but seriously, don't you think I'm a bit . . . inexperienced?'

Ian was very positive. 'It'd be a matter of organisation, mainly – and I'm sure you're good at that. I attended a trial in the Central West when I was working at Warren, and from what I can gather, the main elements are the venue, obstacles and sheep.'

'Plus a judge, a timekeeper and some stewards,' Fiona added. 'There'd also be a few other details to arrange: trophies, for starters, and then there's catering for the handlers and spectators.'

'There you are. You're on the ball already,' Ian said with a grin.

Fiona had been struggling to hide her disappointment at Ian's lack of interest in her, but with this warm encouragement, she began to feel better.

'I dare say you could talk to a sheepdog person or two and find out the ins and outs of the business,' Lachie said to Fiona. 'There's sheepdog cranks in both Longreach and Roma.'

'Are you sure you won't mind that it takes some of my time away from Nelanji?' Fiona asked her father.

'Absolutely not!' exclaimed Lachie, 'It's a great idea and I'm right behind you.'

'Good show!' Ian beamed. 'If we can't get wethers closer in to Murrawee, we'll use our cull maiden ewes. And I tell you what, you could have a couple of our Belted Trio to order about at the trial.'

'Belted Trio?' Fiona asked with raised eyebrows.

'That's what I call Peter, Ted and Gerald – our three jack-aroos – because of their identical belts and pouches. They ought to get a kick out of being your offsiders.'

Fiona's courage momentarily deserted her again. The thought of telling the men what to do was daunting. 'Seeing you're so au fait with what's wanted, shouldn't you be running the show?' she asked.

'Honestly, you'll do a much better job than I would. And I don't have the time. It will be a great occasion – perhaps the start of Murrawee's rejuvenation,' Ian said. 'I'm looking forward to it already!'

'So am I,' agreed Lachie.

Seeing Ian and her father's enthusiasm, Fiona suddenly wanted, more than anything else, to prove to Ian Richardson that she could do it.

# Chapter Seventeen

When Trish Claydon heard by bush telegraph that Ian had been to Nelanji for dinner, she was determined to get in before anyone else extended Ian another invitation, and invited him for afternoon tea. She had no doubt that Fiona had her eye on Ian, and Trish wanted him unspoiled.

Ian wasn't keen on going to the Claydons. Too many people had warned him about Trish for him to feel entirely comfortable in her company. But he could hardly decline a visit to Bahreenah after going to Nelanji. Visiting the neighbours was the kind of public-relations exercise Leo had told him would be part and parcel of his role as owner of Kanimbla. There was also the fact that Alec used Kanimbla rams. Anyone who spent as much money on rams as Alec merited at least one afternoon of his time. Besides, Ian quite liked him and respected his interest in merinos.

The surrounds of the Bahreenah homestead were not as well kept as Nelanji, but an expansive, faded green lawn gave some relief from the dry red earth that bordered it. The garden consisted of some large trees with dark green leaves that

Ian couldn't identify, and some rose bushes that were very much in need of pruning. The homestead was large, with the ubiquitous gauzed verandahs. A high fence surrounded the lawn and homestead, and outside the gate a wisteria struggled to climb the pergola beside a roofed carport.

Trish met Ian at the top of the homestead's steps. Her strapless white dress was split up the side, as usual, revealing a fair proportion of one long, smooth thigh. It was a rather inappropriate outfit for a casual afternoon tea, Ian thought, as he tried to avoid looking at her cleavage. Trish wore just enough eye shadow and lipstick to subtract a few years from her age.

'It's lovely you could come, Ian. I'm sure you've got lots to occupy you at Kanimbla,' Trish said as Ian walked hesitantly up the steps.

'Thank you for inviting me, Mrs Claydon,' Ian said in his usual well-mannered way.

'You must call me Trish. We're your closest neighbours, after all, and I expect that we'll be seeing quite a lot of each other over the next few years,' Trish oozed. God, but he is gorgeous, she thought as she looked at him in his light-coloured trousers and blue linen shirt.

Ian smiled wanly. 'Where's Alec, Trish?'

'He's in Roma Hospital. Nothing serious, just a small operation he's been putting off for some time. The date became available and I didn't like to postpone your visit,' Trish said smoothly. 'And the girls, of course, are away at uni and school.'

'Will Alec be away long?' Ian asked, feeling a stab of concern that briefly overtook his nervousness at being alone with Trish.

'Not very long. He'll need to take it steady for a few days and then he'll be as right as rain,' Trish said. She led the way into a very comfortable lounge room with sliding doors that opened out to a verandah. The room was furnished with large leather lounges and a glass-top table. The view out through the doors was of a huge area of silver and green bushland.

'Make yourself comfortable, Ian. What would you like to drink?' Trish asked.

'I'd like an orange juice, if you have one.'

Trish disappeared, to return a moment later with a jug of juice in one hand and a tall glass in the other. As she walked towards Ian, she appeared to trip and the juice splattered all over her white dress.

'Oh, look at that. I'll have to soak it straight away, Ian. Sorry. Will you unzip me, please? It's down the back, here,' and she turned her back to Ian so that he could do as she asked.

Unsure how to react, but not wanting to appear impolite, Ian stood up and pulled down on the zip. Trish's dress fell away to reveal a tanned body devoid of any undergarments. Before he could think, Trish had turned to face him, glass and jug still in hand. Ian stood as if paralysed.

Trish felt she had him. When she saw Ian's eyes rove over her, she was already imagining the hours of pleasure she would have with this gorgeous young man. She believed that, deep down, all men were the same, and that she could trap any man into sleeping with her.

'I'll put this dress in the tub to soak,' she said calmly. 'Here. Please take these,' and she handed the jug and glass to Ian, who put them on the table. Then she walked away with the dress over one arm, confident that Ian would follow her. She threw the stained dress through the bathroom door and kept walking towards her bedroom.

When she discovered that Ian was not behind her, she walked back to the lounge room. The poor boy is probably very shy, she thought; so much the better. But Ian was not to be seen, and as she ran to the front door, she heard the car start up and then saw it go down their drive. She stood in her nudity and watched until the Mercedes was out of sight. For the first time in her life, Trish Claydon had been stood up. 'You don't know what you've missed, Ian,' she spat angrily.

Trish didn't remain angry for too long, however. She only had a limited time before Alec was back, and intended to make the most of it. If Ian wasn't up for a bit of fun, she knew someone who would be.


After breakfast the following morning, Ian told Mrs Heatley that he needed to see Leigh Metcalfe but would be back for lunch to meet a ram client who was due at about two o'clock. He put Gus in the front of the ute and drove away to Top River.

Ian could never go past the rise above Leigh's bungalow without stopping to enjoy the view of the river. This morning, he got out of the vehicle and leant against it as he looked down the slope towards the house. But instead of the usual tranquillity, he saw two people running down the terraced steps, yelling. It was Trish, with Leigh hot on her heels. Both were completely naked and Leigh held a leafy branch, which he was applying to Trish's backside at frequent intervals. Trish's squeals and cries of 'Don't, Leigh!' carried clearly through the still morning air, and despite her protests, Trish was clearly enjoying herself. By the time she had fallen into the river, and Leigh had jumped in on top of her, Ian had started the ute, backed it across the road and was headed towards the homestead. Leigh had obviously forgotten Ian was coming and he could hardly interrupt.

'You're home early,' Mrs Heatley said when he walked into the kitchen. 'Yes,' Ian said, sniffing the aroma of freshly baked biscuits. 'Leigh was otherwise engaged.'

'Don't tell me – he had a "friend" there,' Mrs Heatley said with a sigh.

'Yes. They didn't see me,' Ian said, sampling a biscuit.

'Lordy me,' she uttered under her breath.

'Mmm, these biscuits are good, Mrs Heatley.'

'I'm pleased you like them. They're a different recipe. There's salmon patties for lunch,' she said. She knew these were Ian's favourite and was glad she'd chosen to make them today, as Ian seemed a little shocked by whatever he'd seen at Leigh's.

'Lovely,' Ian said, reaching for another biscuit. Mrs Heatley put a cup of tea beside him.

'What makes a woman behave like that, Mrs Heatley?' he asked.

'You mean like Trish Claydon?' she asked. She needed a few moments to get her thoughts together on this question.

'Yes. She has a husband, yet —'

What an innocent he is, thought Mrs Heatley, but how refreshing to find a young man who was honest enough to seek an answer to things he didn't understand.

'Well now, Mr Ian, I'm not sure I'm the person you should be asking about that.'

'Well, I can't ask my mother now can I, Mrs H? You don't mind me calling you Mrs H do you? So if I can't ask you, I don't know who I can ask,' he said.

Mrs Heatley was touched that Ian felt he could confide in her, and knew she had to try to provide an answer that made sense. She took a deep breath.

'Women have different reasons for wanting men. Of course it might be that she simply wants to experience sex with another man, or it might be that it makes her feel good to seduce a man away from his wife. I suppose there's a feeling of satisfaction and power that comes with that. Then there are women who like to seduce and manipulate young men because they offer so much in bed. Trish Claydon might be one of those women.'

Ian was still looking puzzled, so she went on.

'Basically, it's quite apparent that Trish enjoys sex. It's a great shame you had to be exposed to that behaviour,' she said.

'*Exposed* is the operative word,' he said and laughed.

Mrs Heatley smiled at Ian's joke. 'Some people just aren't satisfied with their lot in life. There are plenty of women who work closely with their husbands or partners. But from what I can gather, Trish has never been very keen on property life, except what it can give her in the way of material things – expensive clothes and holidays in fancy places. You do have to feel a bit sorry for her and the fact that she gets her kicks with other men. They're like a drug she's got to have. It wouldn't surprise me if she gets a rude shock one of these days. It wouldn't surprise me at all.'

'She hasn't shown any interest in my proposals for Murrawee,' Ian said.

'Trish doesn't have much to do with the community. She leaves all that to Alec. So how is the Murrawee project progressing?' Mrs Heatley asked.

'Slowly,' Ian said with a wry smile. 'There's still some opposition. Well, that's not exactly right. There's a mixture of apathy and timidity. And a kind of xenophobia, if you know what I mean . . .'

'So some aren't warming to the idea of tourists traipsing about Murrawee?'

'That's exactly what I mean,' Ian said. 'You'd think that people prepared to live in Western Queensland would be more adventurous.'

'You've got to bear in mind that there's a lot of older people, some retired, in the area. You'd hardly describe them as get-up-and-go types. They've worked hard and they're probably fairly set in their ways,' Mrs Heatley pointed out.

'Yes, I know, but I'm still surprised that they can't see the benefits of a more prosperous township. It will be a lot easier to attract a retired nursing sister or ambulance officer if we can inject some new life into Murrawee – and closer medical help would surely be a great benefit to everyone.

'Anyway, we'll keep working. The few remaining business-people are all for my suggestions and the younger people in the district would agree to just about anything that livens the place up. Once we get something actually started – and that's not far off – I'm hoping some of the doubters will come to the party,' Ian said.

'And how is Jim doing with his pilot training?' Mrs Heatley asked.

'Remarkably well, by all accounts. He's been flying solo for several weeks. His night flying clearance is his next objective. He'll be bringing our new Cessna home very soon.'

'Is Karen coping with the idea, do you think?'

'I know she's been apprehensive about the whole thing, but I think she sees the sense in it. One thing you can be sure of, Mrs H, is that's that I won't be going in that plane. Not unless I'm in mortal danger. I still remember, as clearly as if it happened yesterday, how I felt when the ranger came and told me that my father and mother had been burnt to a crisp in that damned plane. I still miss them,' Ian said.

'I'm sure you do.'

'They explained everything to me,' he continued. 'They never left me groping for answers. I know that they were proud of me. But I also know they would have loved me whoever I was – that's an amazing thing, don't you think?'

Mrs Heatley nodded.

'I used to have nightmares when I was at Harrow. They were about how my father and mother must have felt when the plane began to dive towards the ground and they knew I would become an orphan. Can you imagine the agony they would have suffered in that death dive?' he asked.

'I believe I have some notion,' she said, thinking of her son and his motorbike accident. 'But for an eight-year-old boy, the sudden loss of both parents is especially tragic. They were both very clever too, weren't they?'

'Oh, yes, they were. My father had begun to talk to me about his dream of working in a different field, of saving people from disease. I think my parents felt it was a kind of luxury to be spending so much time and effort on dogs,' Ian said reflectively. He felt as if he was looking down a long dark tunnel and trying to imagine what lay at its end. He was learning a lot more from this Australian sojourn than he had ever imagined.

'A lot of things have become clearer to me lately, Mrs H,' he added.

# Chapter Eighteen

Ian shut the door of the ute and opened the passenger door for Billy just as Leigh Metcalfe sauntered out onto the verandah.

'G'day, Ian. What brings you up here this fine day?'

'I need your expert opinion,' said Ian.

The two sat down at the big table that looked out over the river. Billy squatted beside Shelley who, as usual, sat obediently beside his owner. After setting Billy up with some drawing paper and pencils, Ian continued. 'I've been trying to draw up some plans for the caravan park and aviary, and am finding it very difficult. Originally, I had envisaged placing the caravan park adjacent to the river with the motel next door. It's a delightful spot with a great view of a long stretch of river and majestic gums. Aesthetically, it's the best place for the caravan park, but the river poses a problem. If families stay there, as we hope they will, children could very easily come to grief in the river. This could only be prevented by erecting a child-proof fence right across the paddock, which would spoil the look of the place to some extent.'

Leigh nodded, 'Go on.'

'Well, then I thought we could place the native bird enclosure there, but this wouldn't help the aesthetics because it would mean an even higher fence. River access is so important, Leigh. I don't want anything built that will deny access to people who want to have picnics and go fishing. I realise this is no light matter that can be changed on a whim – the whole complex has to be approved by the shire council.'

'And don't forget that the bird enclosure will have to be approved by the Queensland Parks and Wildlife Service,' Leigh added. 'Have you thought about the size of the park at all?'

'Well, no, I haven't got that far.'

'You wouldn't be able to compete with the big bird complexes over on the coast in terms of numbers or actual layout. It would cost more money than you've got and you aren't proposing to put all you've got into the bird park. Also, you're starting from scratch so you're going to have costs galore even if you discount volunteer labour. I think the way to go is to concentrate on the endangered and vulnerable parrot species because then you'll be contributing something really worthwhile and different. Sure, have some of the more popular varieties because they're showy and easy to buy, but put most of your effort into the scarce varieties.

'What you've also got to consider is that you can't just throw in a whole lot of male and female parrots and expect them to behave. You can run a lot of males together but if you want to propagate birds, you'd have to run them in pairs – male and female. Some species are more troublesome than others. Bluebonnets are fairly aggressive, so I wouldn't go overboard with them – one pair for starters. Rosellas would be best kept on their own too. I think you could run princess parrots, cockatiels and budgies together, but males only, to be on the safe side.'

'Are there some species you could run with ground birds like quail?' Ian asked.

'The dove varieties would get on okay with quail, but bear in mind that ground birds like quail need grass cover,' said Leigh.

'I'd like to have one or two walk-through aviaries so that people can experience the birds up close,' Ian suggested.

'Good idea.'

'What about the endangered species? Can you buy breeding stock?' Ian asked.

'You can, but some are very difficult to get. Some are reasonably priced and some cost a packet. The golden-shouldered parrot is endangered and expensive. It breeds in termite mounds on Cape York. The hooded parrot is from the Northern Territory and breeds in much the same conditions. Now, look, if you go ahead with this park, I wouldn't be too ambitious at the start. I'd stick to a few seed eaters that aren't difficult to handle and don't require special feed or conditions. And that's another thing: how do you propose to look after these birds? They can't be neglected or Parks and Wildlife will take away your licence. You'd need somebody on site all the time.'

'Well, Leigh,' Ian paused, 'I was hoping you might want to get involved, at least part-time anyway.'

Leigh shook his head, 'Sorry to disappoint you, matey, but I wouldn't cope with having to talk to a lot of tourists. That said, I'm more than willing to help you from behind the scenes – to tell you what to buy in terms of feed and so on – but I wouldn't want to be your front man.'

Ian was crestfallen, but moved on quickly, 'So could you recommend someone else to run the park?'

'What could you offer them?' Leigh asked.

'Not much to begin with. Later, if we could propagate some of the more endangered species we might be able to sell some to help with expenses. I'm going to put a couple of on-site vans next door and whoever we find to manage the park could stay there rent free. I thought it might suit an older retired person who's keen on fishing and wildlife,' Ian said.

'Hmm. I wonder . . .' Leigh scratched his beard in thought.

'Does that mean that you know of someone who might fit the bill?' Ian asked.

'Maybe. There's a bloke I know – a bush poet, knocked about a fair bit in his time: Luke Weir. He's been working on a property at Longreach but he reckons he's too old for it now.'

'Is he reliable?' Ian asked.

'He's been on the same property for a long while. He wouldn't have lasted that long if he wasn't reliable.'

'Does he drink?'

'Occasionally, but he's not a booze artist. He's a clever old bloke. He can turn his hand to just about anything.'

'He sounds promising. Can you mention the bird park and see what sort of a reaction you get?' Ian asked.

'I'll do that.'

Billy looked up from his drawing, 'Look Ian, I drawed a bird.'

'That's beaut Billy. How about you draw Leigh a picture of Shelley now? I'll bet he'd like to put your drawings up on his wall.' Ian winked at Leigh.

'Sure would,' smiled Leigh.

'Okay.' Billy settled down next to the dog again.

'But we're still stuck with the problem of position, Leigh. Where can we put the birds?'

Leigh paused and gazed at the river for a moment. 'Let's look at your proposal in a different way,' he said.

'What do you mean?' Ian asked.

Leigh pointed a finger towards the river. 'The stuff in there is the answer to making your proposal a success.'

Ian was perplexed. 'I don't follow you.'

'You're driving in western Queensland, the temperature is forty-plus and there's no relief in sight from more of the same. What would you be wishing for?' Leigh asked.

'Somewhere nice and cool and a dip in a pool,' Ian answered.

'Exactly. You've hit the nail right on the head. The first thing you've got to do with your Murrawee complex is to set it up as a kind of oasis and promote it as such. Now, what are you doing for water for the park?' Leigh continued.

'We're proposing to pump water from the river into an

overhead tank so we can reticulate it throughout the area. The existing bore is hot and while that is going to be an asset when we eventually put down the swimming pools, it wouldn't be any good for other purposes,' Ian explained. 'Here's a survey map that shows the position of the bore.'

Leigh studied the map for a moment, then reached for some writing paper and began making a few rough sketches. 'The way I see it, the first thing you've got to do is create something that is going to make an instant impression on your visitors. That means a great entrance. You need a rain-forest with ferns, cycads, cordylines and the like, and running water. You drive through this entrance to the caravan park and bird complex, and then take either a left or right fork. The swimming pools would be on the right-hand side of the complex. Here,' Leigh pushed the piece of paper he'd been sketching on across the table to Ian.

Ian stared at it for a little while and then closed his eyes. 'Yes, I can see it.'

'"The Oasis of Murrawee" or something along those lines,' Leigh said. 'You'd place tables and benches under greenery and there'd be a trickling fountain and a pond. You'd have a watering system set up to keep everything fresh on even the hottest day. All that and the river close by – but you need trees and plants galore. Understand?' Leigh asked.

'Perfectly. So one of the first things we'd need to do would be the plumbing. We'd get the overhead tank erected, lay the pipes and then set out the gardens,' Ian said.

'That's right. You'd need to fit larger gauge steel piping

from the hot bore and cap it near where you're proposing to put the swimming pools because that bore is plumb in the middle of your bird aviaries. I don't know which water you'd use for your cold water pool. Probably bore water too, but allowed to cool down. You'd also need rain-water tanks for drinking water,' suggested Leigh.

'Frank Morton thought we should request council funding for an ablution block and toilets that would serve both the caravan park and the main reception area,' Ian said.

'Yeah, well, that sounds okay. I reckon that you should be able to dig up enough blokes to do the plumbing work and erect some fences, but I'd recommend that you employ a top gardener or landscape designer to lay out the gardens. Tell him what you want and let him have his head. It wouldn't be cheap, but it's the recipe for success.'

'The more I think about it, the more I think you're right about the "oasis" concept, Leigh. It's different, and that difference might be just the magnet to pull people into Murrawee. If we get that right, we can build everything around it. But I would like to get some big aviaries constructed and also some smaller ones for breeding,' Ian said.

'You've got to provide shelter for all the birds so they can get out of the wind and rain. That means proper sheds, not just hollow logs. They breed in hollow logs but they need to be under cover. The more natural you can make the set-up, the better. I'd put a lot of thought into the fresh water aspect too. All birds need little pools to splash about in,' Leigh said.

'What I've had in my head is that people first walk amongst

the birds in the big walk-through aviary. The birds would be perched up high or flying overhead. And then what I'd really like would be a series of large cages that you enter through fences of vines if you follow what I mean. Like a series of new discoveries,' Ian said enthusiastically.

'Sounds good. Who have you got in mind for drafting the proposal for the council and the Parks and Wildlife people?'

'Frank told me he uses Geoff Greenaway, a retired building inspector in Roma. He used to be with the shire and he knows the business backwards. It seems that he's fished in Murrawee and wouldn't mind getting involved. Retirement doesn't suit some blokes,' Ian said.

'Yeah, well, you could be on a winner there. If there's one thing I can't stand it's red tape and bureaucrats.' Leigh grinned as he ruffled Billy's hair.

'Here's Shelley,' giggled Billy and held up his drawing for the men to see.

'That's great, Billy,' said Leigh. 'You've been a good little fella sitting there for so long. So what do you reckon? Do you think it's time we got you something to eat?'

'Yeahhhh!' Billy cried, and then jumped up and ran up and down the verandah.

## Chapter Nineteen

Fiona was putting a huge effort into the trial. Ian had deputised Peter Cross, who was good with sheepdogs and attended every meeting, to act for her, along with a couple of local property owners, one of whom put Fiona in touch with a sheepdog trialler in Roma called Lou Rydge. Lou came to the second meeting and laid out what would be required. It seemed fairly simple the way he had described it, but there had been days when Fiona had wondered whether they'd ever get there. Someone had to make sure that there were sheep at the ground and that they'd be taken away and fresh sheep brought to replace them. Her preoccupation with getting every detail right and her concern that something might go wrong elicited a mild reproof from Lachie. He very seldom had occasion to find fault with his daughter, of whom he was exceedingly proud, but on this occasion, Lachie had little doubt that most of Fiona's anxiety stemmed from wanting to prove to Ian Richardson that she could make a real success of the trial.

'Can't you delegate some of these jobs to the rest of the

committee?' Lachie asked as he and Fiona had driven to Toowoomba to select trophies. Ian was keen that placegetters receive trophies and ribbons to remind them of the trial in Murrawee, and Kanimbla had donated some money to buy these. On top of this, Fiona had managed to persuade a few private companies to donate some extra funds, so they could afford some impressive trophies.

'They're all busy too, Dad,' she replied. 'There's just so much to do.'

'Well, don't exhaust yourself completely, or you won't even make it to the big day!'

Lachie and Fiona had stayed overnight in Toowoomba and were amazed at the development taking place. So much there and so little in Murrawee, thought Fiona as they drove down from the motel on top of the range. But instead of depressing her, she felt more inspired than ever to put Murrawee back on the map.

Bearing in mind her father's advice, Fiona had called Ian and asked if she might meet with him, Leo and Peter to finalise some important details. The four of them sat at a table on Kanimbla's verandah.

Fiona looked down at her list. She had been so busy with the trial that she had found herself less distracted by her feelings for Ian. Yet she knew that one look into his tanned, handsome face, and her resolve would melt. 'If you don't mind, I'll get straight to the point,' Fiona began. 'We need a truck to take sheep to and from the ground and someone to be responsible for that side of things.'

Ian looked at Leo. 'You can use the Kanimbla truck if you like, and Peter, can you be responsible for driving it?

'No problem,' said Peter.

'What sheep will you need?' asked Leo.

'I've talked to Joe Barker and he says we can use his wethers but that we'll have to transport them in batches. There's a field next to the trial paddock where we can run them, but we'll need to rig up a portable yard so we can load them,' Fiona said.

'Righto,' said Leo. 'We can provide equipment for the temporary yard. Peter, can you also see to that?' Leo said in his usual brisk fashion.

'What else, Fiona?' Ian asked.

Fiona continued to avoid eye contact with Ian, and instead addressed Leo. 'Who should we get to judge the trials?'

'Good question,' Ian remarked. He was especially cheerful today and did not seem to notice her avoiding his gaze. 'A big name judge could go a long way towards attracting triallers to Murrawee.'

Leo folded his arms across his chest. 'I suggest that we invite David MacLeod. I know he's a very busy bloke so he might not have the time, but we've used a couple of his rams, and that might go in our favour.'

'I'll call him today,' said Ian. He'd heard MacLeod's name mentioned many times since arriving in Australia and was keen to meet him; he had the feeling that David was a man who'd be able to teach him a great deal.

'Will you work Gus, Ian?' Leo asked.

'Oh no. I couldn't ask David MacLeod to judge one of his own dogs. It wouldn't look right if Gus won the trial,' Ian said. 'And the MacLeods can stay with me so you won't have to worry about sorting out their accommodation, Fiona.'

'That will be nice. Thanks.' Fiona glanced at Ian. He was such a considerate man, and so handsome in his white short-sleeved shirt, she thought to herself. If only . . .

Leo interrupted her reverie. 'If you've got any problem sheep-wise, or man-wise for that matter, and I mean in terms of staging the trial, don't get in a stew about it, Fiona. You can bet your life we'll be able to help you.'

'Thank you, Mr Blake. You'll be pleased to know I've got *Queensland Country Life* interested in doing a story about the trial and I'm sending press releases to all the major rural newspapers.'

'Great stuff,' Ian said warmly. 'And now, I have some news to report about the Murrawee developments. The plans for the caravan park and aviary have gone to the shire council. Geoff Greenaway says there shouldn't be any problem with either project. At this stage we've only pencilled in the areas that would be used for the motel and swimming pools because we're still chasing finance on those,' Ian explained.

'That's great news Ian,' Fiona said warmly and felt a sudden urge to hug him. How inappropriate that would be in the circumstances, she smiled to herself.

'We don't yet have permission in writing, but Geoff doesn't think there'll be any holdups. Most shires are all out for keeping people in the country – they don't want townships to die. And they're very aware that tourists can do a lot for the bush,' Ian said.

What he didn't tell Fiona, Leo and Peter was that the wire and piping for the first stage of the Murrawee project would be paid for by Kanimbla. He knew that once they got the fencing and water sorted out, it would be so much easier to get financial backing for the motel – the next big phase.

# Chapter Twenty

'Will I be safe?' Fiona asked with a laugh when Ian rang to invite her to visit Leigh Metcalfe.

'You'll be safe with me,' Ian replied. Fiona had obviously heard about Leigh's weakness for women. 'Anyway, you told me you wanted to see Top River,' he added. He'd heard that she had been working too hard on the trial and that this might make a nice break for her.

'Only joking. Of course I'd love to come,' Fiona said.

When Ian pulled up in the twin-cab ute to collect Fiona, with Billy in his little seat in the back, she was a little disappointed. Billy was a lovely boy, but having a third person along put a different complexion on the trip. She wished Ian had mentioned Billy when he'd phoned her. However, as soon as Billy clambered out of his seat and put his arms around her neck, her disappointment dissolved.

Ian had begun to take Billy with him when he visited Leigh. Despite Leigh's eccentricities, Billy seemed to like him and Leigh was obviously becoming fond of the little boy. Billy had also become great mates with Shelley, who was incredibly patient with him.

When Ian pulled up on the rise beside Leigh's bungalow, the big grey German shepherd was the first to greet them.

'Sherry! Sherry!' Billy screamed as Fiona opened the door of the ute and the little boy jumped out to greet the dog. Shelley licked his face while Billy's arms went around his furry neck.

'Looks like they know each other,' Fiona smiled.

Ian was relieved to find that Leigh was relatively spruced up for their visit, in green cotton trousers and a faded but clean blue cotton shirt. His socks were no doubt holey, but they were hidden by his laughing-side boots.

'Fiona, this is Leigh,' Ian said, introducing them. He was sure Leigh wouldn't want to be called anything else.

'It's great to meet you, Leigh – Ian has told me a lot about you,' Fiona said, shaking his hand.

'Has he now? Not *too* much, I hope.' Jeez, but she is a great looker, thought Leigh. What a lovely smile. If Ian isn't having it off with this girl, there is definitely something up with him.

'How's the swimming coming along, Billy?' Leigh asked. He knew that Billy had been learning to swim since the staff swimming pool had been completed.

'I can go all the way to the other side now!' Billy thrust out his little chest.

'Look over there,' Leigh said to the little boy, and pointed to where a rope had been tied over the thick limb of a red gum that protruded out over the river. 'I put that up for you. Think you could hang on to it and then drop into the river?'

'But he's only little,' Fiona protested, 'and a river is very different from a swimming pool . . .'

'Shelley will bring him out. You've got to give boys – even small boys – some challenges, I reckon,' Leigh said.

'What do you think, Ian?' Fiona asked, obviously concerned.

'I think it's up to Billy,' Ian replied calmly.

'I want to, I want to,' Billy said, dancing with excitement before sitting down to pull off his boots.

'You better take your shirt off, at least,' Leigh said.

Billy undid the buttons and handed his shirt to Ian. Leigh showed him how to hold on to the rope and told him to let go only when he was over the water. Billy didn't need any further instruction. The next moment he was swinging out over the river. Although he was surprisingly strong for someone so young, Fiona had her heart in her mouth. He dropped into the water with a splash and, like a flash, Shelley was in the river and swimming for him. But Billy came up laughing and dog-paddled back to the bank with the big grey dog beside him. 'Again!' he was saying before he was even out of the water.

After three more swings and splashes, Leigh decided it was time for something to eat.

'That's enough for today,' he said. 'Ian, you'd better get his pants off and dry him. He can wear the towel until his shorts dry. They won't take long in this heat.'

219

Lunch was corned beef and tomatoes with slabs of damper and billy tea. They had it at the big table and watched the river while they ate. It was very quiet along the banks at this hour of the day. There was little birdsong and only an occasional squawk from the white cockatoos that perched in the topmost branches of the gums.

'This is a great spot, Leigh,' Fiona said. 'I can see how it would be perfect for a writer.'

'Yeah. Those first settlers knew what they were on about when they acquired this stretch of country.'

'So what are you working on now?' she continued.

'Oh, nothing in particular.' Leigh clearly didn't feel comfortable discussing his work with someone he'd only just met, so he changed the subject. 'What are you planning to do with yourself now that you've finished school, Fiona?'

'I've decided to have this year off and maybe next year too. Dad's a bit lost since Mum died. I'll see how things are at the end of next year. Mum wanted me to go to uni – and I might, eventually, but I can't leave Dad at the moment,' she said, with all the weight of that responsibility heavy in her voice.

Leigh nodded. 'What are you interested in studying?'

'I'm not sure. I got good enough marks to do medicine, but I'm not sure I'm committed enough. If I'm keen on anything, it's the land, and there's only me to carry on at Nilanji. If I go to uni, I might do an ag degree. That way I could use what I learn, even if I don't make a career of it,' Fiona said.

'Makes sense,' Leigh agreed. 'You've got a big lump of a

place and a lot of stock. It should be enough to give you a good living. That's if you want to stay on there. But a degree is no load to carry. It means you've always got something to fall back on.'

Fiona wasn't especially keen to discuss her future with Leigh, but she knew that Ian regarded his opinions highly. She supposed that some women would find Leigh attractive. He had a kind of magnetism in his dark eyes and there was something about his thoughtful brow . . . She looked from Leigh to Ian as they talked, and wondered how two such different men could hit it off so well. Ian, clean-shaven and fair-haired, was almost twenty years younger than Leigh who had dark, unruly curls and a bushy beard.

Leigh noticed that Fiona had fallen silent, and tried to draw her back into the conversation. 'Ian tells me you've got the job of organising the sheepdog trial. How's it shaping?' Leigh asked.

'It's going well. Now it's just a matter of promoting the event and hoping the trial workers will come. Thanks to Mr Blake, we're going to have a great judge: David MacLeod.'

'Yes, I've heard he's a good bloke,' said Leigh. 'Anyone want any more tucker?'

'Want to get your duds, Billy?' Leigh asked when they'd finished lunch.

As Billy made to run down the wooden steps to the clothesline, Ian put a hand out to stop him.

'Just a minute – what have you forgotten?'

'Boots!' Billy laughed, looking around for them. Karen always made sure that Billy didn't go anywhere without shoes on, and the little boy seemed to understand. He sat on the verandah and pulled on the small boots before skipping down the steps.

There was a low growl from Shelley as Billy jumped up and down to pull his pants from the line that Leigh had rigged between two trees.

'What is it, Shelley? Dogs?' Leigh queried as if Shelley were another person at the lunch table.

Shelley growled again and followed Billy. He'd almost reached him when there was a cry from the little boy. Leigh was on his feet instantly, running towards him.

'It bit me!' Billy said, pointing towards the slim brown snake that was now slithering away towards the river. Leigh wanted to kill the snake, but knew his first priority was the little boy. He picked him up and carried him back to the table, giving instructions calmly but precisely as he walked. 'Clear all those things away, Fiona. I'll get the bandages. Ian, you ring Leo – get him to find Jim Landers and have him prepare the plane. You can take Billy straight to it. Get Leo to ring Roma Hospital, too, so they can be ready for Billy,' Leigh said. 'And just check that they've got some brown snake anti-venom.'

Fiona watched as Leigh removed Billy's boot and bandaged his leg from his ankle, where the snake had penetrated the skin, all the way up to his thigh. He then placed a splint against the leg and bound it to Billy's good leg to completely immobilise it. Billy was very good, only whimpering a little. Fiona held his hand, and spoke to him gently about Shelley, to keep his mind off the dangerous situation he was in. They didn't want to alarm the boy.

'Did you get on to Leo?' Leigh asked Ian once the bandage was in place.

'They'll be ready for us,' Ian said.

'Right, let's get a move on. Help me carry Billy over to the car. The main thing is to keep his leg completely still.'

Leigh and Ian settled Billy in the back seat of the ute with his legs outstretched and his back against Fiona.

'You'll keep me informed?' Leigh asked and Ian nodded.

'Do we need to take the snake?' Ian asked. He didn't know a lot about snakes but he had learned that it was best to know the type of snake you were dealing with because there were different anti-venoms for different snakes.

'No. It's a brown snake. And the hospitals have venom-detection kits now, anyway. Get a move on, Ian. Timing is critical,' Leigh said urgently.

'Bye, Leigh. Bye, Sherry,' Billy said bravely as Ian gunned the utility forward.

Leigh and the big grey dog stood and watched until the vehicle was out of sight. Then he tied Shelley up and went in search of the snake. He found it near the river and belted it. He reckoned it would be touch and go – the snake hadn't been large, but Billy was still small and there was not as far for the poison to travel. Even with the plane it would take them a while to get to Roma.

There was silence in the ute. Fiona looked at Ian. He was pale and struggling to hide his anxiety.

Too afraid to speak, he drove as fast as the road would allow. Trees rushed at them and then passed in a kind of blur.

When they reached the homestead, the gates into the landing field had been opened for them and they saw with relief that Jim had the plane out ready for take-off. Karen, Leo and Judy were beside the plane. Karen's face was wet with tears, but she was calm and ready to follow instructions. Leo opened the door of the ute and helped Ian move Billy to the plane. 'Get her started, Jim,' he said. 'Karen, you get in. We'll put Billy on your lap and you can keep his legs still.'

Leo and Ian backed out of the plane, closed the door and watched as the machine gathered speed across the bitumen runway. There hadn't been time to discuss Billy's condition; they all knew that what mattered was getting him to Roma as fast as possible.

'What happened?' Leo asked Ian.

Ian gave him the facts, and then his voice cracked with emotion. 'It was my fault. If I hadn't taken Billy with us to Top River, he'd be okay.'

Fiona touched his arm. 'Oh, Ian, you can't think like that.'

Leo shook his head. 'She's right. It could have happened anywhere, Ian. Billy isn't the first child to be bitten and he won't be the last. Snakes are a constant hazard in this country. And you can't wrap kids up in cotton wool. Jim killed a snake in their yard last summer. They're a damned menace, but they're here and we have to live with them – and teach our kids how to deal with them.'

'Leigh had fixed up a rope so Billy could swing out and drop into the river. Billy thought it was great,' Ian said.

'Let's hope he can go back and do it again one day,' Leo said and put his hand on Ian's shoulder. 'You weren't to blame, remember that.'

The four of them drove back to the homestead and sat on the front verandah. Mrs Heatley brought them tea and scones, which they could barely touch. The housekeeper could see the concern on all their faces, especially Ian's. All sorts of scenarios were forming in his mind. If Billy died, Kanimbla would never be the same again. They would probably lose Jim because Karen would want to leave. He thought about Billy at the hospital and the deadly venom that was probably creating mayhem in his small body. He thought about his own life and how today might change the course of his future. He thought about what he would have done differently if he had the chance to live this day again . . .

After the Blakes left, Ian and Fiona remained on the verandah. Fiona put her hand on Ian's arm. 'Would you like me to stay for a while?' she asked.

Ian shook his head. 'No, you go on home. But thank you. I know you're still busy with the trial. I'll keep checking with the hospital. Whatever the news, I'll let you know. I'm sorry the trip finished like this.'

'Ian, listen. You're not to blame yourself. Snakes are a fact of life in this country. All right?' Fiona said.

'Billy was my responsibility while I had him, and I slipped up. I should have watched him more closely. How will I ever make it up to Jim and Karen?'

'I should think that agreeing to replace your uncle's plane and giving your support to Jim's desire to fly would go a long way towards it,' Fiona said.

'Those rotten useless things – God, I hate snakes. In England we don't have to worry about them. Here, you have to watch for them all the time,' Ian said fiercely.

Fiona looked at him in surprise. It was the first time she had witnessed any real anger in him. Suddenly, he seemed more vulnerable, more human.

'And you the son of two zoologists!' she said, trying to inject some lightness, if not humour, into the conversation.

'Two doctors, Fiona. And if they were sitting here, I'm sure they'd be as concerned as I am,' Ian said quietly.

Fiona wouldn't give up in her quest to make Ian feel better. 'There are plenty of poisonous snakes in Africa, aren't there? And your parents took you there with them. I never knew them, but I'm sure that they, of all people, would have been fully aware of the risks they took in their life and work. Were they watching you twenty-four hours a day?'

'No, they weren't. But I had a custodian who was. His name was Kinshi – well, that was what I called him because I couldn't pronounce his proper name. My father told him that his job was to look after me and that nothing was to divert him from it. When my parents were away from the camp, Kinshi gave me my meals and we talked a lot. He told me about his people's customs and about ivory smugglers. He was always concerned about leopards because they were such silent killers. And he watched for mambas – a deadly snake. I was never worried while he was close to me. So that's why I feel especially bad about Billy. I wasn't as watchful of Billy as Kinshi was of me . . . ' Ian ducked his head, but Fiona could see his eyes were moist.

'Poor Ian,' she said, and reached out across the table and took his hands in hers. Fiona knew that if ever there was a time that Ian needed support it was now. And she was right. He did not pull away, and they sat like that for a while, just holding hands. But eventually Ian got to his feet and Fiona knew it was time to leave. She hugged him goodbye, asking him to call her if there was anything she could do, though she suspected that he'd weather this crisis without her help. He had, after all, been coping since he was eight years old.

Ian phoned the hospital every hour or so for the rest of the afternoon and evening, but couldn't get much information. Billy had been injected with anti-venom, but remained in a serious condition in the intensive-care unit. After dinner, Ian tried to do some study but couldn't concentrate. Finally, he phoned Leo to give the Blakes a last update for the day.

'Bloody snakes. If anyone can tell me what good they are, I'll take off my clobber and walk to Murrawee,' Leo said.

'St Patrick was supposed to have rid Ireland of all its snakes and other reptiles. If this was true, it was probably the best thing he ever did, saint or otherwise,' Ian said. 'Snakes are a menace to humans and animals alike. I reckon we ought to try and get rid of all our snakes too.' A few weeks ago, Ian had seen one of Peter Cross's young kelpies after it had been bitten by a brown snake and its horrible death had sickened him.

'That seems a bit radical,' said Leo, 'but I get your drift. The cost per annum of animals lost as a result of snakebite must be colossal. I've lost dogs and horses as well as sheep and cattle.'

'Someone ought to protest about this policy of protecting highly venomous snakes. Why would you want to protect something that can kill you? It doesn't make sense,' Ian said vehemently.

Billy Landers was very sick for several days, and until he was declared 'out of danger', Ian could hardly live with himself. He considered driving to Roma to see Billy, but Jim insisted it wasn't necessary to drive all that way and that he needed to stay at Kanimbla. Jim and Karen took turns keeping watch at Billy's beside, returning to the motel paid for by Ian. Jim's voice seemed strained and distant in the brief conversation he'd had with Ian, and Ian began to worry that his negligence might have caused irreparable damage to his relationship with the Landers family. After speaking with the doctors at Roma, he'd put aside his science papers and directed his anxiety and energy into a concentrated study of snakes and their venom. There was a great deal of up-to-date information on the Internet. He found that the poison of the eastern brown snake causes muscle paralysis and contains toxins that interfere with blood clotting. It can also cause kidney failure. One of the critical factors in snakebites, apart from the actual toxicity of the individual variety of snake, is the amount of venom it injects, and this is determined by the length of the snake's fangs and also by its aggressiveness. Aggressive varieties like the tiger snake often bite more than once and inject a lot of venom. Ian admired the scientists who had 'milked' dangerous snakes for their venom and developed anti-venoms. And the whole time, he wished there was more he could do for Billy.

In the end, a number of things saved Billy. The snake had been fairly small and only one of its fangs had lightly penetrated the skin. The other fang must have encountered his boot. Or, according to the hospital superintendent, the second fang may have been broken. Ian had discovered that although the brown snake's venom is the second most deadly in the world, its fangs are relatively small, so it does not inject such a large dose of venom. A kind of miracle had saved Billy Landers.

It was a much happier group of people who waited for Jim and Karen to bring Billy back to Kanimbla. The Blakes and Fiona sat with Ian in the Mercedes with their ears pricked for the sound of the Cessna. The plane finally came into view but, before landing, it flew upriver and made two sweeps across Leigh's bungalow. Man and dog looked skywards, Leigh – and perhaps Shelley too – with intense relief.

When the Cessna landed, Ian was the first to greet Billy. Jim had told Billy that but for Mr Metcalfe's quick bandaging of his leg and for Ian's plane, he might still be in hospital (or much worse, Jim had thought). He'd warned Billy that he had to be more careful where he walked in future.

Leo helped Karen down from the plane and she turned to Ian and hugged him. 'Thank you,' she said with tears in her eyes. And when Jim shook Ian's hand and nodded, Ian felt his own tears welling. He had been so worried about Billy, and whether Karen and Jim would blame him for their ordeal. He should have known they were far too generous and forgiving for that.

Ian bobbed down to give Billy a hug. 'I saw Sherry from up in the sky,' Billy said excitedly. 'He was looking at me.'

'You can go and see him tomorrow, Billy,' his father told him. He turned to Ian, 'Karen wants to go to Top River to thank Leigh for his quick action.' Ian was full of admiration for Karen at this moment. He knew that she didn't feel comfortable with Leigh.

'I think we'll have to get you a pony to keep your feet off the ground, Billy,' Ian said with a laugh.

'A pony? Then I could go riding with you and Fiona,' Billy said.

Judy saw the momentary look of alarm on Fiona's face. This arrangement was obviously not quite what Fiona would be hoping for, but still she said kindly, 'That would be lovely, Billy.'

Ian gave Fiona a grateful look.

'Mrs Heatley has lunch waiting and I happen to know that she's got some special goodies there for you, Billy,' Judy said.

The next day, Ian issued a clean-up directive to his men. All tall grass near buildings was to be mown and all sheet-iron and timber was to be raised off the ground. Any cover that could hide a snake was to be eliminated and things were to be kept that way. In the course of the resulting clean-up, several snakes were discovered and destroyed.

The following week, a half-page advertisement appeared in the *Western Courier* and ran for the next four weeks. It read:

### REWARD

The sum of $10 will be paid for every dead venomous snake (any variety) delivered to Kanimbla station.

Leo did not approve of the advertisement. 'I appreciate that you're making a protest, but frankly, Ian, I'm opposed to Kanimbla money being used in this fashion.'

'I don't see why we can't categorise it as pest control,' Ian responded. 'Snakes certainly come into that category. But I'm not going to argue with you, Mr Blake. I'll pay for everything from my own account.'

There was a lot of discussion in the district about whether the advertisement was a hoax or fair dinkum until several bushies decided to test the water. They turned up with dead snakes and received their reward. The word spread and more people began bringing in snakes.

Ian had paid out nearly fifteen hundred dollars by the time he received a phone call advising him that two National Parks officials would be calling on him the following morning. He had been expecting something like this and didn't know what the outcome would be. But in the meantime, he couldn't help feeling glad that there were one hundred and fifty fewer snakes around the district than before.

The rangers arrived about ten the next morning. Ian invited them to sit on the front verandah and offered them cool drinks. Leo had asked Ian whether he could sit in on the meeting.

'Are you aware that it's an offence to kill native animals except by special decree, such as in the case of an open season on kangaroos?' the older ranger asked.

'I'm not killing native animals,' Ian said simply.

The ranger produced Ian's advertisement and spread it out on the table.

'I haven't killed a single one,' said Ian. 'I'm simply paying for the dead snakes people bring here. They could have been run over on the roads for all I know.'

'You're encouraging people to kill snakes, which are a protected species,' the younger ranger said, trying to conceal his anger.

'Up in one of those cottages is a great little boy who came very close to dying after he was bitten by a brown snake. If he'd died I was going to bring an action against whoever was responsible for drafting the idiotic legislation that protects killer snakes and for whoever was responsible for enacting it. Those people would have been culpable.'

'Culpable? How could anyone be culpable?' the older ranger asked.

'Snakes are your responsibility, aren't they?' Ian asked.

'Yes, I suppose they are.'

'Then you should be responsible for any damage they cause. That's the drill in every other walk of life. If one of my animals gets out on the road and causes damage to a vehicle or a driver, I'm responsible. In effect, you're condoning the most venomous snakes in the world. It's like having loaded guns all over the country – except that snakes are more dangerous than loaded guns. At least with guns we're supposed to keep them in locked containers,' Ian said.

'You'd be wasting your money taking that route. You'd never succeed,' the younger ranger said.

'Don't be too sure of that. There's been a lot of legislation overturned in recent years. It's just that no snake protection outfit has yet been charged with culpability. If keeping certain kinds of guns is illegal because they're more dangerous than others, I don't see that protecting snakes that can kill humans and animals is any less of a crime,' Ian said evenly.

'Snakes have their place in the ecosystem, like dozens of other highly venomous or dangerous creatures,' the older ranger said.

'But we kill dingoes because they attack our sheep and calves,' Ian continued. 'Why should snakes be treated differently? If a fellow broke into your house and threatened you or your wife with a weapon, wouldn't you try and do something about it?' Ian asked.

'But snakes only attack when they are frightened or provoked —,' the older ranger began.

'A snake is a threat to every person and every animal,' Ian interrupted. 'One of my jackaroos lost a good young sheep-dog to snakebite just the other day. It was probably worth at least a thousand dollars. But more than the money, it's the suffering caused.

'If I send you an account for Peter's dog, or for any other animals killed by snakes, will the Queensland National Parks and Wildlife Service cough up the money to pay for them?' Ian asked.

Both rangers sighed and shook their heads.

'So you tell me *you're* responsible for the brutes, yet you want me and all the other landholders to bear the cost of the animals they kill. I'll tell you what I'm going to do. If I lose any more animals to snakes, I'm going to send a bill to your department and then I'm going to contact all the major current affairs programs and advise them of what I've done.'

'But the law simply states that it is illegal to kill snakes,' said the younger ranger, who came across as the more aggressive of the pair. 'You will be breaking the law.'

'Then the law is an ass and should be changed. You can make all the laws you like, but it won't stop people from killing snakes. The average bush person has got a lot more common sense than the pie-in-the-sky bureaucrats who drafted that ridiculous clause in the *Nature Conservation Act*. I'm all for preserving native animals and I'm full of regret for the species that have been made extinct, but where were the gentlemen like yourselves when over half a million harmless Queensland koalas were massacred in 1927? Now if you'll excuse me, I've got a great deal of work to do,' said Ian as he showed the rangers to the door.

# Chapter Twenty-one

Ian found it hard to believe that a year had passed since he first arrived in Murrawee. It was only when the sheepdog trial began that he realised just how much had been achieved in that time. The trial might not have been the biggest event ever staged in Murrawee – it was a moot point whether it was bigger than the annual gymkhana – but it was memorable for the fact that it was the district's first. It was also a landmark occasion because the man who came to judge it was a legendary figure in the pastoral community. David MacLeod was a renowned kelpie breeder, and owned a merino stud that produced some of the best sheep in the country.

Ian had invited David MacLeod and his wife, Catriona, to stay at Kanimbla for a couple of days prior to the trial. He was keen to hear David's opinion on their sheep and also to go over the trial courses with him.

Ian was waiting to greet them on the front verandah when they pulled up in the late afternoon. David was a tall, wide-shouldered man, now grey at the temples, who could still turn heads. But it was Catriona who captured Ian's attention. She was lovely: fair with warm brown eyes and a tall, slender figure. Her clothes seemed made just for her and she walked with a quiet confidence. Ian was immediately reminded of his mother. As the pair walked towards the homestead it was clear from the way that they looked at each other that they were still very much in love. It was just how Ian remembered his mother and father, and he was suddenly overcome by a mixture of sadness and a kind of gratitude to the MacLeods.

After smoko on the verandah, David and Catriona asked whether they could see Gus. They stood in the gathering dusk and looked at the dog David had sold to Ian's uncle more than five years ago. 'He's a typical MacLeod kelpie. On a scale of one to ten for natural ability, I'd have scored him eight and a half – that's pretty good. The best I've ever rated a dog was nine and a half, but I regard anything from eight up as worth keeping for breeding purposes,' David said.

'For a long time I scored way below eight on David's scale,' Catriona smiled.

'But what matters is what you score now, Catriona,' Ian said, returning her smile.

'Good for you, Ian,' David said with a laugh and thumped him on the back. It was an affectionate thump, but Ian preferred not to think about how it would feel to be on the receiving end of something less friendly.

The Blakes and the Landers joined Ian and the MacLeods for dinner at Kanimbla. It was the first time the big dining room had been used since Ian's arrival. Billy came too because David and Catriona had wanted to meet the brave boy who'd survived a snakebite. Billy was on his best behaviour and knew that he had to go to bed as soon as dinner was over. But he was captivated by David and forgot all about eating. David talked about his ponies and the ponies his children had ridden. He gave Billy an account of the first time he'd ridden up Yellow Rock, a notoriously difficult hill on the MacLeods' High Peaks property. He told him about the eagles that rode the thermals above the Rock. And he told him about the wethers that found sanctuary on the mountain and how you needed a very good dog to winkle them out. Billy's wide eyes widened even further when David talked about the 'eel bashing' picnics in the creek on High Peaks.

That night the yarning went on for a very long time. Over Mrs Heatley's delicious buffet meal of hot and cold meats, baked potatoes, green beans and salad, the guests chatted about their lives on the land and their love of the bush. With the exception of Ian and Karen Landers, they'd all spent a large part of their lives in the bush.

Ian was impressed by Catriona. She was fascinating to talk to, obviously highly intelligent, and stylish yet down-to-earth. What a couple she and David made. Fiona would enjoy meeting her, he thought.

Well after midnight, Jim and Karen said they'd have to take Billy – now asleep on Ian's bed – home, and the Blakes also got up to leave. Ian, usually so keen to escape an evening of entertaining, was reluctant to say goodnight, but apologised for keeping David and Catriona up so late after their long drive and urged them to sleep in the next morning.

'Ha, you must be joking, Ian,' Catriona laughed. 'Nothing would make David stay in bed. Believe me, I've tried! I'm resigned to enjoying my lie-ins on my own.'

'Remember this when you team up with your Miss Wonderful, Ian,' David advised. 'You can't win with women. They're either complaining that you're neglecting them or scolding you for being under their feet.'

After some cheerful, loud protests from Catriona and Judy, they all went off to bed.

The next morning, Ian took the MacLeods riding. He gave his biggest gelding to David because of his size, and his own favourite, Major, to Catriona. Both David and Catriona sat horses as if they were part of them, and they rode for most of the morning. Ian took them down along the river, where the white cockies called shrilly from the gums. Eventually they dismounted and sat on a log to drink tea from small flasks and enjoy Mrs Heatley's biscuits. 'This must be quite a contrast to your hill country,' said Ian.

'Sure is. But we do own a couple of properties on flattish country. We grow our best sheep there,' David told him.

'The wool market's a real worry, isn't it, David?' Ian commented. 'Our ram sales are down a heap, as they seem to be everywhere. Seems like cattle are the big thing.'

'Cattle have had their low periods too. We haven't been too badly affected so far,' David said. 'We don't have the ram numbers that Kanimbla has, and were able to breed some finer rams.

'We don't have the option of going finer,' said Ian, 'or we'll lose size, and this is not fine-wool country anyway. I don't want to convert Kanimbla to an all-cattle operation either, but we're going to have to take some hard decisions about where we're going with sheep. Maybe reduce the numbers of rams we breed and look at meat production.'

'There's plenty of that going on,' David agreed. 'I'm having a look at it myself, in fact. I'm thinking of putting some of our wether lambs into a feedlot to top them off. I've got one butcher interested if he can get a constant supply. But that's a bit hard to arrange when you've got fixed lambing times.'

'Wether lambs in a feedlot? That sounds interesting. Would it pay to feed them?' Ian asked.

'Our sums say it would.'

'Very interesting,' Ian mused. 'Well, we'd better make tracks. I can see that we're boring Catriona.'

Catriona smiled, but didn't argue.

They returned to the homestead for a salad lunch. Soon after, Leo and Jim arrived to collect David to show him the Kanimbla rams and stud ewes. Ian told them that he'd talk to David about the sheep later, and elected to stay at the homestead with Catriona.

It was so easy to talk with Catriona, and they spent most of the afternoon on the verandah, chatting. Mrs Heatley brought them afternoon tea. 'It's amazing how much you resemble my mother, Catriona,' he said, after a while.

If Catriona was surprised by his remark, she didn't show it. 'Do you remember your parents very well?' she asked.

'I was only eight when they died, but yes, they're still clear in my mind,' Ian said quietly.

Ian went on to describe the years since his parents' death, and Catriona listened intently. Despite the difference in their ages and background, she seemed to understand completely his unhappiness during his years at school, his attachment to his stiff grandfather, and his love for the English countryside.

'So how did you feel when you learned that you'd been left this great property?' Catriona asked.

'Honestly? I was confused. I thought it was a huge complication.'

Catriona gave him a questioning look, and he felt encouraged to continue. 'You see, I began studying a science degree while I was at Wongarben, and I'm continuing it here, keeping my options open. But I know that if I do return to Cambridge, I'll be regarded as the most ungrateful creature on God's earth. Ownership of Kanimbla definitely gives me a certain standing in the community. And it's a pleasant enough occupation – I don't have to work hard because the staff do all the physical labour. My role is more public relations with our ram buyers. And that's going to be a declining role, the way the wool industry is shaping. It's going to be a hard decision,' said Ian.

Catriona gazed at the gardens thoughtfully for a moment before replying.

'I think you should do whatever will give you the most satisfaction, Ian. David has stock and land on the brain – it's all he's ever wanted and he wouldn't be happy doing anything else. He's worked very hard but he's had his share of luck too. His parents were battling on a hill country property when a neighbour offered to sell them his property – an offer they couldn't refuse. David's parents were great people; hard-working and incredibly unselfish. I admired them very much, and compared to them, I realise now I was far from the perfect mother. Before the children went to school, I had a nanny for them because I wanted to be with David all the time. If I'd been a different kind of mother, I wouldn't have sent them away to boarding school either. David tried to talk me out of it, but I wanted to work on the property.'

'I'm sure you did a wonderful job raising your children, Catriona. All children think their parents are very special, no matter what they choose to do. Mine realised it was risky taking me to Africa, but they wanted me to be with them. It was horrible after the crash – I remember being terrified. But if I'd been left behind in England, I think I'd have taken their deaths a lot harder.'

'It must have been terrible losing your family. Do you have a girlfriend yet? Someone to share your life with? I can't imagine waking up in the morning without David beside me.'

Ian hesitated. He felt he could tell Catriona anything, but was afraid that if he opened up, it might be his undoing. 'Not really,' he said, looking at his hands.

'Oh, come now, Ian. Mrs Heatley told me last night that

you see a lot of Fiona McDonald. She sounds like a lovely girl.'

'She is,' Ian replied, 'but really, we're just friends. Would you like another cuppa?'

Catriona knew the boy was uncomfortable, so steered the conversation back to safer topics.

'No thanks. I'm quite full. So how are you going with your studies?'

'Not bad. It's a lot of work, but I'm really enjoying it. It's almost as if I'm leading a double life – boss of Kanimbla by day and dedicated student at night.'

'Good on you. Life's short, and in the end, I believe we should all do what we feel we do best. Our oldest boy, Dougal, did well at school and went on to become a vet. David was disappointed that he chose not to stay on the property, but he realises now that Dougal made the right decision. And our other two, Moira and Angus, are both stock and land cranks so David's got good company there.'

Ian smiled. He felt relieved to be understood.

After David had returned and showered, he joined them for pre-dinner drinks. Ian had invited Fiona and Lachie so that Fiona could meet the trial judge.

'I hear you've been working hard setting up the trials,' David said as he shook hands with Fiona.

'It's been very rewarding. I've learned so much,' she replied. 'From what I can gather, there seems to be a lot of concern about the lack of cast in many of today's kelpies and collies. Some blame the yard trials, though more seem to blame motorbikes. The way we've set up this trial, good casting dogs will gain extra points.'

David nodded, 'Good stuff. The cast is very important in hill country dogs, though it's easy to see why it's deterio-rated in flat country where bikes are used a lot. I love to see dogs working at long distances from their handlers when the country is too steep or rough for bikes or horses. You've done well to organise things so efficiently.'

'Thank you, Mr MacLeod, but it was Ian who encouraged me to organise the trial. I couldn't have managed without him. He's been a great help,' Fiona said.

The following morning, a day before the trial was to begin, Ian took David, Catriona and Fiona in to Murrawee and they went over the details of the event.

Unusually, the Murrawee trial was to take place at two different locations. The first venue was a bush paddock just outside the township. Here, the course was set up so that when sheep were released, a dog had to cast blind to pick them up. The dogs that succeeded in casting blind were allotted twenty-five points. There were only two obstacles at this venue – a race and a pen.

The second part of the trial was to be run on the Mur-rawee oval, where the gymkhana was usually held. The layout was the conventional three-obstacle course combined with a yard trial off the oval. A dog could score well in both sections of this trial, but if it hadn't scored the points for blind cast-ing at the bush venue, it was behind before it started.

'Do you have any problem with these courses?' Ian asked David, after they'd seen the set-up.

'No. They look good. The better casting dogs will go to the second venue with the extra points, but they'll still have to work well there to earn the overall title,' David said.

'Right. Once the trial begins you're the boss man. If you have any problems, talk to Fiona. She'll be at the timekeeper's table.'

The night before the trial, the dozen rooms at the pub were all booked. This was despite the fact that most of the sheep-dog workers had either brought their own accommodation (the oval was surrounded by caravans) or had been happy to camp wherever there was a roof. The evening was warm and everyone was out and about. The township hadn't seen so many people for a long time. Helen Donovan was busy in the café for several hours after she'd planned on closing. She'd offered to coordinate the catering, which she did every year for the gymkhana, and had hoped to close early. But she certainly couldn't afford to turn down business.

At daylight on the morning of the trial, the first draft of a line of young cull ewes provided by Kanimbla was trucked in to the paddock. Soon after, the gentle September sun was shining and the trials had begun.

The paddock stage of the trial resulted in a great deal of good-humoured banter because some dogs lost their sheep, and Peter and his kelpie, Jake, had to retrieve them and work them down to the holding pen at the far end of the paddock. Only about a third of the dogs managed to blind cast without crossing, and there were nods of appreciation when a dog successfully picked up its sheep. Ian was relieved that the handlers appeared to enjoy this leg of the trial, as it was a bit of an experiment, and a departure from the other trials held in Queensland. David thought it added an interesting twist to the event, and reminded people to think about the importance of good casting.

Fiona was timekeeping under a tent containing a table, a couple of benches and several bales of straw that served as spectators' seats. Beside her, Lachie made his announcements over the microphone.

Once the events began, Fiona became so absorbed in the sport that she forgot the nervousness she'd felt about the success of the event. She talked to dog handlers from all over the country, who were impressed by her interest and knowledge, and especially by her organisational skills. Despite this being the inaugural Western Districts Championship Utility Trial, with the added complication of two separate venues, things were running very smoothly indeed. The handlers all asked Fiona about her own dog. She explained that, although she would have liked to be competing, she knew she wasn't quite ready yet. But the handlers told her that they were certain they'd see her out there before long.

Around noon, Ian took Fiona, Lachie, David and Catriona for lunch. The usual gymkhana tucker was on offer (ham and salad rolls, meat pies and hamburgers plus large mugs of tea and coffee) and everyone was hungry.

During the afternoon, Ian noticed Catriona sitting beside Fiona at the timekeeper's table. He thought back to his own conversation with Catriona, and wondered what the two of them were talking about. They seemed to be laughing a lot. He wished he could join them but as the owner of Kanimbla he felt he should at least make an effort to socialise and welcome visitors to Murrawee.

On the second night of the trials, dog workers, visitors and townspeople all gathered for a giant barbecue. Storms had been forecast, but the meteorologists were wrong on this occasion and the weather held out for the duration of the trial. The party went on into the small hours, and was notable not only for the amount that was imbibed, but for the atrocious yarns that were pitched. But as the noted historian C. E. W. Bean once quipped, if you couldn't tell lies about sheepdogs, what could you tell lies about.

As a younger man, David MacLeod hadn't been much interested in parties, but his years selling stud sheep and cattle had matured him, and he was more at home at such functions now. For this reason, he stayed on to talk to the many people who were eager to meet this legend of the sheepdog world. Catriona, who'd written a family history of the MacLeod family, was a charming woman in her own right, and there was always a knot of people around the pair.

After two and a half days, the competition came down to seven dogs in the open final – five kelpies and two border collies. In the end, a kelpie that had picked up extra points for casting blind won the supreme champion ribbon. Its owner, Kevin Hunter from Eugowra in New South Wales, was delighted and made a speech praising the warm hospitality he'd received in Murrawee, the efficient running of the trial and the added interest of the blind cast. Kevin had been badly injured in a riding accident and had become very depressed when he could no longer do any demanding physical work. A friend suggested that he might find it interesting to breed and train sheepdogs, and he'd never looked back. Kevin was a popular figure on the trial circuit and his words were echoed by all the competitors and other spectators. 'We'll be back,' they said.

Fiona was over the moon that the trials had been such a success. She knew they could not have run without the massive support of Kanimbla, but was confident that next year they would be able to raise more funds themselves. She was especially chuffed when Ian presented her with two CDs on sheepdog training, in recognition of her efforts. She also scored a kiss on the cheek, but didn't allow this to raise any hopes – Ian was, no doubt, just being polite in front of the crowd.

'I'd like to be able to enter Glen in next year's trial,' she said to Ian.

'You should be able to do that, Fiona. You'd have seen what was needed, and I saw you talking with David. I'm sure he offered you some good advice,' Ian said supportively.

'After talking with David, Kevin Hunter and other handlers, I know I've been making some mistakes with Glen, but

I know exactly what to do now to remedy them.' Dreamily, she imagined spending time out in the paddocks with Ian and Gus, but stopped herself before she got too carried away. Ian had seemed rather preoccupied these last few weeks.

Ian hoped that David and Catriona might have been able to stay longer, but they were due home and had to leave the next morning.

'I realise you're a busy man and I'm grateful you found the time to come and judge our trials,' Ian said as David and Catriona packed their vehicle in the rain. 'If we had an annual trial as good as this one, it would really help put Murrawee on the map.'

'Indeed it would,' David agreed.

'Jim Landers will be down soon to look at those two rams you spoke about,' Ian continued. 'If we buy one or both of them, I hope it will go some way towards compensating you for the time you've given us.'

David smiled and shook his head. 'You don't owe me anything, Ian. I'd have come for nothing if only to see old Gus again. And I really hope you can come and see us sometime.'

Catriona put her hand on Ian's arm. 'It was lovely to meet you. Thanks hugely for your hospitality. Your homestead is beautiful. Please thank Mrs Heatley again for us, too,' she said, kissing him on the cheek.

# Chapter Twenty-two

Support for Ian Richardson's proposals changed quite markedly for the better with the news that finance for the project had been approved. Up to then Ian's proposals had not been taken too seriously by all but the solid core of people who were right behind him. It was Fiona's idea that had sparked the shift. She'd sent a press release to a major city newspaper, and a journalist and photographer had come to town to write the whole Murrawee development story over a big double-page spread, with photos of Fiona, Ian, Leo and Mrs Donovan. Of course all the country papers had followed suit, and the story of how people were pulling together to rejuvenate a dying township touched a lot of hearts. Then there were some radio interviews, and when it looked like the story might make it to a current affairs show, Ian convinced a very reluctant Fiona (and excited Lachie) to be interviewed. Suddenly, so it seemed, there were important people who wanted to meet with this rural benefactor, two of whom were in a good position to give material support – the State Member, Stuart Duff, and the Federal Member, Alan Moore.

Moreover, no sooner had the story gone to air when Lachie and Fiona had a visit from Joe Barker. Joe had gone cold on the proposals when he realised there was little money to be made, but after seeing all the media attention, his opinion had begun to shift. Although it was not widely known, Joe was a generous philanthropist and regularly donated to the children's hospital in Brisbane.

Joe and Lachie were old friends, and on this occasion, Joe came straight to the point. 'Do you reckon Ian Richardson is fair dinkum about what he wants to do, Lachie?' he asked as Fiona handed him a plate of freshly made pikelets.

'Absolutely,' Lachie replied firmly. 'He's spent his own money to acquire that land in Murrawee and he's not out to make a quid for himself. Like he says, if the town and the district get behind him, he'll donate the land. How much more fair dinkum can you get?'

'Hmm. The thing is, I give a fair bit of money to the National Party and if you think Richardson's proposals are okay, I might be able to get some government money,' Joe said.

'That would be wonderful, Mr Barker,' Fiona said enthusiastically.

Joe enjoyed Fiona's attention, but tried his best not to embarrass her by betraying his pleasure. He'd never married, and always had a soft spot for Fiona and her mum. They'd been like family to him. 'I guess it would make a big difference to the district if there was a motel there and a swimming pool. I didn't know about that bore,' he said.

'It seems no one else did either,' said Lachie.

'So how come young Richardson is so keen to do something for Murrawee?' Joe asked.

Lachie looked at Fiona before he answered. 'He thinks that if someone doesn't do something, Murrawee will go down the gurgler, Joe. He comes from a place with many great little villages and can't believe we'd sit by and watch ours die. More than that, I've got the idea that Ian wants to make up for his late uncle's deficiencies. What do you reckon, Fiona?'

'Dad's right, Mr Barker. Ian is very interested in human welfare and has plans to study medicine after his science degree.'

'Hmm. Well if you and Lachie think he's all right then we'll have to do something about it,' Barker said.

'Thank you, Mr Barker!' Fiona exclaimed as she pushed the plate of pikelets towards him.

'Your pikelets are as good as your mother's, Fiona,' Joe said with a smile.

Ian Richardson was in his laboratory when Mrs Heatley announced Joe Barker had arrived at Kanimbla. 'I'll meet him in the lounge room,' Ian said to Mrs H as he removed his dust coat. He never took anyone into his lab.

'Sorry to keep you waiting, Mr Barker,' he said as he walked into the lounge room. 'I had to wash up. What can I do for you?'

'I saw Fiona's interview on the telly, and the stories in the paper. I'd like to help,' Joe said without any preamble.

'I don't mean to be rude, Mr Barker, but it was my impression that you weren't so keen on my proposals,' Ian said politely.

'I wouldn't put it quite like that, Ian. I reckoned you were biting off more than you could chew. I didn't think you'd get the support you needed.'

'And now?' Ian asked.

'It seems there are more people in favour than against. It'd be a great thing for the district if you could pull it off, but you'll need a lot of help financially. Not so much for the bird park because a couple of working bees could knock that up, but if you want a motel and swimming pool, that's a whole different kettle of fish,' said Joe.

'You're right about that,' agreed Ian.

'It's going to cost you a lot more time and money, not to mention a fair bit of worry, beyond what you've already contributed, and I don't think it's right for one bloke to carry the whole load, seeing as how the whole district would benefit. So I'd like to take some of the load off your shoulders, Ian,' Joe said sincerely.

'That's just great, Mr Barker. What are you proposing?' Ian leaned forward, a sparkle in his hazel eyes.

'I reckon I'll give you some money,' Joe said as he took his cheque book from his pocket. 'Who do I make it out to?'

'You're a good man, Mr Barker. Make it out to the Murrawee and District Development Association,' Ian said.

'And I suppose you put up the money to get that started?' Joe smiled.

'A nominal amount, Mr Barker,' Ian said modestly.

Barker scribbled out a cheque, ripped it out and handed it to Ian. 'That should help you to get things moving. I'd like most of it to go towards the motel when you get around to it, but if you need some of it for your caravan and bird park, feel free to use what you need,' he said.

Ian looked at the cheque and then at Joe. 'That extra zero is not a slip of the pen is it, Mr Barker?' asked Ian in surprise.

'No fear. You'll need all of that and more. What you're proposing for Murrawee would be the biggest and best changes attempted in my lifetime. If you need more, let me know,' Joe said generously.

It had been almost two years since Ian's arrival at Kanimbla, and in that time he had heard a bit about 'western generosity' but Barker's cheque completely floored him.

When he'd seen Joe off, Ian immediately rang Fiona. 'Joe Barker was just here,' he told her excitedly.

'Was he? He's been here too. What did he say?' she said.

'He's given me a cheque for two hundred and fifty thousand dollars,' Ian told her.

For a moment, Fiona didn't grasp what Ian was getting at. 'What for?'

'For the Murrawee projects, of course!' exclaimed Ian.

Fiona was dumbstruck.

'Are you there, Fiona?'

'That's fantastic, Ian!' Fiona almost yelled down the phone line. 'Dad's going to be thrilled!'

'Mr Barker said he'd like most of it to be used for the motel, but that we can put some of it towards the caravan and bird parks,' Ian said.

'Wow!' Fiona said excitedly. 'When can we start?'

'Well, Geoff Greenaway called last week to say that approval has been granted for us to make a start with the caravan and bird parks, though it's not yet in writing. Alf Zeller, Frank Morton's plumbing contractor, told him that he'd superintend the plumbing for cost, which will be a huge help. As soon as the electricity is connected, we can make a start. If I print up some notices about the first working bee can you help me distribute them?' he asked.

'As long as we don't have to do it on horseback,' Fiona joked happily.

Initially it was proposed to hold two working bees on consecutive Saturdays, but in fact some preliminary work had already been done. The electricity had been connected and there were poles to carry it through the park.

In the flyer he and Fiona had posted throughout the district and displayed in the township, Ian had asked for two weekends of working bees with particular emphasis on people with plumbing and welding skills, though there would be jobs for everybody.

Before the working bees, however, there was a considerable amount of preparatory work to be done. An overhead tank had to be erected and pumped full of river water to be used for concreting and other purposes. That was followed by the arrival of two new caravans which were parked in the area designated for the caravan park.

At the end of term, Rhona returned to Kanimbla to visit her parents and to carry out one of her regular checks of Kanimbla's computer system. Ian had been out for the day helping Alf Zeller and his team with the tank and pipework for the parks. He was pleased to hear of Rhona's arrival and had invited her for a drink after she finished her computer checks.

After a couple of glasses of wine, Rhona found herself telling Ian what a mess she felt her life was in. She was a highly qualified academic but lately seemed only to be marking time – marking time and marking papers. It wasn't exactly what she had imagined when she began her university career. The final straw came when her boyfriend, Graeme, had cleared out after she'd loaned him a heap of money. And there'd been some cutting remarks from some of her competitive colleagues about her being an easy target for men. They hurt.

'I've started having nightmares. It's always the same dream. I'm in a lifeboat in the trough of a wave and there's this wall of water towering above me. Then just as it begins to crash down, I wake up in a sweat, feeling terrified.'

'That must be awful,' said Ian.

'I don't know why I'm dumping all this on you. It's my own fault for having such poor judgement where men are concerned, but I just don't know what to do,' Rhona's eyes brimmed with tears, but she wasn't a person given to crying, and didn't want to break down in front of Ian. He was only young, but there was a maturity about him, an empathy that made him different from anyone she'd ever met.

She remembered her first meeting with Ian, and how she had left Kanimbla in a great hurry to avoid making a fool of herself. Ian was utterly gorgeous and years younger than her, but was the only man she'd ever met who seemed to respect her for who she was. Since that first encounter, she'd only met him on one other occasion, yet her fine opinion of him had grown even more. This was a huge concession for Rhona because she didn't have much time for graziers, despite the fact that a grazier's money (via her father's salary) had paid a substantial part of her university fees. Initially, Rhona had lumped Ian into the lucky class of young men and women who inherited property without lifting a finger to earn it. Ian certainly fell into this category, but what she was to learn about him soon changed her opinion. Ian wasn't made in the mould of many young graziers. He could have sold the great property and walked away with millions, but he hadn't done that. He'd improved conditions for his employees and set out to make Murrawee a more liveable township. As if that wasn't enough, he was studying science externally and had even built a small laboratory to aid in this endeavour. This suggested a man of exceptional merit, and one in whom she felt she could confide.

'Maybe I should just chuck it all in and take off travelling? God knows I need a fresh challenge. I really admire how you've settled down here, especially as it wasn't what you had in mind when you left Harrow. I don't know how you manage to do all you do, Ian. You're such an inspiration.'

Ian leaned back in his chair and allowed his gaze to wander across the big lawn to where the giant red gums stood sentinel over the river.

'That's very kind, Rhona, and I'm flattered that you feel you can confide in me. I guess you've just got to do what makes you happy. Many people have changed careers midway through their lives, and if you're not content with what you're doing, perhaps you should consider that.'

'What do you mean?'

'Well, why not combine travel with a change in vocation? With your qualifications you shouldn't have much trouble doing another degree in the UK or the United States,' Ian said.

Rhona allowed his suggestion to sink in. 'It's a great idea, Ian, but I simply couldn't manage financially. I gave Graeme most of my savings, and I just can't ask my parents for any more handouts – not after all the support they've already given me. And they're close to retiring; they need all the money they can get.'

'I'll tell you what I can do to help you, Rhona,' Ian said at last. 'There's a nice little complex attached to Lyndhurst. It's where my grandfather's batman lived before he went into the village. Why not stay there while you take a sabbatical and decide what to do? You could look into courses and use Lyndhurst as your base. It won't cost you anything,' he said.

'Oh, Ian! That's so incredibly generous. But is there any

point in looking into studying when I couldn't possibly pay the course fees, let alone support myself for any length of time while studying?'

'Of course there is. I can lend you the money for the course fees and you can repay me when you're earning again.'

'Ian, post-graduate courses are very expensive and Dad would go off his rocker. I couldn't possibly accept your money. He might even object to you giving me rent-free accommodation.'

'Let me talk to him. I think a very great deal of your father and mother and by helping you I would be repaying some of their kindnesses,' said Ian.

Rhona stood up suddenly and leaned over to kiss Ian's cheek. 'You are just the most special man, Ian,' Rhona said gratefully. 'I feel awful dumping my problems on you. You must think me dreadfully inadequate.'

'Not at all. I'm delighted to be in a position to help you,' Ian said gently. He felt that by helping Rhona he was repaying Leo for staying at Kanimbla well past his anticipated retirement date. Without Leo, and for that matter, Judy, he'd have found the going less tolerable. Leo took so much responsibility off his shoulders that he was able to indulge his passion for science.

Rhona returned to Sydney, her head in a whirl. Ian had shown her a way out of her impasse.

# Chapter Twenty-three

It was actually happening. It really was. And anyone driving through Murrawee on this particular Saturday could be excused for thinking that a circus was in town, there were so many vehicles on River Road.

This was the first of the two working bees, and the roll-up had surprised Ian. Only two men were left to look after Kanimbla; the remainder were all in Murrawee, including Jack Greer, who was to liaise with Helen Donovan about the catering. Leo Blake had warned Ian that putting these two 'top dogs' together was a sure-fire recipe for disaster. So Ian had had a word in Greer's ear and then talked to Helen Donovan, and they both assured him that they would put aside their differences. This assurance of harmony lasted only until the two of them got together to discuss the lunch.

'So I'll bring meat and vegetables for a —' Greer began, before Helen interrupted.

'That won't be necessary. A stew means they'll need plates and knives – too much fuss and bother. Rolls and sandwiches are all that's needed for a working bee. If you want to cook something you could make some damper for smokos,' Helen said.

Greer puffed up his chest. 'Ian told me I was to give everyone a decent lunch and he's the boss. So I'll be putting on stews. You can still supply rolls and sandwiches if you like, and they can take their pick.'

Helen's face flamed with indignation, but she held her tongue – after all, she'd promised Ian there'd be no dust-ups.

The park's venue became the scene of increasing activity as trucks began to arrive with fencing material, poly pipe and timber. Both Judy Blake and Fiona McDonald, to mention only two of the women who came to help, worked with Helen Donovan and Jack Greer to provide the smokos and lunches for everyone.

Ian put up the approved plan for the complex on a blackboard so everyone who came to help knew more or less what had to be done. As Leigh Metcalfe had pointed out, the laying of piping and other plumbing was the first essential, though there was some fencing that could be erected while the plumbing was being done. This included the low fence fronting the river, with a child-proof gate, and the concreting-in of some of the very tall steel poles that would hold the bird-proof mesh on top of the cages. Shorter posts were also concreted in for the first shelters. During the morning three loads of ready-mixed concrete arrived from Roma. These loads were poured into the boxing that had been prepared for the pathways.

By lunchtime, water was available from half a dozen taps,

and at that point Jack Greer stole a march on Helen Donovan and announced that lunch was 'on'. There were plenty of people with good appetites who didn't say no to his stew. Ian looked at Leigh Metcalfe and grinned. 'So what do you reckon, Mr Bird Man?'

Leigh, who had temporarily set aside his dislike of company in his enthusiasm for Ian's project, grinned back. 'I think that maybe this thing is going to work.' He and Ian had spent most of the morning pegging out the overall plan for the aviaries and it was no small task. It had to be done because the post-hole diggers would be going into action after lunch. Every cage would be planted with Australian native plants that produced nectar, seeds or berries, and the holes had to be dug before the cages were wired and meshed. Initially, more than five hundred trees were being planted. Most of these were trees especially favoured by birds. The trees that would grow tall, like pink flowering ironbarks, were planted outside the cages.

Just before darkness set in on that first Saturday, Leo Blake got everyone together so Ian could speak to them. As usual he came straight to the point because they'd been hard at it all day and were pretty exhausted.

'I just want to thank all of you for your amazing efforts. We've made a great start. Next weekend we'll need welders, and only one post-hole digger as most of the holes have been dug. We'd also like lots of hollow logs, and rocks, preferably big ones. If you've got any, please throw them on a vehicle and bring them next Saturday.

'During the week our landscape designer will arrive and he'll be laying out the gardens. Kanimbla will be providing some manpower to speed things up.' Here Ian paused and looked sideways at Leigh Metcalfe. 'And next Saturday night the lights will be switched on and we'll be having a party . . . with kegs.'

This announcement was greeted with loud cheering and much clapping.

The landscape designer arrived mid-week. Lindsay Gayford and his two offsiders, Rick and Paul, were from Brisbane and had laid out some of the city's best new gardens. Their services cost a mint, but Ian agreed with Leigh that it was crucial to employ professionals who could work with the climate to produce the best results.

Lindsay had assured Ian that he could do it and then told him what he'd need on site. There'd be loads of loam, compost, manure, pine bark, rocks and railway sleepers. They'd be bringing other gear on his truck. He said he'd fax through exact quantities after he'd seen the council-approved plans. Ian told him he could let him have three men who would work at his direction – Peter Cross, Ted Beecham and Gerald Bradshaw. The young jackaroos had experienced just about every kind of work associated with the land, and Ted said he'd regard the gardening work as a 'bit of a break'.

The landscape designer and his team of five were hard at it when Leigh Metcalfe's mate, Luke Weir, arrived out of the blue. Well, almost. He rang from Longreach and told Leigh that he was on his way. He arrived in a green 1966 HR Holden utility packed with gear including a swag, three large flagons of port and several tea chests full of books.

It seemed that in their most recent conversation, Leigh had happened to mention that there would be a significant 'party' the next Saturday evening and this had hastened both Luke's retirement plans and his departure from the Longreach district.

Luke Weir was a slightly larger version of Leigh Metcalfe, though his beard was more profuse and he had guileless blue eyes that promised an unfailing sense of humour. His pet sulphur-crested cockatoo, 'Kolar', accompanied him everywhere. He could whistle a treat and quite often repeated Luke's more colourful expressions. Luke had named the bird after the distinguished Austrian ornithologist, Kurt Kolar, when he read that the learned doctor had created something of a splash on his 1963 visit to Australia. He'd told the waiting media on arrival at Sydney airport that he had an 'invitation to study the galahs in Canberra' and that 'Canberra is supposed to be the best location for this'.

Ian and Leigh drove in to meet Luke late on the Wednesday evening. They found him sitting at one of the log tables that Lindsay had placed for his team to eat at. Luke seemed quite at home talking to Lindsay and greeted Metcalfe with a kind of subdued enthusiasm before turning his attention to Ian.

'So you're the young Pommy that's set this township on its ear,' Weir remarked wryly.

Ian let the 'Pommy' bit slide. 'I take it that you're interested in being involved in what we're doing here,' Ian began.

'I wouldn't be here now if I wasn't,' Weir said simply.

'As Leigh told you, we can't afford to pay you anything yet. What we're prepared to do is give you free rent of that on-site van over there and pay for your electricity. Later, if things progress as we hope, we may be able to pay you a small weekly wage. We may also be able to offer you better accommodation a year or two down the track,' Ian said.

Luke waved his hand in front of his face. 'Oh, I don't need to be paid. I've got me pension. That'll keep me going. And it's a nice spot, here. Leigh tells me you want me to look after the park and keep the tucker and whatnot up to the birds you're going to bring here.'

'That's about it in a nutshell,' Ian agreed.

Luke looked at Leigh, who nodded. 'That's about it, Luke. The idea is to attract people to Murrawee so that the township doesn't go down the gurgler in the same way that a lot of other bush towns have done and will do.'

Luke looked at the work in progress and nodded. 'It looks to me as if you've made a pretty damned good start.'

'Wait until you see what happens next Saturday,' Ian said with a smile. 'So the job's yours if you want it, Luke.'

'I reckon it will do me fine.'

'In that case we'd better unlock your van and you can get settled in,' Ian said.

'Is there anything you want me to do straight off?' Luke asked.

'I've got my three jackaroos here to help Lindsay Gayford and his two offsiders, so he should be right for men. There's a heap of trees and shrubs arriving tomorrow so you might be able to help get some of them in the ground. When we've got the shrubs in place and the water connected to all the cages, we can start hanging the wire. Here's a plan of the area so you'll know what's what,' Ian said and took a sheet of paper from his coat pocket and handed it to Weir.

'Oh, if you aren't set up for food tonight, I can get you a meal at the café or pub,' Ian added.

'Thanks, that would be great,' said Luke.

Ian put out his hand. 'Good to have you with us, Luke.'

# Chapter Twenty-four

'I've had a call from Lachie.' Leo held the door open for Ian as they walked into the homestead. 'It seems that Joe's generous donation has sparked the interest of a few other graziers. They want to get involved in the motel.'

'Really? That's great news,' said Ian.

'It sure is. But don't look so surprised, there's some good blokes in Queensland. I've heard there's a fellow in Toowoomba who's given twenty million dollars to local charities,' said Leo.

'So what's next?'

'Well, they'd like to have a preliminary meeting. I think next Saturday would suit most of them. I thought you might prefer to have it in your study where you've got access to everything,' Leo said.

'All right. Make it for ten o'clock Saturday,' Ian said.

The meeting got off to a promising start with Mrs Heatley's hot scones and freshly made biscuits. Helen Donovan, as spokesperson for the Murrawee and District Development

Association, was there, as were Lachie, Fiona, Joe Barker, Sean Driscoll and Will Roper.

Lachie addressed the gathering in his usual, no-nonsense style. 'The fact of the matter is that we're very impressed with what's been done in Murrawee,' he said. 'Ian, you've talked about fitting a motel into the park and those of us here today would like to discuss the pros and cons of actually building one. Have you done any cost calculations?'

'I've done quite a bit of research. Initially, I'd only imagined a small motel – say, six units. But the moteliers I spoke with told me a six-unit motel wouldn't be viable. We'd need at least ten units, preferably twelve,' Ian said.

'And costs?' Lachie asked.

'It depends which way we go. We can have the units prefabricated in Brisbane and put together here for twenty-five to forty thousand a unit. They'd be all electric and each unit would require a TV, fridge, toaster, kettle, crockery and maybe a hot plate and a microwave. You'd have two beds, a sofa, wardrobe and table and chairs. Oh, and linen and other bedding. Plus there'd be bathroom fittings, plumbing and a septic tank to install.'

'Is prefabrication the only alternative we have?' asked Lachie.

'There's also the possibility of getting hold of some of the mining accommodation no longer required in the mining towns. I'm assured that some of this is still in very good nick and could be used for a motel,' Ian said.

'What about management?' queried Fiona. 'Wouldn't

you need someone to look after a motel and maybe cook breakfasts?'

'I've thought about that. One of the keys to making the motel pay would be in keeping costs down. My inform- ants suggest offering free board and one of the units to a caretaker-cum-housekeeper, as we're doing with the caravan park. Also, I'm not convinced that we would need to offer breakfast. One way around that would be to provide break- fast vouchers so that guests could get their breakfasts at Mrs Donovan's place or at the pub. That way we'd add to *their* revenue,' Ian said.

Helen Donovan smiled openly at this suggestion.

'Wouldn't most guests prefer breakfast laid on at the motel?' Joe queried.

'Perhaps,' answered Ian, 'but let's not make this a sticking point.'

'We'd definitely need a caretaker-receptionist if we build the hot and cold swimming pools,' offered Fiona. 'They'll require some looking after.'

'That's right,' agreed Ian. 'Ideally we'd be looking for a settled couple, one of whom is a retired nurse or ambulance officer. Free rent and fishing close by might just attract the right person,' Ian said with a smile.

'Okay, so what about the profit side of things,' queried Sean Driscoll. 'The first thing we need to know is, will it pay?'

Ian had been well aware that this was the question Sean and the other graziers would ask. Ian had not been able to answer questions about the motel's profitability at the town meeting back in February, but this time he was armed with much more information.

'Sean, I'll be honest with you and say that I doubt there'll be any great profit in a motel in Murrawee. I think the return on investment would be small, especially in the first couple of years, though I might be wrong. Still, there might be some benefits tax-wise and I'm looking into that, but I'm more interested in the extra business a motel might bring to the town. I don't want to badmouth the pub because it has been the only accommodation in Murrawee for some time, but the fact of the matter is that most people don't want their vehicles parked in the street and they don't want to have to carry luggage a long way. They like their cars outside their doors and they want en suite facilities.

'Wouldn't you all like to be able to tell your clients that there's a motel available for them in Murrawee?' Ian said. He looked across to where Helen Donovan sat in his big leather sofa. 'What do you think, Mrs Donovan?'

'A motel would be just wonderful for Murrawee. I suppose its profitability would depend on how well we promote our town, as well as how much the tariff is. If it's lower than at the motels in the bigger places, that could be a plus. The "Oasis in the West" slogan could work very well to pull in travellers. But I'd have to think about the breakfast side of things. I'd like the extra business but how would guests take to leaving their rooms for breakfast? We could offer them a real bush breakfast and that might be an inducement.'

Mrs Donovan continued, 'But of course the big question is whether the district will come up with the money. I dare say if it was a prefabricated job, we could count on some voluntary labour but there's plumbing and electricity and that has to be done properly.'

'I've done a bit of work on this for Ian,' Fiona cut in. 'If we decide to go ahead and build a motel we can use Mr Morton, whether we build it from the ground up or use prefabricated units. We've talked to him and he's been very helpful. Mr Zeller has agreed to do the plumbing and Mr Petersen the electrical work. Mr Greenaway referred us to an architect in Roma, who will draw up the plans for the council,' Fiona said.

Joe smiled at Fiona, 'Good work.' Ian marvelled at her newfound confidence. After all her work on the sheepdog trials, and her interviews for newspaper and television, Fiona had seemed much more self-assured, and he had been pleased when she offered to take on the project management of the motel.

'So do you have an estimate of what it will cost?' Will Roper asked. Will ran a big Santa Gertrudis stud and was seriously well off. He conducted an annual stud sale of his cattle, and being able to book some of his buyers into a motel in Murrawee would be a big plus.

'If we allowed fifty thousand dollars per unit and a hundred thousand overall for furnishings, bedding, TVs and other electrical gear we'd be close to the mark. Of course it depends on how many units we settle on. Our advice is that it would be better to build a twelve-unit motel than a ten. One of those units would be taken up by the caretakers,' Fiona said.

'So we're talking seven hundred thousand?' Will Roper asked.

'Not exactly,' Ian interceded. 'We've already got nearly a third of that amount.'

There was a general swivelling of heads towards Ian after this announcement. He smiled at Fiona who was clearly enjoying herself at this meeting.

'You mean some people have already promised that much?' Will Roper asked.

'More than promised. We've got the money in the bank, Mr Roper,' said the ever-courteous Ian. 'Actually, we've got a great deal more than that, but the government grant wasn't for the motel. It was to be used for the caravan and bird parks' amenities block and office, and for the swimming pools. We'll need about four hundred thousand more for the motel.'

'We should be able to raise that,' Roper said.

'Yep,' agreed Sean Driscoll.

'Thank you gentlemen,' said Ian as he shook hands with each man present, 'I know you won't regret it.'

# Chapter Twenty-five

Ian sat with Jim in the Kanimbla ram shed. A new client had been impressed with their sheep and left an order for ten rams. This bucked the trend for a downward spiral of ram orders as disenchanted woolgrowers got out of the wool business in favour of either meat breeds or cattle.

'Jim, as you're well aware, today's order is unusual. Overall, our ram sales have dropped quite drastically in line with a statewide decline. In the last twenty years, Queensland's sheep population has dropped by more than seventy-five per cent. As I told Mr Blake, I don't propose to keep breeding good rams that end up at the abattoirs. However, I'm not going out of ram breeding entirely. What we're going to have to do is reduce the number of rams we breed and improve still further the quality of those we do breed.

'When David MacLeod was here, he spoke about a couple of rams he'd set aside for us to examine. They're from a special family he's developed from a New England stud. These sheep push out a lot of wool – so much so that they'd need shearing every eight months. This will increase shearing costs, but we'd produce three clips in two years and that would help to make up for the downturn in ram sales. That's one avenue open to us and I'm proposing to take it,' Ian said.

'It's a good one, Ian,' Jim agreed. 'But you could also consider meat sheep or prime lambs. Of course, it wouldn't be as simple to implement here as in the cooler country. It would be a real challenge, no doubt about that.'

'Jim, I want you to take a trip down to Merriwa and have a look at those two rams David MacLeod spoke about. If you like what you see, bring either one or both of them back.'

'You'll leave it to me?' Landers asked.

'Of course,' Ian said. 'I've spoken to Mr Blake and he's agreed that I should appoint you Assistant Manager. I'm proposing to increase your salary to go with your new status, Jim – assuming that you'll stay.'

'I'm not planning to leave in the short term,' said Jim, 'unless perhaps a manager's job comes up elsewhere.'

'That's settled then,' said Ian.


The meeting began at nine o'clock in Ian's study. Leo, Jim and the three jackaroos were in attendance. Peter Cross, the senior jackaroo, had been promoted to overseer now that Jim was assistant manager.

'Thanks for coming, gentlemen,' Ian began. 'I've already spoken to Mr Blake and to Jim Landers about where I think Kanimbla should be headed and now I want you all to understand quite clearly what your roles will be in the future. What I'm hoping is that these roles will provide incentives for you to stay at Kanimbla and also make your lives a lot more interesting.

'Peter, as overseer your main role will be to look after the stud sheep and to show them. We'll be reducing the number of rams we breed by fifty per cent, but we'll still get stuck into showing. I'm hoping you will be taking teams of our sheep to the big shows down south so we'll be mixing it with the best sheep in the country,' Ian said.

Peter nodded his assent.

'As you know, the two MacLeod rams Jim brought back from David's are from a family he's been developing that produce a lot of wool. Jim, with Peter's help, you will be developing this factor using an artificial insemination program. Hopefully, and before very long, we'll have a line of these sheep which will mean three shearings every two years. The extra returns should help to compensate for the reduced ram sales and additional shearing costs.'

Jim piped up, 'There's a big push on to produce merinos with faster growth and more meat. Gerald could take a trip around the country and have a look at this whole situation. He could talk to Roger Fletcher at Dubbo and get a handle on the mutton picture. And there are a few fellows down that way who are big on Dohne sheep.'

'Good idea, Jim,' said Ian.

Jim continued, 'I've been thinking that we could mate some of our lesser ewes to Dohnes and then use the half-bred ewes to mate with Texels or some other prime lamb sire.'

'When would you want me to go?' Gerald asked Ian.

'As soon as possible,' said Ian. 'You'd better take the new utility. I'll give you some cash, but keep a record of your costs.'

'Righto,' said Gerald.

'In the first place we must ensure that our young stud sheep are fed right so they'll grow well. That means oats and lucerne – lucerne because we'll need hay and chaff. We'll also need a fair area of oats for prime lambs. I'm also concerned that we don't have enough stored feed for cattle. I want to put down a big quantity of silage which we can use for our best stud cows if things get tough. I believe corn silage is what most dairy farmers use though you can use a range of crops including forage sorghum.'

'But what about irrigation for all this?' asked Ted.

'We've got a licence to pump more water than we've ever utilised,' Ian replied. 'In the future we're going to make the most of whatever water we're entitled to. When Gerald gets back from his trip I want you to look into the silage business to see whether it's better for us to cut and manage the silage or, alternatively, bring in a contractor.'

'Okay,' said Ted.

'I want you to be responsible for all the farming. That will be your number one priority. You'll put in the crops and look after the irrigation. How does that suit you?' Ian asked.

'It sounds like a challenge,' Ted smiled.

Ian felt confident that he had helped put Kanimbla on the right path to maintain its future profitability. He knew it would take some time to implement these changes, but he had a great deal of faith in Jim Landers, and in his three young jackaroos – they'd do a fine job.

# Chapter Twenty-six

Trish Claydon, who initially had not exhibited any great interest in the Murrawee developments, pricked up her ears when she heard that the construction of a motel had been approved. It seemed to Trish, who had some experience of assignations in motel rooms, that a motel in Murrawee offered some definite advantages hitherto unavailable in the township.

When Trish noticed that work had well and truly begun on the units, she called Ian to tell him that she'd be happy to be involved with any aspect of planning for the motel, especially the selection of bathroom fittings, electrical goods and furnishings – after all, she was an expert at spending other people's money.

Ian discussed Trish's offer with Helen Donovan as the chairperson of the Murrawee and District Development Association.

'I'd give her a list of what you need and let her get some quotes, Ian. Trish has got good fashion sense even though she wears those outrageous outfits from time to time,' said the ever-practical Helen Donovan. 'There are some good places in Toowoomba where you can buy sheeting and furniture fairly inexpensively,' she added.

So Trish, who was never reluctant to have an outing, drove to Toowoomba to get some quotes, and to select some sample linen. It was a drive of several hours, and she planned to spend the night there. It would probably take all day to do the rounds of the shops, with time off for a nice lunch, and she wasn't going to return late in the day, as it would mean driving in the dark. So she planned to skip breakfast in Toowoomba and get away early on the second day. And this is exactly what she did – the car stacked with curtains, towels and other linen, some of which she'd bought for Bahreenah because they'd been on special.

When she reached Murrawee, she decided to inspect the developments in River Road. She drove across the railway line and headed down towards the stretch of river that had so captivated Ian when he saw it for the first time. As she passed by the caravan park, she noticed Leigh Metcalfe's four-wheel drive out the front.

Leigh and Luke had been working hard on the bird park. It had taken a long time to set up each of the cages in readiness for their new occupants, and on this day they were celebrating the arrival of a pair of princess parrots with their distinctive long tail feathers. This wasn't an endangered species, but was considered vulnerable, and its habitat ranged across the west of South Australia's western region, and easternmost Western Australia. This pair had come from a bird fancier who happened to be a mate of Leigh Metcalfe.

The men were sitting outside Luke's van enjoying a game of poker. Trish couldn't resist the opportunity for a flirt with her old flame, so she stopped her car and joined them.

'G'day, Trish. Fancy a hand?' Leigh asked in high good humour. 'You've met Luke, haven't you?'

Trish hesitated. She noticed an empty wine bottle under the table and another on the table top. She liked poker and she liked red wine, but drinking and playing poker with two men in a caravan park in Murrawee wasn't what a grazier's wife was supposed to do.

Leigh pushed a glass of red wine towards her. 'That's a great drop, Trish. Won a gold medal some damn place.'

Trish picked up the glass, sniffed the wine and then took a swallow. It was very smooth and it did lovely things inside her. Two glasses later Trish was playing poker.

After a few games, the last of which she won, and several more glasses of red wine, Trish decided she'd better head back home. She wasn't feeling the best, so she put one of the sample towels on the front seat. It would come in handy if she were sick.

'Are you all right to drive, Trish?' Leigh asked. It seemed that the wine had had very little effect on him or Luke. But Trish, in her determination to retain her figure, had had very little to eat before she left Toowoomba. Leigh and Luke had eaten good breakfasts.

'I could drive back to Bahreenah with my eyes closed,' Trish boasted.

It may have been that Trish was testing this boast or it might have been that she was driving a shade too fast for her condition. Drowsy from too much wine, she didn't see the big red roo as it left a patch of scrub and hopped across the road. Trish slammed on the brakes and the Fairlane spun sideways, hit the roo, jumped the gutter and slammed into a small ironbark. The roo jerked convulsively a couple of times and then lay still.

Ian, on his way in to Murrawee to meet Luke and Leigh, was the first car along the road and he saw the big dead roo before he saw the stationary Fairlane. He slowed to a stop and saw Trish Claydon sitting on the ground with her back against the right front wheel. She had a cut on her forehead and a lot of blood had run down her face onto her blouse.

Trish put her hand above her eyes to shield them from the sun so she could look up when she heard Ian approach. She essayed a weak smile as Ian stood over her. 'It's the lovely Ian come to the rescue,' she giggled.

Ian thought at first that she might be concussed, but moving closer realised she was drunk. 'Where are you hurt, Mrs Claydon?' he asked.

'I'm Trish. Trish, Trish, Trish,' she burbled.

'All right, you're Trish,' Ian said to humour her. 'Where are you hurt?' he repeated.

'My head hurts and I've got a pain here,' she said and pointed to her rib region. 'Ouch!'

Ian decided she was probably both concussed, drunk and may even have fractured ribs. 'Do you think you could get up?'

'If you help me,' she said weakly.

Ian took her hands in his and pulled her slowly to her feet. She wanted to fall against him, but the pain in her ribs was excruciating, so she had to settle for his strong arms encircling her shoulders as he steered her gently to the front seat of the Fairlane. He used the towel from the front seat to wipe the blood from Trish's face, then he stood back from her and assembled his thoughts. Ian Richardson dealt with problems in sequential layers. The first priority was to get Trish attended to, so he used his mobile to ring Jim Landers. He explained the situation to Jim and asked him to get the plane ready so he could fly Trish to Roma Hospital. He then tried to ring Alec, but couldn't get an answer – mobile phones were notoriously unreliable in this area.

Ian walked to the dead roo and pulled it off the road by its thick tail. It was huge and took some effort to shift. He knew he couldn't have left it on the road because it might have caused another accident.

He went back to Trish and helped her into the Mercedes. She groaned in pain as she settled into the front seat. He called Helen Donovan and asked her to get a message to Luke and Leigh that he'd have to skip their bird park meeting.

Trish looked very pale. 'Feeling any better?' Ian asked.

'I think I need to be sick.' Ian pulled the car over so Trish could lean out the window. It must have hurt her ribs, but she didn't cry out.

'We'll get you to a doctor before you know it,' said Ian.

# Chapter Twenty-seven

Ian drove up to the manager's residence in the Mercedes and collected Judy. Trish was out of hospital and he wanted to take Judy to visit her at Bahreenah.

Mrs Heatley had been critical of Ian's decision to visit Trish Claydon. She had a low opinion of Trish, quite apart from the fact that she believed her accident had been self-induced. Of course, an accident could happen to anyone, especially in roo country, but it had been clear to Glenda as she helped Trish on to the Kanimbla plane that the woman had been drinking. She'd been sick on her clothes and there was an unmistakable smell of wine.

'I can't *not* visit her, Mrs H,' Ian had said. 'It's the neighbourly thing to do. Alec buys Kanimbla rams, and he's spent a lot of money here. He's still committed to merinos and I want him to keep buying Kanimbla rams.'

'I suppose it would be difficult to keep Alec onside if you ignore Trish,' agreed Mrs Heatley. 'She is his wife, even if she has been unfaithful to him. Perhaps the pottery classes will give her a new interest, and keep her at home more.' Mrs

Heatley sincerely hoped so. For now, she had to admit that Ian's decision to visit Trish at Bahreenah was typical of his behaviour generally. And while Alec and the girls were with Trish this time, she couldn't help feeling relieved when she heard that Judy Blake was accompanying Ian.

When they had left the main western road and were on the track into the Claydon property, Ian pulled off to one side, turned off the ignition, unclipped his seatbelt and shifted his body so he could talk to his passenger.

'Why, Ian, if I weren't an old duck, I'd say this was an assignation,' Judy said with a smile.

'You aren't an old duck and never will be in my eyes. What I have to tell you is for your ears alone,' Ian said with an answering smile. 'How much you feel disposed to tell Mr Blake is up to you.'

'How mysterious you sound,' Judy said.

'It's about Rhona,' he said.

'What about Rhona?' Judy looked alarmed.

'She's been going through a rough time. Her boyfriend cleared out with most of her savings. His betrayal brought things to a head and she felt that she'd come to a dead end and wasn't doing anything really worthwhile with her life. To cut a long story short, Rhona felt she needed a change in direction, but couldn't do it without help,' Ian said.

'Why didn't she come to us?' Judy asked.

'She was very much against doing that because she was aware you and Mr Blake need what money you have for your eventual retirement. She's applied for a sabbatical to

Cambridge and I've offered her Lyndhurst as a place to stay.'

'Oh. I can't believe she didn't confide in me,' Judy felt close to tears.

'She knew you would jeopardise your own future to help her, Judy. Rhona will pay me back when she gets on her feet again . . .'

Judy looked aghast. 'You mean you have loaned her money?'

'Just to help her on her way. The money's nothing, Judy. Rhona will get it back to me but I'm not concerned whether she does or she doesn't,' said Ian.

'But Ian, Leo would never allow it.'

'Why does he have to know? Couldn't she have won a scholarship?' said Ian.

'You're asking me to lie to my husband, Ian. I don't know if I can do that,' Judy looked out the window at the endless blue sky.

'Rhona feels guilty that it was her own poor judgement that landed her in this predicament. She trusted someone she shouldn't have, and he let her down. She's also aware that her father had already paid her way through university.'

'But none of that matters, Ian. What matters is that you've put me in a terrible predicament,' said Judy, wiping her forehead nervously.

'I'm sorry, Judy. I didn't mean to cause any bad feeling. I just wanted to help,' Ian said, crestfallen.

Judy looked across at Ian and her heart went out to

him. Sometimes it seemed to her that he really was only a boy.

'Let me speak to Leo,' she said gently. 'I'm sure he'll be okay about Rhona staying rent-free at Lyndhurst. Perhaps once she's over there we can deal with the rest,' Judy patted Ian's shoulder comfortingly. 'And thank you for trying to help,' she added. 'Now let's see how Trish is faring.'

Ian started the car.

Alec Claydon was alongside the Mercedes as soon as it stopped. He pumped Ian's hand vigorously. 'I don't know how to thank you, Ian. Trish and I have had our differences but . . .' he trailed off.

'It was nothing, Alec,' said Ian.

'At least let me pay for the use of your plane,' Alec offered.

'I wouldn't think of it. It'll be listed as a property expense. How is Mrs Claydon?' Ian asked.

'She's pretty good considering she copped broken ribs, a broken collarbone and a shattered kidney,' Alec said.

Trish Claydon was seated in a big lounge chair flanked by her daughters Cyd and Maureen, who had come to see their mother after her accident. Both girls were now studying at university in Brisbane.

Trish got up carefully and kissed Ian on the cheek after he handed her the flowers.

'A small present put together from a rather bare garden,' he said.

'Judy,' Trish said with a smile and the two women embraced.

'I had to come to see how you were,' Judy said.

'That's very sweet of you,' Trish said. Judy kissed Cyd and Maureen and then stood back as Ian more circumspectly shook hands with both girls. He didn't know them well enough to greet them with a kiss.

'You look very well, Mrs Claydon,' Ian said.

She was wearing a soft wool skirt, white blouse and a navy cardigan. Cyd and Maureen were wearing jeans and pretty blouses.

'You've done a lot since we were here last. The park is lovely, Ian,' Maureen ventured.

'Yes it does look great, but I couldn't have done any of it without the generous help of all the amazing people of Murrawee. Helen Donovan's been a brick; and Joe Barker, who was one of the early doubters, put up a lot of money, which got the others on board – oh there's too many to name,' said Ian throwing up his arms in mock exasperation.

'Hasn't Fiona McDonald been your main partner in crime?' asked Trish.

'I'm sure Fiona has been a *big* help,' teased Cyd.

Trish shot Cyd a look that said, 'Enough!'

'Well actually, she's been amazing, Cyd,' said Ian, 'I would have soon lost my temper with all the red tape, but she's been patient and organised – a real gem. I couldn't have done it without her.'

'The park should be a real asset to Murrawee,' said Alec. 'I reckon there's a lot more optimism in Murrawee now with the park and an annual sheepdog trial.'

'I've no idea where you get all these ideas, Ian. Your brain never seems to stop!' Trish exclaimed.

'I haven't finished, yet,' Ian smiled, 'I've bought the old butcher shop in Murrawee and I'm thinking of opening it again. Norm Higgins's son is keen to have a go at running it.'

'That would be lovely! To be able to buy our meat locally again, like years ago,' said Judy.

'We'll be feeding wether lambs and we'll have crossbred lambs in the future. We could easily feed a few steers in a small feedlot and offer grain-fed beef. We'll advertise and promote it as "the best meat in the west"! Someone could even run some turkeys and we could sell them through the shop, especially at Christmas. The shop was cheap and it was lying idle,' Ian said.

'You exhaust me with your ideas, Ian,' Trish said kindly, 'I think it's time for morning tea.'

'So you're studying science,' Trish remarked as she stood up to pass Ian a slice of cake. 'What do you plan to do when you get your degree?'

'I've got a way to go, Mrs Claydon, and I'm not sure yet. I'm hoping to do medicine as well,' Ian replied.

'I can't imagine why you would want to be a doctor when you've got Kanimbla,' Trish said as she sat down again. They were sitting at a table on the gauze-enclosed side verandah, and the smoko was quite impressive. Ian had never imagined Trish as a cook, yet her sponge cake compared very favourably with Mrs Heatley's masterpieces.

'I wouldn't be the kind of doctor you probably envisage,

Mrs Claydon,' Ian answered. 'I expect to be looking through microscopes quite a lot. I eventually hope to specialise in medical research.' Ian saw the look of interest on Maureen's face. He knew she'd just started a veterinary science degree.

'It all sounds terribly important,' said Trish.

'There are diseases that are killing millions of people in developing countries, Mrs Claydon, and I want to see if I can make a contribution in combating those diseases.'

'But if you go, what will become of Kanimbla?' asked Alec. 'Will I still be able to buy Kanimbla rams?'

'Yes, you'll still be able to buy Kanimbla rams, hopefully for some time to come. To compensate for lower wool prices, we're homing in on sheep that need to be shorn every eight months, which will mean three shearings every two years,' said Ian.

'I'm damned pleased to hear that,' said Alec. 'I'll have a vet here in Maureen, at least for a while, and we could do some artificial insemination work to help establish Kanimbla's genetics program.'

'Sounds good,' said Ian.

As much as she was interested in genetics, Maureen would have liked to get Ian to one side so she could discuss his medical research aspirations. She was particularly interested in diseases that could be transmitted from animals to humans, known as zoonotic diseases, but it was clear that her mother wanted to be queen bee of this gathering, so there was no chance of initiating such a discussion. She liked Ian a lot, and if Fiona hadn't been on the scene, Maureen would have been interested in getting to know him better.

Afterwards, the whole Claydon family came out to the car to say goodbye. As Ian was about to get into the car he turned back and looked directly at Maureen. 'If you feel like doing a post-graduate course when you finish and would like to do it in England, you could use my place as your base. It's a big house with plenty of room. Cambridge offers some interesting degree courses in biological sciences,' he said.

'Why thank you, Ian,' said a stunned Maureen.

He nodded and got into the Mercedes. The family watched it as it drew away from them.

'Well, lucky you, Maureen. Imagine having Ian Richardson to look out for you. He might fancy you,' Cyd said.

'As if!' replied Maureen.

Alec jumped in, 'I reckon he'd only be thinking about what he could do to help Maureen's career. He's a damned nice bloke. He treats everyone the same, no matter who they are. You keep Ian's offer in mind, Mo.'

Maureen looked at Cyd, 'Anyway, Fiona McDonald has stolen Ian's heart. That's common knowledge.'

'Humph! Well someone had better tell Ian that, because from where I stand, he doesn't seem all that keen on her,' Cyd said.

'I'm not sure you're right about that,' Trish interposed, watching as the Mercedes disappeared over the rise.

'That wasn't too bad, was it?' Judy asked Ian as they left Bahreenah. 'You got waited on hand and foot, and that cream sponge was lovely.'

'Hmm,' Ian replied absently.

Judy glanced across at him. He seemed rather distracted, which wasn't a mood she had noticed previously. 'Is there something wrong, Ian?' she asked.

Ian concentrated hard on his driving for a few moments before answering. 'I'm still concerned about whether I did the right thing with Rhona, Judy. It seemed right at the time because Rhona was in a trough and needed help. She wouldn't go to you or Mr Blake, and had no other option, so I offered to lend a hand.'

'Don't worry about it, Ian. I can see from your offer to Maureen that this kind of generosity is just part of who you are. Rhona will find her feet again. Ten to one she'll find another bloke and Graeme will be a distant memory.'

'I hope so,' said Ian, clearly not convinced.

'Actually, there's something else I've been meaning to talk to you about,' Judy said, her voice serious.

Ian looked at her with a worried expression.

'It's about Fiona,' explained Judy. 'She came to see me last week – in tears.'

Ian looked straight ahead, dreading what was coming next.

'Ian, she adores you. Why do you think she's been doing all of this work for the Murrawee projects? It's not really for the town; she's doing it for you. It's almost as if she's trying to prove that she's worthy of your love.'

Ian ran one hand through his fine hair and shook his head slowly in exasperation.

'Judy, it's not what you think. She's an amazing person

and I care about her deeply. I'm just confused. I'm not sure I'm ready. There's so much I want to do with my life. I don't want to let her down. It doesn't seem fair to expect Fiona to wait patiently while I slog away studying for years.'

'But don't you see, Ian? That decision should be hers to make, not yours,' Judy said passionately. 'I didn't really want to live in the outback for most of my life, but I love my husband, he's a good man and I was willing to make that sacrifice. Then I had the two girls and I began painting and I never looked back. The big question is whether you want to live *without* Fiona. You might think you're doing the right thing by leaving her here with Lachie, but she might prefer to be with you in England no matter how difficult the circumstances. And she needn't sit at home and twiddle her thumbs while you do your medical stuff. She could do a uni course too,' Judy stopped and let all of this sink in.

'But what about Lachie?' Ian said. 'He'd be on his own.'

'Daughters leave home all the time, Ian,' replied Judy. 'That's life. Lachie wouldn't want to hold Fiona to him. He's a strong man, with a good heart and he'll just want his daughter to be happy.'

Ian wiped his brow and glanced at Judy. 'Thank you,' he said as they pulled up outside the bungalow. 'You've given me a lot to think about.'

'It's a pleasure, Ian. I know you'll make the right decision,' she said kindly.

# Chapter Twenty-eight

It was a great day for Murrawee. Granted there was still the odd local who was anti-tourist, but the benefits accruing from the 'Oasis of Murrawee' would soon take care of their whingeing. The garage reported increased sales of petrol, the café more meals and the pub more business. More travellers were calling in at Murrawee. It would be true to say that no one in the district had ever thought they'd see a motel built in their township. Now, they not only had a motel but a caravan and bird park, and plans for a swimming pool to be built adjacent to the motel.

On the day prior to the official opening, two snow white marquees were erected adjacent to the motel, one filled with chairs and the other with several trestle tables covered in white linen. The tables were for the lunch and liquid refreshments which were supplied, co-operatively – and remarkably – by the Murrawee Café and the Murrawee Hotel.

There were several dignitaries at the opening. These included the Federal Member, Alan Moore; the State

Member, Stuart Duff; two mayors and other representatives of local government as well as media from Roma.

Helen Donovan opened proceedings. 'As president of the Murrawee and District Development Association it is my pleasant duty to welcome you here today. I'd like to begin by thanking most sincerely the members of the syndicate who supplied the finance to build our motel. Their faith in the future of this part of Queensland, when so many small towns are in decline, can't be praised enough,' Helen said, and paused while there was a round of applause.

'But the motel wouldn't have been built except for the generosity of Mr Ian Richardson of Kanimbla station who donated this thirty-five acre block and then with great energy and enthusiasm proceeded to convince us that our town *had* a future. It is due largely to this man's efforts that we're here today. Ian is going to say a few words so please welcome him,' Helen urged.

Ian walked to the front of the marquis to the accompaniment of prolonged clapping.

'Thank you, Mrs Donovan. I'd like to echo Mrs Donovan's remarks by also thanking the members of the syndicate who generously provided finance. They've shown faith in this district, a faith I hope will be rewarded, if not by decent profits, then by a more prosperous future for the township. Just alongside you'll see that there are three caravans in the park and during this coming week, we'll have two coaches calling in to visit the bird park – a clear sign that we're now on the map!' Ian said with pride.

'I'd like to thank several people, in particular, for their part in getting the motel, caravan and bird parks up and running: Mr Frank Morton, for his superb building management; Mr Lindsay Gayford and his team for the landscape design; and Mr Geoff Greenaway for his help in liaising with the shire council. Countless local people have been involved in the construction of the parks and motels – Alf Zeller, Frank Morton to name just two. Mrs Donovan and Mrs Trish Claydon were responsible for choosing the furnishings for the units, which you'll all be able to inspect very shortly. I'd especially like to thank Fiona McDonald, who did a lot of the costings and project management. Thanks to you and to the many other people who assisted.'

Helen Donovan returned to the front of the marquee. 'Thank you, Ian. I'll now call on the shire president, Mr Les Peters, to officially open the motel after which the rooms will be open for your inspection. Lunch and drinks will be available in the adjacent marquee. Thank you,' Helen Donovan finished.

It was here that Ian first met Eddie and Katie Fisher, who would be the motel's caretakers. Eddie had worked in the Queensland ambulance service for more than forty years, and Katie had been an 'ambo' too before she married him. They had two grown-up children, who were both doing well. Eddie had handled hundreds of people who'd been the victims of accidents or suffered heart attacks – he'd even delivered babies. He was a big man with a head of thick white hair and keen blue eyes. Katie was a pretty brunette who had allowed her hair to grey naturally. She had only ever loved one man, and she was married to him. Eddie had looked forward to retirement so that he could more fully indulge his passion for wildlife photography. He liked to fish, too, but that came second to the camera.

'So you're the man who started all this,' Eddie said to Ian and waved his arm in a sweeping motion towards the motel and bird park. Helen Donovan, who'd interviewed Eddie and Katie for the caretakers' position, had taken Ian aside so he could meet them.

'I plead guilty,' said Ian, smiling.

'It must have come as a bit of a shock to the locals,' Eddie said.

'You could say that,' said Ian, 'but their support meant we got it done. Are you happy with your rooms?'

'They're very nice,' said Katie.

'I hope you'll be happy here. I'm so pleased to meet you. It's been a worry not having any kind of medical service in the town. We've had to use the Kanimbla plane for emergencies. Have you had a chat to Helen about what you'll need?' said Ian.

'I've had a brief word with Eddie,' said Helen.

'Good,' said Ian. 'So you're keen on wildlife photography?' he directed his question at Eddie.

'Yes,' replied Eddie.

'We'd love you to take some pictures of the parrots in the bird park. We'd like to print a brochure about the motel and park, and it would be great to include some photos of the rarer birds,' said Ian.

'No problem. I'd been thinking I'd like to take some photos next door,' said Eddie.

'Talk to Luke Weir. He's your counterpart at the bird park. Welcome to Murrawee, Eddie and Kate,' said Ian. He shook hands with the couple and then turned away to talk to the politicians.

For young Billy Landers the best thing about the day was the appearance of Luke Weir with Kolar the white cockatoo sitting on his shoulder. Luke had come across from the park for the opening and although Billy didn't know it, Luke and Kolar would pass into legend.

'G'day, minister,' Luke said with due deference as he passed Alan Moore in the marquee and stopped to introduce himself, 'Luke Weir. I look after the bird park.' This important personage from Canberra looked with interest at the animated bird clinging to Luke's shoulder.

'G'day, Luke. So who's this then?' the minister nodded towards the bird. He didn't point, because he didn't like the look of Kolar's beak, which appeared formidable enough to take off a finger.

'This is Kolar,' Luke said with obvious pride.

'Are you pissed again?' Kolar squawked.

Luke was mortified, but the minister was a good sort and doubled up with laughter.


It was typical of Ian Richardson that he didn't let on about his twenty-first birthday until after the event. Fiona got it out of him, albeit with difficulty, about a week afterwards.

She'd called in at Kanimbla on her way back from Murrawee and found Ian in his study. He was working on a science paper, and had asked her to stay and join him for lunch.

Over lunch she'd remarked that he hadn't celebrated any birthdays since his arrival. 'Surely you must have an important birthday coming up soon,' she probed.

'Mmm,' he answered.

'What does "mmm" mean?' she asked with a smile.

'It means I did have what you might call a significant birthday,' he answered.

'And what do you mean by "did"?'

'It was last week,' said Ian calmly.

'Ian!' exclaimed Fiona with loud exasperation. 'Did anyone know?'

'No. Nobody knows.'

'Not even Judy or Mrs Heatley?' Fiona pressed.

'No one. I've got no close relations, so I knew I could get away without a big kerfuffle. You know how I feel about crowds.'

'But we must have some kind of celebration for you, Ian. Even if it's a little one.'

'I'm not a party person, Fiona. Really I'm not.'

'But we must have a dinner at least,' Fiona said and looked up as Mrs Heatley appeared in the doorway of the study.

'Mrs Heatley, Ian's just told me that he turned twenty-one last week and that nobody knew! Isn't that the limit?' Fiona said with more than a tinge of outrage in her voice.

'Mr Ian! How could you not tell us?' Mrs Heatley scolded.

'I thought you'd make a fuss, and I'm just not comfortable with fusses,' he answered truthfully.

'Well, you'll not get away without a dinner at least, Mr Ian. With Leo and Judy, Fiona and her father, and perhaps Jim and Karen. Do you agree?'

'I suppose so,' Ian said, 'if it's not too much trouble.'

'Will you listen to him! "If it's not too much trouble!" Of course it's not too much trouble. It would be a pleasure. And we must have a cake,' said Mrs Heatley warmly.

'Don't go spreading the news around, will you Mrs H?' Ian pleaded. 'I was dead scared that if Mrs Donovan found out she'd want to do something big. It's only a birthday after all.'

'But it's your twenty-first, Ian. You should have told someone!' said Fiona. But what she meant to say was that he should have told *her*. Surely they were close enough for him to at least confide in her. She would have respected his wishes and not made a fuss. But Ian was Ian. He hated a fuss. He got his kicks from making things happen for other people.

# Chapter Twenty-nine

Ian sank into the reading chair in his study, relieved to have some time to himself. He glanced at the small pile of letters that sat unopened on his desk. Between the motel opening, his studies and the birthday dinner, he'd not had much time to keep up with his correspondence. He riffled through them – letters from the university, a couple of late birthday cards, a few bills – then one envelope in particular caught his eye. It was postmarked London, and Ian recognised the name of the prestigious legal firm that took care of his parents' estate. He opened it carefully, and found a covering letter along with a slim envelope, yellowed with age, and with his name handwritten on the front. He knew at once that it was his father's writing. Trembling, he released the flap, and took out the letter.

*My dearest boy,*
*If you receive this letter, two things will have happened. The first is that I shall have passed away and the second is that you will have turned twenty-one. This letter is a safety measure because I am well*

aware that your mother and I often find ourselves in areas that pose great risks. Africa, with its terrible diseases and wild animals, is not a safe place, and that's without considering the internecine conflicts and political upheavals that plague the continent.

You may have thought me harsh to advocate that you spend a period of your post-school career out in Australia. But I felt that you should have the opportunity to gain experience on an Australian property in case this kind of life appealed to you. I didn't support the idea of you gaining this experience with my brother Jack because, quite frankly, he wouldn't set you the right example. Jack is too fond of a good time. People say that your grandfather is too straight and autocratic, but if you go to him he'll look after you well.

You should know that I think you are a very special boy. Remember how you used to say that you wanted to be a scientist when you grew up? With your intelligence and patience I have no doubt that this is exactly what you are pursuing. However – and this is my most important message to you, Ian – although your mother and I have spent our whole careers in the zoological field, I want you to know that we had always planned to transfer our attention to medical research. Through our work in developing countries, we have become painfully aware that more work must be done to search for cures for diseases such as AIDS and malaria, which continue to decimate their populations. Philanthropic organisations provide huge amounts of money for research, but the death toll is still intolerably high.

If you receive this letter it will mean that we did not get the opportunity to see our hopes realised. I would urge you, then, *with all my heart, to consider working in this field, because you would have the opportunity to contribute very meaningfully to the amelioration of major health problems.*

*I want you to know what joy you brought us and how much we hated to be separated from you for even short periods. God bless you, my dear boy, in all that you do.*

*Dad*

Ian put the letter to one side and sat with his head between his hands. Tears flowed down his cheeks and soaked the papers on his desk. To receive a letter like this so many years after the deaths of his parents and grandfather was a tragic reminder of how much he had lost. It was also a reminder of the choice he would now have to make. Fiona McDonald had walked into his life two years before, and while he had buried himself in his study, his responsibilities at Kanimbla, and the Murrawee projects, it had become harder and harder to imagine a future without her. But now his father's letter had arrived, and while it reinforced his personal goal, the fact remained that he had commitments at Kanimbla and in Murrawee that he couldn't walk away from.

His grandfather had often told him that one of the worst things that a man could be was a quitter.

'You take on something, you finish it, Ian. You don't quit. A fellow that quits isn't a man at all. It might be tough to keep going, but when you're done you can hold your head high. Understand?'

'Yes Grandfather,' he'd answered. He hadn't really understood the significance of this advice. Not then. But he understood now. There were still things to be done, things he'd initiated that weren't quite finished. The motel units were done, but the swimming pools were not yet underway. There were changes to be made at Kanimbla, too. The shot was to take a different path – breed fewer, but even better rams and diversify as much as possible into the meat side of things. And that's just what they were doing, but it was still early days. There was a lot to do. All of these things flashed through his mind as he read his late father's letter.

There was also another disclosure in the same envelope. It explained that a safety-deposit box, the property of his mother, was now available to him, and that it contained some very valuable rings.

Mrs Heatley put her head around the study door to tell Ian that lunch would be ready in a few minutes. She noticed that he looked very strained and pale.

She glanced at the opened letters on his desk. 'What is it Mr Ian? Bad news?'

'It's a letter from my father. It was to be opened after my twenty-first birthday and only after his and my mother's deaths. And there was a note about my mother's jewellery. It's all a bit distressing, Mrs H.'

Mrs Heatley walked to Ian's desk and put a hand on his shoulder. It wasn't the kind of gesture a housekeeper would normally make, but she knew that Ian had no one else to offer sympathy or understanding.

Ian looked up at her, 'Thanks Mrs H. I thought I'd put my past behind me. But now it's all come back. Have I told you about the day the police came to tell me that my father and mother were dead? There was a clear blue sky, a beautiful African day, except that I no longer had my parents. There was only Kinshi to look after me until good old Britain took over and got me to my Grandfather in Cambridgeshire. I never saw Kinshi again.'

Ian stopped and gazed out the study window.

'You needed eyes in the back of your head, Mrs H. There were leopards, silent killers that could drop on you from trees. And lions, and a snake called the mamba. But my parents took me with them because they couldn't bear to be separated from me. I don't regret that.'

'So what does your father say, if you don't mind me asking?'

'He wanted me to do medicine and medical research. That's what I'd be doing if Uncle Jack hadn't left me Kanimbla,' said Ian with a sad smile.

'Forgive my impertinence, Mr Ian, but the impression you give is that you'd rather not have Kanimbla,' Mrs Heatley said.

'Kanimbla has complicated my life, Mrs H. The wool industry is going down the gurgler what with low prices, high costs, and dingoes – dingoes and drongos if you listen to Leigh Metcalfe. He doesn't mean that the growers are at fault, just that the administration has been less than efficient. Some of the blame has to be sheeted to agri-politicians who've kept too many fingers in the pie without agreeing on the best marketing strategy. I realise you don't think much of Leigh, Mrs H, but he's a clever man and he doesn't have an axe to grind where wool is concerned.'

'But what can you do?' asked Mrs Heatley.

'The easiest answer is to sell Kanimbla because I could get so much money for it that I wouldn't have to work again, but that would be unforgivable. I've got to try to keep the place viable.'

'But you're doing that aren't you?'

'I hope so.'

Mrs Heatley was determined to cheer Ian up. 'Would you like your lunch now? It's a very nice piece of corned beef.'

Ian looked up at his dear housekeeper. 'When things are bleak, there's always corned beef,' he joked.

'That's the shot,' she said. She could have hugged him.

# Chapter Thirty

'How about we take a couple of hours off and throw a line in the river?' Ian asked Leo Blake. They were in the shed looking through rams Jim Landers had set aside for a client.

'Sounds like a good plan, though towards evening would be best for that,' Leo replied. 'What about bait?'

'I'll get Ben to take some time off stable duties to dig some worms and we can use them and the lures,' Ian said. Leo knew that Ian rarely took time off to go fishing, and that when he did, he usually had something on his mind. He'd been looking pale lately – not his usual self – and Leo wondered what was bothering him.

'What say I take something to eat and we boil the billy and have afternoon smoko there?' Leo suggested kindly.

'That sounds fine to me,' Ian said. 'I'll pick you up about three.'

They drove down to what Ian referred to as Fiona's Picnic Ground. It was where he had taken her on the first occasion he had invited her to Kanimbla. Ian had brought in some extra log benches and tables, and these had made it a popular place for picnics. The river was reasonably deep here, and there had been some good-sized cod and yellow bellies, or golden perch, caught in this very hole. The river here was clean and there seemed to be plenty of food for fish.

A squadron of wood ducks lifted off the river as Ian nosed his utility into the picnic area. Leo set about getting a fire going in the rock fireplace and Ian took the rods and fishing baskets from the back of the vehicle and placed them against the trunk of a red gum. When the billy was boiling, Leo threw in some tea leaves and then went to the front of the utility for the picnic basket that held their smoko supplies. There was milk in a small bottle, a tube of condensed milk, sugar, scones and Anzac biscuits.

Leo put his mug of tea to cool on one of the rough log tables and took up his rod for a quick cast. He chewed an Anzac while he watched the line drift sideways with the slight current. Presently, he came and sat beside Ian. 'I know something has been gnawing at you lately, Ian. What's the problem?' he asked.

Ian hesitated, testing his line before answering.

'Mr Blake, I'm going to have to go back to England.'

Leo could never get over the fact that his boss refused to call him anything but 'Mr Blake', even though he had asked him repeatedly to call him by his Christian name. Ian had replied just as often that he was entitled to the respect he had earned.

'Well now, what's brought this on? I was beginning to

hope you might be staying, especially now that you and young Fiona seem to be such a team,' said Leo.

'Fiona's a good friend, Mr Blake. Because of the respect I have for you, it is important that you of all people understand why I have to go back to England,' Ian said. He took his father's letter from his shirt pocket and handed it to Leo. 'Maybe this will help,' he said.

Leo took his time to read the letter before he handed it back to Ian. 'I reckon your father must have been a fine man. But still, I don't understand why you need to go back to England. Couldn't you do medicine in Brisbane or Sydney?'

'There'd be too many distractions in Australia. I've got automatic entrée to Cambridge because of my pass at Harrow and I'm on the way to getting my science qualifications. I don't want any distractions. I need to go at this medical course full bore and hopefully, if I finish up with honours, I'll be offered the best opportunities in research. It's important I don't think about anything or anyone else, Mr Blake.'

'When you put it like that . . .' Leo began.

'By the way, I think you've got something on your line,' Ian interrupted. Leo's rod, which he had stuck in the bank while they were yarning, was headed for the river.

Leo retrieved it, and after a few minutes of effort landed a cod that he put at almost ten kilograms. 'Look at that! I'll split it with you,' he said to Ian.

Ian smiled half-heartedly, 'That would be great,' but he was clearly still distracted. 'Actually, Mr Blake, there was something else I wanted to talk to you about. I wanted to make sure that you didn't mind me offering Rhona the use of the flat at Lyndhurst.'

Ian paused, waiting for Leo's response. He had expected an argument, even an outburst, but was surprised when Leo said calmly, 'Don't worry about it. Judy has explained everything. Rhona's leaving for England next week. She's seemed a lot happier the last few times we've spoken.' Leo cleared his throat before continuing. 'Er . . . there's nothing between you and Rhona is there? I mean, because you're going back there and she is too?'

'Oh no, Mr Blake. Nothing like that. Rhona might not even decide to study at Cambridge, she's keeping her options open for the moment.'

'Well, I reckon it'll be good for her, Ian, and I can't thank you enough for helping her out in this way. She might be a bit of a rough diamond, but Rhona will do right by you and pay back anything she owes.'

'I have no doubt about that,' said Ian.

'Well Ian, now it's my turn to share some news. I know this probably won't come as a surprise given my age, but it's time I retired. I've got a block of ground over on the coast and I want a few years fishing before I become too useless to do anything. To be honest, I probably should have done this a few years ago, but I couldn't walk out and leave you in the lurch either.'

'Mr Blake, the last thing I want is for you to leave Kanimbla but I appreciate that there comes a day in every man's life when he realises it's time to let go. I'm very appreciative of the extra work you've done here. It's meant a lot to me,' Ian said.

'Actually, I was ready to retire when your uncle and aunt were killed. I couldn't run off after that happened. I felt I owed it to your family to wait a while. And then you arrived and somehow I didn't want to leave any more. Not for a while anyway. I wanted to see what decisions you'd make for Kanimbla and then you got started on Murrawee. There are things I want to do before I get any older. I've had fifty odd years in the bush and I reckon that's long enough to be in this game. Some of it hasn't been easy on Judy. She wants to have a trip or two and I reckon I owe her that.'

'I'm very grateful to you, Mr Blake. Kanimbla won't be the same without you. You've made a huge contribution and you've been an immense help to me personally. I would have found things a lot tougher if you hadn't been manager here or if you had resented a young bloke like me taking over,' Ian said.

'I never thought of you in that light, Ian.'

'I'm sure you didn't but some men would have felt threatened having someone like me being handed Kanimbla on a plate. You've been more than a manager, you've been a friend and that goes for Judy too,' he said.

'The men think a lot more of you than they ever did of your uncle, Ian,' Leo said.

Ian nodded and looked out over the river before he spoke again. He looked at Leo sitting there with his rod in his hand – big, solid, ever-reliable Leo, with his lifetime of knowledge of the bush and property management. The small lines beneath his eyes testified to thousands of hours spent in the open air, in hot and cold conditions and all the variations in between.

'I suppose some people will wonder why you left here but I doubt that anyone will forget you in a hurry,' Leo said.

'Better a has-been than a never-was,' Ian said with a grin. 'Now, I propose that we offer the manager's job to Jim Landers. I've watched Jim closely and I think he has the ability and commitment to manage this place. What do you think?' Ian asked.

'I think Jim would do a great job.'

'Good. Now, how would you feel about becoming a pastoral consultant?'

'Meaning what, exactly?' Leo raised his eyebrows questioningly.

'I'd pay you a retainer and you would report to me on the state of play. This would only involve you coming back here a couple of times a year. Jim's employment as manager would be contingent on him accepting your role. It's not a new idea. A lot of the big grazing companies employed pastoral inspectors. After three years Jim would be on his own. If he were to leave Kanimbla I might need to ask you to step in temporarily but we'll handle that if and when the situation arises. There's Peter Cross coming along nicely and he's potential assistant manager material. What do you say?' Ian asked.

'Well . . . I'm sure I could fit in a couple of trips a year,' Leo said.

'If Jim accepts the manager's job he'll move into your house. When you come back you'll stay at the homestead. If Mrs Heatley isn't here, you can bring Judy to look after you,' Ian said.

Leo nodded. He was impressed with Ian's plan. Ian was playing things safe appointing him to a watching brief. 'I think you'll have to say something to the men though.'

'I'll talk to them,' said Ian

'Right. Well we'd better get this fella back to Mrs Heatley then,' said Leo, sliding the big fish into the esky.

Ian felt much better having talked to Leo about his decision, but he was yet to tell Fiona, a conversation he knew would be the most difficult he'd ever had in his life.

# Chapter Thirty-one

Fiona was in the big kitchen setting the table. She was wearing a denim skirt and white blouse, protected by a pretty blue and white apron. Her soft curls fell around her face and she smiled happily as Ian entered the kitchen.

'Hi.'

'Hi to you too,' Ian managed to smile. Now that he was leaving, she seemed to him to be even more beautiful than ever and he felt a spasm of regret. He pushed it away.

'Would you like to have a drink before lunch? Dad's going to have a beer,' Fiona said.

'Thanks. I'll have a beer with him,' Ian said.

Ian joined Lachie on the verandah and they talked about the usual topics – the weather, the price of sheep, cattle and wool – before settling down to lunch. After the roast beef and four vegetables she produced fresh strawberries and cream – his favourites.

'That was a really terrific lunch, Fiona. I'm so full,' he smiled, and patted his stomach. 'Can we walk some of it off?'

'What a good idea,' she agreed.

They raced through the washing up and Lachie said he'd have a look at the paper while they were gone.

They walked up the track that led to the shearer's quarters and then took a branch track to the big wool shed. Fiona walked to the steps that led up to the wool room and he followed her. There were several bales of crutchings stacked against the back wall and Ian sat down on one of them. There was an unmistakeable smell of sheep in the shed and a less pungent smell of greasy wool.

Ian wrinkled his nose. 'I'll never forget the smell of an Australian wool shed.'

Fiona sat on a bale and looked sharply at him. 'What do you mean "forget"? What is it?'

He stared at her, trying to find the right words. 'I'm leaving Kanimbla, Fiona. I'm going back to England.'

'What? You're not serious!' Fiona jumped off the bale and stood before him, a lump rising in her throat. She wanted to run from the sudden pain she felt in her chest.

'I'm serious, Fiona.'

'But why, for God's sake?' she asked, holding back tears.

'It's just something I have to do,' he said simply. 'I have to finish my science degree and then I'll be doing medicine at Cambridge.'

She shook her head, eyes brimming, 'I just don't get it. How could you give all this up, all these people who love you, to spend years studying at university and hospitals? It's just . . . stupid.'

Ian saw her distress and felt moved to comfort her, but knew it would make her feel worse. 'If I'm completely honest, Fiona, I never really wanted Kanimbla, but I took it on to honour my father's and grandfather's wishes. It was the least I could do. I've given it a good go, but I feel it's my destiny to be a medical researcher. Science is in my blood.'

'But what's in your heart, Ian? What kind of person can give up everything for a microscope? I don't know who you are anymore,' Fiona said hotly.

'It's not for a microscope, Fiona,' he chided her gently. 'It's for people. Did you know that three thousand people die from malaria every *day* and that most of these are little children? Children like Billy . . . '

He let that fact sink in. 'And that women are twice as likely to die from malaria if they are pregnant? Each year there are over three-hundred million cases of malaria and that's five times as many as all of the cases of tuberculosis, AIDS, measles and leprosy put together.'

Fiona folded her arms, knowing that what he said made sense, but not wanting to hear it.

'There's a strong possibility that malaria could even be introduced to Australia,' Ian continued. 'What's more, scientists believe that global warming and other climatic changes could increase the areas prone to malaria.'

'But what can you do, as one man? There are heaps of brilliant researchers working in this field, Ian. Don't you think they'll come up with a cure for malaria long before you're even ready to begin work?' she asked fiercely.

'If everyone felt that way, we'd make no progress at all medically,' he said. 'Scientific opinion is that it may take twenty years to come up with an effective vaccine to prevent malaria. The available drugs are becoming less effective because of resistance to them. Malarial mosquitoes have been around for millions of years, so they're very hard to knock out. But there'll always be diseases that need controlling, and it's the combined knowledge of scientists everywhere that helps find solutions,' Ian said.

'Why couldn't you stay and research ways to rescue the wool industry? God knows it needs a saviour,' she said savagely.

He ignored her tone. 'Why don't you?'

'Me? And I suppose you'd offer to help me like you're helping Rhona Blake,' she said huffily.

'Of course I would,' he said softly. 'I'm only repaying the kindness of the Blakes by helping Rhona. I'd do the same and more for you.'

'Oh, Ian,' she sighed. She tried to imagine studying for years, weighing it against the life she had at Nelanji and the fact that she would have to leave her father whom she loved. She also thought of how very difficult it would be to get used to the idea of marrying someone other than Ian Richardson, someone second best. It was all too much for her and she fell against him and sobbed.

He held her tightly. 'Hush, Fiona. It's okay.' After a while he moved her gently away from him and stroked her arms. 'I'm so sorry. I know you think I've let you down.'

Fiona wiped her eyes and nodded.

'But looking back, I think I'd made my decision long before I came to Kanimbla. You've got to look at what your priorities are and get on with your life too, Fiona,' he said.

'Ian, can't you see? I simply want *you*. I've wanted you from the very first day I met you. If you stay at Kanimbla we could have a wonderful life together,' she said between sobs.

'Oh, Fiona,' he held her close again and could feel her lovely shape against him. 'You've been such a dear friend — my best mate. But I've got a huge amount of work to do. I couldn't do justice to a relationship with *any* woman. It's not just you. I'll be working all hours, sometimes at Cambridge's training hospital and when I finish there I'll be doing another course,' he said. When he felt her sobs ease he handed her his handkerchief and sat her down on the bale beside him.

'I must look awful,' she said.

'You always look pretty good to me,' he said.

She felt a stab of grief, and pushed it back down. 'But not good enough apparently,' she said as she dabbed at her eyes. How had she allowed herself to hope for all this time that he might one day return her love? She got up off the bale and walked across the room to the back door of the shed.

'Have you told Dad yet that you're leaving?' she said, with her back to Ian.

He got up off the bale and joined her. 'No, I wanted to tell you first.'

'Have you told anyone else?' she asked.

'Only Mr Blake.'

Fiona turned to him suddenly, 'Did it ever occur to you that you could have me and your medical research too?'

'Of course it did,' he said earnestly. 'I've agonised over that, but I'd be neglecting you for a lot of the time, and it would be unfair on you – perhaps even unbearable.'

'How do you know it would be unbearable for me?' Fiona almost snapped. 'You don't seem to have much faith in me. Haven't I supported you in everything you set in motion in Murrawee? Did I ever let you down? Did I? Well, if you think I'm an emotional lightweight then perhaps this is for the best.' Fiona turned away from Ian, quickly negotiated the woolshed steps and ran back to the homestead. She had intended to tell him what she might do in England, but Ian seemed to have made up his mind so what was the use? Was Rhona Blake the stumbling block? Surely not. And according to Judy, Ian was only helping her. It just didn't make sense.

Ian walked slowly back to see Lachie and explain his decision. Lachie's handshake was firm and sincere. He was disappointed when Ian told him he was leaving, but more worried about how his daughter would cope with the news.

As Ian drove off, a single tear slid down his cheek. He brushed it away quickly and took a deep breath. He was on a path now. It was going to be a long and arduous journey, and in his right-minded way, he couldn't see how it would be fair to expect Fiona to take it with him. How little he knew about women . . .

318

# Chapter Thirty-two

Ian Richardson sat on a log beside the river and looked down at the handsome black and tan dog at his feet. Of all the decisions he'd had to make at Kanimbla, sending Gus away was one of the toughest. This dog was in a class above the ordinary working dog, and Ian knew he'd never own another like him. His sadness at losing Gus was only partly eased by the fact that the dog would be going to Catriona, who would be sure to look after him very well.

He could have kept Gus longer, but was worried that a snake might get him before he could sire some pups for David MacLeod. Maybe Gus would sire some famous dogs of the future; he was such a great animal. What he could do with sheep was incredible.

Ian sat with the dog, stroking his head gently. 'You can't understand why I'm sending you away, but it's for the best, old mate. I'm going to be very busy. Some day I'll write about you and this place but that won't be for a long while.'

Jim and Karen Landers drove down to the homestead, bursting with curiosity. Ian had sent for them, and they figured it must be serious, as Leo and Judy were looking after Billy.

Ian sat them down in his study. 'Mr Blake is retiring and will be leaving here in a couple of months, though I'll be retaining his services as pastoral consultant. Now this may not come as too much of a surprise, but I'm also going to be leaving. I'll be going back to England about a week before Mr Blake and Judy leave Kanimbla.

'Do you mean you're leaving to live in England permanently?' Jim asked.

'That's right. But I'll be coming back from time to time. I'll be studying medicine at Cambridge. It was actually what I was planning to do before I inherited Kanimbla.'

'We'll all miss you,' said a suddenly tearful Karen.

'And I'll miss you, but I will come back and see you all again. And now for the best part of my news. Jim, I'm offering you the position of manager. If you accept, there'll be a substantial increase in your salary and you'll be living in the manager's house. You would be the boss of Kanimbla, though Mr Blake would occupy a kind of watching brief for three years. After that period, and all being well, you'd be on your own,' Ian said.

'You'll always be the boss of Kanimbla, Ian,' Jim said. He wasn't put out about Leo being retained because he knew that was par for the course with the big pastoral companies.

'I'll be the boss in absentia. You'll be the boss in residence. So do you want the job? Or do you need more time to think it over?' Ian asked.

'No, I don't need time to think it over. I'll accept it and thank you for offering it to me,' Jim said.

Ian looked at Karen who, he noticed, had suddenly become very quiet. 'Are you happy about Jim's decision?'

'Yes, fine. We figured that when you made Jim assistant manager to Mr Blake that you'd probably eventually offer him the manager's job,' Karen said.

'But are you sure you're okay with this? I had the feeling that you didn't really like being here,' Ian pointed out.

Karen was embarrassed by Ian's uncharacteristic directness, but rationalised that he was probably under a lot of stress.

'Jim being manager makes a big difference. I'll have to do more entertaining when Leo and Judy leave,' she said, 'which means more of a social life, if not a challenge.'

'Ah, yes. We'll have a look at the manager's residence and see if it needs any repairs or renovations before you move in,' Ian said kindly.

'One more thing, Jim. I was hoping you might keep an eye on the sheepdog trials in Murrawee. Fiona has been convenor of the trials and I'd like you to give her any help she needs in the way of sheep and manpower. Would that be agreeable to you?'

'No problem, Ian,' Jim said.

'We'll talk again over the next few days. You're pretty good on the computer so we can keep in touch by email and fax and I'll talk to you from time to time,' Ian said.

Karen kissed Ian on the cheek before she and Jim went down the steps of the front verandah. 'Thank you,' she said. 'For this and for everything else you've done for us since you came here.'

'Ability and good service should be rewarded,' said Ian. 'People like you and Jim are the future of rural Australia.'

Ian found Leigh working at his long table on his covered front verandah. The table was littered with dozens of sheets of paper, some of which contained only a few lines of writing. But it was Leigh's appearance that stopped Ian in his tracks. One eye was half-closed and the skin around it varied between black and yellow while both lips were badly swollen and the top lip was cut.

'Did he catch up with you?' Ian asked.

'Who?'

'Alec Claydon.'

'How did you know?' Leigh asked.

'Let's call it an educated guess,' Ian said.

'Jesus, he hits hard,' Leigh mumbled through his swollen lips.

'So what's the upshot?' Ian asked.

'I'll just have to lay low for a while, I guess.'

'Perhaps a long while,' Ian suggested.

'Yeah. Well maybe you're right,' admitted Leigh.

'Judy says Alec and Trish became a lot closer after her

accident. She's taken up pottery and been doing some lovely pieces featuring birds. Luke could sell some of them at the park. Tourists might like to take something away,' said Ian.

'I'll mention it to him when I see him next,' said Leigh.

'That might be a good way to make amends to the Claydons,' said Ian. Leigh shot him a sideways look, but let the comment slide.

'So what are you working on now?' Ian asked as he sat down beside the table. 'It looks impressive,' he said.

'I'm writing a script for a musical about Thunderbolt.'

Ian raised an eyebrow.

'He was a bushranger who held up coaches in northern New South Wales, though he ranged over a wide area. His real name was Fred Ward. He was killed near Uralla by a police constable who went on to become Commissioner of Police. Funny thing, there's someone still putting flowers on Ward's grave one hundred and twenty-odd years after he was killed. There's dozens of stories about Thunderbolt. He was a great horseman and he never killed anyone. He mostly rode the rough country of the Great Dividing Range. He got down as far as Moonan Flat in the Scone district. "Only the crows know where he goes." Anyway, what brings you to this house of iniquity?'

'I've come to tell you that I'll be leaving Kanimbla in a few weeks. I'm going back to Britain and Cambridge. I didn't want you to hear the news second-hand,' Ian said.

Leigh put down his pen and gave Ian a concerned look. Eventually he said, 'It's a wonder you lasted this long!' and his face broke into grin. 'Well, good luck to you. How did they take it down at headquarters?'

'I believe surprised would be an understatement. I doubt that anyone really understands how much work I've got in front of me, you excluded,' Ian said. 'Jim will be taking over when Leo retires.'

'At least Jim Landers knows his way around a computer and is a good sheepman. Yeah, I reckon Jim might be all right,' Leigh conceded.

'I'll try and get back here once a year if I can,' Ian said.

'I suppose you'll end up a blooming Florey and win a Nobel prize,' Leigh joked.

'That's the last thing on my mind right now. I just want to get through so that I can make it into a top research establishment,' Ian said.

'Well, I'll miss you. I never thought I'd say that about another bloke. What you've got going in Murrawee is bloody amazing. If I was wearing a hat I'd take it off to you, Ian,' Leigh smiled broadly. 'Feel like a drink o' tea? And I made a fresh damper this morning. How about a bit of that and some cockie's joy?'

'Why not. It might be the last I'll have for a very long time.'

'You should take a camp oven back with you and show your Pommy mates how to bake a damper. Probably go over well.'

'Yes, it probably would,' Ian agreed, taking a piece and biting into it.

'Could be a good sideline for you . . . importing camp ovens, I mean. Ah, well, Australia's loss is England's gain,' Leigh said.

'I'll be having a small function. It's a farewell for the Blakes, mainly, and for me, I suppose. I'd like you to come if you could see your way clear to join us,' Ian said.

'I'll have a think about it. They're decent enough people but they're all dead from the neck up. The only Shelley they've ever heard of is the one under the table there,' Leigh said.

'It's up to you. So will you stay on here?' Ian asked.

'You mean forever? God knows. I like it here and I probably wouldn't find anywhere better. Is the damper okay?'

'Terrific,' Ian acknowledged. 'Actually, there's another piece of news that will interest you.'

'Don't tell me you got Fiona McDonald in the sack with you.'

'No, Leigh. Sorry to disappoint you. Rhona Blake has gone to England too,' Ian said.

'She's what?' Leigh asked quickly.

'Rhona's thinking of studying at Cambridge. She came to see me in a bit of a mess. Her last boyfriend left her after she'd loaned him a great deal of money. She told me she needed a change.'

'Well, I'll be blowed. You and Rhona haven't been playing up, have you?'

'You sound like a cracked record, Leigh,' said Ian with genuine annoyance. 'Just because I help a woman doesn't mean I'm sleeping with her. She's Mr Blake's daughter and she needs a hand. I'll help her with a place to stay, but the rest will be up to her.'

'A bit touchy today, aren't we?' Leigh smiled.

Ian sighed, 'I guess it hasn't been an easy decision to leave.'

'I'm sure it hasn't, and I'm sorry to have made light of it before. How has Fiona taken it?' said Leigh.

Ian looked at Leigh with surprise. Despite his friend's claim to preferring his own company, he was remarkably astute about other people. He'd known from the day Fiona visited Top River with Ian that there was something special between the two of them, and that Fiona was not the kind of girl to give up easily.

'She hasn't taken it too well. But Fiona is a friend, Leigh. That's all she is. And I've never led her to believe otherwise.'

'Never?'

'We kissed once, early on, but I felt it wasn't right, especially as I wasn't sure I was going to stay,' Ian said.

'Well I hope you don't regret not making her more than a friend,' Leigh said.

'I'll have to take it on the chin,' Ian said. 'In the meantime I just want you to know how much I've enjoyed our friendship and that I'll think about you, and Shelley, and this place quite a lot when I'm back in England.'

'Especially when you've got snow everywhere and a wind that would freeze your balls,' Leigh laughed.

'Especially then,' Ian agreed.

'I'll expect great things of you,' the writer said.

Ian scribbled down his English address on a page of his small notebook, tore it out and handed it to Leigh. 'I hope you'll send me anything you have published. The best of luck with Thunderbolt,' he said.

'Thanks. We'll be talking again before you leave?'

'Of course.'

They walked out to Ian's utility and shook hands. 'Be seeing you,' said Leigh as Ian started the engine. He watched as the ute disappeared out of sight, the sound of its engine growing fainter and fainter until Leigh could hear only the screeching of the white cockatoos in the river gums. He shook his head and went back to the litter on his table.

# Chapter Thirty-three

Ian was very pleased that he had entrusted Gerald and Ted with specific fact-finding missions. They had both done a very good job collecting the information that was needed to set Kanimbla on its new path, and showed a lot of enthusiasm for their new roles. Consequently Ian had been able to formulate, in best marketing fashion, five- and ten-year plans for the property. A few weeks before he was due to leave, he called his core staff together for a final strategy meeting. Leo Blake was there, as were Jim Landers and the jackaroos.

'As you may have heard, Mr Blake will be retiring soon and Jim Landers will become manager. Fortunately we won't be saying goodbye to Mr Blake for good, as he's agreed to act as my pastoral adviser for the next three years and will be coming back here two or three times a year.

'Nothing I can say would be adequate to convey my appreciation for the job Mr Blake has done at Kanimbla. We'll be having a send-off for Mr and Mrs Blake and I'll say more on that occasion.

'As for Kanimbla's future, my aim is obviously to keep the operation viable. The merino stud will be retained, albeit a smaller version. There will be an even bigger commitment to quality and Kanimbla sheep will be widely shown. Only when we've won the Stonehaven Cup will I admit that we've made some progress in that area,' Ian said with a smile.

'We'll be making a big push towards developing sheep that can be shorn every eight months giving us three shearings in two years. This is a factor we'll be promoting for our rams and a reason for woolgrowers to stay with merinos. And, if all goes according to plan, I'm hoping we can stage an annual on-property sheep sale.

'We'll be classing off a line of merino ewes to mate with Dohne rams and the ewe portion of this first cross drop will be mated to prime lamb sires. We'll also be looking to lot feed a line of wether lambs. I've got a couple of Brisbane butchers interested so we'll give it a go. This will entail us erecting a couple of big shelter sheds with feed and water troughs. As you know, Norm's son is interested in running the old butcher's shop. We could put our own lambs and beef through the shop. Maybe install a small feedlot here for steers and advertise grain-fed beef.

'There'll also be an accelerated farming program to grow oats, lucerne, corn and forage sorghum and we'll be taking up all the water we're allowed. We'll also be laying down a lot of silage, principally for the stud cows.

'The last announcement I'll make today is that I'll be leaving Kanimbla to return to Britain shortly before Mr and

Mrs Blake depart.' He could see that this had stunned the three younger men because Leo and Jim had not thought it their place to inform them yet.

Although there had been rumours in Ian's early days that he might return to Britain, as time passed they had come to believe that he was going to stay. This view was reinforced when their boss began his push to do something for Murrawee. Then there had been Ian's close friendship with the beautiful Fiona McDonald. It didn't make sense.

'You mean for good?' Gerald Bradshaw exclaimed.

'I'll be coming back from time to time. Hopefully, once a year,' Ian said.

'But we all thought you'd be staying,' Gerald said.

'Life is a matter of priorities, Gerald. There are things I need to do and Britain is where I want to do them. Kanimbla will be in good hands, and Mr Blake and Jim will keep me informed about everything. You've got some interesting projects and you don't need me here to do them.'

'Can you tell us what you're going to do?' Ted Beecham asked.

'Medicine, Ted.'

'You mean to be a doctor?'

'Not the kind of doctor you're thinking of. Ultimately I'll be aiming to do research work,' Ian replied.

'That'll involve a lot of study, won't it?' Ted asked.

'A huge amount. I've only done the equivalent of three years of one course, and there are at least six more years to go. That's why I can't have any distractions,' Ian said.

Jim Landers came to Ian's rescue. 'Well, we wish you well, Ian. Karen and I are very thankful for all that you've done for us and Billy. I think I can speak for the whole team and say that we'll miss you.'

Every man present realised that Kanimbla would not be the same without Ian. He had breathed life into the place. The great homestead, temporarily enlivened by Ian's presence, would be empty again and who could say when a Richardson would return to it.

A week later and not many days before Ian Richardson was due to leave Kanimbla, Leigh Metcalfe came back from checking his getter-guns to find an envelope marked 'Leigh' on his table. He picked it up and ripped it open. There were two sheets of paper. One was a copy of a letter to Ian Richardson's legal firm authorising them to take steps to excise forty hectares, with house thereon, from the Top River section of Kanimbla Station, and to transfer the said forty hectares to the ownership of Leigh Metcalfe.

The second sheet contained a brief note.

*Dear Leigh*
*I hope the enclosed instructions to my lawyers will convince you to stay where you are. I can't imagine anyone else taking your place. It's perfect for you and Shelley.*
*Very best wishes*
*Ian Richardson*

Leigh held the two sheets of paper in his hand and looked eastwards towards Kanimbla and the road Ian would be travelling.

'That son of a gun has made me a bloody landowner, Shelley!' he shouted.

## Chapter Thirty-four

The send-off was really for Leo and Judy Blake, though everyone knew that Ian Richardson would actually be leaving for Britain a week before them. It was held in the shearers' quarters and there was food and drink galore – big juicy steaks, chops, sausages, onions and salad and a keg of beer. And Leigh Metcalfe came too – he figured it was the least he could do given Ian's generous gift.

After everyone had finished eating, Ian Richardson asked them to be quiet because he had something to say. 'As you all know,' he began, 'Mr and Mrs Blake are leaving here after twenty-five years. It gives me great pleasure to present this cheque in recognition of their long service. I know you'll all join with me in wishing them a long and happy retirement,' Ian paused until the noise of cheering and clinking glasses subsided.

'We pondered long and hard about what to give you as a farewell present and finally decided on something you'll be sure to find useful,' Ian continued, and on cue, Peter, Ted and Gerald pushed a spanking new tinny and outboard from around the back of the quarters.

'Speech, speech,' the three young blokes chanted.

Leo was overcome with emotion. 'I don't know what to say. I'm not a great one for speeches.' Leo paused to regain his composure. 'Ian, I just want to say that Judy and I would never have stayed as long as we did if you hadn't come to Kanimbla. It's been a real pleasure working with you, even though you've spent a lot of your time looking down a microscope!' This comment induced a burst of laughter. 'I'd like to thank all my loyal staff for their dedication and hard work. Their input makes a job like mine a shoe-in.'

'Thank you, Mr Blake. I'm not here to steal your thunder. This is your night. Three cheers for Leo! Hip hip . . .'

'Hang on, hang on!' Leigh Metcalfe stood on a chair and interrupted Ian.

'Look, I know this is Leo's night, but I've got something to say and I'm going to borrow it from *The Scarlet Pimpernel*.'

'Who?' Jack Greer muttered to nobody in particular.

*'They seek him here, they seek him there,*
*Those westerners seek him everywhere.*
*Is he in Oz with the heat and the flies?*
*Or back in the Old Dart scoffing pork pies?*
*Half Pommy, half Aussie, he burns in the sun,*
*That damned elusive Richardson!'*

Loud cheering and clapping erupted from the group. Leigh got down from the chair and walked over to Ian, 'Thanks for the house and land,' he said quietly. 'That's a mighty big gift and I can't see that I'm worth it.'

'It's not all that much in the overall scheme of things. You've been a big help to me, Leigh. I'll sleep a lot easier knowing you and Shelley are at Top River,' Ian said.

Later, after several beers, and much laughing and joking, Leo took Ian aside.

'I got a phone call from Rhona today,' said Leo.

'How is she?' asked Ian.

'Well, she's settled in well – she's very happy,' Leo smiled. 'Of course, Judy's a bit upset that she didn't get a proper send-off, but you know Rhona. She just took off when she felt the urge.'

'Well that's brilliant news, Leo,' said Ian.

'I thought you might have heard from her by now yourself,' suggested Leo.

'I'm sure I will in time,' said Ian. 'I'd given her all the contact information so there was no need for her to make any formal arrangements with me.'

Leo patted Ian heartily on the back, 'Looks like we need another keg,' he said as he wandered off.

Needless to say the party went on for a long time and there were some sore heads next morning.

If Ian had imagined he would be able to slip away with only a Kanimbla staff do, he was very much mistaken – the people of Murrawee had organised a party the likes of which had never before been seen in the district. Of course, Helen Donovan had been at the helm of the organising committee, and with the help of Mrs Heatley, Judy, Trish, Karen and a few other faithfuls, had managed to keep it a complete surprise. Her only disappointment was that she could not convince Fiona to come. Fiona had claimed she was ill, but Helen knew that this was probably a ruse.

It had been hoped to hold the send-off at the bird park but the amenities were inadequate for such a gathering, so it was transferred to the oval. Hundreds turned up and the motel was fully occupied for the first time.

Ian seemed overwhelmed by the tributes paid to him. He was even more overwhelmed when he was presented with a top-notch microscope (Leigh Metcalfe's idea) even grander than his own.

When Ian stood in front of the crowd to thank them, there was absolute silence on the oval.

'Thanks to each and every one of you for this night. I've made some wonderful friends here and am leaving part of my heart in this district. There's a saying that every person marches to the beat of a different drum. I believe that my destiny lies in science. I hope that doesn't sound pompous or pretentious. It's just something I feel very strongly about – so strongly that it pulls me away from this life at Kanimbla.

'The gift couldn't be more appropriate; thank you. I didn't expect it or this night, and I'm touched to the point of embarrassment that you've made so much of what I've done.

'The most amazing thing of all is that you dinky-di Australians should do this for a half-baked Aussie, though, to my credit, I did have an Australian mother. This, I understand, bestows on one the right to play cricket for Australia *or* England!'

There was laughter and cheering.

'Thank you again for this night. I'll never forget it.'

That night was the first in Ian's life in which he really let loose. He even drank enough to dance with Judy Blake and Helen Donovan, but despite all the rowdy merriment and fun, despite all the declarations of friendship and promises to catch up in the future, he felt a kind of emptiness, as if there was something, or rather someone, missing.

The next morning broke clear, warm and cloudless. The birds were singing in the garden and in the trees above the river as Ian sat with Mrs Heatley.

'I'll miss sitting here and hearing so many bird calls,' Ian said.

'Do you have to go, Mr Ian?' Mrs Heatley asked.

Ian nodded and wondered again how he could explain why he had to leave. 'Yes, I have to go, Mrs H,' he said gently.

'I don't understand why. You've got so much to keep you here. The men think you're great, and the new things you've initiated will guarantee them their jobs for some time at least. And there's a certain young woman not far away who thinks you're wonderful. I realise it's not my place to question your decisions, but I must say that I think it very strange that you should want to leave. I must also say that I'll miss you very much, Mr Ian,' Mrs Heatley said.

'I shall miss you, too, Mrs Heatley. You've set me on the right path about a lot of things.'

'If you don't mind me saying, Fiona seems very upset about you leaving,' Mrs Heatley said. 'We all tried to get her to come to the party, but she said she couldn't bear it.'

Ian hesitated before answering. 'I am sorry about that, but really, there's never been anything between us except friendship. I'm sure Fiona will find contentment and happiness. Nelanji will be hers some day, and she'll find a nice young man whose heart is with the land.'

'If you don't mind me saying, Fiona has always thought you were that young man, Mr Ian.'

Ian looked away. First Judy, then Leigh and now Mrs H. How many more people were going to give him a hard time about Fiona? With so many people questioning his decision, he began to wonder if he had been really honest with himself. Had he really avoided a relationship with Fiona because he was afraid of letting her down? Or was he afraid of something else?

Mrs Heatley interrupted his reverie. 'I suppose I'll go back to live in Murrawee now that you're leaving.'

'Oh no, Mrs H. If you'd like to stay here instead of going back to live in Murrawee, you are quite welcome to do so. But if you decide to live in the township, I'd like to pay you to come out here for a day a week to keep the place in order. Mr Blake will be returning a couple of times a year for the next three years and he'll be staying in the homestead. He'll contact you and let you know his movements. Judy may or may not accompany him. If you're happy with that arrangement, you can let Jim Landers know, as he'll have charge of the cheque book in future,' Ian said.

'When will you come back, Mr Ian?' she asked.

'I'll try and come back from time to time. It will depend on university vacations and how much cramming I'll have to do. The university year is from October to June but they have summer schools and at this stage I don't know if I'll be involved in any of those,' Ian said.

There was so much she wanted to tell him. Ian had filled a great hole in her life and had become almost like a son.

'I won't forget you, Mrs H. You know, you could always come over and stay at Lyndhurst and have an inexpensive holiday,' he said with a smile.

'I had once thought of going to Britain. I wanted to see the Lake District and parts of Scotland. Oh, and some places in Europe,' she said.

'Well, there you are. You could make Lyndhurst your base while you make those trips,' Ian said.

'You're very generous, Mr Ian,' she said.

'There's a quid pro quo. You might find time to cook me some of your lovely meals,' he said.

'So I might,' she said, her voice breaking a little.

Later that day, Ian spent a while saying goodbye to each of his men. They all seemed genuinely sorry to see him go, as much as he could ascertain from their laconic Aussie manner. He asked Ben to take good care of his horses and to ride them occasionally.

The night before he left, Ian invited Leo and Judy Blake, Jim and Karen Landers and Lachie and Fiona McDonald for a meal at Kanimbla. And of course Billy Landers came too. The little boy was very cut up about Ian's departure. The reasons were beyond his boyish comprehension.

Fiona was still very upset and had, at first, contemplated refusing to attend. She could be excused for missing the party, seeing it was such a big, public event. However, refusing a private invitation to someone's home would be a breach of good manners and would reflect badly on her father too. She loved her father dearly and simply couldn't do that to him. And deep down, as upset as she was, she didn't want Ian to leave with a poor opinion of her.

It had been a very restrained gathering. Lachie and Leo had talked bush generalities and Judy and Karen had talked about houses and furnishings. Fiona picked at her food and barely spoke. Judy's heart went out to the poor girl – she knew what an effort it was for her to be there. Ian also noticed Fiona's downcast demeanour, but was embroiled in discussions about Kanimbla's future with Jim and Leo. Billy Landers managed to put away three lots of strawberry ice-cream before Karen stopped a further foray.

'Is it too cold for ice-cream in England?' Billy asked Ian.

'It isn't cold all the time, Billy. We do get lots of warm days. People play cricket in summer. Some of the grounds are quite beautiful, very green and people sit on canvas chairs until late in the evening because it doesn't get dark for ages,' Ian told him.

But the overall mood was subdued because each person realised that it would probably be the last time they would all meet for dinner at Kanimbla. Ian would soon be in England and Leo and Judy Blake would be on the coast. Fiona didn't know what she'd be doing because Ian's departure would turn her world upside down. She had the weird thought that Ian's sojourn at Kanimbla could be likened to the appearance of a shooting star that flashed across the sky and then disappeared.

Eventually, Lachie couldn't bear seeing his daughter's grief for a moment longer, and he made his excuses for an early departure. The Blakes and Landers followed soon after, but not before making arrangements for taking Ian to the bus depot.

After they left, Ian sat by himself on the verandah. He would be returning to England in the Northern Hemisphere's autumn, when so many trees were aflame with colour. The gentle transitions between western Queensland's seasons would be replaced by sharply defined harbingers of winter and summer. One early settler to Australia had written home to England to say that everything was 'upside down'. The country that had once been regarded as a giant jail for Britain's unwanted citizens was now the land of promise for people of just about every country in the world. If you wanted blue skies, magnificent beaches and a laid-back lifestyle, Australia was your country. Yet here he was, turning his back on all that and more.

Ian walked inside to his study. Mrs Heatley had left a few

papers for him to sort out before he left. He sighed as he sat down to leaf through them. One was an airmail letter from the UK. He opened it carefully.

*Dear Ian*

*I hope this letter reaches you in time. I didn't want to email you – it's so impersonal, and I didn't want to risk leaving a garbled message on your answering machine. I want to thank you again for your kindness and generosity in allowing me to stay at Lyndhurst. If you hadn't offered to help me when you did, I don't know how much lower I would have sunk.*

*And now I wanted you to be the first to hear my good news. I've met the loveliest man, Robbie, and am moving to Edinburgh. I know it sounds all too fast and too good to be true, but it feels so right. He lectures in philosophy at the university and is certain I will be able to find work there. It'll be work I'm already doing, so I'll have to put any ideas of further study on hold – at least for the moment. I'm so in love, he's just the most incredible man I've ever met (well the most incredible man who was my age!).*

*And do you know what the most exciting part is? Robbie has introduced me to philosophy, and I know I sound like a giggly teenager, but I'm utterly inspired. I've been reading the work of all sorts of amazing writers and thinkers and there's one I just have to share with you. His name is Rainer Maria Rilke, and this is probably his most famous quote:*

'For one human being to love another: that is perhaps the most difficult of our tasks; the ultimate, the last test and proof, the work for which all other work is but a preparation.'

*When I read it, it got me thinking about my life, and how I'd always seemed to choose men who had let me down – men who had failed the ultimate task that Rilke speaks about. And then I thought about you, Ian, and how hard you have been trying to avoid love. Mum told me what has been happening with you and Fiona, and I just hope you've decided to let her into your heart. I'm glad I let beautiful Robbie into mine.*

*Better go now,*
*Love and a big hug*
*Rhona*

Ian put the letter down and shook his head. He sincerely hoped that this time Rhona had met a genuinely decent man. He'd half-hoped that Rhona might move into the sciences – perhaps even study microbiology. She had a great mind and could make a valuable contribution. For the moment, however, she had decided to put love first, and although he wished her well, he began to wonder about his own decision.

He felt suddenly hot – no, anxious, even confused. He stood up, and began pacing in his study. All tiredness left him – it would be a long night.

## Chapter Thirty-five

It was the morning of Ian Richardson's departure. Lachie McDonald was up making his usual early-morning cup of tea. Fiona was still in bed – while she didn't rise as early as her father (unless it was shearing, crutching or lamb-marking time), she seldom stayed in bed after seven.

Lachie heard a car drive up their track and stop at the back gate. When he heard the click of the gate, he looked through the kitchen window and saw Ian Richardson walking up the path. All his instincts told him that Ian hadn't come to see him. He walked quickly to Fiona's bedroom and woke her.

'Ian Richardson has just arrived. You'd better throw on a gown,' Lachie told her.

Fiona looked at her watch. Five past six. Ian had never before arrived at such an hour. But of course he was leaving today. What did he want? Her curiosity got the better of her and she ran for the bathroom, washed her face, combed her hair and added a smear of lipstick.

Ian was standing in the kitchen when she walked in. Lachie had diplomatically departed.

344

'Ian, is anything wrong?' Fiona asked.

'No, there's nothing wrong except that I don't have much time. Fiona, I want you to come to England. Not today but as soon as you can arrange it. I've been a complete fool. I thought it wouldn't be fair to ask you because I'd be so occupied, but Judy said that if you love me you wouldn't mind any of that,' Ian said in a rush.

Fiona took a step backwards and stammered, 'But . . . why? What changed your mind?'

'I thought about the reality of leaving, and how I might never see you again. I don't want to spend my life without you, Fiona. I'd like you to come over and see if you can bear it,' he said.

'You mean live together?' she asked.

'Not the way you probably think. Lyndhurst is a very big house. You could have your own rooms. But we'd be together. You could do a uni course if that's what you'd like. Later, if you think it's not all too much for you, we could get married,' he said.

Fiona clapped her hand over her mouth as if stifling a cry. 'Oh Ian,' she managed to choke out before he encircled her in a gentle embrace and kissed her tenderly.

'Will you come?' he asked.

'Yes, of course I'll come, but I won't be able to leave straight away. I'll come as soon as I can organise things here. You're a duffer for being such a slow coach,' she said. 'Why didn't you tell me all this when we were in the woolshed? Surely you could see how I felt about you?'

Myriad thoughts flashed through Fiona's mind — the experiences they could have shared, and now there was no time.

'I'm not that big a dumbcluck, Fiona! If I'd known I was staying at Kanimbla, I would have asked you long ago. But I'm going to be devoted to medical research for such a long time, it seemed unfair to expect you to settle for so little time together. Then there was Lachie here all on his own and, well, you seem so cut out for a life on the land. You've got your horses and your dogs . . .' Ian trailed off.

'You didn't consider that I just might be cut out for a life with you? Women are very adaptable, Ian,' she said with glowing eyes.

'That seemed too much to hope for,' said Ian.

'But why? Haven't we always got on well? Have we ever argued? Did you ever hear of me going anywhere with another man? You're usually so bright, Ian. How could you not know how I felt about you?'

'I guess I was afraid that you'd find it all too hard and you'd end up leaving me,' Ian said quietly.

'Oh, darling! I'll never leave you,' said Fiona and they held each other for a long time.

'I'm sorry I've been so slow. Leigh told me I was crazy to keep you at arm's length,' Ian said.

'I'll bet that's not all he said,' Fiona laughed.

'Granted,' Ian said and laughed too.

'So where does Rhona Blake fit into your plans? I can't imagine living in the same house as Rhona. People might imagine you've got a harem at Lyndhurst,' Fiona smiled.

'You don't have to worry about Rhona, darling. She's met a halfway decent bloke and moved to Edinburgh with him. Between you and me, I don't think she's planning to join me in the research work,' said Ian.

'If you're looking for a research partner, why can't it be me? I don't think I'd want to do medicine even if I could get into Cambridge, but I could do a science degree. That way we'd be studying together for some of the time. I got a distinction in science, so there's every chance I'd be accepted. What do you think?' she asked.

'I'm floating!' Ian grabbed Fiona around the waist and danced her around the kitchen.

'Hang on!' Fiona laughed, breathless from the dancing. 'Haven't you got a coach to catch? We'd better tell Dad.'

They found Lachie on the back verandah trying to appear as if he'd been reading the newspaper. The fact that the paper was upside down made that a virtual impossibility, suggesting he'd been more interested in what had been discussed in the kitchen.

'Ian's got something to tell you, Dad,' Fiona said, and flashed her father a smile.

'Fiona and I, well, we're sort of engaged, Mr Mac. I want Fiona to come to England to see if she'll be able to tolerate the lifestyle. I don't want her to commit to marriage until she knows what she'll be letting herself in for. If it suits her, we'll get married,' Ian said.

'You mean you'll live together first? This isn't how I'd expect you to behave, Ian,' Lachie said sharply.

'No, I don't mean that. Fiona can have her own rooms. Lyndhurst is a very big place. I've suggested that perhaps Fiona could study. But we'd be together and we'd be able to see each other,' Ian said.

The tall grazier looked at his daughter and what he saw on her face told him all he needed to know. 'It's up to you, Fiona,' he said.

'I've told Ian that I'll go to him. Not immediately, but when we get everything sorted out here,' Fiona said.

Lachie stood up and held out his hand. 'Congratulations, Ian. It looks like I've got myself a future son-in-law.'

Fiona kissed her father warmly before taking Ian's hand. 'Would you like me to cook you some breakfast?'

'That would have been lovely, Fiona, but I told Mrs Heatley I'd be back for an eight o'clock breakfast,' he said.

'Did you tell her where you were going?' Fiona asked.

'Yes, but I didn't say why. She probably imagines I'm saying goodbye to you,' he said.

'Which you are,' she said with a laugh.

'But not for long, I hope. Now I'd better rush. Pack plenty of warm clothes when you come over Fiona,' he said. 'I'll arrange your ticket as soon as you're ready.'

Lachie smiled as they walked down the path hand in hand. He reckoned that his daughter's future was assured. Fiona was made of good stuff and there was no way she'd bail out if the going got a bit tough. A pity that Ian had left it to the last minute to make his feelings known – it would have been great to organise an engagement party for them.

Fiona watched the Mercedes until it was out of sight and then she walked back up the path to where her father stood on the verandah. 'I'm sorry, Dad. I couldn't say I wouldn't go,' she said.

'Of course you couldn't,' he agreed. 'Blokes like Ian Richardson don't grow on trees.'

'I've wanted to be with him since the first time we met,' she said. 'I knew no other boy would do.'

Lachie looked past her to the garden his late wife had loved so much. 'I think your mother would be very happy about this, Fiona.'

'I think so too, Dad,' she said and kissed her father's rough cheek affectionately.

# Chapter Thirty-six

Mrs Heatley clucked about Ian as he loaded his luggage into the Mercedes, worrying that he wouldn't be warm enough when he got to London.

'Don't worry, Mrs H. I've got enough clothes to see me through the first few days. I'll buy some warmer ones when I get there,' Ian told her.

'And what about Fiona?' she continued. 'Is she coming to see you off?'

'I doubt it, Mrs H. We've said our goodbyes. She has a lot to get sorted out.'

Mrs Heatley had seen the happiness in Ian's face when he returned from his 'drive' that morning and immediately surmised the truth. She was so thrilled that Fiona would be joining him in England that she'd forgotten her usual good manners and given him the biggest hug.

Ian drove with Leo beside him in the front seat and Judy and Mrs Heatley in the back. The Landers were following behind them. Ian had been surprised when Mrs Heatley told him she wanted to come along to see him off. She said she wasn't going to forego that pleasure just because Leigh Met-calfe would be there. She also packed a basket of food and utensils because, as she told Ian, Leigh was a 'rough sort of cook'. The fact that he could make a damper to die for didn't elevate him in her eyes one little bit.

Leo had offered to drive Ian all the way to Sydney airport, but Ian had said he wouldn't hear of him doing any such thing. Jim Landers had also offered to fly him to Brisbane or Sydney or any place he wished to go, and Ian had replied that he wouldn't fly in a small plane for love or money.

'I'll return to Sydney the way I came – by coach. I like them, they're very comfortable. I've got a lot to think about and travelling in a coach will give me the time to do just that.'

When they had left Kanimbla and were on the road in to Murrawee, Ian looked across at Leo and grinned. 'Well, Leo, this is the last trip to Murrawee for a while.'

'After all this time you finally call me Leo!' Leo exclaimed with an answering grin.

'I'm an absentee owner from this point on and a medical student to boot. Or almost,' Ian said.

When they arrived at the park, the atmosphere was far from subdued. Leigh had gone in quite early in his utility as he and Luke wanted to get the fire going so the damper would cook nicely in the camp oven. He and Luke had the billy boiling and the camp oven covered with embers. Mrs Heatley put a tablecloth on one of the tables and set out butter and jam and golden syrup and knives. Helen

Donovan had badly wanted to come too but the coach's passengers stopped at the store for lunch and she had to have food ready for them.

'Soon be cutting up bodies, I reckon, Ian,' Leigh said cheekily. 'But don't let it put you off your smoko.'

'It won't,' Ian said. He knew Leigh would kid you up a gum tree and chop it down behind you.

Mrs Heatley shuddered. The thought of her lovely Mr Ian cutting into human corpses was too much for her. It was her private opinion that he would make the best possible doctor but she knew that his aspirations reached beyond a GP's practice or even a specialist's rooms.

Leigh hooked the camp oven out of the fire, lifted the lid and using a cloth Mrs Heatley handed him removed the beautifully risen damper.

'Good one, Luke,' he said and nodded to the old bush poet who'd been responsible for preparing the damper. Leigh cut it into slices, buttered one, smeared it with golden syrup and handed it to Ian. 'That'll stick to your ribs,' he joked.

Ian chewed his way through two slices of damper and sipped at a large mug of billy tea sweetened with condensed milk and looked around him. It was another gorgeous day – not a cloud in the sky and a soft breeze blowing from the south-east. It was a day to marvel over: a day for fishing or for riding, not a day to get on a coach to begin a journey that would ultimately land him back in Cambridgeshire.

Presently he left the others and walked with Leigh through the park to take a last look at the large aviaries and their beautiful, endangered inhabitants. Some of them, like the orange-bellied parrot, they had been able to acquire because of the park's status. It was very satisfying to see them flying freely in such large cages, flashing like coloured jewels as they darted in the bright sunlight. In one cage there was even a pair of the endangered Gouldian finches from northern Australia.

This was a good beginning. The swimming pools were yet to be constructed, but they would come. Helen Donovan had assured him that she'd work closely with the rest of the Murrawee and District Development Association to continue work on the pools and assist Trish Claydon with her pottery project.

Leigh's voice cut into his thoughts. 'What would really put this park on the map, bird-wise, is a pair of night parrots, *Pezoporus occidentalis*.'

'Is that a possibility?' Ian asked.

'Oh, I'd say it's roughly equivalent to finding a Tasmanian tiger or a chook with teeth,' Leigh mused.

'*That* hopeless?'

'Well, there're two schools of thought about the night parrot. The first is that it's extinct and the second is that there may be some birds still out there, but their habitat ranges from western Queensland right across the Northern Territory and northern South Australia to the Kimberley region. A dead night parrot was found beside a road north of Boulia in 1990 and there have been a couple of supposed sightings since then. There could be anything from twenty-five to a hundred left, but estimates are almost impossible because their habitat is so broad. They're very secretive green and yellow birds that fly, but live a bit like quails, staying amongst tall grass and dense vegetation. They only come out to feed and drink after dusk,' Leigh explained.

'So there's not much chance of us acquiring a pair,' Ian said with a wry smile.

'Not unless you were prepared to offer someone a lot of money to try and locate a pair,' said Leigh.

'How much?' Ian asked.

'A lot. And in the unlikely event that we got our hands on a pair, we'd probably have to duplicate their environment to some extent to get them to breed. But a bird man can dream . . .' Leigh trailed off.

'There's no harm in dreaming, Leigh,' said Ian reflectively. 'Some of humanity's best endeavours start out as dreams.'

'You're deep and meaningful this morning,' Leigh remarked.

'Well I've got a bit of good news. Fiona's going to join me in England as soon as she can.'

Leigh gave Ian a hearty pat on the back, 'That's the best news I've had all year. Good on yer mate! So will there be a wedding?'

'I haven't asked her to marry me yet, but if she likes living in the UK, we'll go from there. It's going to be a bit of a shock for a girl who's been on the land for most of her life.'

'She'll be fine,' said Leigh. 'Fiona's a top sheila. Now you'll have to promise me that you'll have the wedding at

Kanimbla. I reckon I'll be able to dig out a clean shirt for the occasion.'

Ian laughed, 'Whoa there! You're moving too fast. Let's just see how things go.'

'Okay. But I expect to be the first to be notified of the wedding date,' Leigh smiled. 'After her father, of course.'

'Of course,' Ian grinned.

When they returned to the smoko site, Leigh pulled a sheet of paper from his shirt pocket and held it in front of him. He cleared his throat, 'Ian, Luke and I have put a few lines together and we'd like you to hear them before you leave us.'

Ian smiled expectantly as Leigh began reading.

*'He came to us a new chum,*
*What use to us out here?*
*"Another swell from England",*
*We swore into our beer.*
*How could we know,*
*What he would sow*
*This Pommy bloke*
*We thought a joke,*
*This Ian Richardson.'*

Leo, Judy, Jim, Karen and Mrs Heatley clapped and smiled, though Billy Landers clapped the loudest. Leigh handed the paper to Luke and he began to read his own contribution.

*'Ian's leaving us for England,*
*Leaving us behind,*
*To be a bloody doctor*
*Of a very special kind.*
*There's grieving at the station*
*And on Nelanji too,*
*Cause blokes like Ian Richardson*
*Are mighty bloody few.*
*He dreamt how things could be*
*And in spite of all the narks*
*In a tiny town called Murrawee*
*At last we've got our park.'*

When the clapping died down, Leigh took another sheet from his pocket. 'If you'll humour me, I have one more.

*'Brown ducks floating by the reeds.*
*Bush bees humming in silver trees.*
*Will you remember these?*
*Will you remember our golden days?*
*Our laid-back Aussie ways?*
*When bitter winds are blowing,*
*And snow is all you see,*
*Will you remember all of us in little Murrawee?'*

Ian smiled. 'Thank you, Leigh. Thanks Luke. That's a very nice way to say farewell.'

There were a few moments of awkward silence because

the small group at the table recognised there wasn't much more anyone could say and that in not much more than an hour Ian Richardson would have left them.

It was Judy Blake who broke the silence.

'Leo and I just want to say how glad we are that you've asked Fiona to join you in England.'

'Thanks Judy. I am too,' Ian said.

'So what will you remember most about your stay here, Ian?' she asked.

'That's a hard question, really hard,' Ian rubbed his chin in deep thought.

'I think it would have to be the salt of the earth people of western Queensland and the way they work together when something needs to be done.'

'Hear hear!' Leigh cried out.

'Do you have any regrets?' Judy asked.

'Not now that Fiona's going with him!' joked Leigh, and everyone laughed.

'I suppose the biggest disappointment would be what's happened to the wool industry. I've watched the greatest wool clip in the world going down the gurgler, and while a huge amount of growers' money has been hived off to support the industry, there's not a lot to show for it. Granted there have been some technical advances in production, but no consistent promotion. We've got some brilliant advertising people in this country, but where is the advertising that tells consumers about wool's softness and elasticity? It seems to me that the industry needs to "sell" wool with a simple but telling slogan like Paul Hogan's "throw another shrimp on the barbie", so that you'd have something like, "Now it's getting colder, throw on a super-soft Aussie wool sweater."'

Ian stopped and looked at Leigh, as if for approval of this suggestion. He knew Leigh's razor-sharp mind could cut to the core of a subject very quickly.

'Yeah, a simple message and well put,' said Leigh.

Ian felt encouraged to continue. 'The industry has had fifty years to get its act together, yet growers are bailing out because they see no future in wool. The huge downturn in Queensland's sheep numbers is proof of that. Kanimbla has had to change tack to remain viable. But I'm rambling now. Time to get off my soapbox,' Ian finished, and everyone laughed.

Ian shook hands with Luke first and then with Leigh. 'Thanks for all your help, both of you. Good luck with your next book, Leigh.'

'I owe you a hell of a lot more than you owe me, Ian. If you don't come first in that bloody medical course I'll have something to say,' he said, then called Shelley from his ute to shake hands with Ian.

Ian shook paws with the big dog and felt a lump in his own throat. 'Look after him, Shelley. And keep a lookout for those dingoes.'

After Ian had watched Leigh drive off, he stood beside the Mercedes and looked back at the place that Leigh had dubbed 'The Oasis of Murrawee'. And it was a kind of oasis, with its lush vegetation and its water fountains – the kind of place that travellers would welcome after a long drive. On one side there was the long, lovely stretch of gum-shaded river and on the other the leafy aviaries where some of Australia's rarest parrots and finches were being encouraged to breed to help ensure their survival. There was also a motel with its caretakers, Eddie and Kate Fisher, who were both retired ambulance officers. The two swimming pools, a project under the steerage of Helen Donovan, would make a difference too. There was a lot more to see and do in Murrawee now, and people were coming.

Leo, Judy and Mrs Heatley waited patiently in the Mercedes as Ian took one last look at all he'd helped achieve for Murrawee. It had come at a price because of the long postponement of his personal needs, but he knew he could leave now, confident he'd left the township in a better state than he'd found it.

Ian's next stop was the Murrawee café. When he got out of the car, he handed the keys to Leo Blake who, with Judy and Mrs Heatley, would drive the Merc back to Kanimbla.

The gold and brown coach was parked outside the café and its exodus of people had just about finished their lunches. Ian dropped his bags beside the steps of the café and the four of them went inside.

Mrs Donovan greeted them warmly, 'Just enough time for another cuppa,' she said.

'That's very kind of you,' Ian said. He looked at her and smiled, and she remembered how it had been when he had got off the coach nearly three years ago.

'You fooled me properly that first time you came in here,' she said. 'I thought you were just another jackaroo going out to Kanimbla for experience.'

'You were partly right, Mrs Donovan. I certainly acquired some experience,' Ian said with a laugh.

'You'll never be forgotten here, Ian. Ray and I wish you well. I daresay Glenda will keep us informed about you,' she said. She knew that a lot of the locals would be asking for news of him.

'I'm not going away forever, Mrs Donovan. And I've some news for you; Fiona will be coming over with me, so with a bit of luck, I'll be back for my own wedding.'

'Good on you, Ian!' said Helen. 'I saw the look that passed between you on that first day. I said to myself, those two are destined for each other.'

Ian smiled, 'Thanks for agreeing to keep things humming here. Maybe the swimming pools will be in action when I come back.'

'Oh yes, they certainly will,' said Helen.

'Looks like it's time to go,' Ian said.

The Kanimbla contingent followed him out to the coach where he shook hands with Jim Landers and then with young Billy, who jumped up into his arms for a big cuddle.

A teary Karen hugged Ian and kissed him affectionately on the cheek. 'Thank you for all you've done for us,' she said, and whispered in his ear, 'I'm pregnant again. If it's another boy, I'm going to call him Ian.'

'That's wonderful, Karen,' he whispered back.

'Very best wishes, Mr Manager,' he said to Jim Landers. 'Kanimbla is in your hands now. You've got a big program but I know you'll manage.'

He turned to Leo Blake and they shook hands like good friends do. 'I can't tell you how much I've appreciated having you with me, Leo, and you too, Judy. It's made a huge difference. I'll miss you both,' Ian said.

He was embraced by Judy, who held him tightly. 'Our love to Rhona if you see her. We'll be coming to Edinburgh before long and we'll drop in to Lyndhurst on the way. The best of everything at Cambridge. We'll miss you,' she said and turned away with tears running down her cheeks.

Mrs Heatley stood back from the others while Ian said his goodbyes. She watched as the driver put Ian's luggage in the side compartment of the coach.

Ian stepped up to her and took her hand. 'What I owe you I can't put into words, Mrs H. If you'll come to England in my summer break I'll try and make some of it up to you. We'll go and see the Lake District and anywhere else that takes your fancy.'

'I knew you were special from the very first day, Mr Ian. I knew it from when you told me you wanted to have breakfast in the kitchen,' she said.

'Just as well I did or you might have formed a very different impression of me.'

He hugged her and kissed her on the cheek. Then, just as he stepped up into the coach, a car screeched to a halt beside the bus, sending a cloud of dust over the surprised little group. Fiona McDonald leapt out of the driver's seat and rushed over to a startled Ian, throwing her arms around him and kissing him passionately.

'It could be months before I see you again. This kiss needs to last a long time,' she said, her eyes sparkling with tears.

'It's time for me to go, darling,' he said to Fiona as the coach driver nodded to him. Fiona backed down the steps and stood next to Judy, who put her arm around her shoulders.

Ian turned at the top of the steps and looked back at the silent group. 'I'll be seeing you,' he said. The door slammed shut and they lost sight of him. They watched as the big coach pulled away from them and moved like a great over-sized slug down the wide road towards the east. Leo Blake looked at the three tearful women around him and shook his head.

The last thing Ian saw of Murrawee was the two trees that stood out starkly against the red soil. 'Two silver trees shimmering in the breeze,' came immediately to his mind. And then they were past the trees and the tyres thrummed as the coach picked up speed, heading for Roma and then Sydney. Ian Richardson closed his eyes and the paddocks of western Queensland faded from his vision.

# *Epilogue*

Five weeks had passed since Ian's departure for England, and Fiona was struggling with the idea of leaving her father. She was torn between wanting desperately to be with Ian again, and wanting to look after her father. She knew he would be terribly lonely when she left – how could he be otherwise? This would be the second time that he'd lost the person dearest to him.

The post office had sent a card notifying Fiona that there was a registered parcel to collect, so she'd headed into Murrawee. After stopping off to talk to Luke at the bird park, she drove to the store to pick up Nelanji's groceries.

'Have you heard from Ian, Fiona?' Helen Donovan asked.

'Oh, yes. Ian's rung, Mrs Donovan. He's started at Cambridge and seems very excited about it,' Fiona said.

'Imagine that. And while he's going into winter, we're heading into summer,' Helen said.

'Yes. He said it was cool, but not yet really cold,' Fiona remarked.

'There isn't a day goes by but someone asks about him.

363

I never would have thought anyone could rate so much attention. Nobody else ever has,' Helen said. 'Funny thing, but I knew he was different the first time I set eyes on him. It wasn't only that he was so polite, and that he had class, but he seemed to have something that nobody else had. It isn't that he cares about people, either. Ian has a lot of concern for people. But there's more to him than those things and for the life of me I can't decide what it is.'

'I think I know what you mean, Mrs Donovan,' Fiona said. How could she explain that Ian's mission in life was to save millions of people threatened by fatal diseases, and that few had the talent and dedication to follow that path? So she didn't try, and said that she had to go to the post office.

The parcel was from Ian. She took it out to the four-wheel drive and eagerly tore off the wrapping and padding. Inside was a letter enclosing a small red velvet-covered box. Which to open first? She slid a finger along the flap of the envelope and extracted a single sheet of paper on which was the Lyndhurst letterhead:

*My darling Fiona,*
*I'm sending you my mother's engagement ring by way of proxy until we have the time to select something to your liking. Will you wear it until you arrive, and then together we can select one of your choosing? The setting might be a bit old-fashioned by today's standards, but at least it will show that you are adored!*
*I should explain that when Mum went off with Dad on their*

*field trips, she only ever wore her wedding ring and a wristlet*
*watch. All her jewellery was left behind in a safety deposit box.*
*Some of these pieces are quite valuable and you may wish to*
*have some of them reset.*

*I'm missing you, my sweet, and am trying to wait patiently*
*for your arrival. I realise you have a lot to organise before we*
*can be together.*

*My kindest regards to your father.*
*Fondest love, darling*
*Ian*


Fiona opened the small box and gasped. The ring was stunning – a large diamond surrounded by smaller stones. She
slipped it on her finger and felt an immediate uplift of spirit.
She was actually engaged, and to the man she'd wanted from
the first day she met him. 'Oh, God,' she breathed. She realised that her future lay with Ian, and that she'd have to go to
him as soon as she could.

Fiona drove back to Nelanji with a light heart and the
germ of an idea in her head. Helen Donovan had told her
that Mrs Heatley was at Kanimbla that day and so Fiona
decided to pay Glenda a visit. Having no mother to share
her happiness about the engagement ring, she felt that Mrs
Heatley would appreciate seeing it.

It didn't take that perceptive woman more than a few
seconds to understand the reason for Fiona's visit.

'Congratulations, Fiona. You don't have to tell me. I can
see it on your face,' Mrs Heatley said warmly.

Over a cup of tea and a scone, Fiona told Mrs Heatley about the letter that had come with Ian's ring.

Mrs Heatley nodded. 'That's just like Mr Ian to be so thoughtful. Few men probably appreciate the thrill a girl gets to receive a ring that signifies love and commitment. Mr Ian probably thinks a proxy ring is better than no ring.'

'It's a lovely ring. And yes, it would be nice for Ian and me to choose a ring together, but I'm not sure I'd find one better than this. Ian loved his mother and her ring was given with love, and I'm very happy with it,' Fiona said.

'I would be too,' Mrs Heatley agreed.

'How are you finding Kanimbla with Ian gone, Mrs Heatley?' Fiona asked.

'I miss him a lot. After I lost my husband and then my son, my life didn't seem the same. I wouldn't say I had a high opinion of Jack Richardson, but looking after Kanimbla at least kept me busy. And then Mr Ian arrived and it was almost like my Miles had been returned to me. If you don't mind me saying, the three of us – that's you, Judy Blake and me – were good for Ian. It must have been hard for him having a grandfather who'd been a general and then having to go to a big boarding school for boys.' It was obvious that she loved talking about Ian Richardson.

'I'm glad you said that, Mrs H. It means you understand why I have to go to Ian. My future is with him. I've got lots of misgivings about leaving Dad. I've tried to be a companion to him since I came home from school because I could see how much he was missing Mum. Dad takes very little interest in the television or radio apart from the news and weather and stock reports. I've worked in Mum's garden with him and played chess with him and I know he's going to miss all of that,' Fiona said.

'I didn't know that your father was keen on chess,' Mrs Heatley said.

'Oh, yes. He and Mum were regular combatants. I took over after I came home from school, but I'm not in her class,' Fiona said.

'I haven't played for years, but I used to love chess,' Mrs Heatley said with a sigh.

'I'm sure Dad would enjoy a game with you,' said Fiona. 'Really?'

'Oh yes,' said Fiona. 'Actually, Mrs H, I have a much bolder suggestion to put to you. How would you feel about looking after Dad? You could still keep coming to Kanimbla but maybe go to Nelanjii three or four days a week. Dad isn't a fussy eater. If you could keep an eye on him and perhaps play some chess, he wouldn't be so lonely. It'd be such a relief if I knew you were going there,' Fiona said.

'Well now, I'd have to think about that, Fiona. Have you mentioned any of this to your father?' Mrs Heatley asked.

'No, I haven't, but it's been at the back of my mind ever since Ian left. Receiving this engagement ring has made me realise I have to go to him. We've wasted enough time, and I don't want to waste any more,' Fiona said.

'Then the first thing you should do is talk to your father to see what he thinks of the idea. If he's agreeable you could both come back here to discuss it further,' Mrs Heatley said.

'So you wouldn't be against it?' Fiona asked.

'Not if your father is agreeable, but he may not like the idea of another women at Nelanji. Your father and mother were very close, Fiona.'

'Dad wants the best for me and he knows I'm reluctant to leave him on his own. But . . .'

'Men like Ian Richardson don't grow on trees,' Mrs Heatley said with a smile.

'That's exactly what Dad told me,' Fiona said with an answering smile. 'But I love him, Mrs Heatley. I've loved Ian from the very beginning. But his head has been so full of science, and doing something for Murrawee and putting Kanimbla on a different track that he wasn't able to, well . . .'

'See where you could fit into his life?' Mrs Heatley suggested.

'That's exactly right, Mrs Heatley. It wasn't until he was about to leave that he realised he really loved me. He thought science would be enough for him and that he could get along without me. And then, as Ian explained, reality hit him,' Fiona said.

'I'm delighted, Fiona,' said an obviously pleased Mrs Heatley.

A fortnight later Fiona waved goodbye to her father in the international lounge in Brisbane, and boarded the plane. She knew he had a long drive back to Nelanji, but Mrs Heatley would be waiting there when he arrived and would look after him. Mrs Heatley was very good at looking after people.

Ahead of her was Britain and Ian. She realised that some of what lay ahead wouldn't be easy, but with Ian, she felt she could face just about anything.

*Dear Dad,*

*Lyndhurst is really lovely. The house is much bigger than Kanimbla and it has a beautiful old garden and orchard. The front fields run down to the River Ouse. The soil is amazing, pure black, and it's supposed to be the richest in Britain. You'll be pleased to know that I'm living in a self-contained flat in the back part of Lyndhurst. It's very comfortable. It was where Sir Nicholas's batman lived and where Rhona Blake lived before she cleared off to Edinburgh.*

*Cambridge and the university are only about half an hour's drive from Lyndhurst. It's a very selective university, probably the most selective of all, and only about twenty-five per cent of all applicants are successful, and of these only about ten per cent are from outside the UK. I've missed my chance to attend Cambridge this year so I'll have to make some enquiries about beginning a science course externally.*

*Ian took me for a canoe trip on the River Cam, which was really lovely. The sun came out for about ten minutes so it gave me some idea of what being on the river in summer would be like. Ian said we had to go before the very cold weather set in. We came back and had afternoon tea in a quaint little tea shop before driving back to Lyndhurst. What bliss to be with him again!*

*I hope everything is going okay at Nelanji. I'm sure Mrs Heatley has everything well and truly under control. She's a gem.*

*I miss you, Dad, and I miss my dogs and the horses. You'll have to try and come here in the spring so we can talk about the wedding.*

*Ian has a long summer break from university in June and that seems the obvious time to get married. I can't wait to see you.*

*Love*
*Fiona*


Lachie McDonald looked at his daughter's letter for a long time. Although another man had taken her away, he knew that she would always be part of him. Perhaps, just perhaps, a grandson or a granddaughter, a Richardson, would once again live at Kanimbla. He hoped he would live long enough to see it.